MARY WITHALL was born near Epsom in Surrey. Having spent some thirty years as a lecturer in various colleges of technology, in 1988 she retired to Argyll where she began a new career as a writer. She has published six other Eisdalsa novels and three non-fiction works about the area in which she now lives, the Slate Islands of Netherlorn.

Crisis of Conscience

MARY WITHALL

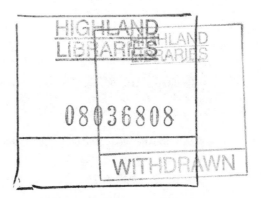

Luath Press Limited

EDINBURGH

www.luath.co.uk

For Petre

First published 2009

ISBN: 978-1-905222-19-3

The paper used in this book is recyclable.
It is made from low chlorine pulps produced in a low energy,
low emissions manner from renewable forests.

The publisher acknowledges the support of

 Scottish
Arts Council

towards the publication of this volume.

Printed and bound by
Bell & Bain Ltd., Glasgow

Typeset in 10.5 point Sabon

Foreword

Like my other Eisdalsa novels which traced the history of general medical practice through the nineteenth and twentieth centuries, *Crisis of Conscience* is a work of fiction based on fact.

As one who has witnessed medical services in this country from a childhood in the 1930s, and who has made good use of the NHS when a student, as a young mother and latterly as an OAP, I can offer first-hand knowledge of the system from the receiving end. My teaching work in the field of sciences applied to medicine provided much of the academic background to this book and I also enjoyed the privilege of teaching nurses and nurse tutors in the course of a long career in Further Education. My researches included discussions with GPs and other doctors, in particular, Willie McKerrel and George Hannah, who between them have served the Easdale community where I live for a period which covers more than forty years of the sixty since the scheme was inaugurated. Statistical details owe much to a remarkable little volume by Graham Cannon, *A Short History of the NHS*, published in 1988. Historical references are drawn from the biographies of some distinguished politicians of the day, in particular, Aneurin Bevan and Michael Foot. I would like to thank my editor Jennie Renton for her wise counsel and my husband Petre for his technical skills with the computer, offered, always with the greatest patience, at every howl of frustration on my part.

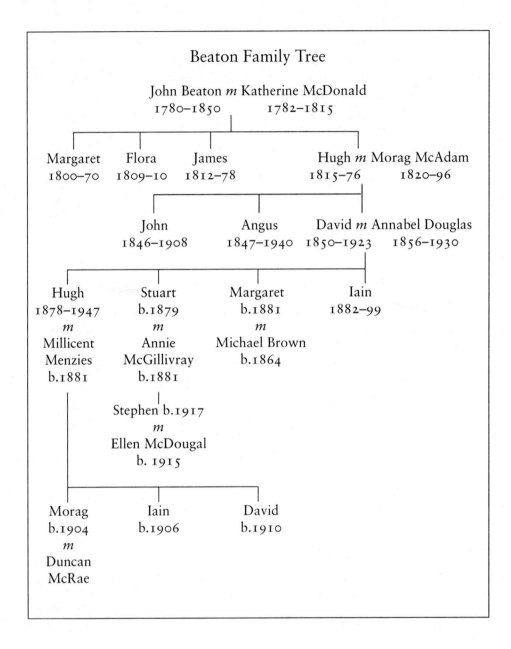

Beaton Family Tree

John Beaton *m* Katherine McDonald
1780–1850   1782–1815

Margaret   Flora   James   Hugh *m* Morag McAdam
1800–70   1809–10   1812–78   1815–76   1820–96

John   Angus   David *m* Annabel Douglas
1846–1908   1847–1940   1850–1923   1856–1930

Hugh   Stuart   Margaret   Iain
1878–1947   b.1879   b.1881   1882–99
m   *m*   *m*
Millicent   Annie   Michael Brown
Menzies   McGillivray   b.1864
b.1881   b.1881

Stephen b.1917
m
Ellen McDougal
b. 1915

Morag   Iain   David
b.1904   b.1906   b.1910
m
Duncan
McRae

I

IT WAS ONE of those April days in the Highlands when nature throws off the bleak drabness of winter and everything suddenly springs into life. A warm sun had drawn the fresh green leaflets of hawthorn and hazel from their brown buds and primroses peeped shyly from beneath the overhanging willow wands whose soft grey catkins scattered yellow dust on the dark sleeves brushing past. Daffodils glowed in the long grass beside the slate grey of the cemetery wall and here and there a flash of purple showed where an over enthusiastic violet had already dared to show its face. Beyond the wall sheep grazed, heavy with lamb and startlingly white after the recent showers, while a crown of golden gorse marked the horizon between green hillside and the brilliant blue of the western skies.

The church had been full to overflowing. They had chartered a bus to bring in the mourners from Oban and every one of the small fleet of vehicles which served the islands had arrived crammed with passengers. There were a few bicycles belonging to those who could attempt the steepest hills but most of the island people had walked along the narrow lanes, across the hills and over the bleak moor where the dead bracken crunched beneath their feet and the heather, just tinged with green following the snow, soaked boots and shoes especially polished for the occasion. Many had made the ferry crossing from the adjacent islands, for Hugh Beaton's medical practice included all the inhabited islands in the Firth of Lorn.

Everyone had stories to tell about the doctor who had been such an important part of their lives for so long. Some spoke of having had to call him out on a wild night to make a sea crossing or to make a treacherous journey across the hills, on foot through fog or snow. They remembered how on such occasions he would arrive clad in waterproofs looking more like the fisherman pictured on sardine tins than their doctor. On these occasions he had never been heard to complain. Some even had stories to tell of emergency operations carried out on a kitchen table with only an oil lamp to see by, for the war had interrupted plans to bring electricity to the islands. Many could claim experience of a long night vigil to save a life or to draw one peacefully to a close.

Ellen Beaton drew back a little from the crowd gathered at the graveside. Despite their warm welcome and all their kindnesses, she still felt herself to be an outsider at this moment of family grieving. While she had grown to know and love Stephen's parents, Annie and Stuart Beaton, she had met Hugh and his family only once before, when she and Stephen were married here, just a year ago. Then, Stephen's aunt, Millicent, had been kindness itself, insisting that the reception must be held at Tigh na Broch because Annie and Stuart's cottage on Eisdalsa Island was far too small for such an important event.

Ellen's first visit to Eisdalsa had been very short. Stephen's three cousins, all doctors, had taken special leave from their war duties to be at the wedding, but all three had gone by the next day. She had managed only a very brief exchange with Morag before she returned to her hospital job at Inverlinne, while Iain had left with his brother the following morning at crack of dawn to return to his regiment. Ellen had exchanged no more than a few words with David, the younger of Hugh and Millicent's two sons. He had seemed rather quiet, she thought, almost withdrawn compared with his lively, outgoing siblings. She knew he held an important post in psychiatric medicine, and wondered if his work had some bearing on his somewhat distant manner.

While Stuart and his nephews, all three splendid in full Highland dress, took their places beside the coffin, Stephen placed himself opposite them. The most suitable outfit he had been able to lay hands on at such short notice was his full dress RAF uniform. How distinguished he looked standing there alongside the other mourners in their dark Sunday suits, men who had been lifelong friends of Hugh, either from the earl's estate or from the village. When she and Stephen had taken their seats with the rest of the family in church that morning, Ellen had noticed a number of curious glances from the congregation, for those who understood the significance of the bands on the sleeve of Stephen's tunic and could interpret a row of medal ribbons, might well be surprised. There weren't that many medics in the RAF who had achieved the rank of Wing Commander or were entitled to wear the ribbon of the DFC.

At a pause in the proceedings, Ellen turned to the woman standing beside her. She had noticed her earlier, in the church. A solitary person immaculately turned out in the uniform of a district nurse. Ellen had at first supposed her to be one of the official representatives of the Local Authority, of whom there seemed to be a great many, but now she could see from the woman's strained white face and sad eyes brimming with tears, that her pain was very personal.

'Did you know Hugh Beaton well?' she enquired, gently.

'We worked together for a long time,' the nurse replied, 'and he has always been our family doctor. I grew up here on the island. In fact I once shared a desk with Iain Beaton in the village school.'

The nurse's recollection raised a smile, which quite transformed her, making her younger and far more attractive.

'I'm Alma Livingstone,' she held out a gloved hand.

'I'm Ellen. Ellen Beaton, Stephen's wife.' They shook hands.

'I already knew who you were,' Alma confessed. 'I was in church the day you were married.'

Ellen looked a trifle embarrassed, feeling perhaps that she should have recalled their meeting. Alma added quickly, 'You wouldn't have noticed me. Everyone attends weddings and funerals here. You don't wait for an invitation. We're like one huge family.'

Ellen recalled the ceilidh they had had in the village hall after the official wedding reception. There had been so many people, she had wondered at the time how Stephen managed to amass so many friends when he himself had grown up in Glasgow, coming here only in his school holidays.

'For a short while Stephen was at the village school too,' Alma told her. 'He was in the infants when Iain and I were in the top class. When his father returned in 1918, towards at the end of the first war, they went off to Glasgow. We didn't see a lot of the Stuart Beatons after that.'

Ellen tried to imagine Stephen as an infant in the village school and couldn't help smiling at the image the thought conjured. She regarded her companion with renewed interest.

Alma's voice broke a little when she added, 'It was Dr Hugh who recommended me to the Matron at the Cottage Hospital in Oban where I did my nurse training. I believe it was his word got me the job here. I owed so much to him. He was always very kind to my mother and me, especially after Dad died.' The tears began to well again.

To spare the nurse's embarrassment, Ellen turned her attention to the activity at the graveside and saw that Iain was looking in their direction and pointing them out to Stephen. He gave a smile and an almost imperceptible wave and when Ellen turned again to Alma, she noticed a flush in the nurse's cheeks which had not been there a moment ago.

So the nurse had also seen Iain's gesture. Whether it had been meant for Alma or for herself, she could see there was little doubt about Alma's interpretation of that moment of recognition!

So that's it, Ellen told herself. Well, it was high time one of Hugh's sons found a wife. Iain must be past forty and David was only a year or two younger. Realising that her thoughts were straying, Ellen tried to focus on the proceedings, which were now reaching a climax.

Spanning the open grave, Hugh Beaton's coffin rested beneath the Union Jack. Upon it lay his RAMC cap and cane from the Great War. Despite the fact that it had been the effects of that conflict which had blighted the remainder of her husband's life, Millicent had insisted that Hugh would have wanted his military service recognised in this way.

'It's an impressive line-up.' Stuart Beaton murmured to his nephews as they waited for the minister to take his place. He pointed out the Chief Medical Officer, who was conversing quietly with the Lord Lieutenant of Argyll. 'I reckon old Hugh would have been pretty pleased with this send-off.'

The minister stood with his back to the afternoon sun. His unruly shock of white hair, blowing in the breeze, stood up like a halo around his shining, wrinkle-free brow and as he took up his position at the head of the coffin, his gown flapped around him like the wings of a raven preparing for flight.

The Reverend Archibald McCulloch spoke in a sepulchral voice loud enough to reach the furthest corner of the cemetery.

'Man that is born of a woman has but a short time to live and is full of misery...'

Hugh's widow clung to her daughter's arm, wondering if she would be able to see this thing through to the end without giving way. For years she had struggled to maintain a calm outward appearance no matter what the turmoil within, and all those years of suppressing her true feelings had taken their toll. After a long week nursing her husband as well as holding the household together, she had been near the end of her tether by the time Hugh finally succumbed to the influenza virus. The disease had struck like a lightning bolt in the villages at the beginning of March and had kept both Hugh and Stuart on duty day and night with very little opportunity for sleep. Stuart had retired officially, the year before, but he could not stand by while his brother was run off his feet so despite Annie's protestations, he too had joined battle with the disease and since Hugh's death he had been running the practice, single-handed.

'I must ask the CMO for the name of a good locum,' Millicent told herself. It helped to think of practical matters. If she kept her mind busy with other things she did not have to be forever blaming herself, as she had been doing all week. Hugh had succumbed to the flu virus himself soon after an epidemic had been declared and rather than have him removed to the hospital, Millicent had undertaken to nurse him in the same way she had cared for him through all his troubles since the day the Army returned him to her, drained and disillusioned in 1918.

There had been many times in recent months when it had all got too much for her but rather than let Hugh see her distress, she would busy herself in the dairy or climb the hill behind the house and sit on the rocks gazing out to sea until she had calmed down. Since his death, however, she had been overwhelmed by self-recrimination.

'I should have stopped him,' she murmured, so quietly that Morag had to strain to hear what she was saying. 'He ought never to have taken all those night calls in that freezing weather. I should have made him take more time off. I should have insisted he ask for help from the Chief Medical Officer.'

Morag squeezed her mother's hand.

'You did all you could, Mummy, much more than anyone should have expected of you.'

Millicent was not the only one to shoulder the blame for Hugh's demise. As his doctor, Stuart Beaton was convinced he could have done more to prevent his brother's death. He had confessed as much to Stephen and Ellen when he had met them from the train the day before.

'In the old days I would have accepted the situation with a good grace,' he admitted. 'There was nothing one could do once pneumonia had set in but wait and hope for the best. Now of course we know that a shot of penicillin might have cleared the trouble up at once. I couldn't get hold of any. Even Morag, with all her contacts, was unable to help.'

'Penicillin is still in short supply, everywhere,' said Stephen. 'Even though we get a little, for our worst burn cases, we're still expected to play God by deciding who can have it.'

Stuart nodded.

'You're right of course,' he agreed. 'It should be reserved for those who will benefit most. We've known for ages Hugh was living on borrowed time so it's quite possible the penicillin wouldn't have saved him anyway.'

'*We give thee hearty thanks, for that it hath pleased thee to deliver this our brother out of the miseries of this sinful world...*'

As the service drew to a close, dark clouds began to gather on the horizon and a chill wind threatened to bring on the rain. The crowds melted away, the congregation hurrying to take shelter as best they could. At last, only the immediate family remained at the graveside. Millicent Beaton standing beside the open grave gazed on her husband's coffin for the last time. With a strangled cry she turned away and clinging for support to an arm on either side, she allowed her two sons to escort her to the iron gateway which led out onto the road.

2

MILLICENT HAD INSISTED on holding the wake at Tigh na Broch. Stuart and Annie had tried to persuade her to engage Dougie McGowan from the Eisdalsa Inn to do the catering but she would not hear of it.

'If I cannot make a few sandwiches and scones for my husband's funeral tea, what use am I?' she insisted and Stuart, seeing this as her way of picking up the pieces and getting down to the business of living, argued no further.

All the women of the family had been up since dawn and the dining room table creaked under its load of sandwiches, scones and pastries.

Now islanders, family friends and medical colleagues alike mingled cheerfully, tucking into the splendid feast like a hoard of locusts descending on a ripened wheat field. The first few drams loosened tongues and gradually conversations which had begun with the weather and its being a perfect day for a funeral, had turned to a thousand and one memories of Dr Hugh Beaton, some of them serious, others amusing.

'What's wrong with that?' Annie wanted to know, when Stephen commented on the party atmosphere. 'Hugh was a good man. He had a long and eventful life. It's only right that it should be celebrated. He would have wanted people to have a few drams and a joke or two at his wake. Don't you agree, Millicent?'

Her sister-in-law nodded absently, dabbing at her eyes with a damp, lacy handkerchief.

Stephen cast a professional eye over Millicent and saw that underneath her composed exterior she was quite exhausted. Her life had been changed so suddenly and so dramatically, he wondered how she was going to manage on her own. There was so much work here with the house and the farm. He supposed it would all be sold eventually. Millicent could do with a smaller place, perhaps a cottage like his mother's. Maybe she would go and live on Eisdalsa Island. That would be nice for both her and for Annie.

'Why don't you two girls go into the conservatory,' he suggested. 'It's quieter there. I'll see if I can get someone to make you a cup of tea.'

'Oh, would you dear,' said Annie. 'That would be lovely. Come along Millicent, it's not every day we get a chance to be waited on.'

Annie led the way through the milieu and into the conservatory. It was pleasant to be away from the bustle and the noise. They settled, out of sight of the guests, in an arbour which had been created by the luxuriant growth of tropical plants, prominent among which were the orchids which had been one of Hugh's consuming interests.

'Isn't it strange.' Millicent spoke as though she were thinking out loud. 'For all these years I have had to shoulder most of the burden of this place but now that Hugh's gone, I just don't know how I am going to manage without him!'

Annie said nothing to interrupt Millicent's flow now she had, at last, started talking about what really mattered to her. For the past week Millicent had carried on running the household as before, showing little sign of her true feelings. It was time for her to let go.

'It's not that I didn't love him,' Millicent continued. 'It was just that the man who returned from the war was not the man I married. He would never talk about the experiences that had changed him so much, but sometimes he would wake up in the night bathed in sweat, shouting out unintelligible things.'

Annie needed no telling. In 1918, her own husband had been returned to her by the Navy after three years, when everyone but she had believed him dead. There had been many nights when his experiences of war had returned to invade his dreams. Stuart's response had been to immerse himself in his work. It had not been an easy life for a general practitioner between the wars. The patients that needed the most help were the ones least able to pay, but he had used the fees from his wealthier private patients to augment the meagre allowances provided by the various insurance schemes of the friendly societies to which most working men subscribed.

Hugh's rural medical practice was very different. The slate quarrying operation which had sustained the economy of the area for two hundred years had fallen into decline. Many of the men had gone away to find work, leaving behind wives, children and elderly dependants, who, like the agricultural workers, were living at subsistence level. Hugh would never have been able to support his family solely on his work as a general practitioner. Between the wars he and Millicent had depended heavily on income from the family farm at Tigh na Broch. Few people realised that it had been Millicent who shouldered much of the responsibility for the management of the farm and who, with the help of a couple of hired hands, had undertaken the physical work as well.

'The boys were too little to have remembered what their father was like before he went away but Morag was different,' Millicent was saying. 'As a wee girl she idolised Hugh, following him everywhere he went. In those days he adored his *wee princess,* as he always called her. They were inseparable. Often he would take her on his rounds and teach her all kinds of things to do with his work. I'm sure that was what inspired her to become a doctor. Morag never said anything,' she went on, 'but I used to see the bewilderment in her eyes when Hugh was sharp with her. She must have wondered what she had done to upset her father so. He took so little interest in what was going on with his children. What a good thing it was that her grandfather was there to encourage her.'

Annie couldn't help but smile at this. Hugh's father, David Beaton, had been a tower of strength to them all during those terrible times when Hugh was in France and Stuart missing, believed drowned; but as for encouraging his granddaughter, well, that was absolutely untrue. David had been totally opposed to his Morag becoming a doctor. It was Annie and Morag's headmistress, Elizabeth Whylie, who had persuaded Hugh and Millicent to let their daughter study medicine. Millicent had taken a long time to convince. She had been quite adamant that medicine was no profession for a respectable young woman.

For a while the two women sat in silence, enjoying the peaceful interlude. Millicent, who had slept so little in the past few days, began to nod. She came to with a start when Annie suddenly got to her feet.

'Stephen must have been waylaid,' she said. 'I'll go and fetch that tea myself.'

Leaving Millicent alone with her thoughts, she rejoined the fray.

Amongst Millicent's visitors that day was someone who believed he was the man to solve all her problems. Dermot Cameron owned the largest tenanted farm on the Isle of Seileach, grazing much of the better agricultural land as well as running a flock or two of sheep on some of the uninhabited islands in the Sound. It was his flocks which dotted the hillsides like confetti, and his ewes, with their young lambs, which found a way through poorly maintained fences in order to wander the village streets and destroy the plants in the tiny, well sheltered gardens by the shore. Fortunately for Dermot wool prices were still inflated following the war. His store cattle, a scruffy looking herd of carelessly interbred beasts, held the dubious distinction of commanding the poorest prices at the local market. His dairy herd of cross bred Friesians and Ayrshires, which provided milk for the surrounding district, faced slaughter once the Ministry of Agriculture began to enforce testing for bovine tuberculosis.

Dermot had long admired Dr Beaton's magnificent prize bull and his herd of Highland cows, with their healthy calves and high milk yield. Taking the opportunity to catch Hugh's widow at a low ebb and maybe strike a bargain that could lift him out of the clutches of the bank manager, he elbowed his way through the throng and found her sitting alone in the conservatory. This glassed-in extension spanned the front elevation of the house, giving access to the garden, with magnificent views across the meadows towards the rocky shore a few hundred yards to the west.

'A grand send-off, Millicent,' Dermot greeted her, 'Old Hugh would have been delighted to see so many in attendance.'

Millicent smiled up at him, wanly. 'It was good of you to come, Dermot,' she replied automatically.

'It was an excellent service,' he continued, following the prescribed pattern to the letter. Millicent had heard it a dozen times already and scarcely listened.

Dermot allowed his gaze to rest on the prize bull grazing in the lower pasture.

'What a fine old fellow that is. It will seem strange not to see him down there by the road as one drives past.'

Millicent turned a questioning gaze on him.

'How do you mean?'

'I naturally assumed that you would be giving up the farm. After all, it was Hugh's hobby, wasn't it?'

Dermot found it difficult to disguise his excitement at the thought of acquiring this herd of Highland cattle which had won awards all around the county and was the envy of every professional stockman. It seemed so unjust that a rank amateur should have done so well as a farmer.

Millicent regarded Dermot with a curious expression as though she had just woken up and was trying to remember what she had been dreaming about.

'Give up the farm?' she repeated. 'Why should I give up the farm?'

'I merely assumed...' Dermot was at a loss to continue.

The output from the Beaton herd was insufficient for it to be a competitor for Dermot Cameron's milk round. It was however famous locally for its butter and a unique range of cheeses. With the help of a single stockman and a couple of women from the village, the doctor and his wife had maintained the farm as a modest investment. Recently Hugh had spent more and more of his time amongst the animals, finding in their company the solace lacking in his human relationships. Sorlie McKinnon had looked after the day-to-day management of the stock when Hugh was otherwise occupied and the dairy had always been Millicent's responsibility. The idea that things should not continue as before had never crossed her mind.

Placing her cup carefully on the little rattan table at her side, Millicent rose to her feet. 'You will have to forgive me, Dermot,' she said dismissively. 'I really must attend to my other guests.'

Dermot followed her with his eyes as she mingled with the crowd in the drawing room. Perhaps it had been a bit precipitate of him to raise the question of the herd just now. Maybe he should wait a while before he approached one of the sons.

3

BY LATE AFTERNOON the last of the guests had departed and while the women of the household were busy in the kitchen clearing up, the men had gathered in the sitting room to discuss the future now that the head of the family was gone.

As Millicent reached for a tea towel, Annie stopped her.

'You have done quite enough for one day Millicent,' she said. 'Leave it to the girls to finish up now.'

'That's right, Mother,' Morag agreed. 'You too Aunt Annie, it's time you had a break. Why not go and join the men? Otherwise they will have your entire future mapped out for you before you have a chance to express any opinion.'

The two older women, grateful for any excuse to sit down, departed, giving Morag her first chance to become properly acquainted with her cousin Stephen's wife.

Ellen Beaton lifted a pile of plates.

'Where do these go?' she asked, glancing around the generously proportioned kitchen. Generations of Beatons with their large families had accumulated great stocks of china and glass and rather than dispose of what was no longer wanted, they had provided more and more cupboard space to house it.

'Best let me put away,' suggested Morag. 'Mind you, it's so long since I had anything to do with running this house, I shall probably put everything in the wrong place! Perhaps you could deal with the cutlery.' She indicated a large drawer in one of the dressers. 'You can't go wrong there!'

Ellen watched as Morag bustled about confidently. She had the bright auburn hair which distinguished all the members of the Beaton family, but unlike the men, the pale complexion of her Viking ancestry did not extend to invisibly fair eyelashes and brows. Her grey eyes were framed by long brown lashes, which gave them a peculiar radiance. Her high, intelligent brow, broad and as yet unlined, accentuated her finely cut features.

Both young women worked steadily, all the while exchanging their impressions of the events of the day. Gradually, as they began to feel more comfortable in one another's company, the discussion rested upon more personal matters.

'Do you have plans to return to Australia soon?' Morag asked suddenly. 'I seem to remember some mention of a visit to your parents at the wedding breakfast.'

'Stephen had to stay on at the hospital while his boss went back to New Zealand to settle some family business,' Ellen explained, 'but Mr McIndoe is back now, so it should soon be Stephen's turn for some leave. We're hoping to get away in May. It will be autumn in Australia by then, a more suitable climate for Pommies.'

The reference to 'home' introduced a distinctly antipodean twang into Ellen's speech.

'You must miss your family, being so far away,' Morag sympathised. 'I don't get home all that often, but I do have the consolation of knowing that if there is an emergency, I'm only a couple of hours' drive away. Where do you two think you'll live eventually?'

'Stephen seems undecided about what he is going to do,' Ellen confided. 'I envy you and your brothers. You all seem so settled in your jobs and confident about the future. Down south, the whole medical world appears to be in a state of upheaval. Stephen's colleagues can talk of nothing but this new National Health Service.'

'I can't speak for the men,' Morag told her, 'but I don't think the new arrangements will affect me much.'

'You're not going to involve yourself in the political wrangle then?' Ellen asked.

'No. I might continue to do some consultancy work, but I think it's time I paid more attention to my home and Duncan. We have both been so occupied with our work these past years, we've had precious little time to enjoy one another's company.'

Ellen remembered Stephen telling her that Duncan McRae, older than Morag by some ten years, had made a lot of money from the manufacture of armaments. Morag had no need to work once she was married. She had continued with her job at Inverlinnie only because she wanted to.

'What about you Ellen?' Morag asked. 'Will you go on working once Stephen leaves the RAF?'

'It depends where he decides to go,' Ellen answered. 'There's not a lot for me to do in East Grinstead. I've taken a job with the local vet but overfed moggies and pet poodles, not to mention their owners, are not my scene. I'm far happier dealing with farmers and their livestock. What I'd really like to do is carry on with the research programme I was engaged in when the war started.'

'I thought you worked for the Ministry of Ag and Fish?' Morag recalled.

'Only after war broke out,' Ellen explained. 'I came over on a research scholarship, and was attached to the Veterinary College in London. As a matter of fact, the ideal place for me to continue with the research is back home, in Australia. It would be nice if Stephen could find an opening there.'

'I don't think Aunt Annie would be too keen on that idea,' Morag observed. 'Besides which,' she gave the draining board a final rub down and tossed the wet dish towel over the radiator, 'I've never had a female cousin before. I don't want you to go rushing off before I get to know you properly.' Morag was pleased to have such a good rapport with Stephen's wife. They had a lot in common, each having succeeded in the struggle to gain a foothold in a man's world.

Brought up within a typically Edwardian family, in which her mother had insisted upon maintaining the myth of the supremacy of its male members, Morag had had a supreme battle to become a surgeon. Once established in her profession, she had encountered few females in whose presence she felt really comfortable. Of the women who had featured in her early life, only Aunt Annie had understood her burning desire to make a career for herself.

'Is it quite common for a woman to train for a profession in Australia?' she wondered. 'My mother nearly had an apoplexy when I announced I was going to be a surgeon.'

'I'd always had a way with animals, especially horses. My mum and dad seemed to take it for granted I'd be a vet.'

Morag envied Ellen her freedom from the social barriers erected by the narrow, middle-class values upheld by her own parents. 'How did the men treat you at the university,' she asked.

'I was the only girl in a class of thirty men. They never expected me to complete the course.'

'I know the feeling!'

Morag could laugh now but there had been many moments of despair during in her long climb up the ladder of her profession. She grinned as she turned Ellen around and untied her borrowed pinafore.

'C'mon, it's time we joined the others!'

Ellen stopped to glance in the hall mirror and adjust her hair. Fine blonde tendrils clung to her sweaty brow. Reaching for her handbag which earlier in the day she had thrust beneath the hallstand out of the way, she pulled out a powder compact to make a few repairs.

Seeing her, Morag felt obliged to do the same.

'What a mess!' she exclaimed running her fingers through her tousled mop. She shifted a pile of hats, scarves and gloves to one side in search of her own bag and quickly gave up in disgust.

'I don't know how Mother manages the house these days, with just a daily help,' she surveyed the chaos left by the departing guests. 'There was always a live-in cook and a nanny in the old days. Now the only women employed here are in the dairy, and that's only because the operation of the farm is subsidised by the Ministry of Agriculture.'

'You have to face up to it Morag, the days of house servants are long gone,' laughed Ellen. 'I can't see any of those young girls who have been in the Services or working in the factories ever accepting domestic service as an alternative, can you? The wages they demand will be far too much for most people to afford.'

Morag remembered the interviews she had conducted only last week at Achnafroach and how embarrassed she had been to offer the post of housemaid to a woman who six weeks earlier had been commanding a platoon of ATS on a parade ground somewhere in the Borders.

'I suppose it depends on how much they need a job,' she said. 'Well paid work for women, no matter how talented, is not that easy to come by, especially up here in the Highlands.'

Ellen, having replaced her lipstick, put her bag back on the hall stand.

'I'm ready,' she announced.

4

'SOMETHING HAS TO be decided about the practice, Mother. Uncle Stuart is not fit enough to take on the job on his own. After all, he's supposed to be retired. Naturally, if the practice is put up for sale, the house will have to go with it. In any case, it's far too large for you to manage alone.'

David Beaton, irritated by his mother's endless string of sentimental reminiscences had perhaps put his point rather too bluntly but it was the subject they had all been trying to get around to for the past half hour.

Millicent regarded her son with the severe expression he remembered from their nursery days.

'I was just waiting for Morag and Ellen to join us,' she said testily. She motioned to Ellen, indicating the empty chair beside her. Morag joined her husband on the window seat.

'It was your father's wish that the practice should stay in the family,' Millicent reminded them. 'With four of you doctors, that can't be too difficult. Surely there's one of you will take it on? I realise it could be difficult for Morag, but what about you boys?' She appealed to Iain who had propped himself against the mantle shelf while he cleaned his pipe, irritating her by allowing the dottle to fall into the grate. She held back the reproof which rose to her lips and turned to her younger son. 'David?'

'I know it means a lot to you, Mother,' David said, 'but I, for one, am not prepared to give up my career to bury myself in the country, lancing the occasional boil and dishing out a few aspirins. I've been offered a post as Superintendent of one of the London County Council Psychiatric Hospitals in Surrey and I have every intention of accepting.'

'Congratulations Dave! That's splendid news,' exclaimed Stephen.

David, while accepting his cousin's congratulations with good grace, looked to his brother for support in the question of the practice.

'What about you, Iain?'

'Perhaps we should hear what Morag has to say first,' Millicent intervened. 'After all, she is the oldest.'

Morag grasped hold of Duncan's hand before replying.

'General practice was never in my plans, Mother. As a matter of fact I've been offered an interesting research job which I can manage very well from home and I'll probably be giving up my consultancy at Inverlinnie to do that.'

She smiled at Duncan as she spoke and he squeezed her hand affectionately. It was a relief to know she had made up her mind at last!

'What about you, Iain?' Despite his annoying habits, Millicent regarded her second child with affection. Of them all, he was most like the man she had married more than fifty years ago. Tall and broad shouldered, with that same shock of curly auburn hair; even his voice sounded like Hugh's.

'Well,' he began hesitantly, 'I can't say that I haven't thought about it a great deal over the years, especially when I was out there in France during that last long winter. I used to dream of nights by the fireside here and envied Pa his convenient list of well documented patients, most of whom were folk we had grown up amongst. D'you know, I even fancied myself carrying on the farm.'

He paused for a moment. The lengthening shadows emphasised the deep frown that grim memories had drawn across his brow.

'When mutilated bodies are passing through your hands so rapidly that you don't have time to put a name to them before they're sent on down the line, you begin to see yourself as just a cog in a machine. There's no satisfaction in that kind of medicine. I longed for the opportunity to watch just a few of my patients recover from their wounds. I used to think about Grandad and Father and how they had often boasted of caring for individuals from the cradle to the grave. If it were possible, I would gladly take on the practice. Unfortunately, it's out of the question.'

'Why?' Millicent demanded. 'What is there to stop you?'

'Money. I don't have any and that's about the size of it. Do you have any idea what this practice is worth today? It must be thousands.'

'Why should that bother you?' Millicent asked. 'Have I said one word about you having to buy it?'

'No, Ma, but let's be realistic. The others have a stake in the family business and anyway, there's your own future to be considered. You have to have something to live on. The sale of the practice would provide you with a decent little annuity; enough to keep you comfortably for the rest of your life.'

Millicent would have protested, but he continued before she could interrupt him.

'No, Mother, I'm quite determined. Unless I'm able to buy the practice outright, I don't want any part of it.'

'Now just a moment,' Morag intervened. 'Let's look at this thing logically. If it was Dad's wish that one of us should carry on the practice, then we ought to give the matter serious consideration. When we believed that none of us was interested, it was okay to talk of selling up. Now Iain's saying that if he was in a position to, he would buy it.' She glanced across at her brother, seeking his confirmation.

Iain nodded.

'Well then, I don't see any problem. Personally, I want nothing to do with the practice, and as for my share of the inheritance – I have everything I shall ever want. I'll happily sign over my interest in the business to Iain.'

David remained silent. He had not anticipated anything from his father's estate as yet, but he was not prepared to relinquish all interest.

'If you will forgive me…' Stephen intervened hesitantly.

Iain turned towards his cousin suspiciously. Was Stephen going to make a claim after all? The practice had been started by their great grandfather and carried on by their grandfather. Stephen had as much right to be considered as any of them. What was more, as a Wing Commander, his gratuity from the RAF would have been far more than either David's or his own. He was probably in a position to offer enough money to buy the practice.

'I don't know how much attention you people have been paying to the discussions which have been going on at Westminster,' Stephen continued, 'but I understand that private practices are likely be subsumed by the National Health Service. Where the incumbent agrees to sign a contract with the Government, the authorities will pay rent for the business premises and assume responsibility for the cost of maintenance of that part of the building. What that means is that Aunt Millicent could expect a steady income from the surgery, waiting room and dispensary. The important thing is for Iain to be well established in the practice before the take-over, so that his appointment within the new set-up is assured.'

'What would happen if Iain decided to pull out at a later date? How would that leave mother?' David asked.

'As I understand it, the house would remain Aunt Millicent's,' Stephen hastened to reassure him. If she chose to repossess the doctor's premises, the Health Authority would have to provide suitable accommodation for the practice elsewhere.'

'There, you see,' Millicent smiled happily at them all, 'Iain can come back here to live. I shall keep house for him and look after the farm with help from McKinnon. When the time comes that Iain needs the house for himself and his family, I shall move into the farm cottage. With a little fixing up, it will be ideal for a widow woman all on her own.'

'You make yourself sound a hundred years old!' laughed Morag. 'But still, it seems the ideal solution. What do you think, David?'

David frowned. And what was going to happen when Millicent died? Chances were that Iain would end up with everything... house, farm, medical practice, the lot. He couldn't help feeling unwilling to kiss his rightful inheritance goodbye. Accustomed as he was to analysing people's reactions to every situation, he wondered whether these doubts arose from a genuine concern for his mother's interests or from old sibling rivalries tinged with jealousy. Suspecting the latter and not liking himself for it he shrugged noncommittally but could not bring himself to express any agreement.

Morag's husband, with the insight of the outsider and the mind of a businessman, appreciated David's quandary and ventured a compromise.

'Even within a close-knit family circle such as this,' he observed, 'it is a good idea to have matters of property set out within a legal framework to avoid argument and recriminations at a later date. Why don't I have my solicitor draw up an agreement for you?'

'That makes a lot of sense,' said Stuart approvingly. 'What do you say, Millicent?'

'I can't see that it's necessary to be so formal,' was Millicent's emphatic response.

Morag glanced at her youngest brother, willing him to say something constructive. David was clearly relieved that Duncan's suggestion had made it unnecessary for him to put forward a similar proposal.

'Sounds okay to me,' he assented.

Iain breathed more easily. An hour ago he had been resigned to the loss of the prize he had dreamed of for so long. Now there was every prospect that he might remain here at Eisdalsa after all.

'Trust you to come up with the obvious solution,' he said. 'Thanks, Duncan.'

He shook his brother-in-law by the hand, kissed Morag on the cheek and returned to his place on the couch where David, smiling now that things had been settled to his satisfaction, was helping Millicent get to her feet.

When Iain attempted to give his mother a hug to show her how pleased he was, she ignored him and glared at Duncan. 'No doubt that is the way things are done in business, but Hugh was always suspicious of lawyers. I'm quite certain we can get by without any legal rigmarole. Iain will take over the practice and I shall remain here with him. As for the inheritance, you children will just have to work things out for yourselves when the time comes.'

This new Millicent, so forceful and determined, was someone none of them recognised. For a moment the family was left speechless.

Ignoring the uncomfortable silence which followed her outburst, Iain thanked her effusively, promising to take care of her always. 'We'll get along fine together, Ma,' he assured her.

Millicent released herself from his embrace and studied him at arm's length. 'Don't expect me to go on taking telephone calls at all times of the day and night,' she told him. 'I've had a lifetime of that. It's time you settled down properly. The sooner you get yourself a wife, the better!'

She had not meant it as a joke and seemed surprised when everyone laughed. Nevertheless, the tension had been broken.

'I for one am delighted that the practice will stay in the family,' Stuart declared. 'So much so, that I'll volunteer to continue to hold the reins until such time as Iain is relieved of his duties in Edinburgh. Only, don't make it too long because I've committed myself to becoming the district representative for the BMA and will be obliged to attend quite a few meetings as we get nearer to July of next year.'

Stephen was taken completely by surprise at his father's announcement. 'Fancy keeping something like that to yourself, you old dog!' he exclaimed, 'That's great news. Congratulations!'

'Now we can be sure that the new Health Service will be in safe hands,' Iain agreed, following suit with his own congratulations.

Stuart however, could not share their confidence. Already he had attended some meetings where he had found himself to be a lone voice in favour of Mr Bevan's proposals. The majority of his colleagues appeared to be more concerned with their own position than with the extra benefits that might be enjoyed by their patients. If the top echelons of the British Medical Association were to have their way, Aneurin Bevan's dream of health care for all, free at the point of delivery, was doomed to failure. While he acknowledged the family's congratulations with a rather embarrassed smile, Stuart Beaton could only pray that they were right and he would be proved wrong.

5

ALISON MCKENZIE EMPTIED the steel pan in the sluice and thrust it into the steriliser with such force that the metal rang like a bell. The effort was sufficient to dispel at least a little of her anger. She rinsed her hands under the tap and dried them, pushing a wisp of hair out of her eyes as soon as she had done so.

Blast Sister! How did she imagine a girl could keep her hair tidy hauling patients in and out of bed and shoving furniture from one end of the ward to the other all day? Not a single word of appreciation for the fact that she had been the one to notice that Mrs McTavish had changed colour and was struggling for breath. The old girl would have died if she hadn't called the crash team in time! As the experts went in with their resuscitator, all Sister had had to say to her was, 'Fetch the monitor, Nurse, and be quick about it.' When she returned pushing the massive trolley with its electrical cables dangling, it was, 'Really, Nurse, don't you know better than to leave wires trailing like that? You could trip someone up.' And, 'For goodness sake, girl, straighten your cap and tidy your hair, you look as though you had been dragged through a hedge, backwards!'

As Alison had fiddled with the pins which trapped her unruly curls beneath the ridiculous little cap, the woman was on at her again. 'Answer that bell, Nurse. It will be Mrs Smithers wanting a bedpan.'

How had she known? Alison wondered. She'd probably forgotten that the poor old dear had asked her ages ago and was still waiting. Anyway, by the time Alison had got there it was too late and that had meant yet another bed to be stripped, the third on this shift!

She glanced at the fob watch attached to her apron. It was six thirty, another hour and a half before the night staff came on duty. Her feet ached, her back ached and her head was splitting. The nurses in those pre-war Dr Kildare movies never seemed to have such problems. Had she known it would be like this, she might have gone into a bank like her friend Kirsty or become a teacher like Katy Swinburn. It was those films that had made her decide to be a nurse. Those, and the way her mother's eyes had lit up when she had said what she wanted to be. Lew Ayres was her film star pin-up. She had an autographed photograph stuck inside the lid of her desk at school. One of her cousin's GI boyfriends had got it for her. Ever since she could remember, her one ambition in life had been to marry a doctor just like Dr Kildare.

As she made her way along the corridor past the bathroom and ducked to avoid being seen from Sister's office, she caught a glimpse of the new surgical registrar all the girls were swooning over. It was unusual for Sister not to be hovering nearby. She seemed to have an instinct for knowing when doctors were on the ward and immediately went to them. This time, however, Alison aimed to reach him first. She checked that her fountain pen was still in her top pocket in case he wanted her to take notes.

Iain Beaton glanced up as she approached.

'Ah, good,' he said, 'just the girl. Fetch me a chair, will you, Nurse. I'd like a chat with Mrs McDougall, just to let her know what we will be doing tomorrow.'

Alison felt the blood rushing to her cheeks and moved quickly to carry out his request. Sister was approaching rapidly from the far end of the ward. When she reached Mrs McDougall's bed she halted, watching with pursed lips as Alison slipped past her carrying the chair.

'Thank you, Nurse,' she murmured, through clenched teeth. 'You may go.' As Alison turned away she called after her, 'There is still the linen to be sorted for the laundry collection.'

Sister placed herself at the end of the bed, hands clasped in front of her, making it quite plain that she disapproved of the doctor's casual approach to a patient in her charge.

Iain glanced up, smiled broadly and greeted her in a friendly manner.

'Good evening, Sister Charles,' he said cheerfully. 'Just having a word with Mrs McDougall about tomorrow's wee operation. We won't keep you from your other duties!'

Sister Charles sniffed, disgustedly. This young man had a lot to learn about hospital etiquette. She must have a word with Mr Delaney. The principal consultant in surgery was unlikely to put up with such cavalier behaviour from his junior staff. Without another word she stalked off and Iain, grinning broadly at his minor victory, rubbed his hands together to warm them before placing them on Mrs McDougall's swollen abdomen.

'Yes, that's an uncomfortable lump, Mrs McDougall,' he said. 'Better out than in, don't you agree? Now, this is what Mr Delaney proposes.'

As Iain left the ward some time later, he collided with an untidy pile of bed linen approaching rapidly from the far end of the corridor.

'Whoops, sorry Nurse,' he said, as a couple of sheets fell from the top of the heap. He stooped to pick them up and found himself looking into a pair of green eyes as bright and sparkling as the Eisdalsa seas.

'Where are you going with that lot?' he asked, as Alison straightened up and re-balanced her load.

'Just in here, Doctor,' she indicated the door to the linen room. 'Would you mind opening it?'

He reached around her to grasp the knob and the sleeve of his white coat brushed her bare arm, setting off a tingling sensation which almost made her gasp out loud. In spite of the overpowering scent of iodoform and carbolic soap, she could still detect a hint of the expensive pipe tobacco he smoked. It was her father's favourite brand, Balkan Sobrani. The odour evoked memories of a childhood whose happiness had faded with the death of her mother in the first year of the war.

'Thank you,' she mumbled as she eased her burden past him and dumped it on the floor ready for counting into the laundry basket.

She turned, half expecting him to be gone, but Iain lingered in the doorway.

'You're new here aren't you?' he asked.

'This is my first time on a surgical ward,' she explained. 'My last assignment before I take my finals in June.'

'How's it going? Sister a bit of a tyrant, is she?' His sympathetic enquiry was almost too much for Alison. Despite every effort to control her emotions, she felt her eyes brimming with tears.

Sister Charles was a dragon where her staff were concerned but Iain could vouch for her knowledge and expertise. She was never slow to advise medical students and inexperienced housemen when she thought they were likely to slip up. Although she probably did not remember it now, there had been occasions in the past when Iain had had cause to be grateful to Sister Charles.

'Don't let her get you down,' he said, alarmed to see tears trickling down Alison's cheeks, 'her bark's much worse than her bite.'

He could see that she didn't believe him.

'No, honestly,' he added hastily. 'She was around when I was a student here, years ago. I promise you, if you stick it out, she'll make a fine nurse of you. Her girls always do best in the exams.'

Alison tried to smile. She rubbed the back of her hand across her eyes, fiddled with her cap and tried to hide those unruly brown wisps which had once again escaped capture.

I'll bet she's a cracker out of uniform, thought Iain. He would love to get a proper look at those chestnut curls.

'Best let you get on, before Sister comes back.' He smiled broadly. 'See you around,' he added brightly. 'Keep your chin up!'

He was gone through the swing door at the end of the corridor before she could reply. She watched until he was out of sight and then, with an unladylike sniff, rubbed her back where the pain was greatest and picked up the laundry list, checking off each of the items as she placed them in the basket.

An hour later, as the first of the new shift began to arrive, Alison was completing her reports before she went off duty. She looked up from the chart she was studying, to find Sister standing at her elbow.

'Ah there you are, McKenzie,' exclaimed the older woman. Alison wondered at the bright red colour in her cheeks. Could it be that Sister was embarrassed for some reason?

'Mr Standish, the cardiologist, has just been in to check on Mrs McTavish. It seems that had you not observed her distress when you did and called for help, we would have lost her. Well done, Nurse!'

She stalked away, leaving Alison staring after her.

Perhaps it had not been such a bad day after all. She had at last made contact with an unmarried member of the medical staff who was under fifty and who, if not quite as handsome as Lew Ayres, was neither fat nor bald. What was more Iain Beaton was an inch or two taller than herself. Alison at five foot ten in her stockings, often towered over her dancing partners. It was a pity about that flaming red hair, but his eyes were nice. Then to round off what had turned out to be a pretty perfect day, the old dragon had shown a chink of humanity in that brittle armour of hers.

6

IAIN BEATON HAD returned to Edinburgh in a glow of euphoria. The local Medical Officer of Health had accepted his uncle's recommendation that he take over the Eisdalsa practice, so the only task left was to deliver to the Superintendent the unwelcome news that he was about to lose his surgical registrar of only six months.

The wind caught him as he rounded the corner of the building, ruffling his hair and threatening to tear the papers out of his hands. Only in Edinburgh would you encounter a piercingly cold northeasterly like this in mid-May. That was another good thing about his decision to move back home. The Argyll winds were sometimes stronger but they were rarely as cold as this, even in midwinter. Iain put his head down and clutching the documents to his chest as he crossed the open square, he mounted the steps to the oldest part of the hospital.

Constructed of red granite, the infirmary had been built to last for centuries and presented every appearance of having already fulfilled its purpose. Chipped and stained stone mullions surrounded row upon row of small square windows which overlooked the dismal streets of downtown Edinburgh. The building presented such a miserably bleak façade to the outside world, it was small wonder the older citizens regarded the hospital as a place where you came only to die. Inside, the windows did little to relieve the gloominess of the endless corridors with their highly polished marble floors and dark green tiled walls, unrelieved by ceilings which had not seen a coat of fresh cream paint since before the war.

Swing doors on either side gave access to wards, every one identical to its neighbour. Each contained twenty-four beds, aligned precisely at the designated distance apart as if laid out by theodolite. Not a chair, not a water-jug, not a patient's chart was out of place. Patients obeyed strict rules as to where they could sit, when they could walk about, what they could have in their lockers and on them. Woe betide anyone who sat on a bed or whose counterpane showed the slightest wrinkle.

How patients ever recovered from their ailments in this regimented atmosphere, Iain could not understand. Possibly their determination to escape from the place helped them to get better!

He entered the glassed-in office which was Sister Charles' domain and stopped abruptly at the sight of Alison McKenzie on her knees, searching through the contents of the bottom drawer of a filing cabinet. It would be difficult to say who was the more startled.

'Oh,' he said, lamely, 'I thought Sister would be here.'

'She's at a meeting in Matron's office,' said Alison. 'I'm in charge for the moment. Can I help?'

'I'm looking for some patient histories. I have to bring them up to date for the new man before I leave.'

'Are you going somewhere?'

What a stupid thing to say! She could have kicked herself. If he was leaving, of course he was going somewhere!

'Going into private practice,' he told her.

'Oh? Won't that be a big change from hospital work? I had the impression that you were dedicated to surgery.'

'I had my fill of cutting and stitching during the war,' Iain told her. 'Direct contact with patients satisfies me more. It's not easy to form a personal relationship with a liver or a pair of kidneys.'

Since their first encounter, Alison had never missed an opportunity to observe him at work on the wards. She had noted how he treated every patient as an individual. They would open up to his friendly approach. Even Sister must appreciate his bedside manner, for she would invariably approach Dr Beaton if there was something unpleasant to tell a patient. He had his own particular way of inspiring confidence, even in the most hopeless cases.

Alison had got to her feet while they were talking and laughed outright at his reference to surgery.

Iain noticed her even, white teeth and the delightful way in which one eyebrow seemed to rise up when she was puzzled. There were precise little lines at the corners of her mouth when she smiled.

'Look,' he said, 'I shall be leaving on Saturday. How about having dinner with me on Friday night? They tell me you can get a really decent meal at the Italian place that's just opened in the Canongate.'

'That would be lovely, only...'

'Don't tell me you're on duty? Or you have to wash your hair, or something!'

'No, it's not that. I usually go to visit my grandmother on Friday evenings.'

She realised that as an excuse it sounded feeble but it was true. Her grandmother had practically brought her up after her mother died and now, living all alone on the top floor of a tenement, the old woman relied on Alison to take her the few necessities of life.

'Oh, well, it was just a thought.' Iain turned away, disappointed.

'What about your patient records?' she called after him.

'Oh yes, of course, thanks,' he said, turning back. 'These are the ones I need.'

He handed her a short list of names and for the next few minutes watched her rifling through the files, withdrawing the necessary folders.

'There, that seems to be the lot.' She handed them to him with a smile. 'About Friday. If you wouldn't mind waiting for me while I take Granny a few bits and pieces for the weekend, we could eat later.'

'All right.' He brightened up instantly. 'Tell you what, why don't I come to visit Granny too? It'll save time if we both leave here together and go straight on to the restaurant afterwards.'

Alison's heart missed a beat. Could she really take him to the tiny two-roomed apartment where her grandmother lived? She cringed at the thought of the shared lavvy on the landing and her grandmother's perpetual moaning about a neighbour who never took her turn at scrubbing the stairs. He might think she had been brought up in such surroundings. She had, of course but there was no need for him to know it.

'I have seen a tenement before you know! I shared a single end with a couple of guys during our final year at Uni.'

'I know she'd enjoy meeting you,' Alison could imagine how impressed old Maggie would be to receive a visit from Dr Beaton.

7

'IT'S BEEN A lovely evening. Thank you.'

They were standing in the shadows, carefully concealed by a stone pillar, just a few feet from the entrance to the Nurses' Home.

'I hope we didn't tire your gran too much.'

She had made the most of her unexpected visitor. Iain was treated to a blow by blow account of how Mr Gillespie had removed the old lady's gallstones and she spent twenty minutes hunting for the little bottle containing the evidence of her operation!

'She had the time of her life,' laughed Alison. 'I hope you didn't mind all that stuff about me at school. I was the first in our family to progress beyond elementary school, so she takes a lot of pride in me.'

'She never mentioned your father.'

'After Mum died, Dad took to going down the pub every Friday, football or dogs on Saturday and drinking again on Sunday. He and his pals used to take the ferry to a hotel in North Queensferry so they could claim to be bona fide travellers. We hardly ever saw him.'

'A tough life for a wee girl.' Iain was gazing at her approvingly. 'Still, it didn't stop you getting your school certificate, and now, State Registration.'

'We'll have to see about that, won't we,' she answered rather sharply. 'There's only a few weeks to the exams and I've loads of revision to get through.'

'Oh come on, I'm sure you'll be okay. Sister Charles' girls never fail.'

'Only because they'd be too frightened to face her if they did!'

'Anyway, does it matter all that much?' He had been standing with his hands loosely beneath her elbows but now he tightened his hold, grasping her around the waist with one hand while tracing the contours of her face with the other.

'A pretty girl like you doesn't want to waste her talents running after Matron and kowtowing to a bunch of middle-aged medics, all for a few pounds a month.'

'I have to earn a living somehow,' Alison said.

'You'd be much better off getting married and having a couple of kids.'

A few weeks ago she might have agreed but now, for some reason, his complete disregard of her professional aspirations really annoyed her.

'Not every girl you meet is looking for a husband,' she retorted.

'Oh, I'm sorry.' Iain hadn't meant to be sound dismissive. The fact was, he really admired her spirit. From what he had seen of her on the wards, she made an excellent nurse but if he said so now she'd only think he was trying to get back into her good books. Best to let it go.

'What a pity we didn't get around to doing something like this earlier,' he said instead. 'I shall be far away from here by tomorrow at this time.'

'While I shall be starting night duty.' Her tone had softened. 'The old ladies on the ward are going to miss you. They all look forward to your rounds. No doubt we shall be left to mop up the tears. I wouldn't be surprised if Mrs Riley comes to live over on the west coast, just so she can have you for her GP!'

'Will I see you again, Alison?'

'Only if you come to Edinburgh.'

'We could write.'

'We'll both be busy for a while.'

She might write to him, but would he bother to answer? She suspected not.

The city clocks began to strike the hour taking up their cue one from the other. Alison started... eleven o'clock already!

'I must go in! The porter locks up on the dot.'

Far from their parting kiss being the lingering romantic moment Iain had been working up to, they exchanged a light touch on the lips and she was gone, slipping in through the door with a cheery 'Goodnight' for the porter before disappearing into the dimly lit forbidden regions of the Nurses' Home.

Iain watched after her for a while, regretting his foolishness in not making the most of his opportunity and cursing his clumsy reference to her work. He would write... that's what he'd do. It was always easier for him to express himself on paper. Full of resolve, he made his way back along the road to where bright lights from the hospital's emergency entrance flooded the forecourt. A white city ambulance pulled in with a screech of brakes. It was followed by a police car which drew up alongside, its bell still clanging from the wild dash through city streets. Instinctively, Iain began to run forwards but then, remembering that he was no longer part of the emergency team, he pulled up short and looked on as porters, nurses and doctors poured out through the doors and surrounded the motionless figure covered by a bright red blanket.

8

'DR BEATON? IT'S Alma Livingstone.'

'Alma?' Iain raised his eyebrows questioningly at his mother.

'District nurse,' Millicent whispered. 'You must have met her at the funeral.'

Iain remembered. She was the woman he'd seen talking to Ellen in the cemetery.

'Welcome home.'

There was a short pause. Surely she was not ringing at eight o'clock in the morning just to say that.

'Thanks,' Iain replied.

'I'm sorry to bother you so soon, Doctor, but I think you should come and have a look at Tam, Thomas McFarlane that is. He lives in one of those little cottages beside the castle.'

'Can you tell me what's wrong?'

'He came home from his work last evening talking very oddly. He was rambling on about all sorts of things so that at first Mairi, that's his wife, thought he was drunk. She got him to bed expecting him to sleep it off but he didn't sleep, just kept on rambling. He has been feverish and delirious all night. When I made my usual call on old Mrs Moran first thing this morning, Mairi waylaid me as I was leaving.'

'Where does Mr McFarlane work?'

'He's only recently been demobbed. He started back at his old job in the quarries about six weeks ago.'

Iain recalled the fellow now. They had been contemporaries at school. Tam was one of the tough kids in the school yard. Iain could imagine him becoming a stonemason. 'And where was he stationed during the war?'

he demanded.

'India or Burma I think. Somewhere in the Far East.' Alma cursed herself for having failed to ask the obvious questions.

'It could be any one of a number of things, but my bet is malaria. I don't suppose you thought to ask if he's had it?'

'No.' Alma had so wanted to make a good impression and the new doctor had already found her wanting.

'No reason why you should have recognised it,' he said reassuringly. 'I'll get over there immediately after morning surgery. Where are you speaking from?'

'I'm at the castle lodge. The factor kindly allowed me to use his phone.'

'Will you be passing McFarlane's again?'

'I can do.'

'Tell Mrs McFarlane to make sure her husband gets plenty of fluids. If necessary, she'll have to force him to drink. It's important he doesn't become dehydrated. Sponging down with tepid water might help to reduce the temperature but she mustn't allow him to get chilled and she should keep him as quiet as possible.'

'She has three children... are they in any danger?'

He was taken aback by her apparent ignorance of the disease.

'Not if it's malaria, no. Just in case it's something else, tell her to keep the kids out of the way.'

'I'll tell her and I'll say you'll be there as soon as possible.'

'Thanks.'

He was going to put down the phone when he had another thought.

'Miss Livingstone, we really ought to meet some time soon. Did you have a regular time for swapping notes with my father?'

'Thursday mornings. Surgeries are usually pretty quiet then. I would call in at about ten thirty to have a talk and then Dr Beaton would usually go on into town to visit any of his patients in the hospital.'

'Where are you staying?'

'It's a cottage at Clachan, you can't miss it. Next to the bridge. Mrs Beaton knows.'

'Look, to save you a trip over here, I'll call in on you tomorrow on my way into town. Shall we say eleven o'clock?'

'That will be fine. I'll look forward to it.'

He heard a click and the line went dead. Replacing the receiver he turned to his mother.

'What did Dad think of Alma Livingstone?'

'They always seemed to get on well enough. I never heard him say anything derogatory about her, but then of course, your father looked for the best in everyone.'

At the mention of Hugh, Millicent felt her eyes beginning to fill and fussed with the breakfast dishes. Would this go on forever, she wondered? Every day she woke up determined to get on with things, only to find herself thinking of him in everything she tackled. Half a dozen times a day she would imagine she saw Hugh climbing the stairs or crossing the broad landing. Sometimes she thought she caught a glimpse of her husband's shadowy figure disappearing into the dimly lit corridor which connected the entrance hall with the surgery...

Iain was spreading his toast thickly with butter and digging his knife into the marmalade pot.

'Oh, I do wish you'd use the spoon,' Millicent said sharply, 'Just look at all that butter in the marmalade!'

Iain glanced curiously at his mother. What was making her so scratchy this morning? She didn't usually reprimand him, even for this most heinous of crimes!

'Sorry,' he murmured and used a clean knife to dig out the offending butter. 'Is Alma State Registered?'

'Oh, I wouldn't think so,' Millicent replied. She took little interest in the professional qualifications available to women. In her opinion, marriage was the only respectable occupation for a well bred girl. 'Alma went to work at the West Highland Hospital soon after she left school,' she said. 'As far as I know she remained there until she got this job with the Council. Do they train nurses for State Registration in a cottage hospital?'

'Unlikely.' Iain swallowed his final mouthful of tea and brushed the crumbs off his shirt front. At this point, his father would have sunk his head into yesterday's *Scotsman* and ignored everything going on around him.

'What happened to the daily paper delivery?' he asked, suddenly aware that he had seen no sign of a newspaper since his arrival.

'When Hugh was ill, the papers just piled up unread, day after day,' said Millicent. 'In the end I told Donnie to stop delivering them. I'll re-order if you want.'

'Thanks, Mum.' Iain got to his feet and came around the table to give her a peck on the cheek. 'I suppose I ought to keep abreast of what's going on in the world. At the very least I should know what's happening in the world of football. My patients won't think much of a doctor who doesn't know whether Rangers or Celtic are winning this season.'

Millicent couldn't help laughing.

'The football season's already finished!'

'I didn't even know that! It just shows how important it is to take a daily paper. Who knows what such fearful ignorance might lead to!'

There was a ring at the surgery door.

'First customer, right on the dot. Best get to it.'

He hurried out, drawing on his jacket and straightening his tie in a manner which reminded her of his father.

'There I go again,' Millicent brushed away a tear and began to clear the table.

9

THOMAS MCFARLANE WAS a shadow of the burly youth Iain remembered. The man's skin was drawn tightly over his skull, his eyes deep sunk in their sockets. Iain pulled back the covers to expose a torso which was little more than a skeleton covered in skin. He had seen nothing like this since those terrible scenes he had witnessed in 1945. As commander of an advance medical team, he had been one of the earliest witnesses to the full horror of the Nazi concentration camps.

Iain looked up at Mairi, seeking some explanation.

'That's how they sent him back to me,' she said. There was no emotion in her voice, no tears in her eyes, just desperation.

'From where?'

'Burma... he was a prisoner for four years.'

Iain nodded. No need for further explanation. Everyone knew what had befallen those who had been prisoners in the hands of the Japanese.

'He's been in hospital for three months. They discharged him six weeks ago. Fit for work they said, when he went back for a check-up last week.'

Mairi pursed her lips. There was no doubting her opinion of Army doctors.

'Nurse told me he has already started working at the quarry.'

Iain found it hard to believe that anyone would employ this man for such heavy work.

'Tally clerk, that's all,' Mairi told him. 'It's not much money but it's better than being on the dole. Mr Fergusson was obliged to have him back you see, but he couldn't work as a mason. He had to give that up after a couple of days. They must have felt sorry for him, I suppose, because they offered him a job in the office though how long he's likely to keep it is anybody's guess. He's nor exactly cut out for writing and figuring, my Tam!'

'Surely he'll be getting a pension?' Iain could not believe that any ex-serviceman in this condition would be expected to fend for himself.

'He applied. They said because he wasn't actually wounded and had only been a prisoner of war, there was nothing they could do about a pension. *Only* a prisoner of war! Can you believe that?'

'Has your husband ever mentioned having had malaria, Mrs McFarlane?' Iain asked.

'No. He won't talk about anything that happened to him out there.'

Iain examined his patient for signs of swelling in the spleen and what he found confirmed his suspicions.

'He began by complaining of the cold, I believe. Was there intense shivering?'

She nodded. 'When I felt him though, he was boiling hot. He sweated something awfu'. Wringing wet all night.'

'Until I've had your husband's blood analysed, I can't be sure we are dealing with malaria, but it seems highly likely. I'm going to put him on a course of Quinacrine. In my grandfather's day they used to call it Peruvian bark. Nowadays it's refined and mixed with other ingredients to make it more effective with fewer side effects, but he may complain of ringing in the ears and his skin will turn a bit yellow. Oh, yes, and his urine will be yellow too but there's no need to be alarmed. The colouration will disappear as soon as he stops taking the drug.'

'Why would he have something like that?' Mairi demanded. 'I thought malaria was what people got in the tropics.'

'This is almost certainly a recurrence – your husband must have picked it up in Burma. The malarial parasite can remain in the human body for years and every now and then the disease breaks out again. Attacks can occur for some years but in people who are otherwise healthy, after each recurrence the body becomes a little more able to put up a fight until complete immunity is achieved. There's no great danger in these secondary attacks provided your husband receives proper treatment and gives himself time to recover.'

At the sound of childish murmurings, Iain looked around to see, grouped in the bedroom doorway, three children varying in age from around four to twelve years. They were wide-eyed and fearful, responding to the doctor's friendly greeting with silent stares.

'It's not infectious,' he said, turning back to Mairi, 'but your husband needs rest and quiet. It might be as well to park the children out for a few days.'

Mairi snorted. 'Tam and me's nae family in these parts and such friends as are left have nae mare room than oursels!'

The McFarlane's cottage was built to the same plan as all the workmen's houses in the district. The kitchen and bedroom were separated by a closet that ran from back to front of the house. The front part formed a small lobby into which the front door to the house opened. Behind this was a pantry and also, approached from the kitchen, a narrow box bed, scarcely large enough to accommodate the three children, with two of them approaching their teens.

'Well, do your best to keep him as quiet as possible.' Iain snapped shut his medical bag and stood up. 'Try not to worry too much, your husband will be back on his feet again in no time.'

Mairi scarcely acknowledged his reassurances.

'*Wha!* What're they doin? Oh God no. *No!*'

Startled, Iain turned again to the bed, where Tam McFarlane, semi-conscious and clearly delirious, had begun to toss agitatedly from side to side. Suddenly he sat bolt upright, stared fixedly at the opposite wall for a few moments and then screamed out, 'Na! No' again, ye bastards. Dinna hit me again!' He covered his head with his arms and bent sideways as though to ward off a mighty blow.

Shaken by the sudden outburst, Iain reopened his bag, fumbled for a sedative and plunged a hypodermic needle into the bottle cap. When the drug had found its mark and the patient was once more relaxed and apparently dozing he asked, 'How about your husband's general health Mrs McFarlane?'

'He's aye complaining about his heid,' she replied. 'He gets a' frustrated when he cannae hold things. He's gey clumsy at times. Broken three of my best saucers already and him only home a matter of weeks.'

'I'll look into that the next time I see him,' Iain suggested, making a mental note to call within the next day or two. He counted a number of Quinacrine tablets into a small bottle. Thank goodness Alma had warned him what to expect. One would not normally come armed against malaria on the west coast of Scotland!

Giving Mairi her instructions, he began to pack away his instruments.

'The fever should clear up very soon but I'm a little concerned about these headaches. I'd like Mr McFarlane to have an x-ray.'

She looked frightened. Thinking the procedure itself alarmed her, he tried to make light of it.

'Only a precaution you understand. It's quite routine.'

'What'll it cost?' she demanded anxiously.

Now he understood. Remembering she had been employed in factory work throughout the war, he assumed she had insurance cover.

'I stopped the HSA payments when the factory closed down,' she told him. 'Couldn't afford it. Not with just Tam's Army allowances coming in. Then when he came home the allowances stopped and his wages were too small.'

'Well, we won't bother about it now,' Iain assured her. 'Something will be arranged. Meanwhile, you'll need to feed your man up a bit. Give him plenty of butter, eggs and red meat. That's what he needs if we're going to see him playing in the shinty team next season!'

And just how do you imagine we are going to pay for that kind of food, Mairi asked herself, but to Iain she simply replied, 'Thank you, Doctor.' Opening the door of the cottage, she let him out into the bright sunshine.

'I'll get this blood sample to the lab straight away,' he told her as she accompanied him to the gate, 'but I don't think there is any doubt about the cause of the fever. Send for me if you are worried about anything at all. I'll call in again in a day or so.'

He drove out of the sleepy little village under a high, stone wall which separated Creag Castle from the row of workers' cottages, which had been built originally to house the retainers employed by the laird. The wall was crumbling in places, while the great wrought-iron gates, noted for their intricacy of design, had long ago been removed for the war effort. As he passed by the empty gateway, Iain caught a glimpse of the park beyond. The drive, long and straight, was overgrown with weeds. At its far end stood an austere, centuries-old tower house, much altered over the years: the summer residence of the marquesses of Stirling. The park and gardens had been immaculate in the days when his father attended here. Now everything appeared sadly neglected. His mother had mentioned in one of her letters that the house was being used by some government department. That would explain the dilapidation. The offices were empty now and the ranks of camouflaged vehicles which had once crowded into the gravelled courtyard had long departed. His Lordship was going to have a tough time getting the place back to normal after such a long period of neglect.

Iain let in the gear carefully and took his foot off the clutch. He was becoming accustomed to the erratic behaviour of this ancient vehicle. The Armstrong Siddeley lurched forward, sending a shower of mud from beneath its wheels. It must be years since anyone had troubled to maintain the road, which was badly potholed and rutted, the result no doubt of constant use by heavy Army vehicles. He couldn't see his badly worn tyres holding out much longer on roads like this. According to Uncle Stuart, the size of tyre he required was unobtainable. Maybe he should be looking out for another car.

10

'IAIN! IAIN! MILLICENT Beaton placed the telephone receiver face up on the hall table and fetched her son from the surgery.

'A call for you. It's a woman. Alice, Alex, something of the sort.'

'Alison?'

'Maybe. She seems to know you pretty well.'

Iain reached for the receiver.

'Hallo, Dr Beaton here.'

'Oh Iain, it's you. The woman who answered seemed so vague I wondered if I had the right number.'

'Alison?'

'Yes. Are you surprised?'

'Well.'

'Would you believe it, Gran decided she wanted to see Oban just once more. It seems she spent her honeymoon here goodness knows how many years ago. I had some leave due to me so we thought we'd come.'

'You mean you're actually here, in Oban?'

He didn't quite know what to say. Her call had taken him completely off guard. He fingered the little blue envelope he carried in his breast pocket and wished he had found time to answer her letter.

'We're in a guest house in Duke Street, Ocean View. I'd have preferred a decent hotel,' she chatted nervously, 'but Gran insisted on this boarding house. It's where she stayed when she was on her honeymoon. The owners have changed but not much else. The wallpaper looks as though it's been pasted up for forty years and the plumbing has been around even longer!'

'How long are you here for?' he asked.

'Until Saturday week. I wondered how I might get out there to visit

39

you. After everything you told me about it, I can't wait to see Eisdalsa. Is there a bus or something?'

'Well, yes, there is a bus, but only one a day.'

He thought rapidly. Was there some way he could re-arrange his tight schedule to include collecting her himself? No, he really couldn't manage it this week.

'Oh, wait a minute. There are tour buses at this time of the year. They come down to the village most afternoons and give people a couple of hours to look around before returning to Oban. You could get the driver to drop you off at the end of our drive. Tell him Tigh na Broch.'

'Is there one day more convenient than any other?' she asked less enthusiastically. She suspected that if he was really interested in seeing her, he would have offered to come and collect her.

'I should be free Wednesday afternoon,' he replied.

There was a ring at the doorbell.

'Look, I've a patient just now. Come on Wednesday. Bring Granny. My mother will be delighted to entertain you both!'

'Oh, all right. Wednesday it is then. I'll go to the tours office and find out about the bus times. Better let you go now. Goodbye!'

Alison replaced the phone and sat staring at it for a few minutes. Maybe this was not such a good idea after all.

For a few seconds she relived their parting on the steps of the Nurses' Home when, rather shyly she thought, he had made a grab for her and they had kissed. It had been a chaste kiss, like those she had exchanged behind the lavvies in the school yard, years ago, but it had thrilled her just the same. She really liked him. Oh well, it would be a nice ride out for Gran and they had been invited for tea. She pulled on her coat and wandered off down to the pier in search of the tours booking office.

I I

'EISDALSA!' THE DRIVER called out as the coach rounded the bend at the top of the brae and the whole panorama of the Sound of Lorn came into view.

There were gasps of delight from passengers witnessing the view for the first time.

Dozens of rocky islets lay scattered across a wide expanse of ocean. Small boats, their colourful sails breaking up the monotony of blue and silver, darted to and fro. In the summer haze every rocky outcrop appeared to hover a few feet above the surface of the water while below darkly menacing cliffs, a skirt of white foam broke along the beaches. In the far distance were larger islands, their heather-covered slopes sharply silhouetted against the sky.

Alone amongst the spectators, Alison's attention was held by the large white house in the valley below, sheltering in the shadow of an immense outcrop of volcanic rock. Its tall windows reflected the changing patterns of the clouds while above the many-gabled roof of grey slates towered a complex of chimneys.

A narrow lane linked the house with the coast road and behind the main building, lay steadings and another, smaller house, presumably the farmhouse Iain had mentioned. Sheep dotted the braeside and in the meadow which ran down to the shore, shaggy Highland cattle lay or stood in companionable groups, chewing lazily in the warm afternoon sun.

'That must be his home,' she murmured, unaware that she had spoken aloud. Suddenly she felt petrified at the thought of seeing Iain again. What if he made it plain that her sudden appearance was unwelcome? He had sounded so offhand on the phone. Perhaps she had misunderstood.

Had she allowed herself to be carried away by her own romantic imaginings?

'Where?' asked her grandmother, breaking Alison's train of thought.

'Down there. That's Tigh na Broch, where we're going to get off.'

'I don't see the point of coming all the way out here without seeing the village. If it was just tea you wanted we might as well have stayed in Oban.'

'We're going to visit Mrs Beaton, Iain's mum… you know, the doctor I brought to see you that time.'

Maggie sniffed pointedly. She had been talking to others on the coach. Apparently there was a nice gift shop in the village and a place to get pastries and a good cup of tea without having to meet strangers and make polite conversation.

'And hae I to walk all that way up to the house?' she grumbled.

Exasperated, Alison turned to the woman in the seat behind. Mrs McDonald had accompanied them from the guest house.

'Would it be all right if I left Gran with you?' Alison asked. 'She wants to see the village and I have made arrangements to visit some friends, at the house down there.' She pointed to Tigh na Broch.

'Och, I'd like that just fine,' replied the woman. 'Don't you worry, I'll see your granny gets back all right.'

'I expect to pick up the coach on its return from the village,' Alison began, adding as an afterthought, 'Of course, if I were to be delayed… well, if you could see her back to the guest house, I would be obliged.'

'Don't you worry.'

'That all right then, Gran?'

'I wondered when I was going to be asked for my opinion,' Maggie said, disgruntled. 'I don't suppose it would matter much what I have to say about the matter.'

'Oh Gran! You know you'll have a good time. I'll see you later.'

As Alison got off the bus the driver told her, 'If you're not standin' here when I come back, I'll no' be able to wait for ye, lassie.'

'No matter,' said Alison lightly, 'I'll get back under my own steam if I have to.'

She was banking on Iain offering to drive her into town. In a place like this he must surely have a car.

The surface of the drive was roughly dressed with loose slate shingle which caught under the open toes of her flimsy, high-heeled sandals. Several times she had to stop while she took them off and shook out the stones. Realising she was in grave danger of turning an ankle, she gave in and slipped off her shoes, taking to the grass verge in her bare feet.

Rounding a corner, she came abruptly within sight of the house and a wide stretch of lawn, where, to her dismay, she saw a group of deckchairs from which a female figure rose and came towards her. It was too late to replace her shoes now. She must brazen it out just as she was!

'Hallo,' called Millicent, 'I'm Iain's mother. Welcome to Eisdalsa.'

'Alison McKenzie.'

Transferring her sandals to her other hand, she grasped Millicent's. 'I'm afraid my footwear didn't measure up to your roadway.'

'Oh, I am sorry. I hope you haven't damaged them?' Millicent apologised, as she examined the flimsy shoes for signs of scuffing.

'Iain should have told you. It's no place for high heels I'm afraid.'

'It's all right. I quite enjoyed walking on the grass in my bare feet. 'Alison took the proffered deckchair and put her sandals back on with some relief.

'Iain was called out just after lunch. He should be back at any minute.' Millicent was amused to see how Alison's attention kept returning to the corner around which the doctor was due to appear. 'Have you known Iain for long?' she enquired, intrigued at this apparently unplanned visit. Iain's response to Monday's telephone call had left her speculating. She wondered if he had really welcomed it.

Millicent's eldest son was a dark horse where his female friends were concerned. Not once during his medical training, nor throughout his time in the RAMC, had he mentioned a romance of any kind. She supposed that at college he would have been obliged to devote himself to his studies and as Hugh had pointed out, 'A field hospital is an unlikely place to come across the love of one's life.' How she longed for him to find the right woman.

'We met a few weeks ago,' Alison explained. 'Soon after I moved on to women's surgical. It was my last assignment before taking my final exams.'

'Oh, you're a nurse!' Millicent was relieved. A nurse would be absolutely right for a doctor's wife. She would be such a help in the practice.

'Yes, just qualified. I had my exam results last week. That's how I managed to get some leave. It seemed a good idea to use the opportunity to bring my gran away on this trip. She's pretty well housebound these days and I thought a wee holiday would do us both good.'

'That was very kind of you, to spend your hard-earned leave with your grandmother. You must be very fond of her.' Millicent was impressed. Not too many young people would be so generous with their time.

'Well you see, Gran is like a mother to me. She came to live with us when my mother died and kept house for Dad until my sister and I left school. Now she lives just round the corner from the hospital so I manage to pop in and see her at least once a week.

Millicent was a relentless investigator.

'How old were you when your mother died?'

'Twelve.'

'It must have been very hard for you, losing your mother at such a vulnerable age.' Alison, unable to answer, just nodded. Millicent hurriedly changed the subject.

'You must be pleased to have been so successful in your exams,' she said. 'Congratulations.'

'Thank you.' The girl at last managed to conjure a smile.

'Your father must be very proud of you.'

'Well, no, actually. He never wanted me to take up nursing.'

How could she tell Iain's mother of the ridicule her father had heaped upon her? He had complained constantly that her place was at home, looking after him and his only response to the news of her success had been, 'Now meybe you'll come to your senses and get back hame!'

'Your grandmother must be pleased,' Millicent added more hopefully.

'I suppose so.'

Her gran's response had been typical: 'Passed? Of course you passed. How would you do anything else?'

The conversation had come to an awkward halt when, to the relief of both woman, the doctor's car could be heard, its tyres crunching the loose chippings along the drive. Iain parked on the gravelled forecourt and climbed out.

Did Millicent detect the slightest hint of a frown as he strode across the grass towards them? Could she be right in her impression that Iain did not really welcome his visitor?

As he came up to them however, he said in a most friendly way, 'I see you two have introduced yourselves,' and gave Alison a brief peck on the cheek.

'That old bus has just about had it,' he complained to his mother. 'The battery seems to be finished. She won't hold a charge any more. I had to get half the village to give me a push when I left Fraser's. Oh, and there's a slow puncture in one of the tyres. I've had to get out the foot pump twice this afternoon. I'll just have a quick cup of tea Ma, and then I'll have to see what I can do to repair it.'

Millicent got to her feet, suddenly remembering that she had not yet offered Alison any refreshment.

'Where's your grandmother?' Iain enquired as he squatted on the grass beside Alison's chair and examined his oily fingers with disgust. 'I thought she was coming with you.'

'She's gone on into the village with the rest of the coach party,' Alison explained.

'There's not much to see there,' he said, dismissively.

'Oh, I don't know. Mr McColl in the post office has some nice things,' Millicent corrected him, 'and there's the new gift shop on the other side of the harbour. They don't have a lot of stock yet but what there is, is all local craft work.'

There was another awkward pause.

'Well, I'd better see about that cup of tea.' Millicent disappeared inside the house.

'How are things at the Infirmary? Has anyone missed me?' Iain asked, stretching out on the grass and tucking his hands behind his head.

'Sister Charles certainly has,' Alison replied, thankful for the change of topic. 'She's making mincemeat of the new registrar. The poor chap can't put a foot right. Her favourite remarks are, *Dr Beaton didn't do it like that* and *I never had this problem with Dr Beaton.*'

'The fellow must be an absolute nincompoop if he's worse than me,' Iain laughed.

'Well, he's very young... not long qualified.'

'Iain,' said Millicent, returning with a laden tray, which she set down heavily on the rickety garden table, 'Alison has some good news for you. Tell him, Alison.'

She smiled encouragingly.

For a moment Alison could not think what she was getting at but then, realising what was meant, blurted it out. It was not at all the way she had meant to tell him.

'I got my SRN. I didn't think I had a chance but, well, I passed.' She looked down modestly.

'That's splendid news,' he exclaimed, genuinely pleased for her. 'Congratulations!' Raising himself on one elbow he grasped her hand spontaneously and kissed it. Alison felt the blood mounting to her face and turned away so that he would not see her blushes.

'What does that make you now?' asked Millicent politely. There was little she did not know about the ladder of promotion for doctors but the modern day nursing profession was more of a mystery to her.

'Once I receive my State Registration Certificate, I shall be able to call myself a staff nurse.'

'After that, ward sister,' Iain added.

'Not without a great deal more training and experience,' Alison corrected him. 'I don't expect to be around long enough for that.'

She had blurted it out without thinking and at once regretted her statement.

'Why is that?' Millicent wondered. 'Don't you want to carry on nursing?'

'I wouldn't say I was what you would call a dedicated career girl. I hope to get married some day.'

The last thing she wanted was for Iain to hold back because he believed her to be devoted to the nursing profession to the exclusion of all else!

Iain misunderstood her reply. 'I didn't realise there was someone special. Do I know him?' In trying to disguise his dismay he was largely successful.

What was Alison to do? This entire visit had been a bad idea. She felt a complete fool.

Millicent, aware of the girl's discomfort but not the reason for it, thought she had best leave the two of them together to sort out their difficulty, whatever it was.

'I'll go and put the kettle on again,' she said. 'You will have more tea?'

Alison looked at her watch, saw that she had less than ten minutes if she was to intercept the bus on its return journey and got hurriedly to her feet.

'Thank you, Mrs Beaton, but I really must be going. I promised Gran I wouldn't miss the bus back. It's been very nice meeting you. She offered her hand which Millicent shook warmly.

Wearing a somewhat puzzled expression, Millicent turned to Iain.

'Aren't you going to walk with Alison to the road, dear?' she asked. 'She has come all this way to see you and you've hardly spoken.'

'Eh? Oh yes, of course,' he scrambled to his feet. 'I'd have offered to drive you back to town later but there's the tyre.' He shrugged helplessly.

'Please don't bother to come with me,' said Alison, remembering the path and the need to remove her shoes. 'I can find my own way, really I can. It was lovely to see you again.'

She paused, hoping for his protest, but receiving none, she added hurriedly, 'Well, I'd better be going.'

She slung her bag over her shoulder and it was all she could do not to run from the scene. Iain watched after her until she rounded the corner then settled himself into the deckchair she had just vacated and closed his eyes. That was a rum do, he thought. Having waited for his arrival all afternoon, she couldn't get away fast enough.

Out of sight of the house, Alison kicked off her sandals and ran along the grass verge, tears of humiliation almost blinding her progress. Arriving at the road only minutes before the bus rounded the rocky outcrop which marked the entrance to Tigh na Broch, she mopped her face with a tiny square of cambric and prayed the other passengers would attribute her dishevelled state to that last minute dash to catch the bus. As she sank gratefully into the empty seat beside her grandmother, the old woman demanded. 'Well, were they pleased to see you?'

'Mrs Beaton was very nice,' Alison replied noncommittally. 'Did you like the village?'

Hardly listening to the animated description of pretty rows of slate quarriers' cottages, the quaint little harbour and the delicious pastries, Alison closed her eyes to prevent the flow of tears which still threatened. What a blessing her gran had not been with her. Well, one thing was certain. She could forget all about Iain Beaton. Thank goodness this holiday would not last for ever. In just over a week they would be on their way back to Edinburgh. How she wished they were leaving tomorrow!

12

WHEN, A DAY or two later, he had to call upon his mother to help him start the Armstrong Siddeley, Iain decided it was time to consult the professionals. A few enquiries locally convinced him that the man to see was Cyril Lord, who ran a used car and garage maintenance business in town.

He found the garage down a back alley so narrow there was scarcely room for two vehicles to pass one another. As soon as he nosed the heavy old car in between the uprights of two great sliding doors, a mechanic came forward, wiping his hands on an oily rag.

'I wondered if I'd ever see this old girl again when the doctor passed away,' he observed, patting a much dented wing affectionately.

'I'm Dr Beaton's son, Iain. I've taken over from my father.' Iain climbed out of the car and stood back while the mechanic cast his expert eye over the vehicle.

'Good day, Doctor. Cyril Lord. I own the garage. Running all right, is she?'

'Not too badly for an old car, once I can get her to start. The battery seems a bit dicey. I've been keeping it on a trickle charge at night just to be sure she'll start in an emergency, but I need something reliable. I don't suppose there's any chance of getting a new one?'

'Car or battery?' the garage owner asked, amused.

'Battery, for the moment anyway,' Iain was well aware that even if he could afford it, good second-hand cars were like gold dust and new ones unobtainable. 'The tyres need replacing too. I've picked up a couple of punctures already and I've only been here for a short while.'

Cyril shook his head slowly. 'I can try to find a battery. It might take a day or two. Tyres now, that's another matter entirely. They don't make that size any more. Can you leave the old girl with me for a while? I'll give her a thorough overhaul and see if we can improve the starting.'

'I'd be most obliged,' said Iain. 'When shall I come back?'

'Give me a couple of hours.'

Iain wandered through the town, familiarising himself with the changes which had taken place during his long absence. On the south side of the harbour, he took the road past the lifeboat station and along the shore towards the landing for the Kerrera ferry. The island in Oban Bay had an exciting history going back beyond the days of the Vikings and it had always intrigued him. As children, David, Morag and he had been taken there occasionally by their grandfather. They had explored ancient Gylen Castle and examined the strange rock formations of amazingly contorted strata. Great land movements, millions of years ago, had folded and altered mudstones into slate and much later, a volcano on Mull spewed out magma, which had intruded into the slate and crystallised the minerals in it. Their grandfather had told them stories about the ancient Lords of the Isles and of great battles fought in these waters and across the islands, but as a boy Iain had dismissed most of the tales as old man's fancy. Now he wished he had listened more carefully to what that wise man had had to tell them. He remembered his fear that the crumbling wall of the old castle, standing so perilously close to the edge of the cliff, would at any moment fall into the sea beneath his feet. He could still feel the soapy hardness of those sparkling hexagonal quartz crystals which he had gathered from around the exposed rock faces and stored carefully in his pocket. On his bedroom shelf he used to have a collection of rocks and minerals. He wondered what his mother had done with all the cubes of iron pyrites he had collected from the slate rock lying on the Eisdalsa beaches. He must ask her what had happened to them.

Regretful of the many opportunities which had been wasted during those childhood expeditions and engrossed in his memories of his grandfather, Iain scarcely noticed the slim figure approaching from the direction of the ferry until she was within speaking distance. Even then it was a moment or two before he recognised Alison McKenzie in her tiny shorts, walking boots and Fair Isle sweater. She carried a heavy-looking knapsack, which was probably responsible for her red face and the fact that she was perspiring freely. He could tell by her dishevelled appearance that she had been taking rather more than a casual stroll.

'This is a surprise,' he greeted her. 'I wouldn't have taken you for an outdoor type.'

Alison, who had spotted Iain long before he saw her, had at first considered turning tail and darting away in the opposite direction. Why should I be embarrassed? she wondered, marching on, determined to brazen out their inevitable encounter.

'I'm not!' she replied with forced jocularity, 'but Gran is so wrapped up with the ancient cronies who have befriended her, I thought I might get away on my own for a while. I wanted to explore the castle over there,' she indicated the island from which she had just crossed, 'but I hadn't realised how far it was from the ferry landing.'

'It's years since I was there,' Iain told her. 'What did you think of it?'

'A lovely spot. The castle's a bit spooky perhaps, especially when you're on your own, but well worth the effort. What a pity someone doesn't restore it. It would make a wonderful place to live.'

'I imagine it would cost too much. And anyway, who would want to live so far from anywhere?'

'Oh, I think it would be lovely with the sea and the birds. There were masses of seals off the point and I thought I saw a Golden Eagle.'

He had not taken her for a country-loving girl. He studied her with renewed interest. After a while, they ran out of conversation and in the moments of silence which followed, Iain became acutely aware of the sweet scent of gorse bushes in full bloom and the loud droning of bees which mingled with the sound of surf breaking along the shore. A slight breeze had got up, ruffling the shining, brown curls which tumbled loosely about Alison's shoulders. Despite a complete absence of make-up and even with her untidy appearance, she was enchanting.

'You look awfully hot,' he said, somewhat ungallantly. 'What are your plans for the afternoon? Did you get lunch on the island?'

'I had some sandwiches with me,' she told him, 'but I could kill for a cup of tea.'

'There's a little shack where they sell teas and ice creams back along the path. I could do with something myself,' he said. 'I haven't had time for anything this morning.'

'I mustn't be too long,' Alison glanced at her watch. 'I promised to be back in time to take Gran on a wee boat trip to see the seals off the Isle of Mull.'

'You've time for a cup of tea,' Iain insisted. 'The boats don't leave until three o'clock.'

As children, they had known precisely the times when any holiday trips left the pier. In a town like Oban, even a break of six years for a war would have no impact on the timetable for boats going to see the seals.

They walked slowly towards a green-painted shack whose front had been let down to form a counter. Over it a gaily striped awning had been spread, to attract custom and to provide shelter from the occasional shower.

'Oh dear, I do hope it's not going to rain after all!' Alison pointed out a bank of black clouds moving up from the southwest. 'The forecast on the wireless was for a dry, sunny afternoon.'

'It'll only be a short shower,' Iain predicted, pointing out the patch of blue sky which lay behind the fleeting clouds. 'Here, let me take that.'

He lifted the knapsack from her shoulders and slung it casually over his own. With his free arm he grasped her around the waist and ran with her towards the tea hut. Heavy spots of rain were already falling by the time they reached the shelter of the awning. Laughing breathlessly after their burst of energy, they ordered tea and ice creams.

After the fiasco of Wednesday, Alison had given up all hope of ever seeing Iain again. She had set out to visit him that day with such high hopes, only to have them dashed by his complete indifference to her presence. His mother had been absolutely charming but she didn't want to marry his mother. Had she not been booked into the guest house for the whole fortnight, she would have gone straight back to Edinburgh that evening. Now, quite unexpectedly, here she was alone with Iain Beaton, sheltering from the rain. Shaking off the disappointment of their earlier meeting, she decided to enjoy the moment.

Like a couple of kids they discussed the merits of their ice creams, tasting each others and comparing the different flavours.

'It's ages since I had real ice cream,' she declared as she wiped a stray dollop from Iain's cheek.

'Lovely,' she told the vendor, a tubby little gentleman with a strong Italian accent. 'Do you make it yourself?'

'Since I was a boy,' the man told her proudly, 'I make-a the real Italian ice'a cream for the people of Napoli.'

'What brought you here?' Iain asked, intrigued by the presence of this enterprising foreigner so soon after the war.

'Since Battle of Tobruk I was prisoner, in the Orkneys,' he answered. 'I make'a the ice'a cream for my fellow prisoners. When we are to be sent home, I decide to stay. Is hard to get started but I manage. This is all mine.' Proudly he indicated the wooden walls around him.

It was little enough for a man in his thirties to have achieved in life but Iain had to admire the Italian's enterprise.

'Didn't you want to go home to Italy?' Alison asked. 'Don't you have a wife and children waiting for you?'

'Oh yes. My wife write to me in prison camp. Children is all well and growing up good, but country is mess. She says, *Stay in Scotland, my husband. Get business there and I come to join you!*'

'Well the very best of luck to you,' Iain said. 'I shall tell everyone to come and buy your ice cream. It's wonderful. Will you stay here in Oban over the winter?'

'Maybe, maybe not. I go to Glasgow perhaps. Who knows.' He shrugged his shoulders dramatically.

Their refreshment completed, Alison glanced at her watch and let out a cry of dismay. 'The time has gone so quickly,' she declared, 'I really must go. I'm going to be late for the boat trip.'

She turned back to the friendly Italian.

'Goodbye,' she said, 'and good luck.'

She hurried back to the path leaving Iain to settle the bill.

'You take good care of that lovely girl,' said the ice cream man as Iain turned to follow her. 'Be happy together!'

Iain was relieved Alison had not overheard these parting words. He was surprised the Italian should have mistaken them for a courting couple. They were barely friends, let alone lovers.

Nevertheless, as they walked companionably together towards the town, he began to wonder if she might indeed be the one. The girl his mother was so anxious for him to marry.

At the railway station they parted, Alison to find her grandmother and make her way to the pier and Iain to return to the garage.

'I'm so glad we met again,' he told her as he handed back her rucksack. 'It makes up a bit for last Wednesday. I felt awful, what with the car letting me down and not having time to talk to you properly. Anyway, next time there shouldn't be a problem. The chap at the garage is going to find me a better one, car I mean. I'll be able to give you a lift.'

Unable to believe that he meant anything by it, Alison tried to ignore the reference to *next time*.

'I must run. Thanks for the ice cream.' She turned to go.

'Enjoy the seals!'

He watched after her as she crossed the road onto the esplanade.

'Alison!' he called after her and, as she turned back once again, 'I forgot to ask. Do you know which ward you'll be working on when you go back?'

'Men's surgical,' she answered quickly. A moment later she had disappeared into the crowd.

Iain turned in the opposite direction, headed towards the garage and dodged between hikers staggering under the weight of huge rucksacks and young girls in colourful cotton frocks, teetering on high-heeled flimsy sandals. In his mind's eye he saw only a pair of shapely legs in very short shorts, chestnut brown hair blowing across bronzed and freckled cheeks and a pair of green, laughing eyes.

13

I'VE GIVEN THE battery a boost,' Cyril Lord told him when he got back to the garage, 'but I can't guarantee it'll hold the charge. I've been in touch with the depot at Inverness and they've promised to look out for a new one but can't say how long they'll be, I'm afraid.'

'I can't manage without a car,' Iain said. 'My practice covers miles of open country. It looks as if I might have to take to riding horseback. That's how my grandfather used to make his rounds.'

'What you need is another vehicle,' said Cyril. 'Would you like me to look out for something? It might be easier to find a decent second hand car than a new battery.'

'Really? That surprises me. I would have thought people would be snapping up everything on four wheels.'

'It's the petrol rationing,' Cyril explained. 'Folk are not prepared to licence a car for a whole year with only the vaguest promise of an increase in the petrol allowance at some unspecified time in the future. I know of a few capital cars which have been up on blocks for years, taking up valuable garage space.'

'You reckon there might be someone willing to sell?'

'Any model that's heavy on petrol, yes. That's something that shouldn't bother you.'

Petrol was not restricted for use by the emergency services, including doctors. Iain would have no problems getting the juice to run a gas guzzler.

'I can't promise anything,' Cyril told him, but if you like I'll make enquiries.'

The financial situation might be a bit tight but a reliable car was an essential part of the practice.

Iain felt sure his mother would agree to the additional expenditure.

'Yes, please do,' he answered quickly.

'I'll give you a call if anything comes up,' Cyril promised.

He stepped into the narrow roadway and directed Iain out, backwards. The Armstrong's engine certainly sounded better for its visit to the garage but the thought of something newer, in better condition and even a little more powerful, was exciting. Iain began to hum a tune. Once out on the open road, cresting the steep slope to the south of the town, he broke into song.

'I dream of Alison with the light brown hair...'

14

ARCHIBALD MCINDOE LAID aside the letter he had been reading as Stephen Beaton came into the office and settled himself comfortably in the one unoccupied chair. Stephen drew out his pipe and helped himself from the tobacco jar on Archie's desk.

'Ah, Beaton,' McIndoe greeted him uneasily.

'You wanted to see me, Boss?' Stephen asked.

'We've got our marching orders.' McIndoe pushed a sheet of notepaper across the desk. 'The RAF will begin withdrawing from civilian hospitals at the end of the month. All anaplastics cases are to be transferred to the RAF unit at Halton.'

Stephen appeared unmoved as he read the Ministry memo. They had been expecting these orders for months past.

'Had you taken that job at Halton when it was offered, you'd be sitting pretty now,' McIndoe said. 'There's little chance of a posting in your present rank. No one at Halton is going to move over to make room, even for you.'

The career ladder which Stephen had mounted with so much energy and enthusiasm six years ago was about to be pulled out from under him, and Archie McIndoe felt responsible. In the hectic days following the invasion of France, Stephen had been presented with the choice of taking command of the RAF hospital at Halton or forming a specialist team for the front line treatment of the most severe burns cases. With McIndoe's encouragement, he had decided on the latter.

'The choice was mine,' Stephen assured him, 'and I don't regret it. There'll be plenty of anaplastics work in Civvy Street. There will still be fires, motor accidents and the like. I'm going to take my gratuity and get out of the RAF as soon as they'll let me go.'

'Anything particular in mind?' McIndoe wondered.

'I'll be looking for a hospital post with the opportunity for both teaching and research, preferably in Scotland. But first, I've promised Ellen we'll take a holiday when I get my demob. She hasn't seen her folks for eight years and they're not getting any younger. What about you?'

Unlike Stephen, McIndoe had never been commissioned in the RAF. Already recognised as an authority in the treatment of severely disfigured burns victims, he had been brought in at the beginning of the war as a civilian consultant. Unfettered by military red tape, he was free to resign whenever he wished.

'I've a commitment in the States for the next few months,' he said, 'a lecture tour. Then, I'm going home to New Zealand, for good. It's a beautiful country, Steve. You could do a lot worse than go out there yourself. I might be able to fix a teaching post for you at Otago. They are talking about setting up a new department with a Chair in Anaplastics.'

He had studied at Otago University in Dunedin, under the famous New Zealand surgeon Sir Harold Gillies, who was considered to be the father of modern plastic surgery. At the outbreak of war, both men had been summoned to Britain to advise on the treatment of RAF casualties.

When, during the battle of Britain, he was confronted with horrific burns cases amongst the fighter pilots of his own squadron, Stephen Beaton had sought advice from Professor Gillies and been referred to McIndoe, who was setting up a specialist burns unit at East Grinstead Hospital in Sussex. Stephen had joined McIndoe there in 1942.

'I can't imagine Ellen agreeing to emigrate to New Zealand,' Stephen grinned. 'She wants me to take over her family's local hospital in the outback.'

'You can't seriously be thinking of wasting your talents on a bunch of sheep farmers and jackaroos!' Archie exclaimed.

'No, of course not,' Stephen laughed. 'I don't think I'd find much satisfaction buried out there in the desert. A hospital in Perth or Sydney might not be such a bad idea, though.'

'Have you ever seen Ellen's home?'

'Yes, but that was years ago. It's an interesting place, Kerrera. Ellen's grandfather was a founder member of the town. He emigrated out there in 1913. At that time Southern Cross, the nearest place of any size, was just a whistle stop on the route between Perth and the goldfields. During the next twenty years the entire area underwent development. Kerrera Station itself grew into quite a sizeable town. The sheep farmers have done well out of the enormous demand for wool and mutton during the last six years, and the population has almost doubled. They built a new hospital a year or two back and there's a Flying Doctor Service.'

He paused for an instant, contemplating the prospect seriously for the first time. He had qualified as a pilot in the University Air Squadron before the war and had been very disappointed to be steered into the RAF Medical Service when he joined up. The Flying Doctor Service could be a challenge he'd relish.

'I'd like to continue with the work we've been doing here. There's still so much to learn. As a matter of fact I've written to my old teacher, Professor Dowson at Glasgow University. He might be able to suggest something. Otherwise I thought about trying the States. I'm told there's a great future for plastic surgeons in Hollywood!'

Now it was McIndoe's turn to laugh. 'Somehow I don't see you making vast sums of money improving the appearance of a bunch of ageing movie stars.'

'Whatever else happens, Ellen and I are determined to squander my gratuity on this trip to Australia. We're looking forward to doing absolutely nothing for the five weeks of the voyage and I'm not going to worry about anything at all for the next few months.'

'I'm going to miss you, Stephen.'

A very close relationship had developed between the two men during the past few years. Archie McIndoe regarded his assistant as a close friend as well as a respected colleague. 'Despite Ellen's reservations, I hope you'll both find an opportunity to come out to New Zealand. I'd hate to think this will be the last we'll see of each other.'

'Don't you worry,' Stephen was quick to assure him. 'I'll be on to you every other week for advice about something or other. I can't tell you what this posting has meant to me Archie.'

Too full for further words, McIndoe turned to his filing cabinet and began to search noisily through the racks of patient records.

'One of these days I shall have to write this lot up into a book. Perhaps you'll be good enough to help with the editing?'

'I'd be honoured!' Stephen moved to the door. 'I'll let the boys know about their transfers,' he said, and went out into the silent corridor.

A few months before, the wards had rung with masculine voices. Young men, horribly mutilated and frustrated by long weeks of internment, had roamed the polished corridors. They had occupied the easy chairs in the common room and filled the now empty beds. Loud laughter, practical jokes and a general heartiness had been their way of trying to reassure their doctors, and themselves, that they were ready to return to the fighting.

Today, only two figures occupied the large, airy common room.

Stephen crossed the floor and sat down between the two young airmen.

Flight Lieutenant Charlie Mander's fully loaded bomber had been attacked over France in one of the last air battles of the European Campaign. Having ordered the surviving members of his crew to bail out, he had stayed at the controls of the burning aircraft until he was well clear of the land before bailing out himself. The aircraft had exploded harmlessly over the Channel but Charlie's face and hands had been severely burned. Even after innumerable operations he was still a fearsome sight and although Archie McIndoe had tried to assure him of a good recovery, he was depressed and despondent.

Flight Sergeant Robin Truegood had bailed out of a burning aircraft over France with his parachute already alight and had fallen the final twenty feet unsupported. During the descent his jacket had caught fire and, in addition to fractures in both legs, he had suffered severe burns to his arms and back. It had been three months before he was able to sit in a chair without extreme discomfort.

Stephen drew a deep breath and greeted both airmen, smiling. 'It's all right for some. I wish I could sit around in the sunshine on a beautiful afternoon like this!'

Neither responded.

The doctor tried again. 'You must be getting a little bored with this outlook.' He indicated the neat flower beds and the tall privet hedge which separated the temporary huts housing the burns unit from the red brick buildings of the main hospital. 'I've some good news. You two are off to Halton at the end of the week for a change of air. You won't have to put up with Mac's terrible jokes any more.'

Robin turned his head, very slowly. He was only just beginning to regain the use of his neck muscles. His eyes were wide with alarm.

'What? How d'you mean? I'm all right here. I can't be moved!'

'You're not deserting us. Not now?'

Charlie too was terrified by the prospect of leaving this quiet haven.

Stephen had seen it so often in the past. Frustrated that they could do nothing to escape the constant pain of their wounds, the patients raged and cursed at their doctors, nurses and orderlies and could not wait for their release, but when the moment came, they were frightened by the prospect of having to face the general public. And with good reason.

Out there in the wider world, attitudes were beginning to change. At one time, Archie McIndoe's 'Guinea Pigs' had been welcomed in the local community and made to feel at ease. Already, after only ten months of peace, people were becoming less tolerant of those mutilated ex-servicemen whose disfiguring wounds offended their sensibilities.

Robin Truegood and Charlie Mander had not yet reached the stage of being reintroduced to the outside world. They found it difficult enough to adjust to the smallest changes in hospital routine. A new member of the nursing staff, a student doctor on the wards, even an unfamiliar cleaner was sufficient to set them back days in their recovery.

'How will we get any better without you and Dr Mac looking after us?' demanded Charlie Mander with the self-centred viewpoint of the chronic sick. 'I can't go through any more of this treatment with anyone else. Who's going to do my grafts if you're not around?'

'The chaps at Halton know all about you,' Stephen tried to reassure him. 'As a matter of fact, the fellow who will do your next set of operations was posted here a while back, specifically to find out how we do things. So you see, there won't be any change in your treatment, just prettier nurses and a better view.'

'What if we refuse to go?' Charlie suggested belligerently.

'Oh, I expect they'll simply cover you up in a dust sheet with the rest of the furniture, and leave you behind,' Stephen answered briskly. 'I'm going off to Australia for a holiday and Mac's got a job to go to in America, so I'm afraid it's Halton or nothing for you guys.'

'I hope you'll think of us while you're lounging on deck in tropic seas,' Robin said.

'How could I ever forget you!' Stephen was relieved that Robin, at least, appeared to have accepted the inevitable.

Having successfully disposed of his most difficult assignment, he felt more confident about approaching those patients who were further on in their treatment and weary for a change of scene. Even so, he found his conscience pricked more than a little as, at the end of his shift, he made his way to his quarters to prepare for dinner.

He had been sincere in his commendation of the hospital at Halton and the treatment the men would receive there. Nevertheless, after the relaxed atmosphere which was the hallmark of the East Grinstead unit, he feared his patients were going to be unprepared for the strict discipline of a regular RAF hospital. Maybe the jolt would spur some of them on to make a speedier recovery. If that was the case the move would be shown to have been for the best, but Stephen could not throw off the conviction that he was guilty of betrayal.

15

AS HE STEPPED out into the corridor, Stephen collided with the Senior Nursing Officer, Baggy Gage.

Baggy had already completed his evening rounds. Tucking the boys up for the night, was how he put it.

'I hear you've been telling the lads about the move,' he observed as they walked the length of the corridor together.

'Bad, was it?' Stephen asked.

Baggy was always the one who got the worst end of the stick when disasters of this kind befell them. While the men appeared relatively stoical in front of the medical officers, to Baggy they revealed their innermost fears and grievances.

'Colin and Charlie were the worst. I had to replace Colin's bandages. They were soaked with tears. You can be a tough old bastard when you try, Doc.'

It was not really a reprimand, merely Baggy's way of venting his own feelings about the men whose sufferings he bore as his own personal cross.

Bartholemew Alloysius George Gage, Baggy to his friends, had been a part of Stephen Beaton's life for much of his service career. After a brief encounter at the RAF reception centre in Blackpool, he had again met Baggy, by then a medical orderly, on his first visit to East Grinstead. For the remainder of the war years and after, the two men had worked together.

'You'll be off to Australia then?' Baggy suggested as they entered the dining room.

'Just as soon as I can book a passage,' Stephen replied, nodding a polite greeting to his other colleagues as he took his place at table.

There was little ceremony where rank and professional status were concerned. It had always been McIndoe's conviction that in order to perform its function satisfactorily, the medical team should spend as much off-duty time together as possible. Contrary to accepted practice in both the RAF and any ordinary hospital, everyone, from the most junior nurse to the Chief Medical Officer, ate in the same dining room and relaxed in the same common room. This atmosphere fostered universal understanding of the unit's policy with regard to treatment, cemented friendships and encouraged a mutual respect for the skills and experience of every member of staff.

'Got any idea what you'll be doing, yourself?' Stephen asked while they waited for soup to be served.

'Already sorted,' Baggy announced, stuffing a piece of the chef's own special bread into his mouth and exchanging a conspiratorial smile with McIndoe.

'Baggy's going to take an instructor's course at Halton. He's to become a Nurse Tutor after all.'

'Congratulations, Baggy!' Stephen cried, inordinately pleased at the news.

Baggy had come a very long way from the two-roomed apartment in Leeds which he had shared with his parents and five other kids. Stephen well remembered the inarticulate, sickly little waif he had first met at the RAF Assessment Centre on the Fylde Coast. 'Will you stay in the Service afterwards?'

'I don't know, Doc. I'll wait and see. One step at a time, that's my motto.'

Yes, thought Stephen, that had always been Baggy's way. One step at a time. He had often envied the patience with which the man could persuade helpless, hopeless individuals to make just a single small effort, one step forward every day, until, almost imperceptibly, they regained their confidence. People were lavish with their praise of McIndoe and his surgeons for the work of the East Grinstead Unit, but Stephen knew that without Baggy and his like, even the most outstanding operations in the world would almost certainly fail.

'There's something in the *Lancet* today about nurse training, it's to do with this new scheme of Bevan's. They're suggesting nurses should spend much more of their training time in school, rather than on the wards.' McIndoe, who liked to indulge himself in sniping at establishment attitudes, addressed Sister Knightly, seated opposite. He watched her swallow a particularly stringy piece of beef before she could utter a rather unladylike oath.

'Bollocks! I never heard such nonsense,' she declared. 'Nursing is a practical profession, best learned at the patient's bedside. Besides, hospitals would be unable to operate without the work of student nurses on the wards. Who's going to do all those very necessary but unskilled tasks which they carry out now, while they're learning? Don't tell me Mr Bevan is going to provide every ward sister with a maid to replace her juniors.'

'I dunno, Sister,' Baggy intervened, gently. 'It's pretty tough for a young kid not long out of school and leaving home for the first time. At the end of an eight-hour shift on the ward, doing heavy physical jobs she's probably not used to, a nurse is expected to put in additional hours, attending lectures and studying. It's not expected of other kinds of students, so why should hospital staff have to put up with it?'

'Pie in the sky,' retorted Sister Knightly, who was one of the old school, old enough to have been brought up in the Florence Nightingale tradition. 'If a girl can't cope with a bit of hard work, she's no use to me!'

'But if, at the end of the day, she's going to be as tired as Baggy suggests,' McIndoe interjected, stirring the pot, 'She's not going to be much use to the patients either. It does seem a fearful waste to take intelligent young females with good academic qualifications and turn them into domestic servants, while at the same time attempting to provide them with the technical skills they need to qualify as nurses.'

But Sister Knightly was adamant. In her mind, the established way was the only way. 'Nurses cannot be trained in a classroom. What will they do? Learn to make beds that don't need it? Wash dummies instead of real people? Bandage each other's perfectly healthy limbs? Give injections to oranges?'

'Perhaps that would be better than practising on sick people with no defence against their inadequacies!' McIndoe laughed, and the tensions which had built up were immediately dispelled.

Only Sister Knightly continued to smoulder at the thought of her world being turned upside down. Shortly after, she left the room without saying another word.

'Weren't you a bit hard on her?' Stephen commented quietly to his boss as the dignified figure of the Sister swept out of the dining room.

'It's time for change, Steve,' McIndoe replied. 'The most intractable amongst us are going to have to accept it. Best get our minds into gear in good time.'

Stephen nodded thoughtfully.

'It's strange how, even here, where so many of the SRNs are men, whenever there is a discussion about nurses we only ever refer to them as women. I can't see the men accepting the old regime of the pre-war hospitals, can you Baggy?'

'Never having met Miss Nightingale myself, I can't really say,' Baggy laughed, 'but one thing's for certain, we will never put up with the level of wages the girls are being offered. You can look for a deal more militancy once the men take a hand in the negotiations.'

One did not like to think in terms of a nurses' trade union, but Stephen knew that what Baggy said was true. However tenaciously the Sister Knightlys clung to their old traditions, the world was changing and those who did not change with it would surely fall by the wayside.

16

'I'LL HAVE TO write to the pensions people about Tam McFarlane,' Iain told his mother as they lingered at the table after their evening meal. 'There must be something they can do to help him.'

'I thought you said this bout of malaria would not last too long.'

'It's not that I'm worried about. It's his general physical condition and his mental state. He can't do the heavy work he was trained for and the clerical job he's been given is bringing in less than three pounds a week.'

'Didn't Alma say that he had already applied for a pension?'

'They turned him down. Because he wasn't wounded in combat, it seems he's not entitled to claim a disability pension.' Iain found it impossible to accept the injustice of this decision.

'Well, I suppose the authorities will say that, compared with some of the men wounded in battle, he has come out of the Army relatively unscathed,' Millicent suggested. 'There must be thousands unable to work as a result of their wounds.'

'Oh yes, there are hospital beds and pensions for the wounded but there's totally inadequate support for their families. As for providing psychiatric treatment for discharged prisoners of war, they just don't want to know. The fact is, none of us has any idea what damage was done to the minds of men who were locked up for years on end, underfed, lacking any but the most basic of medical care and often brutalised by their guards. Most of them refuse to talk at all about their captivity. It could be years before the facts are fully known. From all reports, they deserve a medal simply for staying alive in those conditions.'

'Some people are suggesting that all this talk about the brutality and forced labour camps is exaggerated. That it's just so much journalistic sensationalism.'

'Mother, I was among the first to enter Auschwitz, remember. I would never have believed it possible for human beings to treat one another so abominably. I can believe every word that has been printed about the Japanese prison camps. From what Mairi has told me, poor Tam relives his experiences every night in his dreams. It's unlikely he will ever forget them.'

'If the Army is unable or unwilling to look after him, what do you suppose you can do?' Millicent asked anxiously. Hugh would have been the same, worrying himself sick over some individual patient he was powerless to help.

'I can get him some expert psychiatric help. Even when he's fully conscious and quite rational, any mention of Malaya, and his eyes fill with tears. It's pitiful to see a grown man in such a low state, especially a chap who was so strong and fit.'

'At least he has a job,' Millicent pointed out.

'Yes, but for how much longer? Fergusson won't put up with his absences for ever. What's to become of the family if he's unemployed?'

'He'll have to look for other work,' Millicent told him. 'I may sound harsh, Iain, but you can't be expected to fret about every personal setback experienced by your patients. That's the road which led your father into all his problems.'

'I know, Mother, but it's so unfair. It wasn't McFarlane's fault he had to surrender to the Japanese. Anyone would think he had committed some crime by becoming a prisoner. I suppose it would have been more convenient for everyone if our men had just fought to the death when the Japs invaded Singapore, then they'd have been heroes, the thin red line and all that!'

'That's a terrible thing to say!'

Millicent had never heard him speak so cynically before. His bitterness frightened her.

'The least I can do is to write to David about Tam's problems,' Iain decided. 'I'll try to get him up here for a consultation. Meanwhile, I can work on restoring his body weight. He'll need protein and plenty of it. Can we spare some extra eggs and cheese do you think?'

'We can, but will Mairi accept that kind of help? You know how proud people can be. She'll not take charity.'

'I'll think of something to tell Mairi. We can charge a few pennies if it makes her feel any better. I'll tell her the food is subsidised from some special fund.'

'Wasn't Mairi a member of the Hospital Savings Association?' Millicent asked. 'Can't she claim help from them?'

'She tells me she let the payments lapse when Tam came home and she gave up her job. She seems to have been doing engineering work of some kind, in the village. Is the works still in operation?'

'No, they closed the factory down immediately after the war.'

'Pity! That would be just the kind of situation to suit a fellow like McFarlane. You'd have thought someone would have seen the need to keep some kind of light industry going here. What sort of a life is this to offer men who have given the best years of their own lives for their country? No decent jobs... no houses... no future.'

He slammed down his coffee cup with such force that Millicent jumped.

'Let me tell you this, Mother, the ordinary people of this country are not going to stand idly by and watch the Tam McFarlanes of this world be trampled on this time around. If this government doesn't fulfil the promises made when it won the election, we can expect anarchy. You mark my words!'

Millicent didn't know what to say. Was her son becoming a Socialist? Was he too joining the mass of ex-servicemen who were demanding their rights so vociferously these days? They had returned a Labour government a year ago, ousting Mr Churchill from office just when he had achieved the greatest victory of all time. Now by means of their trades unions, the workers were beginning to make extraordinary demands on their employers. Was it possible that the doctors were going to follow suit?

'You've already decided how you'll vote in this referendum, then?' she asked, indicating the headlines splashed across the front page of that morning's *Scotsman*. Alongside, GLASGOW SHIPYARDS ON GO-SLOW and STEEL WORKERS DEMAND 6% RISE ACROSS THE BOARD was a short paragraph headed DATE OF NHS REFERENDUM SET. DOCTORS TO DECIDE.

'I thought you understood,' Iain replied, surprised that she should ask. 'As long as the terms for handing over to the Health Ministry are favourable, I intend to go along with the new scheme. I don't see any alternative.'

'I was reading an account of the proceedings of the British Medical Association in your *Lancet*,' Millicent told him. 'Maybe you haven't had a chance to look at it yet? They are saying that GPs will be allowed to opt out entirely if they choose. It seems there will be no barrier to private practice.'

'You know as well as I do that the list of better-off patients in this district is insufficient to compensate for numbers of those who can't afford to pay. I've haven't had time to read the *Lancet* but I have had a look at Dad's accounts and I can assure you that if it were not for his panel patients, he would have been bankrupt years ago.'

'But surely the panel patients will still come to you?'

'Panel patients will automatically be transferred to the new system,' Iain told her. 'That includes all those who are at present signed up with the Hospital Savings Association or any other insurance schemes. If I were to opt out, the majority of my patients would be transferred to a doctor who is registered with the NHS.'

'But you'll have plenty of extra work when the tourists start coming. And what about all these people buying second homes? They must have enough money to pay for their medical treatment.'

'It won't make that much difference,' Iain assured her. 'Apart from the occasional accident, people on holiday don't often need a doctor. In any case, if they are signed up with an NHS doctor in their own town, patients will automatically receive free treatment when they're away from home.'

'But surely people who have been paying into a private scheme for years will expect to see some benefit from their contributions?'

'They may be offered certain extra benefits; a private room when in hospital perhaps or a place in a convalescent home after they are discharged. I understand that the organisations will continue to make additional payments to those unable to work due to hospitalisation.'

'How do you know you won't have enough private patients?' Millicent was not convinced.

'Stuart and I have already drawn up a list of potential private patients. We wanted to see if it would be possible to run the practice without government support. The marquis himself and maybe some of his staff might opt out of the system and I would expect some of the local landowners to follow suit. There are a few tenant farmers and retired business people who've come into the area to live since the war but, unfortunately, Dad's ledger entries show only too clearly that it's these wealthier patients who are the most likely to hold back payment until the last possible minute. The amount of cash flowing into the practice will be too small to withstand long delays in settling accounts. Without the regular block payments for panel patients the practice simply couldn't function.'

Millicent was forced to admit that Hugh had often complained at the time it took the gentry to pay their bills.

'As for the remainder of the patients,' Iain continued,' there's no question that the majority of the population is going to rely solely on the National Health Service. Why should they spend their hard earned cash on private health care when they are already having to support the State system through their contributions?

'Doesn't it worry you that if you were to become a national health doctor, the most wealthy and influential of your patients might register with a private practitioner, elsewhere?' Millicent wondered.

'You have to understand this, Mother,' Iain replied, his patience beginning to wear thin, 'whatever reservations you may have about the scheme, there is no question that were I to refuse to sign up, the authorities would appoint someone else to look after the registered patients in this area. There's not sufficient work for two GPs.'

'So there really isn't any choice at all?'

'No.'

'But I thought the doctors were intending to put up a fight. If everyone refused to join up to the scheme, it couldn't work, could it?'

'Maybe not, but there are plenty of people, like myself, who want to give it a go.'

'And you're quite determined to sign up?'

'Yes, I am. Providing the administrators do their job properly, it could be the best thing that ever happened to medicine in this country.'

'Your father never had much faith in Hospital Boards and administrators,' Millicent reminded him. 'I remember how Hugh and your grandfather complained about the way the bureaucrats operated their personal empires. What makes you think this system will be any different?'

'It will be up to all of us, doctors and patients alike, to see that it is.'

Believing they had exhausted the topic, Iain stood up. 'I have some reading to do before bed,' he told her.

'Don't go for a minute, I've something to show you.' Millicent disappeared into the adjoining room, returning minutes later with an impressive sheaf of formal-looking documents. 'I've been making a few enquiries of my own,' she told him, handing him the papers. 'When you were tying up loose ends in Edinburgh, I got in touch with Munro and Stewart, your father's solicitors, and asked them to assess the value of the farm, this house and the medical practice. As you can see, they've come up with some surprising figures.'

Iain sat down again, turning the pages slowly, trying to take in the gist. By the time he reached the summary on the final page, Millicent could contain her excitement no longer.

'If we were to sell up everything, there would be more than enough money for my needs. I could buy a little house on Eisdalsa next to Annie and Stuart as well as an annuity to keep me going for another twenty years if need be.' She paused for greater effect. 'But most importantly, there would still be sufficient cash left over for you to buy a private practice in a better area!'

This life suited Iain admirably. He enjoyed being a GP and in taking over from his father and grandfather he had achieved everything he ever wanted. If his mother believed she was offering a tempting alternative, she was quite wrong. He was at a loss to know how to respond without upsetting her.

'There's something you've forgotten,' he said at last. 'How do you imagine David and Morag would feel if you were to hand over the greater part of the family's assets to me? Aren't they entitled to a share?'

'They were happy enough with the present arrangement,' Millicent reminded him.

'Yes, but at the end of the day, the practice, the house, everything would still be here to be disposed of when the time came.'

'You were always going to take the lion's share,' she insisted, 'the others agreed to that.'

Iain was well aware that David's agreement had been wrung from him out of concern for her, not because he felt that Iain should take everything.

'In any case,' said Millicent, 'it's up to me what I do with my inheritance from your father. The house and farm are mine to do with as I choose. If I decide to give you the proceeds from their sale, it's a matter that should concern no one but us. You are the eldest son and legally entitled to inherit everything.'

'That's a pretty old fashioned way of looking at things Ma,' Iain said. 'I'd hate to create a split in the family.'

Why couldn't she accept that all he wanted was to be left alone to work here amongst people he knew and in a place he loved? He really didn't care whether or not it was to be under some government-controlled National Health Service.

'Discuss it with your Uncle Stuart,' Millicent suggested. 'You've always respected his opinion and he has had plenty of time to follow all the arguments over the Health Minister's proposals.'

'I've already discussed it with him, endlessly. However, if it will make you feel any better, I'll speak to him again on Sunday.' Iain sighed, exhausted by the argument. 'But whatever Stuart says, I don't think I can do what you want. Remember, it was you who wanted someone to fulfil Dad's wishes for the practice. That was my main reason for offering to take it over.'

'At least listen to what Stuart has to say,' his mother insisted. 'He will know what's best.'

She had great faith in her brother-in-law's opinion. He was sure to see things her way. It was unthinkable that a Beaton doctor should be forced to give up his independence to become a servant of the State.

'We'll see.' Iain stifled a yawn. 'I'm going up now, Ma. Don't let me sleep in tomorrow. It's going to be a busy day. I've said I would call in on Alma Livingstone right after surgery and then I'm due to introduce myself to the Superintendent at the West Highland Hospital. So far we've only managed the occasional telephone conversation.'

'Don't worry, I'll see you're up in good time.'

Following the pattern of a lifetime, Millicent would be wide awake at six o'clock. Once Iain was married, his wife could tidy the surgery and let in the first of the patients. How she longed to hand over her duties to someone younger!

17

IAIN DUCKED AUTOMATICALLY as he entered Alma's tiny living room, carefully avoiding the inevitable oil lamp suspended from the ceiling. The district nurse's attitude towards him was civil enough, but she gave him the uneasy feeling that she disapproved of him and was just waiting for him to make his first error. He could understand it in a way. She had worked with his father for such a long time, it was inevitable she would make comparisons.

'Will you have a cup of tea while we talk, Doctor?' she asked, when he had settled himself in the old but comfortable chair beside the kitchen range. She left him alone while she bustled about in the narrow kitchen next door.

It was a small room, crowded with an assortment of oversized Victorian furniture. Two tiny windows supplied the only natural lighting and even though her bright chintz curtains and cushions made a brave attempt at alleviating the gloom, they could not lift the claustrophobic atmosphere.

China and glass ornaments crowded every surface and filled the heavily carved, glass-fronted corner cupboard. Despite the clutter however, the room was spotlessly clean. She must spend hours dusting and polishing to keep the place like this, Iain thought.

Despite the summer season, Alma had a fire roaring in the grate and a heavy black iron kettle was simmering on the hotplate.

'I seem to remember your parents' home was in the village. Have you lived here at Clachan for long?' he asked when she returned with the tea-tray.

'I moved in when my aunt died,' Alma explained. 'It was more central to my district. It's very small of course and my aunt's clutter doesn't help, but it suits me. The post office is right next door and handy for receiving telephone calls and with the hotel just across the bridge, there's always somewhere to go in the evenings if I want company. One of these days I'll find the time to shift some of auntie's knick-knacks and get hold of some smaller pieces of furniture.'

Iain could see that Alma's own comfort would always come second to the requirements of her job. It was a lonely existence for an unmarried woman. Most nurses worked as a part of a team, sharing their everyday tasks and helping one another out when things got tough, but a district nurse always worked alone, supported by her local GP. With their patients scattered over such a wide area however, Iain and Alma's paths were unlikely to cross during the daily round.

She squatted on the creepy stool beside the stove and added a couple of shovels of coal to the firebox.

'You must find Eisdalsa a big change from Edinburgh.'

'Time appears to have stood still around here.' Iain grinned.

It was only when he had begun to visit patients in their own homes that he was made fully aware of how far the villages had fallen behind. Women still carried water in pails from the standpipe at the end of the street. Cottages claiming ownership of a flushing toilet were rare. At Seileachan, the public conveniences on the pier represented the only water closets available to villagers and tourists alike.

'Now we have a Labour government, we can expect quite a few changes but it's going to cost a great deal of money to bring the islands up to date.'

'As long as they've earmarked enough for the new Health Service, I shall be happy,' she said. 'That got my vote.'

'You think it's a good idea, then?'

'I wouldn't want to see a return to the old days when the hospitals had to beg for every penny, just to keep their wards open. When I began my training in 1926, we spent almost as much of our time fundraising as we did in nursing the sick.'

'You did your training in Oban?'

'Yes. I wanted to go to Glasgow and study for state registration, but my father wouldn't hear of it. He never really wanted me to go away at all. Anywhere more than a couple of miles from home was bound to be a den of iniquity in his eyes. If I wasn't under his direct gaze, how was he to know whether I was keeping the Sabbath?'

'Were you Free Church?'

She nodded.

'Father was a lay preacher. He kept us on a very tight rein indeed. I can't tell you what a relief it was to get away from home. Even then

I was expected to spend all my off-duty time with my parents and as that usually coincided with a weekend, you can imagine I wasn't too pleased.'

'Under the circumstances, I'm surprised you opted to come back here to work,' Iain laughed.

'Father was dead by then and Mother was helpless without him. She'd become so used to being told what to do, she needed someone with her all the time. The Council considered my hospital experience was sufficient for a district nurse, so I was given a short additional training – a correspondence course with the Queen's Institute and three weeks on the district under the guidance of an old woman who was the nearest thing to Sarah Gamp that I've ever met! It wasn't much of an introduction to general practice, but with your Dad's help, I managed.'

'My mother tells me that he thought very highly of your work,' Iain assured her.

He could not help noticing how his words of praise had made her blush. When her eyes lit up that way, she was surprisingly attractive.

'I can't see myself in this job for very much longer,' she told him, wistfully. 'Under the new regulations, district nurses will have to be state registered and do an extra six months' specialised training at university. I wish I could go in for the proper qualification, but I'm not even sure that I would be accepted for a course, not being SRN.'

'That seems a bit unreasonable when you've been doing the job all this time.'

'Don't misunderstand me,' she replied. 'I believe every district nurse should be properly qualified. I'm only too aware of my own short-comings. That case of malaria is a good example. I had absolutely no idea about the disease, how it's caused, how it recurs or how to treat it. I had to come home and look it up after you told me what it was.'

'There was no reason why you should have recognised it,' Iain tried to reassure her. 'It's not something you would normally encounter in this country, although I don't doubt that with so many troops returning from abroad, there will be cases around for years to come. In any case, it's not your responsibility to make the diagnosis... that's my department!'

Damn it! He hadn't meant to sound patronising.

'I know that,' she replied, 'but it doesn't excuse my ignorance. It would help if there was a better means of communication between us. Dr Hugh and I used to leave messages for one another in the various post offices and in any houses with a telephone. It worked most of the time but there was always the possibility of a long delay before information could be passed on.'

'In the Army we had field telephones,' Iain observed. 'One day I expect they'll introduce something similar for the emergency services. Imagine being able to speak to one another as we drive around in our cars.'

'Imagine driving around in a car,' Alma chided him, 'I have to make do with a bicycle!'

They dismissed Iain's outrageous suggestion with a laugh, and he began to feel much more at ease. He glanced at his watch.

'Good Lord! I've an appointment at the hospital. I really should be on my way. Are there any patients who are giving particular cause for concern?'

'Old Mrs McAllister is really not fit to look after herself,' Alma told him. 'I try to pop in most days, but she can't cope on her own and she can't afford to pay anyone to do the housework. The place is in an awful state. Of course, the situation is not helped by the fact that the roof leaks and the poor old dear has no means of getting it put right.'

'Doesn't she have family? Someone who could come in and give a hand occasionally?'

'Time was when anyone falling sick in the villages would have half a dozen close family members who would rally round. Now, most of the younger people have left for one reason or another and the old folks have to cope on their own.'

'Have you tried to get her a place in St Fillan's?'

The town boasted a number of small hospitals. The West Highland was the general hospital and alongside it stood a small maternity unit of fifteen beds. Both were maintained by voluntary subscription. The Chest Hospital, situated on the outskirts of the town, was funded by the Council, as was the old workhouse which now served as both St Fillan's nursing home for geriatrics and a hostel for vagrants.

'She's very reluctant to go to St Fillan's. Like all the old dears, she reckons that going there will be as good as a death sentence.'

'Which in a way it is,' Iain agreed, 'but then, we all have to die, sometime. Can't you persuade her? At least she'd be comfortable in her remaining years and she must be taking up a great deal of your time, possibly at the expense of other patients with more acute needs.'

'Old people tend to get a bit selfish. They see everything from their own narrow viewpoint,' Alma reminded him. 'She's a nice old lady and I've always tried to humour her.'

She did not mention that the time spent with Mrs McAllister was her own. She visited the old woman most mornings, half an hour before she was officially meant to be on duty.

'Maybe I should have a word with her,' suggested Iain.

'It's up to you,' said Alma, secretly relieved. If Iain appeared as the villain in the piece, perhaps the old lady would lay the blame on the new doctor while Alma remained in her good books.

'I must get going,' said Iain, putting down his cup and brushing away the crumbs of a remarkably fine shortbread. 'That was good. Did you bake it yourself?'

'Heavens, no!' she laughed. 'Whenever would I have time to make shortbread? Jessie Moran is the baker. She lives on Eisdalsa Island. She makes a batch of shortbread every now and again and sells it. You have to be there at the right time, because every piece is snapped up almost as soon as it comes out of the oven.'

Iain was taken aback. He could think of no premises on the island which complied with Public Health regulations regarding the manufacture and sale of foodstuffs. The Medical Officer of Health for Argyll had been at pains to point out Iain's responsibilities in this respect: 'If you see anything, anything at all which contravenes the regulations, it's up to you to report it.'

'It looks as though old Mrs McAllister isn't going to be my only problem in the coming weeks,' he observed, making for the door. He paused with his hand on the latch. 'This has been a very useful meeting, Miss Livingstone,' he said. 'Shall we agree to continue it on a weekly basis, emergencies permitting?'

'I'd like that Doctor,' she replied.

He hesitated, wondering what she would think, 'Do we have to be so formal when we are alone? I knew you as Alma when we were kids.'

'I'd like you to call me that now,' she smiled and as he climbed into his car. 'Next week then, Doctor. I hope you have better luck with Mrs McAllister than I did!'

'Iain.'

'I beg your pardon?'

'Call me Iain.'

'I always called your father "Doctor".'

He slipped behind the steering wheel of the Armstrong Siddeley and tried the starter. The engine turned in a desultory manner, fired once and died.

'It's the battery again. I've got Cyril Lord looking for a new one but goodness knows how long he'll be.'

Iain climbed out of the car, raised the bonnet and tinkered with the electrical connections. Everything appeared to be well tightened down. Short of taking out the plugs and cleaning them, he was at a loss to know what to do.

'I suppose I could bump start her on this slope,' he decided. 'Can you steer, if I give her a push?'

'It'll take the two of us to get her out of those muddy ruts,' Alma said, from long experience. 'You hold the wheel and push from the side and I'll shove from behind.'

Iain felt his shoes sinking in the mud as he gained a purchase on the road surface. With the car in neutral and the handbrake off, he called out, 'Okay, on the count of three. One... two... three!'

They both pushed with all their strength. The rear wheels found some purchase on firmer ground and the car moved forward a few inches.

'She's going!' Iain cried out. 'Once again... on three!'

Again they moved the car a few inches and then as the rear tyres took a firmer grip, Iain found himself running to keep up. They reached the top of a slope and the car began a gentle glide downhill. Iain leapt into the driving seat and thrust the gear lever into second. The engine coughed, turned over once and stopped. Alma continued pushing from behind and the car gathered momentum. Iain threw in the gear once again, the engine coughed and fired and was soon purring smoothly. He pulled in to the side of the road and looked back to where Alma stood, hands on hips, gazing after him. The rear wheels must have spun in the mud, for she was wiping dollops of the stuff off her cheeks. Despite the state she was in, she seemed quite unperturbed. Strangely exhilarated by the sound of her laughter, he called out, 'Sorry about the mud, Alma... see you soon!'

'See you soon, Iain,' she called softly, waving him out of sight.

Alma turned back to the cottage, spattered with mud and with blood running down her leg where she had caught it on the sharp edge of the mudguard. Despite having laddered her last decent pair of stockings, she was still smiling when she closed the door behind her and went in to pour herself another cup of tea.

18

THE WEST HIGHLAND Hospital enjoyed wonderful vistas across the bay towards the islands of Kerrera and Mull. Built of stone with a steeply pitched slated roof, it clung to the side of the hill, fitting so neatly into the landscape that it might have sprung from the rock which supported it. Large windows reflected the bright noonday sun, so that Iain was momentarily blinded as he pulled into the car park before the main doors. The original hospital had been a small building housing two wards of ten beds apiece, an operating theatre, kitchens and laundry. It was soon found to be inadequate to accommodate the growing population of the town, however, and huts added during and after the Great War were still in permanent use as wards.

The elderly porter greeted Iain as though he were a long-lost friend.

'Why, you'll be young Dr Beaton,' he cried, coming forward to shake him by the hand. 'No mistaking you, laddie. Your faither's hair and eyes although maybe just a mite taller all the same.'

Although he took it as a compliment to his father that Hugh had been so well known, Iain wondered if he would ever be allowed to be his own man while he remained in Argyll. Millicent's proposal that he might go elsewhere again sprang to mind. If he was to go to a different place altogether, he might shake off the shadow of Hugh Beaton once and for all.

'I have an appointment with the Superintendent for twelve thirty,' he told the porter.

'I will let him know that you are here.' Despite having lived in the town for the best part of forty years, Angus McDowell still spoke in the muted accents of the Outer Isles. 'I will be a wee minute, just.'

He disappeared along a dark corridor, his heavily studded boots ringing on the marble floor. In a few seconds he was back with a short, balding, almost skeletal figure whose skin was pale but unblemished and whose eyes, a deep, bovine brown, seemed all the more startling because of the absence of any surplus flesh attaching to cheek and neck. It would be difficult to put an age to the man. He might be anything from forty-five to seventy. When he spoke, it was in an accent which reminded Iain of the Polish Brigade whose wounded had been brought into his field hospital in the aftermath of the battle for Arnhem.

'Ah, Dr Beaton, the MOH told me to expect a visit from you. You have taken over from your father, no?' Without waiting for a response he continued. 'I am Jan Kmiecik late of the Polish Army Medical Corps.' He clicked his heels together smartly and made a little bow before holding out his hand.

Iain could not hide his surprise at finding a foreigner in charge. He wondered by what chance this fellow had ended up in Argyll.

Kmiecik laughed at Iain's puzzled expression.

'You are wondering how it is I am here, yes? Well, I will tell you. I escaped from Warsaw with a small group of my countrymen in '39. We stole a civilian aircraft and flew to France just before the Germans marched into Poland. I spent the war as MO with my own countrymen, but when it came time for repatriation I did not want to work under the Russians any more than I wanted to work for the Germans. The Hospital Board must have been desperate to fill the post because, here I am!' He threw his arms wide with such an infectious chuckle that Iain could not but respond in similar fashion.

They shook hands.

'I am very pleased to find you here, Sir.' Iain greeted him warmly. 'I had the good fortune to meet many of your countrymen during the war and I acquired a considerable taste for Polish vodka.'

'Ah, but I, on the other hand, have developed a preference for a good malt whisky,' laughed the Pole. 'The best vodka is very difficult to come by.'

'So is the best whisky,' said Iain.

The Pole laid a finger along his nose in a conspiratorial gesture. 'Not if you happen to have treated the owner of the local distillery recently. Successfully, of course!'

Both men laughed and, in a friendly gesture, Kmiecik placed his hand on Iain's shoulder as they ambled along the corridor together.

'Only in the final few weeks of his life did I get to know your father really well,' said Kmiecik as he led Iain into the insignificant cubby-hole which served as the Superintendent's office. He seated himself in a swivel chair placed behind the desk.

'He would call in from time to time, following the progress of some of his patients. There was one occasion…' he motioned Iain to the second chair but Iain deliberately ignored the gesture, moving instead to the window, where he could gaze out upon the familiar view of the town. He was remembering when, as a boy, he had accompanied his father to this very room.

'…when he consulted me about his problem.'

Startled, Iain turned around sharply.

Avoiding the younger man's eyes, the Pole continued, 'Hugh was a veteran of the 1914 conflict, I believe?'

'Yes, he served on the Western Front in the final years.'

Kmiecik made no further comment, merely nodded, his lips pressed firmly together.

Iain sensed that here at last was someone who was not going to be holding his father up as an example at every opportunity.

Clearly, Kmiecik knew about Hugh Beaton, the man – who, towards the end of his life, had come to rely more and more heavily upon the *uisge beatha* to get him through the day. His patients might have been fooled by the charming, caring front he had put up, but his colleagues must surely have recognised the signs of alcoholism.

As though reading Iain's thoughts, Kmiecik said quietly, 'You must not allow your father's little problem to cloud your memories of him.'

He watched while Iain turned back to the window, trying to gain some control over his emotions.

'His patients were quite unaware of it, I can assure you. Had they ever been in danger, I would have interfered, but that was never the case, believe me. You have to look upon alcoholism as a disease, just like any other. In Hugh Beaton's case, he took to the bottle to try to drown his memories and dispel the nightmares. Once he realised he could not do without alcohol, he moderated his drinking except when he was off-duty. You know, it was really no different from his taking a daily shot of insulin or a handful of pills to keep him alive.'

The kindly Pole stared hard at Iain, willing him to understand. Iain nodded, wiped the back of his hand across his eyes and said, so quietly that he was scarcely audible, 'Thank you.'

He now took the proffered chair, facing his companion across the cluttered desk.

'You discussed his problem with him, yourself?'

'Only the one time. We never mentioned it again.'

'But you kept an eye on him. Thank you for that.'

Iain had often wondered why his father had been allowed to continue working under the circumstances. It was because of friends like this, keeping a watchful eye on him, that he had not been reported.

'I wanted you to understand,' said Kmiecik. 'It is not good for a son to despise his father.'

'I don't think I ever did that,' Iain searched his soul before continuing. 'As a child, I worshipped him. My one ambition was to be just like him. That's why I'm back here now, doing his job. What I find so hard to take is this widely held impression that he was some kind of a saint, when you and I and in particular, my mother, know he was not!'

'You must try not to deprive others of their illusions. For some their memories, no matter how distorted, are the only crutch left to them. What harm can it do to humour them? Ask yourself what damage you might do by exposing their saint for what he really was. And anyway, does it matter now?'

'You're right, of course.' Iain felt strangely relieved as the burden which had troubled him for so long, suddenly fell away. 'Thank you.'

Kmiecik consulted his watch. 'You'll have to forgive me,' he said, getting to his feet and reaching into his tray for a buff coloured manila file. 'I have an appointment in theatre, with a gall bladder. Unless you would like to join me, I fear I shall have to leave you.'

'Thanks for the offer,' said Iain, getting to his feet as well, 'another time perhaps. But before you go, there's something you *could* do to help me. It concerns a returned prisoner of war who worked on the Burma railway. He's in a pretty poor condition generally having recently suffered a recurrence of malaria, but there's more. Possibly it's a psychological problem. From what I'm told, he could become violent.'

'He needs professional help, like the rest of his comrades.' Kmiecik was not unsympathetic. 'Unfortunately there is only one small psychiatric unit, at Inverlinnie and they are so overwhelmed with similar cases, they'll not take him in until he does something to prove he's dangerous.'

'Don't you have access to specialist consultants in a one-off situation like this?'

'I'm authorised to seek help when necessary, of course, but it's finding the right person. Experts are very thin on the ground these days.'

'My brother is a psychiatrist. In fact he'd be ideal for this purpose. He's been specialising in what used to be described as shell shock for some years. Would it be possible for you to call him in for a consultation?'

'Why can't you do that yourself?'

'He's the Superintendent of a fairly large psychiatric hospital in England. I doubt if he would be given leave to come up here unless there was an official request from the Hospital Board.'

Kmiecik hesitated but only momentarily. 'Look, I'm late for theatre. Leave the details on my desk. I will see what I can do.'

'Thank you,' Iain was truly grateful. 'You have no idea how difficult I have found it to get anyone to take notice of this poor fellow.'

He drew out his pen to write on the first scrap of paper that came to hand. Already outside in the corridor, Kmiecik heard him murmur, 'It doesn't take long, does it, for people to forget yesterday's heroes.'

Kmiecik was startled, not so much by Iain's final bitter reflection as by his voice. He might have been listening to Hugh Beaton himself.

19

TAM CREPT CLOSER to the wire. This had to be the place Joe had told him about. The path from the Malay village lay just the other side of the perimeter fence.

He scrambled beneath the overhanging branches and prepared to wait. Hampered by the tropical downpour, he tried in vain to get a better view of the clearing. It seemed to be deserted.

What if the courier had been early and had tired of waiting? In the absence of a watch, he had been forced to rely on the strict routine of the prison guards for timing.

Rain began to collect in the hollow beneath him. Within minutes he found he was lying in a warm puddle.

Despite the poor visibility, he was thankful for the downpour. Not only had the noise of the rain disguised his departure from the camp but the insects had stopped biting.

In his head, he rehearsed the few words of Malay Joe had taught him. Would the villagers accept him in Joe's place, he wondered? He stretched his cramped legs and parted the branches in front of his face. Again seeing nothing, he was about to allow them to fall back, when – what was that? Something had stirred, over to the right. He stared ahead through the dense sheet of water, concentrating on the source of the sound and seeing nothing.

There it was again, a young voice. 'Joe, Joe?'

He heard bare feet squelching through the mud and suddenly the voice was much closer.

'Joe?'

Tam crawled forward into the open space before the wire and rose cautiously to his full height.

The boy gasped, not recognising the figure appearing so suddenly before him. Who was this stranger? His glance darted all about. Had he been betrayed?

'It's all right, laddie,' Tam called softly. 'Joe sent me.'

'Where Joe? Joe plomise come.'

Tam answered, 'Joe's sick.'

How could he tell the child that his friend was already dead? He might disappear into the darkness and this life-saving contact with the village would be lost for ever.

'He get better. He not going die?'

'No.'

'Joe going to take me England,' the boy said, proudly. 'He plomise.'

'You'll get to England,' Tam assured him. The child could be no older than his own wee girl. Would Joanie be this brave in similar circumstances, he wondered? This boy risked his life coming within a mile of the prisoners' encampment and for what? He jeopardised his life for strangers who neither spoke his language nor understood his customs. Men from a strange and mysterious country far across the seas. A place he had only heard of in the mission school.

'What's your name, laddie?' he asked.

'In school we get English name,' the boy said, proudly. 'Me... Tommy.'

'Well, there's a coincidence,' said Tam. 'I'm Thomas too. They call me Tam.'

This was taking too long. He was endangering them both by staying here.

'Look here Tommy,' he promised, meaning every word, 'when we go home, the lads and I, we'll take you along, just as Joe said. But right now, Joe badly needs all the food you can bring.'

'What you bling?'

Tam lobbed his pathetic offerings over the wire: a cheap fountain pen belonging to one of the men on the doctor's sick list and a silver cigarette case taken from a dying officer.

Desperate now to regain the cover of the undergrowth, Tam watched anxiously as the boy searched for the items in the long grass. At last he held up Tam's pathetic little bundle, waving it triumphantly.

'Hurry!' the soldier urged.

There was a blurred movement when the lad stretched back his arm and swung his own package high enough to clear the fence and land at Tam's feet. As he bent down to collect it, a searchlight swept across the clearing.

Tam froze. Had they seen him? Motionless as a marble statue and almost as white in the searchlight's beam, he waited for the light to move on. It travelled harmlessly across to the far side of the clearing, illuminating only the dense undergrowth. Tam remained motionless until he was completely satisfied the light had moved right away. Then, retrieving the precious food parcel with shaking hands, he turned back to thank the child. The Malay had already melted into the shadows.

Time was getting on. He must get to his hut before the next inspection by the guards. Retracing his passage by the markers Joe had carefully set out as a guide, Tam worked his way back into camp. He was half way across the open space which served as a parade ground when he was again brought to a halt, this time by a harsh, barely intelligible command.

'Down on your face... Get down, you... English!'

Tam obeyed instantly, diving to the ground close beside the platform which had been erected for use by the Camp Commandant. Fearing to be caught in possession of the food, Tam thrust his precious bundle out of sight beneath the wooden framework and rolled away.

In the steady downpour, he felt rather than heard the guards approaching. The ground beneath him trembled with the rhythm of their pounding feet.

'Get up!'

A boot landed in his side and he was forced to roll even further away from the stand. As he attempted to get up on his knees, he caught a glimpse of two pairs of uniform trousers tucked into Japanese standard issue canvas boots. Between them dangled a pair of bare brown feet. He did not need to look up to know that they belonged to the Malay child. The guards tossed the little brown body onto the ground some yards away.

Desperate to do something, anything, to help the boy, Tam struggled to his feet. He had almost reached the child when he saw the rifle butt swung into the air above their heads.

'No!' he cried. 'No!'

Throwing himself backwards across the child's body he took the full force of the blow himself. Winded, knowing the sound he had heard was his own ribs cracking, his first instinct was to avoid further damage by rolling into a ball. Drawing his knees up to his chest and turning his face to the ground, he presented the side of his head to his attacker. The second blow fell across his temple, rendering him unconscious. He never felt the dozen or so additional blows which were to leave him crippled for months to come.

When he regained consciousness, Tam found he was lying on his back with the rain still pounding down upon his bruised and battered body. As he lay dazed by pain, he became aware of some kind of movement above him. He opened his eyes. Slowly, cautiously, he turned his head, fearful of what it might be that had disturbed him.

They had raised a makeshift tripod using bamboo stakes and from its apex, hanging by a rope drawn tight about his fragile neck, his sightless eyes staring down into Tam's own, swung his little Malay friend. Tam began to scream.

Mairi McFarlane had been dozing beside the fire when her husband cried out. Fearing he would disturb the children, she rushed to his side, shaking him vigorously to awaken him.

His arm, swinging wildly in an attempt to ward off some imaginary terror, struck her across the face and she felt the warm saltiness of her own blood where her teeth had pierced her upper lip.

'Tam, Tam, wake up!' she cried, wiping her sleeve across her bleeding mouth and trying to hold down his flailing arms. Suddenly he grabbed her around the throat, his huge mason's hands squeezing the breath from her body.

'Let go. Take your hands off me!' he shouted.

With manic strength he thrust his wife away so that she stumbled backwards over a chair and hit the floor with a crash, her head striking the iron fender. Recovering only slowly from the blow, she managed to cry out once again before he lunged at her a second time.

As Tam stumbled blindly about the room, the door flew open and young Tommy came running in with his sister close on his heels. Tommy threw himself upon his father, grasping him around the knees in the rugby tackle which Tam himself had taught him. He sent the distraught man crashing down. With an oath Tam struggled to rise as Tommy retreated, terrified of the consequences of what he had done.

With little fight left in him now that he was fully awake, Tam leaned his back against the wall for support and, as the last ounce of strength left him, sank onto his haunches in the manner he had learned to adopt in the prison camp. As suddenly as the struggle had begun it ceased, leaving Mairi unconscious beside the empty grate and Tam, his eyes wide open, staring blindly into space.

In the silent aftermath, Joan advanced courageously into the room and noticing her mother's deathly pallor, ran to Mairi's side with a strangled cry.

'No, Ma! Don't die!'

At the sound of her child's voice, Mairi stirred and opened her eyes. Painfully, she drew in air through her damaged nose and cautiously fingered her bruised throat. Already breathing more easily, she attempted to rise.

Joan helped her into a sitting position and propped a cushion behind her back.

Mairi could not speak. She held one hand to her head where it had made contact with the fender and moaned softly to herself. Very soon blood began to seep between her fingers and Joan again cried out in dismay.

Joan's voice roused Tam from his stupor. He raised his eyes, focussing slowly on the havoc about him. He stared, not understanding, struggling to recall what had happened. Then, lowering his head into his hands, he began to sob.

A third child, Malcolm, appeared in the doorway clutching a scrap of woollen blanket and sucking his thumb. Tommy moved away to stand protectively beside his little brother. All three children stared in disbelief at the snivelling, pathetic creature who was their father. They had never seen a man cry before.

'Joan, get me something to mop up this blood,' Mairi spoke at last. She pulled herself to her feet, gradually regaining control of her trembling limbs. 'Then go and knock at the lodge. The factor has a telephone. Ask him to call Dr Beaton.'

Mairi's voice sounded thin and strained. Shock and weariness together had taken their toll and added to this she was beginning to feel faint from loss of blood.

The girl fetched her mother a towel from the rail and settled her on a chair. With a word to her brother to fill a kettle and put it on to boil, she ran out into the dark night.

The lodge was a small, stone building standing just inside the castle gate. Whenever forced to pass this place after dark, the children always ran, telling each other tales of monsters lurking behind those tiny leaded window panes.

Filled now with apprehension, Joan approached the iron-studded oak door and lifted the heavy knocker. A tendril from the overgrown vines which threatened to engulf the house touched her cheek. She let out a little squeal of fear, allowing the knocker to fall as she turned, ready to escape. The mournful sound it emitted echoed between ancient walls, bisecting the silence of the night.

Joan, still appalled by the vision of her mother covered in blood, resisted the temptation to run. Instead she waited, straining to detect some hint of movement from within. At last she heard snuffling behind the door, a scratching sound which suggested a dog, wanting out. Through a side window she caught sight of a flickering light approaching. Terrified as she was, the child remained rooted to the spot.

After what seemed an eternity the door opened with a sigh to reveal a tall, thin man in a woolly dressing gown and striped pyjamas, much like her father's. He held a massive black Labrador tightly by the collar.

'Yes?'

His tone was abrupt. It was three o'clock in the morning and the factor was not used to being disturbed in the middle of the night.

'Please, my mother's had an accident. She's hurt her head. She's bleeding... a lot! She sent me to telephone for the doctor.'

The man's tone softened at once.

'Is she alone in the house?'

'No, my faither's there.' Simply recalling this fact appeared to frighten her. 'An' ma wee brothers. They're alone wi' 'im.' Thoroughly alarmed by her own imaginings, she stammered, 'I'll need to get back.'

'You'd better come inside. Monarch, sit!' The factor bellowed at his dog, who, having satisfied himself that the mysterious visitor was no threat to his master, had decided to lick her to death.

The factor led Joan into a small sitting room, which he obviously used as a study. The heavy oak desk, which all but filled the room, was piled high with official-looking documents, while dozens of large, leather-bound ledgers occupied the dark shelving which covered much of one wall. On the enormous desk stood a black telephone.

He pointed the instrument out to the girl who simply stared at it, not knowing what to do. Her mother had once shown her how to make a call from the red call box in the village next to Mr McColl's store, but she had never seen a telephone inside a house before.

'Allow me to make the call for you,' said the factor, suddenly becoming aware of her predicament. 'Do you know the number?'

'It's Dr Beaton,' she told him tearfully. How was he going to help her without knowing the number? You had to tell the lady the number. That's what her Mam had said.

'I see.'

He picked up the receiver and dialled the exchange. At this time of night it would take a few moments for Mrs McWorter to get to the switchboard. At last he heard a click and a sleepy voice answered.

'Eisdalsa telephone exchange, what number please?' To her credit, Mrs McWorter did not enquire who it was had disturbed her slumbers. He would remember to apologise the next time he was passing.

'Can you put me through to Dr Beaton please?'

'One moment caller.' Mrs McWorter used her special voice on the telephone. She had studied the lady telephonists on the movies and she liked to copy their prune-in-the mouth style.

She held the line until Dr Beaton lifted his receiver. 'I have an urgent call for you, Doctor.' She made the connection and hung on just a few seconds longer. People seldom made calls at this time of night and in a village where little enough happened at the best of times, she prided herself in always being first with the news.

Joan listened with tears rolling down her cheeks while her benefactor explained the situation.

'This is Peter Parker, speaking from the castle lodge. I'm calling on behalf of one of my neighbours, a Miss?' he glanced inquiringly at Joan.

The child whispered, 'Joan McFarlane.'

'Miss Joan McFarlane. Her mother is a patient of yours I believe?'

He paused, waiting for the doctor's affirmation.

'It seems that Mrs McFarlane has had an accident to the head and is bleeding badly. I wonder, can you come out to Castle Row?'

Iain, wide awake now, answered, 'I can be with you in about twenty minutes.'

'Is there anything we can do meanwhile?' the factor asked.

Iain hesitated. It was best if they didn't interfere. Nevertheless it would be wise to treat for shock.

'If it's a head wound there's sure to be a heavy loss of blood. It probably looks worse than it is. Try to staunch the bleeding. Keep the patient warm and give her hot, sweet tea.'

Apologising again for disturbing the doctor at such an hour, Peter Parker replaced the receiver and turned to Joan.

'You get along home and make your mother some hot sweet tea. I'll be there in a few minutes to see everything's all right. The doctor will be here soon.'

Joan, troubled, did not move.

'What is it?'

'There's nae sugar ben the hoose,' she wailed.

'Here, take this.'

Without a moment's hesitation, he handed her a little china bowl with a lid.

When Joan had gone, the factor lifted the receiver once again. This time the answer was almost instantaneous but the voice sounded blurred by sleep.

'Police, Constable Christie speaking.'

Peter Parker was a newcomer to the village but the local Bobby was already a good friend.

'It's Parker here, up at the lodge. Sorry to get you up at this ungodly hour, Bill. This may be a false alarm, but I think there has been an attack upon one of my neighbours. I'd be grateful if you would call around and look into the matter.'

'Who are we talking about?'

'Mrs McFarlane. She has a nasty head wound, serious enough for her to have sent for the doctor at this time of night. I suspect that her husband is involved.'

He gave the details as he understood them. 'I'm going round to the house now,' he concluded. 'I'll see you there.'

He put down the receiver and calling the dog to heel, let himself out of the lodge.

20

'I THINK YOU should pay the McFarlanes another visit, unannounced.'
Alma was in determined mood and not prepared to be fobbed off with
some lame excuse about medical etiquette.

'If you're concerned about that incident the other night,' Iain replied,
'Mairi explained it. Tam has these nightmares. He was still half asleep by
all accounts. He wept like a baby when he saw what he had done.'

On his arrival at the McFarlane household Iain had found Tam, full
of self recriminations, bathing the wound on his wife's head and making
a very professional job of it, too.

'When I saw him he seemed as sane as you or me,' Iain insisted, 'but
it so happens that because the factor considered it a matter for the Police,
Bill Christie was obliged to make an official report. The Sheriff wants
an expert psychiatric examination and I've been asked to arrange for a
consultation up at the West Highland.'

He saw no reason to mention that he had already, through the good
graces of Jan Kmiecik, appointed his brother for the task. David had
agreed to come home for a long weekend and would examine Tam
McFarlane on the coming Friday.

While she was clearly impressed by Iain's ability to summon help so
effortlessly, Alma was still not completely satisfied.

'I have serious reservations about Tam being left alone in charge of
the children when Mairi is away at work,' she said. 'What if one of them
upsets him in some way and he lashes out again? We would never forgive
ourselves.'

'I had the impression that the girl is very sensible. She wouldn't upset
her father. How old are the others?'

Alma had to think. 'Joan is eleven, so Tommy must be nine. Wee

Malcolm's the one worries me, he's no more than five or six. Like any wee boy, he gets excited and makes a bit of noise now and again. It seems that Tam can't stand a row of any kind. That's likely to set him off sooner than anything.'

'Are you suggesting that Tam knocks the kids about?'

'Not the girl, he dotes on her. Nor young Tommy who's getting to be a strong lad and able to stand up for himself. It's the wee one I'm not so sure about. Mairi is scared that Tam might hit out at him.'

'Is there any particular reason, apart from the noise he makes?'

'Tam has got it into his head that the child is not his.'

'And is he?'

'Of course he's Tam's child,' Alma replied, indignantly. 'You have only to look at the boy to see his father's features stamped all over him! Tam had a leave before his regiment was shipped out to Singapore just before Christmas, 1941. The boy was born in September of the following year. I remember his birth quite distinctly. It was while Mairi was recovering from her confinement that she received the news that Tam was missing. Months later she heard that he had been taken prisoner by the Japanese.'

'The baby's arrival must have kept the village gossips busy for a day or two,' observed Iain cynically.

'Not once I got a hold of them and pointed out the dates! What I wanted to tell you was that I saw Mairi yesterday. She was nursing a sore arm and I'll swear the red swelling around her eyes was due to something other than the midge bites which she claimed had caused it.'

'You think Tam's knocking her about on a regular basis?'

'I don't doubt it,' Alma replied.

'He was a mild enough fellow from what I remember of him as a boy, powerful of course but such kids seldom find a need to be bullies.'

'He was a good husband to Mairi and after Joan was born, you couldn't have found a more devoted father,' Alma told him. 'Whatever happened to Tam in that prison camp has changed his personality completely. Mairi won't admit it, but I think she is terrified of him. You've seen for yourself that he can be violent.'

'That seems to have been an unfortunate mistake,' Iain interjeced, 'I can't imagine such a thing happening again.'

'The way it was described to me, I would have said the man needs something more than a chat with a psychiatrist,' Alma continued. 'He should be locked up! Of course, I'm not a doctor.'

'No,' Iain agreed with growing impatience, 'you're not. Before you start making assumptions you can't justify, perhaps you should remember that.'

He knew he was being unreasonably prickly and wondered why. Was it because his judgement was being challenged? Did he simply resent her interference, or was it that he knew he'd missed something vital and was also beginning to doubt?

'I have to let McFarlane know about the visit to the West Highland,' he told her, rather more calmly. 'I'll take another look at him then. When would be the best time to find him at home?'

Alma felt the tension subsiding as rapidly as it had arisen. 'Tomorrow's Saturday. The children might be about but Mairi will be at work so you should get a chance to talk to him on his own.'

2 1

DESPITE HIS DISREGARD of Alma's fears, Iain could not get Tam McFarlane and his family out of his mind. He looked forward with interest to seeing for himself how his patient behaved when left in charge of the children. Alma had assured him that Joan was unlikely to be a victim of his abuse but he knew that any little boy could easily provoke an unstable father into activity which he might well regret later.

Saturday morning surgery was unusually busy and when Iain set out for the McFarlanes' cottage, the bright sunshine of early morning had given place to lowering clouds and a cool westerly breeze. By the time he reached Castle Row, a steady drizzle had set in. Seeking shelter beneath the inadequate structure which served as a porch, he lifted the brass knocker, which was stiff and coated in verdigris from long neglect. It took several heavy knocks before he got a response.

Sounds of struggling on the far side of the door were followed by the piercing shriek of tired rusty metal hinges forced open against their will. Protesting loudly, the seldom-used front door was eased ajar a few inches to reveal young Joan.

The child regarded her unexpected visitor with a blank stare.

'Hello,' Iain greeted her brightly, 'is your father at home?'

While she hesitated to let him in, he examined her intently for any signs of physical abuse. To his relief, the skimpy, sleeveless cotton shift she wore revealed nothing untoward.

Still eyeing him suspiciously, she moved aside to allow him to enter. As he crossed the threshold she called out, 'Pa, it's the doctor!'

There was a muffled cough from within and the sound of metal-capped boots scraping on the slate floor.

From his dishevelled appearance, Iain might be forgiven for supposing

McFarlane had dragged himself straight from his bed. He was unwashed and unshaven. What appeared to be yesterday's shirt was only partially disguised by a food-stained waistcoat which, unbuttoned, exposed a pair of gaudy red demob braces. His shirtsleeves, rolled above the elbows, were smeared with soot.

'Yes, what is it?' Tam demanded ungraciously.

'I happened to be passing,' Iain explained lamely. 'I wondered how you might be feeling now you've been back at work for a while.'

'Best come in. It's a mess. I was clearing out the grate.'

Tam retreated into the kitchen, leaving the doctor to follow.

As he entered the miserable little room, Iain consciously avoided colliding with the old oil lamp swinging from a low beam in the centre of the room and stepped in a heap of ashes which had been piled onto a sheet of newspaper in front of the grate.

'Sorry!' Iain exclaimed, removing the ash from his shoe by rubbing it on the back of his other trouser leg.

Tam wrapped up the ashes hurriedly and handed the bundle to his daughter.

'Take this out the back,' he told her, 'and then you'd best get away down to the shop for y' ma's messages.'

Joan looked anxiously from one to the other of the two men, as though reluctant to leave the doctor alone in Tam's company. Fearing to disobey her father, she departed.

'How've you been feeling? Not getting too tired, I hope?' Iain asked.

Without answering, Tam poured water into a bowl and washed his hands, slowly and deliberately. He inspected the result carefully then washed them again. The operation appeared to take all of the fellow's concentration. When he had emptied the water into a bucket, he poured fresh and began to soap his fingers for a third time. Iain realised that what he was witnessing was the bizarre behaviour of someone who is mentally disturbed. Suddenly, as though emerging from a trance, Tam answered the question as if there had been no time lapse since Iain had asked it.

'Malaria's cleared up. I'm not sweating any more at night.'

He paused as though summoning the requisite words. 'I let you down, Doctor, you and Mairi, the other night. I don't know what came over me.'

His hand flew to his left temple, which he rubbed vigorously.

'To tell the truth, I don't even remember what happened. Mairi said I attacked her but I swear to God, I never meant to!'

Iain had been prepared to accept that Tam's actions resulted from having been awakened too abruptly from a nightmare, as he claimed.

Alma could be right however. There might be some deeper significance to what had occurred.

'Headaches no better?' the doctor asked.

Tam shook his head.

He had complained of headaches ever since their first meeting. Iain had given him a thorough examination and found nothing in his eyes which was likely to be the cause of the trouble. Examination of the skull had shown no obvious signs of injury. He had hesitated to say that the headaches were imagined, but this was his conclusion. On Tam's record, *psychosomatic?* was written beside the words *Patient complains of headaches.*

'I've given you a pretty thorough examination already for that,' he said. 'I couldn't find anything wrong. Migraine is a mysterious condition. No one has come up with anything effective in its treatment.'

He paused, wondering how he could introduce the main purpose of his visit without arousing the man's antagonism.

'The other night when Mairi was injured, you may remember the factor called in Constable Christie. The officer was obliged to make an official report and as a result I'm afraid the Sheriff has demanded that you see a specialist who can look into these dreams of yours.'

'I don't need a shrink,' Tam protested nervously, 'just something to make me sleep. If I could just get a decent night's rest for once, I'd be okay.'

'It's out of my hands I'm afraid. A consultant will see you next Friday at two thirty. I've some calls to make at the hospital myself on that day so I'll be happy to give you and Mairi a lift into town.'

'She doesn't need to come, does she?'

'The consultant might want to speak to her. She may be able to tell him things about the episode you can't remember.'

When he had spoken to David over the phone, his brother had been most specific about needing to see the wife.

Still hoping to avoid the doctor's arrangements, Tam protested, 'I'm no' on the panel yet, Doctor. I only work part-time at the quarry. Who's t'pay for yon specialist?'

'No need for you to worry about that, Mr McFarlane. If the Sheriff wants you to have the examination, the Sheriff's office has to pay.'

Iain rose to go.

'I'll need to get time off work.' Tam still sounded reluctant.

'I really do think the specialist will be able help you,' Iain insisted.

McFarlane opened the door to the street and followed the doctor to his car.

'I suppose it will be alright with Mr McWorter.'

It was the nearest Iain was going to get to any assent from Tam. He would have to enlist Alma's help in persuading Mairi of the importance of the consultation.

When the doctor's car had disappeared around a bend in the road, Tam turned back to the cottage. At that same moment, he caught sight of his youngest son, Malcolm, sneaking around the side of the house in hopes of reaching the door before his father saw him.

'C'm'ere!' Tam shouted.

The child stopped, frozen to the spot.

His face was smeared with mud and a trickle of blood meandered down the side of his face from a cut near his eye. The skin around the eye was bruised and swollen as though he had recently received a punch.

'You been fighting again, ye wee De'il?' Tam shouted angrily. 'Get ye ben the hoose. An' hae yersel cleaned up before yer ma sees ye!' He studied the boy more closely and saw that the sleeve of his jacket had parted at the seam and white padding showed through the opening.

'Look at yon coat,' Tam cried. 'D'ye think we're made o' money? Go on, get inside before I tak m'belt to ye!'

He raised his hand and directed a swipe at the child's head. Malcolm slipped under his father's arm and ran into the house, scrambling up the ladder to the attic room he shared with his brother. Once at the top, he slammed down the wooden hatch and sat on it, his knees drawn up to his chin. He knew from experience that his father would be unable to dislodge him. He would be safe here until his mother came home. Cowering in the darkness of the windowless attic, he held his breath, listening for the sound of his father, climbing the ladder to get him. The ladder creaked. He heard Tam's curse as he reached up to begin thumping on the hatch. The door lifted under him, but not enough to shift the boy from his perch.

'Damn!' Once again Tam tried to force the hatch cover, but still weak from fever, he was unable to make it budge. Defeated, he gave up the struggle and retreated down the ladder.

Malcolm, sobbing with relief, dared at last to vacate the hatch-cover and curl himself up on the thin mattress which served him for a bed. Moments later he was startled by violent crashing and banging from the room below. Unmistakeable sounds of glass and china smashing on floor and walls were followed by the splintering of wood as McFarlane, having taken out his frustrations upon every moveable object which came to hand, slammed out of the house and made his way up the path to the top of the cliff.

22

IAIN, EXHAUSTED BY a week in which Tam McFarlane seemed to have commanded almost all his attention, lay in that luxurious dream-like state between sleeping and waking, enjoying a few moments of self-indulgent circumspection.

It was Sunday, the day when even in a one-man practice, a doctor might hope for a few uninterrupted hours. On his desk in the consulting room lay a number of documents which required his urgent attention, several of them concerning the proposals for the new National Health Service. There was the referendum from the BMA to be considered. Upon its outcome would rest the fate of the entire project. After all, you couldn't run a health service without doctors!

A number of parliamentary speeches on the subject had been reproduced by various bodies seeking support from practitioners, either for or against the proposals. Each of these needed careful consideration. If only he had the time to study them properly. Much of what was being suggested sounded too good to be true. Equal access to treatment and care was promised for everyone, from the unborn infant to the senile geriatric, and these facilities were to be free of charge at the point of delivery.

If only he could believe the system was workable. So much depended upon the willing cooperation of a profession which had for centuries enjoyed a unique status in society. Could the physician hope to command the same respect and authority in the community if every man, woman and child was entitled to demand his services as of right? How many of Iain's colleagues would be willing to risk loss of status? In the past, the medical doctor had been regarded as a selfless, caring individual, performing good works out of a generosity of spirit and consideration for the wellbeing of his fellow men. No one questioned how he came by his money. He was a man whose word might be trusted, who vouched for other people's bona fides. In future the doctor would be a servant of the State, paid a regular salary like other people, a sum whose amount would be openly discussed and subject to the will of Parliament. Would he command the same degree of respect when that happened?

If he didn't sign up, Iain was convinced he would be obliged to leave Eisdalsa, something he didn't want to do. The work here was everything he had dreamed of when he was in the Army. Living alongside the people he worked with helped him to make diagnoses he could never reach simply by examining someone tucked up in bed in the anonymity of a hospital ward. He looked forward to watching the children he had brought into the world growing up and having families of their own.

A loud hammering on his bedroom door brought Iain thoroughly awake as his brother, remarkably lively for this time in the morning, burst into the room in a manner reminiscent of much earlier days when they had been children, living together here at Tigh na Broch.

Until this moment, the brothers had scarcely had a chance to do more than exchange greetings with one another. An overnight train journey on Thursday, followed by a protracted session with McFarlane on Friday afternoon had left David exhausted. He had slept late on Saturday and by the time Iain had finished his rounds, had gone off somewhere with his mother.

'Feel like a hike to the top of the Dun?' David demanded, ruffling his brother's unruly mop of hair. 'It'll blow the cobwebs out of that muzzy head of yours and give us a few minutes peace to mull things over together.'

It was a good idea. From the moment her youngest son had appeared on the doorstep, Millicent had usurped every minute of his time. This morning she would be tied up with preparing the Sunday luncheon. It would be an ideal opportunity for them to slip away for a while.

'Okay,' said Iain, rubbing the sleep out of his eyes and stretching luxuriously before swinging his legs over the side of the bed. 'Give me a few minutes. I'll be down directly.'

'Good. I'll tell Mum she can get the breakfast going!'

David took the stairs two at a time. Kmiecik's summons had provided an unexpected and most welcome opportunity for a weekend at home. Standing at the morning-room window, he took in the familiar panorama of the bay dotted with islands and set today, in a tranquil sea. The sun shone in a cloudless blue sky. It wouldn't last of course, so they might as well make the most of the dry weather before the rain came on. He breathed in the tantalising smell of frying bacon and revelled in the freshness of the summer morning. It was just the day for a walk on the braes.

The air began to grow cooler as the brothers struggled up the last two hundred feet towards the summit of the ridge. David shivered and pulled on an old jersey of his father's, which Millicent had insisted he carry with him. He moved cautiously to the edge of the cliff, where the great volcanic dyke of Dun Mor dropped away steeply towards the west, and threw himself down on the springy turf. Tucking his hands beneath his head, he surveyed the cerulean sky above and noticed for the first time the ominous bank of darkening cumulus cloud which was beginning to gather low down on the western horizon.

'I'd almost forgotten how wonderful the views are from up here,' he said as Iain, less agile and shorter of breath, joined him.

'There's been quite a landslip since I was here last.' Iain peered over the cliff to view the recently denuded face. 'The last two hundred feet are a sheer drop to the shore.'

David too inspected the damage done by last winter's storms.

'There's a lamb down there,' he observed, 'stuck on a ledge which can be only a few inches wide. Why on earth should the stupid animal get himself into such an awkward place?'

It seemed that the lamb had, too late, recognised his predicament for it began to bleat dismally.

'Grass is juicier I expect,' replied Iain, watching as the anxious ewe edged towards her offspring, calling encouragement all the while.

'I suppose you're waiting for a report on your McFarlane fellow?' David introduced the subject which had occupied Iain all through breakfast.

'Naturally.'

'He's disturbed. Who wouldn't be after the experiences he's had? But I could find no evidence of any severe mental illness. There's no sign of schizophrenia or manic depression.'

'What about the compulsive behaviour?'

'Ah, yes. That is a recognised symptom of schizophrenia it's true, but it could also be attributed to his excessive feelings of self-recrimination. He becomes so absorbed with his most disturbing thoughts, he forgets what he is doing. We all do that from time to time.'

'Did he mention his experiences as a prisoner of war?'

'Yes, in the end. The nightmares seem to centre on one particular occurrence, although there must have been many equally disturbing events to trouble him. It seems a Malay boy was caught and executed by the Japanese for smuggling food into the camp. McFarlane blames himself for the child's capture.'

'Were you able to do anything to help him?'

'It would take months, perhaps years of therapy to persuade him he was not to blame. The chances of him getting the treatment he really needs, even if he could afford it, are practically nil.'

'Would you say he was dangerous?'

'No, not really, although he confesses to losing his temper easily, largely because of his constant headaches. Now that *is* something you ought to be looking into.'

'I've already used all the usual tests and couldn't find anything wrong with his eyes. I'm not familiar with the latest thinking on migraine but I'm willing to look it up when I have the time.'

'I was thinking of something much more immediate. An x-ray might show up some old injury which is only now causing a build-up of pressure. He mentioned being beaten by the guards on more than one occasion.'

Iain was surprised by this. During his examination, Tam had never thought to mention such an obvious cause as a blow to the head.

'The nearest x-ray unit is at Inverlinnie,' he mused, thinking about the bureaucratic obstacles to obtaining access to the facility. 'I suppose I could pull a few strings. Morag may be able to put in a word.'

'That's the best advice I can give,' David said, drawing out a packet of cigarettes and offering one to Iain.

'No thanks, I'll stick to my pipe.' Iain responded, withdrawing his tobacco pouch. He began to fill a large briar.

David watched him with an amused expression on his face.

'You know, Mum's quite right. You definitely are your father's son! It's no wonder you're her blue-eyed boy.'

It was an old familiar taunt which aroused the same reaction in Iain as it had always done when they were boys. Placing his pipe carefully on a nearby boulder, he took a playful swipe at his brother and for a few minutes they rolled over together in the heather like a couple of young animals. Coming up for air at last, Iain brushed the dried grasses from his jacket and re-settled himself on the rock. Lighting up the pipe, he puffed away thoughtfully for a few minutes before raising the other subject which was bothering him, Millicent's proposal.

'You'll not find this too surprising. Mother is against my signing up to the NHS.'

'What does she expect you to do?' David asked.

'She has very generously offered to buy me a practice in a more affluent area, where it would be possible to remain outside the scheme.'

David experienced a resurgence of those old jealousies which had marred the brothers' relationship in former years.

'What, sell the practice, after all she said about father's wishes?'

'Yes. She's had a valuation made of the entire estate and it seems it's worth much more than she anticipated.'

'Are you going to take her up on her offer?'

'I've already as good as turned it down but Mum wants me to talk it over with Uncle Stuart. I can't think he'll support her idea. He's one hundred percent in favour of the new scheme.'

'So what's your problem?'

'I felt you should know what was being discussed. It didn't seem fair even to contemplate selling up without reference to you and Morag.'

'Good of you to think of us.' David's tone was brittle, despite his anxiety to disguise his annoyance. Had their mother made *him* such an offer he would have refused it too, but it was the knowledge that she would never have considered doing so that he found so galling.

'I've looked forward to working here for as long as I can remember,' Iain confessed. 'This life is everything I had hoped it would be. If it wasn't for Mother's objections to my becoming a Civil Servant, as she insists upon putting it, I wouldn't dream of moving.'

'I suggest you forget all about it,' David told him. 'It's almost certain that the buying and selling of medical practices is going to be stopped. After 1948, there'll be no market for this one. Who is going to buy a practice when, within six months, he can get himself assigned to it for nothing? Government compensation is unlikely to amount to anything like the valuation Mother's been given.'

Iain puffed thoughtfully on his pipe for a few moments. David was absolutely right. Only a fool would part with his money under such circumstances.

'I'll have to raise the question with Stuart this afternoon, otherwise Mother will give me no peace. With you there, we should be able to present her with a united front. If anyone can persuade her to change her mind it will be Uncle Stuart.' He sat quietly for a few minutes before he confessed, 'I feel so much better for having shared this with you.'

David, who spent his life shouldering other people's burdens, managed to shrug off those feelings of resentment which might cloud his judgement. 'It's okay by me whatever you decide, Iain, but if I were you, I'd stick to my guns and stay on here.'

'I suppose there will be a lot of changes coming your way too?' Iain asked.

'It's happening already within the mental health sector,' David told him. 'Under the pretext of winkling out any long term patients who might mistakenly have been put away in the days when lunatic asylums were a convenient place to dump unwanted members of one's family, they've been combing through our inmates, trying to determine who can be released without constituting a danger to the public.'

'Are there many like that?'

'Enough, unfortunately, to make the exercise worthwhile. I think it came as something of a shock to the politicians to discover that before the war more than sixty per cent of hospital beds were in psychiatric hospitals.'

'You hear all kinds of stories about people being put away for no justifiable reason. I've always attributed them to journalistic sensationalism.'

'Not entirely. I have a female patient who was committed by her family because she'd given birth to an illegitimate child. After nearly forty years at Westgate, she's become institutionalised. She thinks and talks like a child. She's harmless, but quite incapable of taking care of herself.'

'It's difficult to believe that in the twentieth century any parent could be so ruthless.'

'It wasn't just the girls either,' David continued. 'We have cases of young rakes getting themselves into trouble with the law who were put away in an asylum so that the family might avoid the stigma of a gaol sentence!'

'I suppose the fees for such patients would have been paid by their families?'

'Exactly! One can understand the government not wanting to continue supporting them out of the taxpayer's money, but after such a long time, even those who were not mentally retarded before, have deteriorated to the extent that they are now incapable of leading independent lives. In many cases they're without immediate family to look after them and while I can imagine a small community like this one absorbing one such misfit without trouble, most of our discharged patients will gravitate towards the big cities. In no time at all, they're going to be sleeping under the arches with the down-and-outs, the meths drinkers and the winos. Sooner or later they'll get into trouble with the law and the courts will send them back to us to be straightened out. It's going to be a vicious circle unless something is done to prepare the way for these people within in the community.'

'You won't be expected to release dangerous patients?' Iain asked.

'Oh no. The criminally insane will remain in places like Broadmoor, although even there there's talk of a time when certain categories of inmates might be considered for parole. The new therapeutic drugs available for the control of manic depression and schizophrenia can keep a patient very well controlled provided he or she takes the medication regularly. The trouble is that, left to themselves, these individuals are likely to stop taking the pills once their condition is stabilised. When that happens, they're going to revert to their former condition and constitute a danger to themselves and their neighbours. Some suitable system of support will be absolutely essential but I can't see the authorities being willing to fund the level of organisation required. It might be a more satisfactory way of dealing with the mentally ill but it's not going save the Health Service any money!'

'With all your patients released into the wide world, it looks as though there won't be a job for you,' Iain observed flippantly.

'Don't you believe it. As a matter of fact, we are likely to be much busier in the future. With the diagnosis of neurological disease becoming more accurate and detection at an early stage more common, we are likely to have greater numbers of patients to deal with in future. On the other hand, they'll not be with us for so long. Our work will become more like that of doctors in the general hospitals.'

'It's quite a challenge,' suggested Iain. 'You must be pleased to be in right at the beginning of a new era.'

'Yes, I find the whole thing very exciting. The only trouble is I have to persuade a staff of very conservative members of the old school that the new regime will benefit all of us, patients and medical staff alike.'

Iain looked at his watch and jumped to his feet.

'Good Lord! It's nearly lunchtime. Mother'll skin us alive if we're late.'

'I'll race you to the bottom,' David shouted and set off at a trot, with Iain protesting loudly that he was being cheated from the start.

23

STUART AND ANNIE Beaton came to Tigh na Broch for Sunday lunch most weekends and cheerful, if sometimes provocative, discussion could be guaranteed.

'Let's hope the Labour Party wins a second term,' Annie observed as Millicent helped everyone to second helpings of clootie dumpling. 'If the Tories get back in before this new Health Service is properly on its feet, they're sure to make a dog's breakfast of it.'

Millicent, always uncomfortable when her sister-in-law introduced politics to the dining table, shuffled uneasily. She was convinced that it was vulgar for a lady to uphold socialist principles.

'How can you say that,' she demanded, defending her instinctive allegiance to respectable middle-class Conservatism. 'Wasn't it a coalition government which introduced the idea of a National Health Service? Didn't it receive the full support of all sides in Parliament? That man who produced the White Paper, Maurice something or other...'

'Willink,' Annie helped her.

'Willink, that's it. He was a Tory!'

'Yes he was,' Iain agreed, 'but what Annie says is quite right, Ma. Lord Moran and his lot will begin to unravel the scheme the first chance they get! They are already advocating a parallel system of private health care for those who would prefer to continue to pay for their own treatment. It's easy to see what will happen. Those with money will be able to jump the queue for both beds and treatment, and the consultants already commanding the highest incomes will continue to feed off the private sector. The wealthy people of this country are not going to forego their privileges without a fight.'

'And then there's the whole question of training,' David joined the argument. 'At present, it's proposed that medical degree courses in the universities will be free of charge, which opens the door to all those people with the brains to become doctors, but not the money. Bevan wants a clause compelling new doctors to work within the health service for a minimum period after qualifying. The big boys in the BMA aren't keen on that and the Tories are sure to throw it out. That means that after qualifying at the expense of the tax payer, many of our best young men and women are either going to disappear immediately into private practice or they'll take posts abroad, where the prospects appear to be better.'

'Mark my words, Millie,' Annie added excitedly, 'The top-ranking consultants are going to fight tooth and nail to make sure their cosy little nest eggs don't go flying out of the window. They're the boys at the peak of the profession, officers of the BMA, consultants to royalty, the men who have both the time and the inclination to put their opinions on paper for organs like the *Lancet* and the *BMJ*. When you tune in to any discussions on the wireless these days, it's these people you're listening to. You're not hearing the views of your ordinary GPs or junior hospital doctors. Their turn will come when they put that cross on the ballot paper. People may be very surprised at the outcome of the referendum.'

'You know what the answer is, Aunt Annie,' Iain chipped in, laughing. 'At the next election, you should run for Argyll on a Labour ticket.'

'Don't underestimate my Annie, any of you,' Stuart defended his wife stoutly. 'If she were to stand for Parliament, she would knock spots off the old guard around here.'

Millicent envied Annie a husband who thought so highly of his wife's talents and supported her so openly. Annie was such a capable woman. She had always been an independent spirit, while Millicent, on the other hand, had relied entirely upon Hugh to make all the decisions. Until he became too ill to manage their affairs, she had never paid a bill or signed an official document. Left to cope alone, she had, until very recently, been totally lacking in self-confidence.

'It's time we cleared the table,' she said suddenly, cutting short any further discussion. 'If you men would like to make yourselves comfortable in the study, Annie and I will bring in some tea when we're finished.'

'Let me help,' Stuart offered. Since his retirement, he shared with Annie responsibility for all the household chores. While it amused Iain and David to see their uncle collecting the dirty dishes, Millicent attempted, not very successfully, to disguise her disapproval.

Annie gave her husband a gentle shove.

'I'll let you off, just this once. Go with David and Iain and do whatever it is you men get up to on your own. Millicent and I have important matters to discuss.'

Stuart Beaton stood with his back to the fire for a few minutes, enjoying the warmth. Even though it was midsummer, the day had turned quite chilly after the rain. After a few moments he sank into an overstuffed, leather-upholstered armchair and fished out his pipe and tobacco pouch.

'I'm inclined to agree with what you were saying just now, about the best of the new graduates going abroad,' Iain said to David.

Stuart was weary of all this discussion about the job. He would have preferred to talk about the coming rugby season or even to have gone over his plans for the sail boat he was having built at McQueen's yard. He'd actually brought them along to get Iain's view on the alterations to the rigging. Unfortunately, it was obvious his nephews were intent on pumping him for the latest information from the meetings he had attended.

'I need your advice, Stuart.' Iain sank into the armchair opposite and in a few brief sentences explained his mother's proposal. 'So you see she's made it financially possible for me to opt out of the NHS if I want to.'

Iain paused, expecting an immediate response.

Stuart made no comment. Instead, with exaggerated concentration, he continued the elaborate process of preparing his after-luncheon smoke. Not until his pipe was drawing to his satisfaction did he make a move, and then it was only to toss the taper into the grate.

Uneasy at his uncle's lack of response, Iain spoke more rapidly. 'It might appear ungrateful to refuse such a generous offer and to do so could prove very foolish if, after all, the new scheme fails to get off the ground. If it's to be the watered-down hotchpotch that everyone is predicting, I'm not at all sure I would want to be associated with it anyway. The question is, should I take Mother up on her offer?'

Stuart Beaton, leaning his grey head against Millicent's crisply starched antimacassar, manufactured a magnificent blue smoke ring. 'I suppose it rather depends upon how you see your role in society,' he replied, surprising Iain with his tone. 'Did you take up medicine as a means of making a living, or did you believe that you had a vocation for it?'

'A bit of both, I suppose,' Iain confessed. 'I never thought of doing anything else.'

'It's one of the drawbacks of belonging to this family that every male child has his life mapped out for him from the day he's born.'

David, who had positioned himself by the window so as not to be included in the discussion, looked up sharply. He was surprised to detect a note of cynicism in his uncle's words.

'I don't suppose they ever told you that, as a boy, I rebelled against becoming a doctor?' Stuart asked quietly.

Iain shook his head and waited.

'I wanted to go to sea,' Stuart told them. 'I'd have gone whaling or deep-sea fishing. In those days a man with his own boat could make a good living. But Dad talked me out of it and in the end we reached a compromise and I joined the Royal Navy as a surgeon. I was a good one too. I found I had a vocation, after all.'

'It would have been awful if you had discovered you hated medicine,' David observed.

Stuart regarded him silently for a moment before continuing.

'That experience showed me that it's possible as a doctor to make a contribution to any situation, no matter what the circumstances, and believe me, there were times when the circumstances were pretty grim.' He paused, remembering that he was not talking to a pair of fledgling housemen, still wet behind the ears. 'You'll have to forgive an old man for rambling. There's no need for me to tell you two what it's like to be a medic in wartime. What I've learned is that money can't buy you happiness; and that if, in pursuit of the comfortable life, you deny yourself the opportunity to exercise your abilities to the full, you will be courting misery. So, Iain, if you're going to continue doctoring, be sure you do it where it's really needed. Work with real people presenting real problems. Don't simply sell your talents to the highest bidder.'

When Iain didn't respond immediately, Stuart wondered if he had been too blunt. Nevertheless, once started, he determined to finish what he had to say. 'As for whether or not the scheme is going to succeed, you have to remember that this Health Service was something devised at a time when people were fighting for survival. Promises were made in the heat of battle and I have no doubt that, at the time, the politicians who made them were sincere in their intentions. Now it's all over and, just as in 1918, many of those who spoke out the loudest for change are beginning to draw back. Unfortunately for them, they haven't reckoned with the mass of the population. The ordinary men and women of this country have had a glimpse of a life denied to many of them before. When the war started, millions of ordinary working-class people who had been forced to stand in a dole queue for much of their working lives and accept pittance wages for what work they could get, suddenly found they had proper jobs to go to and could afford somewhere decent to live. Although there was food rationing, they no longer starved and they were given new clothes to wear, albeit a uniform. People found new strengths and discovered abilities they didn't know they possessed. They learned new skills and in many cases they received a proper education for the first time. You can't handle twentieth-century weapons without some knowledge of science and mathematics and you can't communicate in battle without being able to read and write. With combat training and proper medical attention, those in the armed services were fitter than they had ever been in their lives and if the civilian population didn't have the same advantages, their injuries from bombing were at least treated free of charge. Demobilisation has released a huge workforce of skilled men and women, able to organise themselves through trades unions. It's a formidable machine for reform. Look at the shock the Tories had when Labour won the election in 1945. It was the mass vote of the servicemen which won the day for Labour then and it could be the mass vote of the ex-service medical men who swing the tide Aneurin Bevan's way now. Anyway, I suppose what I'm trying to say is, don't write off this National Health scheme yet-awhile. I think you may be pleasantly surprised at the outcome of the referendum.'

Iain and David had remained silent throughout the old man's tirade. One had to admire Stuart's eloquence, thought David. He must make a formidable contribution to those BMA debates!

Stuart, exhausted by his long speech, puffed once or twice on his pipe before his eyelids began to droop.

Fearful that the pipe would drop out and perhaps burn his uncle's clothes, Iain removed it gently and laid it in the ashtray. Soon the old man's breathing slowed and deepened.

The room was stiflingly hot. Even David had dropped off to sleep where he lay stretched out on the window seat. Iain leaned across his brother's inert form and carefully, so as not to disturb the sleepers, he pulled on the sash cord. The window slid up easily letting in a light breeze, freshened by the summer rain.

From this corner window he could see the view from three sides of the house. He looked eastward towards the head of the glen. To either side, sheer cliffs of volcanic lava rose majestically to a height of a thousand feet or more while in the distance, the woodlands of the Johnstones' estate sheltered the valley from the cruel easterly winds of winter.

Overwhelmed by the ties which bound him to this place and its people, Iain knew he could not leave again so soon. Eisdalsa had always been home to him and he had grown tired of his rootless existence of the past years. Out there in the meadow they had held the village sports every summer. He and David had battled with the likes of Tam McFarlane and Alma Livingston for the cheap little medals they had prized so highly. Where were they now, all those rosy-cheeked children he had studied alongside at the village school? Some were back at work in the fields or on the boats. Others had forsaken village life for a tenement in the city and a job in the shipyards. There were those who, like Tam, had come back terribly damaged by war; some, like young Willy McColl from the village shop, would never come back at all.

Down towards the shore, hoodies searched for carrion along the road, while a buzzard hovered overhead, seeking out any young rabbit or vole careless enough to dart out of the stubble. To Iain's left, further up the glen, the shaggy red coats of his mother's prize cattle made a bright contrast with the green of lush pasture and the backdrop of dry scrub on the lower slopes of the mountains.

From the right Iain noticed a flash of scarlet as the afternoon bus for Oban rounded the base of Caisteal an Spuinneadair. He watched its progress along the shore until the driver changed noisily into bottom gear and attacked the steep slope to the summit of the brae. The vehicle rounded the corner and disappeared from view. He turned his attention to the sea. Out in the bay a commercial fishing boat dredged for scallops and he thought about the boy, Stuart, standing perhaps in this very same spot all those years ago, and yearning to go to sea.

Iain drew in a deep breath and, on hearing a muffled complaint about the cold he turned his back on the scene. Stuart Beaton, huddled beside the fire, must have woken only for a moment because by the time Iain had closed the window, he was snoring again with his mouth hanging open to reveal great gaps between his molars. His lips twitched as he breathed out, creating a slight whistling sound.

'Now, just look at that,' said Annie, placing the tea-tray heavily on the old oak desk which had served generations of Beaton doctors. 'Leave him alone for one moment and he goes right off to sleep. No wonder you don't sleep at night you silly old man,' she scolded her husband affectionately and settled comfortably on Iain's revolving chair to pour the tea.

24

'DID YOU HAVE a nice talk with your Uncle Stuart this afternoon, dear?' Millicent asked, as the three of them settled down to a quiet evening by the fire.

Iain was reluctant to tell his mother what he had decided but he knew he could not put it off indefinitely. Best get it over with while David was still here to back him up. 'Yes,' he said, 'he and David have helped me to make up my mind.' He glanced across the room at his brother, looking for support. 'I've decided to vote "yes" in the referendum and I shall sign the Government's contract.'

'You're quite determined then, despite my offer?' Millicent said, her voice deceptively calm, her face expressionless.

'I have no option.'

'You're going to allow the Ministry to take over the practice?'

'I've told you before this practice can't operate on a privately funded basis.'

'And you will remain here, as a servant of the State?' Her voice was cold. She was obviously offended.

'Don't think that I don't appreciate your offer, Mother,' he hastened to reassure her, 'but I must do what I think is right. If this scheme is the only way in which ordinary men and women are going to receive the health care they need, then I have to go along with it.'

She sniffed disparagingly.

'I can't see what you have against us being Civil Servants,' David observed. 'Haven't we always been somebody's servant? Great-grandfather Beaton was the Marquess of Stirling's servant, so was Grandfather. Dad was employed by the Slate Company. He depended on premiums from the Friendly Societies and payments from the Local Authority. He could never have supported us on the money he got from fee-paying patients. What's going to be so different now? A child with measles, an old man dying of cancer, they're not going to want to know who's paying the doctor's bill. It won't be them, that's all that matters.'

Millicent flinched at the suggestion that the Beatons had always been somebody's servants. It was not a word she would have associated with her husband or any of her children.

In the ensuing silence, Iain searched for some way to explain how much he appreciated what she had tried to do for him, to tell her how important it was for him to stay on here but before he could say anything Millicent forestalled him.

'You've had your chance, Iain,' she declared. 'It won't be any use your coming back to me in a year or two's time, asking for the money to go abroad, or for anything else for that matter, because by then, it won't be available. If you have made up your mind to stay on, I shall take the second option suggested to me by my lawyer.'

Both men looked up, startled by the resolution in her tone.

'I intend to use whatever compensation I'm paid for the practice to reconstruct the farmhouse and restock the farm. With Sorlie McKinnon's help, I'm going to develop the dairy herd and produce more butter and cheese. I intend to make Caisteal Farm products the best in the county.'

Iain knew his mother had been toying with the idea of keeping the herd and she had made no secret of wanting to restore the farmhouse, but she had never mentioned such an ambitious project as this.

David could not disguise his astonishment. 'I expected you to say you were going to sell the farm and move into a little cottage, perhaps take a flat in town or something. Are you sure you're up to full-time farming, Ma? Most people of your age would be thinking of retiring, not taking on an entirely new venture.'

'Don't you, either of you, try to stop me,' she insisted. 'All my life I've had other people telling me what I should or should not do. Just for once, allow me to know what I'm capable of. If you can't find it in your hearts to encourage me, then at least stand back and allow me to get on with my life. If I make a fool of myself then so be it. At least allow me to try to do this one thing on my own initiative!'

This was a mother whom neither man could recognise.

Millicent had been the cornerstone of their family's existence: invariably around when they needed her, ever calm in adversity, always encouraging in their various enterprises, rejoicing in their successes. It had never occurred to them that their mother might have had ambitions of her own which had been left to wilt on the vine, sacrificed in the interests of the family. Far from wanting to oppose her now, both men were filled with admiration for the new Millicent.

'I think it's a terrific idea,' Iain said, completely disarming his mother by sweeping her into his arms and kissing her. 'But there's no need to reinstate the farmhouse. There's plenty of room for both of us here.'

'For us, yes,' she agreed, laughing with relief now that she knew they were not going to put forward any obstacles to her plan. 'You haven't forgotten what I said, I hope. Don't expect me to carry on being the doctor's helpmate. I'm going to be far too busy in future to answer your telephone calls. It's high time you found yourself a wife. And when you do, I shall move out.'

Iain knew he had prevaricated for too long over the question of Alison. From the practical point of view he had to marry as soon as possible, or at least find a receptionist. It would be best if he were married. Patients were uncomfortable having a bachelor for a GP.

He would write to Alison tonight and arrange to see her on his next visit to Edinburgh.

'Looks as if you're doomed, old boy,' David observed.

'I suppose you intend to remain a bachelor for the rest of your life,' his brother asked, almost enviously.

'Not by choice old man, but can you see any woman wanting to move into a house in the grounds of a lunatic asylum?'

'Anyone contemplating marriage to you would have to be a bit dotty anyway,' observed Iain, shielding himself from yet another brotherly attack.

'If you're going to be up in time to drive David to the station, Iain, you'd better both turn in,' Millicent said. 'I'll give you a call.'

Stretching and yawning, Iain got to his feet. 'I'd best go and put the car's battery on charge. We don't want to have trouble starting in the morning.'

'Isn't it time you did something about that ancient banger?' David demanded. 'One of the better things about my job is the decent vehicle that goes with it.'

'I'm dealing with it,' Iain told him, 'You might be very surprised next time you come up.'

25

‘INVERLINNIE GENERAL HOSPITAL.’

‘Good morning, this is Dr Beaton calling from Eisdalsa. I’d like to speak to Dr McRae if she’s available.’

‘One moment please.’

Iain glanced across at Alma. The nurse was sitting forward on her chair, clutching the armrests so tightly her knuckles were white.

Iain smiled sympathetically. ‘Trying to find her,’ he said.

‘Iain, is that you?’

‘Morag?’

‘You’ll be wanting an answer. Can you hold on a minute while I fetch the plates?’

‘She’s gone to get the results,’ he explained to Alma.

In a minute his sister was back.

‘It’s not good news, I’m afraid.’

Morag’s voice faded; the line was poor.

‘Sorry, what was that?’ he yelled, then listened for what seemed to Alma like a very long time, nodding occasionally and interjecting with the occasional ‘Yes, I see.’

‘It’s a tumour,’ Morag was saying. ‘There’s considerable brain swelling which is probably causing the sudden outbursts of temper. The condition is inoperable. All we can do is keep him sedated until the end.’

‘How long?’ Iain asked.

‘It’s hard to say, it could be some time.’ Morag sounded very despondent. He respected her judgement. She would never give up if there was the slightest hope for Tam McFarlane.

‘His wife will want to be with him,’ Iain told his sister. ‘She has children, so she can’t travel back and forth to Inverlinnie. Can Tam be moved back here do you think?'

'Moving him can't make a lot of difference,' she sounded tired. 'I'll arrange for an ambulance. Will you notify Kmiecik?'

'Yes of course. Thanks for doing this rotten job yourself. I'm surprised you were able to. I thought you were a part-timer these days.'

'I am, but it so happened we had a climbing casualty. I've been out with the rescue team most of the night.'

'Did you get the patient down okay?'

'Oh yes. He was suffering from hypothermia, a fractured femur and concussion but otherwise, he's fine. He should make a good recovery despite having climbed Ben Nevis in plimsolls and shorts. He had nothing warm or waterproof with him at all. Luckily his friend was able to call for assistance and guide us to the spot.'

'These crazy people never give a thought to those who have to go out after them,' said Iain bitterly. His sister had been doing this mountain rescue work since the early days of the war. At that time it had been pilots and marines in training who were getting into difficulties. There was some excuse for them, but not for these idiots who went out onto the mountains, untrained, inadequately equipped and without telling anyone where they were going.

'Just you take care,' he cautioned. 'You're too precious to lose over some senseless weekend hiker. How's Duncan?'

'Probably working himself up into a state. He'll be saying exactly the same as you in about half an hour from now. Goodbye, little brother!'

She was laughing as she replaced the phone, all the earlier signs of weariness gone for the moment. Iain was reminded of that new Millicent who had so startled him last weekend. Now he understood where Morag got her remarkable resilience from.

He replaced the handset and turned to Alma.

'McFarlane has a brain tumour. Its inoperable.'

Alma had turned very pale, concerned for Mairi as much as for the patient.

'What happens now?'

'Morag is having him transferred to the West Highland. It seems he has deteriorated in the couple of days he's been at Inverlinnie and she says there's no way he can be nursed at home.'

'Who's going to tell Mairi?'

'That's my job. But,' he added hastily, 'it might help if you were around when I tell her.'

Reluctantly, she was forced to agree.

'There'll be some practical arrangements to be made. Mairi might want to stay in Oban, I know she has friends where she can lodge. We might have to find someone to look after the children.'

'Don't force too much on her at once,' Iain warned. 'This news will come as a shock. Give her a chance to think things out for herself.'

Alma felt a tiny frisson of indignation. You do your job and I'll do mine, she thought, but she remained silent.

How Iain had changed in the short time he had been here. He had arrived with all the bustle and rush of hospital efficiency and now, here he was, telling *her* to ease off and let matters take their course. Despite her annoyance she couldn't help smiling.

'I can't see much to smile about,' he observed, crisply. 'What's the joke?'

'Oh, nothing,' she replied, then added more somberly, 'When do you want to go to see Mairi?'

'The sooner the better. How about later this morning, after surgery? Do you want to come back here and let me give you a lift?'

'No, I have calls to make over near the castle. I'll meet you there.'

She gathered up her things and made to let herself out. Iain followed her to the door. He coloured slightly as he suggested, 'When this business with McFarlane is sorted out, how about coming into Oban with me for some lunch? I have to visit the hospital this afternoon. Maybe you have some calls to make?'

'Lunch would be nice,' she replied trying to ignore his embarrassment, 'and I do need to call in at head office. Thank you very much. I'll see you later.'

As he opened the front door to let her out, the first of his morning's patients filed in.

26

THE LITTLE GABLE-END beside the castle gate had never looked so dreary
and unkempt as it did now. It was not that Mairi McFarlane had always
been a poor housekeeper – far from it. Before her troubles, she had taken
great pride in having a good fire burning in a well-blackened grate and
a table laden with fine home baking. The problem was she was literally
worked off her feet. Always tired, she could not sleep and as one miserable
day followed another, she knew that she was losing any will to get on
with things.

'The neighbours have been very good,' she told Alma, as they
crouched beside an empty grate still dusty from the previous day's ashes,
and supped their tea from an unmatched pair of cracked china cups.

'Mrs Clark gives the children their tea when I'm late back from visiting
the hospital, but I canna ask her to keep an eye on them for the whole of
the school holidays. That means I shall have to take two weeks off work
at Christmas. I just don't know how I'm to manage without the money.'

With the back of her hand, Mairi wiped away tears of despair. 'Mrs
McArthur is going to be looking for another cleaning woman if I keep
letting her down like this.'

'I'm sure she understands,' Alma tried to console her, not daring to
admit that the farmer's wife for whom Mairi worked for two days a
week, had already asked her if she knew of a reliable woman to replace
her. It was past ten o'clock and yet Mairi appeared to be still unwashed.
Her hair had certainly not seen a comb since she rose from her bed that
morning and her clothes might have been slept in, they were so rumpled.
If this was how she was neglecting herself, no wonder Mrs McArthur
was seeking a replacement.

The house smelt of a mixture of dampness, dust and rotting food while Mairi herself moved within an aura of stale sweat and urine, an odour which Alma normally associated with her more elderly patients, those who lived alone unable to care properly for themselves.

Making a mental note to discuss the problem of the children with Iain, Alma tried to find the words which might, without giving offence, persuade Mairi to pay attention to her appearance.

'Are you going to the hospital today?' she asked. 'I wouldn't want to hold you up. The bus leaves in half an hour and you must want to get ready.'

'That's all right,' Mairi replied carelessly. 'I'm as ready as I'll ever be.'

Without showing any sense of urgency, she got up, shifted a pile of papers from one heap to another in search of her purse and, having discovered it on the mantelpiece where she had left it, counted out the few coppers it contained. 'That's just enough for the bus and a wee cuppa while I wait for the return,' she said as though to herself.

Having placed the purse in the pocket of her skirt, she lifted a flimsy, somewhat crumpled envelope which had already been torn open.

'I suppose I'd better take this with me,' she said, 'though I doubt very much if Tam will know the fellow it's from.' By way of explanation she showed Alma the envelope which bore a London postmark. 'It's from someone who was in the prison camp with him. By the cheerful way he writes, he seems to have been quite unaffected by it. The letter is so full of memories of camp life he makes it sound like a Boy Scout jamboree.'

Alma was surprised at the bitterness in Mairi's voice, for it was obvious to her that the men would not want to dwell on the horrors of their experiences. Clearly she resented the fact that others might find anything to joke about from those terrible times. Alma gave only a cursory glance at the untidy hand which had scrawled Tam's address across the cheap envelope. She handed the letter back without comment.

Mairi grabbed a shapeless felt hat from the hook beside the door and pulled on a rusty black overcoat whose sleeves were frayed at the cuffs and whose lining hung down below the hem. The old Mairi would have had that sewn up the moment it happened, thought Alma as she looked on, despairing at the feeble attempt the poor woman made to tuck her mop of unkempt hair inside her bonnet.

They heard the bus the moment it turned into the lane.

'You go on,' Alma told her. 'I'll close up the house.'

The nurse waited until Mairi had climbed aboard and the bus had pulled away from the curb, before she went back to pull the door to. She took one last look at the sad remnants of a once happy home and sighed. The war had much to answer for. They would be dealing with the aftermath for a long time yet.

27

'OH ALMA, HOW nice!' Millicent greeted the district nurse warmly. They saw so little of her these days. Apart from her weekly meeting with Iain, which was usually short and conducted in the surgery, Alma scarcely ever found time to call at Tigh na Broch.

'I was hoping for a word with the doctor,' Alma explained. 'I can only stop for a minute.'

'Is it something Hugh's brother can deal with?' Millicent asked, 'Iain's away to Edinburgh for a couple of days. His uncle is holding the fort.'

As though on cue, Stuart popped his head around the surgery door. 'Do I smell coffee?' he asked hopefully, then seeing Alma, 'Good morning, Nurse. It's not often we see you at this time of day.'

'Good morning Dr Beaton,' Alma replied, smiling.

'Look,' said Millicent, 'There's no point standing here in the cold when there's coffee in the pot and the waiting room empty. Come away in, Alma. You can surely make time for a wee blether, just this once.'

Alma required no further persuading.

'Och well, just for a wee minute then,' she said and Stuart took her bag as she passed by him in the hall.

'What on earth do you carry in here?' he demanded, gasping at the weight of it.

'Everything I'm likely to want,' she replied. 'I can't rely on my patients to have even a bar of soap for me to wash my hands!'

'I don't know how you manage to carry all that on a bicycle,' observed Millicent. 'Don't you find the hills awfully tiring?'

'Not going down,' Alma replied gaily, feeling relaxed for the first time that morning.

'What was it you wanted with Iain?' asked Stuart once they had settled down around the kitchen table with their steaming cups of Millicent's special brew. 'Is it something I can deal with?'

'I don't know,' Alma replied. 'I just feel the need to talk the matter over with someone. You may be able to make some suggestion. It's Mairi McFarlane. She's at her wits end, poor woman. She's neglecting the house, herself and almost certainly the children as well. I can't blame the poor soul. There's Tam up in the West Highland, lingering on, nothing but a vegetable now. Mairi tells me he scarcely recognises her when she goes to see him. He talks to her as if she's a complete stranger. If he does remember who she is, he becomes abusive and sends her away. She has to divide her time between her work, caring for the children and visiting Tam in hospital. She's not coping. It's pitiful. She's not had a haircut in weeks, her clothes are dirty, the house is a mess. And she used to be such a very particular woman.'

'Can you suggest any way I can help?' asked Millicent.

'Well, I don't know, unless you know anyone who might offer her work. Mairi's biggest worry at the moment is how to keep her job while the children are at home from school over Christmas. Her employer is unlikely to want her back if she takes time off to look after them.'

'Iain mentioned the case of Tam McFarlane,' Stuart said. 'Hydrocephalus as a result of a brain tumour as I recall. A terrible business. The only consolation is that it can't go on for much longer.'

Millicent was quiet for a long time while the other two expounded upon the insensitivity of the Defence Ministry's pensions policy, particularly with regard to prisoners of war. They seemed to be completely indifferent to Tam's situation. Injury whilst a prisoner of war did not carry the same compensations as being wounded in battle.

'If it's not in the book, they'll never pay up,' declared Stuart. 'My father worked in Pensions Assessment in 1919. I can remember him fighting many a lone battle over similar cases. A piece of shrapnel or a bullet is easy to recognise, but I suppose the theory is that Tam could have got his blow on the head from almost any source. Without evidence, he can't prove a Japanese guard was responsible.'

'If we were able to obtain the evidence, might they accept that his wife is entitled to compensation?' Alma asked, thinking of the letter she had been shown only that morning.

'I suppose it would help if there was someone who saw him being attacked. We might be able to trace some of his fellow prisoners.' Stuart did not sound hopeful.

'I believe we might be able to do just that,' Alma exclaimed excitedly. She told them about the letter from Tam's friend. 'Maybe he can supply the evidence we need. He obviously spent a lot of time with Tam and he seems to have a very clear memory of everything that happened, mostly stories of how they got the better of their guards.'

'But it must have been more than just a prank that got Tam hit over the head with a rifle butt,' Millicent protested.

'You know what men are like,' said Alma. 'They never want to recall the unpleasant things. They try to make a joke out of everything. Even so, this chap might remember what happened when Tam was hurt.'

Stuart nodded. 'It's right enough, he might come up with something to support Tam's claim. Alma, if you can get the address out of Mairi, I'll volunteer to write and ask him.'

'Will you? That would be grand.'

'Just as long as you don't make too much of it to Mairi,' he cautioned. 'We don't want to raise her hopes only to have them dashed.'

'No, of course,' Alma replied.

'There's also a clinical problem you should know about.' Although reluctant to dampen her enthusiasm, Stuart felt that he must warn her. 'There is no conclusive evidence that a brain tumour can develop as a direct result of a blow to the head. Despite a number of recorded cases of tumour arising after such an injury, there are still those who insist that there is no connection between the two events. They claim that the development of a tumour is more likely to be the result of some hereditary tendency.'

Alma wondered despondently if it would be worth contacting Tam's old comrade after all.

'Oh yes, I think so,' Stuart insisted. 'The hereditary argument may win the day in the end, but it's still worth a try.'

'It occurs to me that I might be able to help with Mairi's more immediate problems,' Millicent observed. 'As part of my plans for the farm, I shall be keeping a few more cows than before and I'm thinking of going into cheese production on a commercial scale. I shall need an experienced person to help me in the dairy. Didn't someone once tell me that Mairi was trained as a dairymaid?'

Alma thought about the miserable wreck of a woman she had seen that morning. Work in a dairy involved close attention to personal hygiene. Could Mairi shake herself out of her lethargy sufficiently to clean herself up? Alma doubted it, but she kept her misgivings to herself. Tam's wife might welcome the opportunity and it could be just the spur she needed to shake her out of her depression. Anyway, it would be up to Mrs Beaton to decide whether Mairi was fit for the job or not.

'Yes, I believe she worked in a dairy before she was married,' said Alma. 'But it's no good her getting a job if she has no one to look after the children.'

'That's just the point,' said Millicent. 'The children could come along too. There's always plenty for the older ones to do around a farm and Joan is quite capable of keeping an eye on wee Malcolm. We can keep them occupied in the holidays. They might even like to earn a little pocket money for themselves.'

'It sounds too good to be true,' said Alma. 'I'll call in this evening on my way home and tell her to come and see you, shall I?'

'Thank you, dear. Yes, that would be best. Don't say any more than that I may have work for her. Leave it to me to explain.'

'Of course.' Alma couldn't have been more pleased had they been making arrangements for her own future.

28

IAIN BENT HIS head to the icy, northeasterly wind which swept across St Andrew's Square. Leaves lifted and swirled along the pavement until they came to rest in soggy heaps at the feet of lamp posts and around the bolls of trees, suddenly stripped bare of their autumnal glory. His only thought was to get inside out of the wind.

As he turned the corner into Princes Street, the rich aroma of roasting coffee drew him towards the fashionable restaurant they had told him about. Once inside, he found to his dismay that many other people had been of like mind. There was not a table to be had.

He cast a glance over the motley collection of shoppers sheltering from the downpour and was pleasantly surprised to see the figure he was looking for, seated alone on the far side of the shop.

As he contemplated making his way across to join her, a pert little waitress, clad in the ubiquitous black dress and frilly white apron of the British upper-class tearoom, addressed him brightly.

'There'a woman by hersel' over there.' She pointed in the direction in which he was already headed. 'Would you mind sharing?'

'Not at all, as long as the lady has no objections.'

He followed the elfin figure as she wove a pathway between tightly packed tables to the rear of the shop. He had not been mistaken. Facing him across a snowy white cloth already laid for morning coffee, was Alison McKenzie.

'Alison.'

'Iain!'

She was not just surprised. She seemed hesitant, discomfited, distant even.

'You don't mind my joining you? You're not expecting anyone?'

'No. No, of course not.'

'I called in at the hospital and they said I might find you here,' he said, trying to defrost the atmosphere. 'It's been a long time.'

'It certainly has,' she replied. 'Six months, almost to the day.'

'I got your letter.'

'Oh?'

When he failed to reply, she had at first, wondered if she'd got the address wrong. Since the envelope was not returned, she concluded that Iain had no interest in continuing their relationship, such as it was.

'I should have answered. It's been difficult taking over a new job and trying to get the practice back on its feet. My father let things slip a bit in the last few years. Sorry,' he concluded lamely.

'It doesn't matter.'

'I knew you'd understand.'

She understood right enough. She had thought that perhaps there might be something between them. His mother had been so nice that day and it hadn't been his fault that they had hardly spoken when she visited Tigh na Broch. Following their second encounter on the day she had visited Kerrera, she had really thought that he was keen on her. It was only afterwards, when he didn't bother to write, that she concluded she had been mistaken. His nonchalant manner now he had delivered his apologies confirmed her opinion.

No sooner had she guarded herself against the emotions his sudden appearance had aroused, than her attitude began to soften.

He had obviously made some effort to find her. If he had been to the hospital asking for her, it must mean he genuinely wanted to see her again.

'How are things going at St James'?' he asked.

'Oh, much the same,' she answered. Then, trying to match his chatty mood, she added, 'Rumour has it that voluntary hospitals will hardly be affected by the changes. The BMA referendum is never mentioned.'

There was an uncomfortable pause.

Iain, by now made fully aware of her coolness towards him, didn't know what to say. He looked like a scolded dog.

It was Alison who eventually broke the silence. 'Sister is up in arms at the way the nurses have been excluded from the discussions. There is even some talk of industrial action, would you believe. Of course there are one or two inducements on the table. We are to be allowed to live out if we choose, though I'd like to know how anyone can afford to pay rent for a flat on our wages. It's all right for those girls with money behind them and the married ones of course. Oh, and that's the other thing. They have agreed to keep married nurses on, provided they can manage to fit their hours in with the staff rota.' She came to a stop, her flow of words stifled by reference to marriage.

Iain was reminded of what his mother had said concerning their domestic arrangements. He forced himself to view Alison in the light of his mother's ultimatum, studying her covertly as she poured a second cup from her already cold coffee pot.

Could she be the one, he asked himself. Her training made her eminently suited to be a doctor's wife. Unfortunately she was a city girl at heart. How would she fare without the bustle of activity that Edinburgh provided? She was a girl who enjoyed nightlife. She liked dancing and eating out, neither of which featured particularly in the Eisdalsa scene.

Her initial visit to Tigh na Broch had taught him nothing about Alison. His mother had taken to her, but then, Millicent had her own agenda. At the time, he had paid little attention to their visitor's reaction to what she had found at Eisdalsa. He could not recall any particular expression of enthusiasm on her part. She had been ill-equipped for country living – he seemed to remember she had worn rather unsuitable shoes. Still, that didn't mean she wouldn't be able to adapt, given time.

'What's brought you back to the big city?' Alison asked, her tone still brittle.

'I had an appointment with the war pensions people and,' he hesitated for a moment only before taking the plunge, 'I thought it was time I got in touch with you.'

'Why?'

'What do you mean, why?'

'You couldn't be bothered to answer my letter so why trouble to seek me out now?'

Alison hadn't meant to put it like that. Iain looked stunned. Maybe he really had meant to keep in touch and had honestly been too busy. With a warmer feeling beginning to soften the heart she had hardened against him, she added rather more kindly, 'Well, anyway, you've found me now.'

'Do you want to order?'

The cute little waitress was standing with pencil poised, at his elbow. He started.

'Eh? Oh yes, I suppose so.' He glanced across at Alison. 'Have you finished? Can I buy you another coffee and what about something to eat? A sandwich perhaps, or one of those.' He indicated the toasted tea-cakes being delivered to the next table.

'Why not?' said Alison. 'Yes, thank you.' To the girl she said, 'Clear away these things will you? The coffee's gone cold.'

Her expression conveying the unmistakable signal that she considered

Iain a very fast worker indeed, the nippie made a note on her pad and removed Alison's tray.

'How was the rest of your holiday in Oban?' Iain asked.

'Oh, all right, I suppose,' Alison answered, noncommittally. 'I would have liked to have done a lot more walking, visited some of the other islands perhaps. Having Granny with me restricted me a bit. She enjoyed herself though. She hasn't stopped talking about it since. In fact she has next year's visit already planned!'

'I hope you'll come back, before that. On your own this time,' he said. 'I can show you Eisdalsa properly and the rest of the Slate Islands. Uncle Stuart might sail us over to Mull if the weather is good. We could go to Iona where they're doing a lot of restoration work to the old abbey. I'm told it's well worth a visit.'

'I'd like that,' she said, surprised at his sudden burst of enthusiasm. 'The only trouble is, apart from a few days I expect to get just after Christmas, I'm not going to have any proper leave until April. That's when my attachment to men's surgical is due to end.'

'There's nothing to stop you coming over to Argyll for those few days after Christmas,' he insisted. 'Maybe you could stretch it to New Year. If you haven't experienced an Eisdalsa Hogmanay, you haven't lived.'

'That would be nice,' she said, warming to the idea despite her resolution to deny him any further opportunity to let her down. 'I'd have to ask Matron about the extra time. I'm supposed to be back at work on the 29th.'

'You could always go sick for a couple of days,' he suggested, wickedly.

'You'd provide me with the Medical Certificate I suppose?'

'If need be.'

They were still laughing when the girl returned, bearing a heavily laden tray. Busily, she arranged things on the table between them.

Iain was thinking that Alison might indeed be the perfect partner for him: practical, level headed and an experienced nurse. What more could a general practitioner want in a wife? Her caring nature was one of her greatest assets and it had certainly endeared her to his mother.

Added to all this, she was young and healthy, neat in her appearance, well spoken and good to look at. Apart from a faint stirring of interest when he had first set eyes upon her this morning, he could not claim any passionate feeling for her, but maybe that was something which would come later. Unlike Alison, he was no longer in the bloom of youth.

Iain was inexperienced in his relationships with women. His studies had taken precedence while at university, and the war years had inhibited any but the most casual of relationships with the opposite sex. Youthful passions had passed him by. What he looked for now was comfortable companionship.

'Do please try to make it at New Year,' he urged as soon as the waitress had departed. 'Mother would be so delighted to have you. It'll be a big gathering, a chance to meet the whole family. You'll like my Aunt Annie, she's quite a character. She was a suffragette you know. A bit of a battleaxe, but great fun when she gets going.'

Alison felt completely bewildered. What exactly did he require of her? When he had failed to acknowledge her letter, she had given up any hope of seeing him again. At the time she had pretended it didn't matter to her. There had even been one or two brief adventures with other men, junior members of staff for the most part. She had caught herself comparing successive conquests with Iain and finding each of them wanting. He was older than those others but in her eyes that only made him all the more attractive. What if she were to accept his invitation? Would anything come of it? Did she really want it to? Was she simply looking for a comfortable existence, an escape from the arduous working life she had mapped out for herself?

Perhaps that was the answer. Iain could offer her a fine house, albeit in the wilderness, a respectable living and release from the monotony of her present situation. If Iain Beaton was not exactly a Ronald Coleman or a Douglas Fairbanks Jr, he could at least offer her a future very different from her own world of sordid tenements with their tiled stairwells and the shared lavvy on the landing. That world of dark, often dangerous closes in which her mother had been doomed to spend her own short life.

'Well,' Iain asked, impatient for her answer, 'What do you say? Will you come?'

'Yes,' she replied. 'Thank you. I'd like to.'

'Good. That's settled then. Give me a ring to tell me the day and which train you're arriving by, and I'll be there to meet you.'

'If the car starts,' she said, reminding him of the reason for his being delayed on her previous visit.

'Oh, I've got another one now. It's a 1939 Daimler, very posh. I'll not let you down this time!'

'I should hope not,' she replied pointedly. Then glancing at her watch she exclaimed, 'I have to be going, I'm on duty at two o'clock.' She stood up, drawing on her coat as she did so. Iain also leapt to his feet to help her, turning her in his arms in order to adjust the top toggle of her duffle-coat. When he had finished, it seemed the most natural thing in the world that he should kiss her. He did so, brushing her cheek with his cool lips.

'I was going to suggest we took in a film this evening,' he said, disappointed that they could not spend the remainder of the day together.

'I'm free tomorrow evening.'

'Unfortunately, I have to be away first thing in the morning. I'm catching the early train. It looks as though it will have to be New Year before we meet again.'

He watched her receding figure until she had reached the door and mingled with the crowds outside on the pavement. Then, taking the morning newspaper from his pocket, he settled down to a second cup of coffee. He may not have had much luck with the pensions people this morning but it seemed he might be close to solving his other problem. The one about which his mother kept on nagging.

29

MAIRI MCFARLANE HAD been sitting quietly, knitting, for the past half hour. Tam was asleep, his body motionless beneath unrumpled sheets. His arms, too long for his striped pyjama jacket, lay outside the coverlet, the long fingers of his pale hands the only part of him that moved. Hour by hour those restless fingers scratched at the starched cotton. They were the only indication to Mairi that Tam was still alive.

She put down her knitting and gazed steadily at her husband with a mixture of compassion and loathing. This monster, with its grotesquely swollen head and distorted features, this was not the man she had married. How could this wreck of a human being be the happy, handsome boy with whom she had run across the fields to school barefoot, for the sheer joy of feeling the soft damp turf between their toes. This was not the youth with whom she had gathered brambles and then swum in the sea-filled quarry on Eisdalsa Island that hot September day when he had asked her to marry him. This was not the man who had gone away to war, marching to the skirl of the pipes with his kilt swinging and his bonnet fixed jauntily, just a little too far over one ear. He had shouted promises to bring the wee bairns exotic gifts from strange lands across the sea, but all he had managed to bring home with him was a battered prayer book, the sole remaining object belonging to his pal, Joe Johnson, whom he had left buried six feet underground, somewhere in the Malayan jungle.

She had gone to meet the train that had brought the remains of his Company into Queen Street Station. The men were so altered she could not recognise anyone she knew. The rags of their imprisonment had been exchanged for new uniforms, but nothing the Army could provide fitted those living skeletons. In the end, it was he who had spotted her in the crowd, and waved. All that remained of her once handsome lover was his smile and even that had appeared less and less frequently during the weeks that followed. Mairi concentrated on his poor, lopsided, swollen face, willing him to open his eyes and make some sign of recognition. If only he would speak her name.

The sound of a bell broke into her troubled thoughts. Visiting hour was over already. While daydreaming, she had allowed her knitting to slip to the floor. She bent to retrieve it and as her eyes came up level with the counterpane, she found herself staring into her husband's face. Startled by what she saw there, she cried out in alarm, bringing the nurses running to her from either end of the ward.

In the few seconds when she had taken her eyes off him a miraculous change had come over Tam. His swollen head had regained its normal size and shape. His parchment-coloured skin seemed to glow with colour as though blood, retained for so long within his tortured skull, had suddenly suffused the tissues of his extremities. Not only his cheeks, but even his fingers took on a more healthy hue. As she stared, speechless, at his still form, she saw his hand sliding across the sheet towards her own, and watched mesmerised, as those fingers grasped hers with a pressure which carried its own message of love and reconciliation.

She examined his face, uncomprehending. The skin, only partially recovering from constant stretching over the past weeks, sagged beneath his jaw and under his eyes, but he was at least recognisable as the man she had married. Her heart filled up with love for him. She flung her arms around him, lifting his shoulders from the bed and hugging him to her.

A firm touch on her shoulder told her that others had arrived to witness the miracle. Reluctantly, she let him go, easing his head into a more comfortable position on the pillow. As she did so, he opened his eyes for the first time in days and looked into her own with every sign of recognition. His lips moved. She bent closer, straining to hear his words.

'Mairi, my wee sweetheart, it's better this way. Tell the bairns I was asking for them.'

His lids fluttered and then stilled, leaving his wide-open eyes staring sightlessly at the ceiling. After a while a hand reached out to close them. One of the nurses guided Mairi gently from the bedside and the other drew the curtains closed around Tam's lifeless body.

The nurse took her to a little room off the main ward and gave her a cup of tea. White-faced and speechless, she sipped automatically. When she had finished, she handed the cup back.

'I can see him again, can't I?' she pleaded.

'Of course.' The nurse took her hand sympathetically. 'Just give Sister a little while to tidy things up, then we'll take you along to the Chapel of Rest. You can stay with him as long as you want.'

30

WHEN ALMA SUGGESTED to Mairi that Mrs Beaton might be wanting a dairymaid and that the job could be just what she was looking for, Tam's widow seemed reluctant even to consider the idea.

'Och, it's years since I made any cheese,' she protested. 'I've forgotten how.'

'Nonsense,' Alma insisted, 'you never forget something like that. You'd soon get the hang of it again, once you got started.'

'There'll be plenty as'll be after a job like that,' Mairi argued, 'women who don't have to worry about what to do with their bairns when school's out.'

Alma, careful not to let slip that the job was not being offered elsewhere, said no more.

On her next visit to one of the cottages below the castle walls, it seemed to Alma that Mairi was on the lookout for her arrival. She invited the nurse into her house, made her a cup of tea, and after exchanging the usual courtesies, went straight to the point. She had been thinking over what Alma had said about working at Tigh na Broch and wanted more information about Mrs Beaton's plans. Had she already found someone to work in the dairy? Was she still intending to resume the cheese making? For how many hours a week was she going to employ someone?

'Look, Mairie, if you're interested in the job, I'll be happy to let Mrs Beaton know,' Alma told her. 'I shall be calling in at Tigh na Broch in the morning. If she agrees to see you, you can ask her all these questions for yourself.'

She studied Mairi's untidy appearance and wondered what Mrs Beaton's reaction might be to such a grubby-looking prospective dairymaid. Assembling all the tact in her armoury, the nurse observed, 'There must be rather strict hygiene rules for working in a dairy.'

'Oh yes,' Mairi agreed. 'as a matter of fact, most of the work is cleaning. Everything has to be washed and polished after every operation. It's hard work, but interesting just the same.'

She looked down at her dowdy black skirt and examined the hands which rested in her lap. They were grimy and calloused, the fingernails engrained with dirt.

'I'll need to find something decent to wear,' she murmured. 'Mrs Beaton will no' be offering me a job looking like this.'

She got up from her chair and examined herself in the fly-blown mirror above the mantle shelf.

'Just look at this hair,' she said, disgustedly, seeing herself for the slatternly person she had become. 'I'll need to get Lizzie Stevenson to cut it.' She pushed the tangled mop back behind her ears.

Her face suddenly alight with anticipation, she turned towards Alma. 'Somewhere, I've got my old uniform dress I used to wear at Bonavie farm. I wonder if it still fits. That was where I worked before I was married.'

At the recollection of those early days when she had been so happy and carefree, Mairi's eyes filled with tears. The spark Alma's suggestion had kindled died as suddenly as it had flared. She slumped dejectedly in her chair.

'I should never have left that job,' she wailed. 'What did marriage to Tam get me, eh? Just look at me. Thirty-five years old and even ma best friends'd take me for fifty. And this place...' She cast a despairing glance around the cluttered room. 'See what thirteen years of marriage have brought me to.'

'This could be your opportunity to do something about it,' Alma insisted. 'Get your hair done. Scrub yourself up properly and find something decent to wear and Mrs Beaton will be happy to employ you. There's no need for you to go on like this a moment longer than you choose.'

Alma set down her teacup, stood up decisively and went across to the door. She had done all she could. Now it was up to Mairi herself.

'Well, do you have a message for Mrs Beaton or not?' she asked, her hand resting on the latch.

Mairi did not reply at once and Alma began to despair of her friend's continued prevarication. After a moment's hesitation however, she answered. 'Would you ask her, would it be convenient for me to call in on Saturday morning?'

Alma stepped into the street. She was too full to make any reply without disclosing her own overflowing emotions. Mairi called her back.

'You've been a good friend to us, Alma. I promise I won't let you down.'

'Just turn up on Saturday looking a wee bit more like your old self,' Alma advised. 'It'll be all right. You'll see.'

LIZZIE STEVENSON AT number twenty-three had cut and styled Mairi's naturally wavy hair into a neat bob. Her old dairymaid's dress had been discovered, neatly folded and reeking of camphor, at the bottom of the clothes press. Mairi had washed and starched it with the greatest care so as to be ready for her interview with Mrs Beaton.

Millicent was happily surprised at the extent of Mairi's experience in the dairy and had no hesitation in offering her employment. She found her neat and tidy in appearance and keen to get on with her work. After just a few weeks she was able to turn over the whole of the cheese-making operation to her new dairymaid, leaving herself more time to concentrate on other matters to do with the farm.

'See here, Mrs Beaton, six brown eggs today. Don't they look just lovely?'

Joan McFarlane laid the basket of eggs on the kitchen table and without waiting to be told, dampened a cloth under the kitchen tap and began to wipe them clean.

Mairi's daughter had blossomed in the short time since her mother had come to work at the farm. Still a pale little girl whose spare frame Millicent put down to poor food and a lingering summer cold, Joan had developed into a serious but happy child. She would be a beauty too, once she began to put on a little more weight.

With a good deal of noise, Joan's younger brothers came bursting into the outside lobby. Their sister thrust open the connecting door and shouted with the voice of a banshee, 'Wull yoos haud yer wheesht the noo, afore I come ben an skelp ye!'

The shouting brought on a spate of coughing, so prolonged that Millicent looked up from her pastry making to see the girl fishing in her pockets for a handkerchief. The boys, sufficiently in awe of their big sister, were silent as they crept timidly into the kitchen

'If you're going to come inside,' observed Joan, recovering both her voice and her poise in Mrs Beaton's presence, 'You're to go up to the schoolroom and play quietly.' Something she had learned quickly during her visits to Tigh na Broch, was that the accents of the school yard were not acceptable in the doctor's house.

'There's nothin' to do,' whined Thomas.

'There is so,' insisted his exasperated sister. 'Did I not start that jigsaw for you only yesterday? The outside's done, you only have to fill in the rest.'

'The outside's the easiest bit,' complained her brother.

'I want to do 'nopoly,' declared Malcolm, who loved the wee silver ornaments which were moved around the board at the throw of a dice. *Monopoly* was his favourite game. He loved to count up the play money, buying and selling properties for hundreds of pounds. Dr Beaton said he was sure to be an accountant or an estate agent one day.

From the day Mairi McFarlane started work at the farm, the children had accompanied her. On school days she walked them the two and a half miles from the castle, leaving them to complete the last half mile of their journey to school, on their own. In the afternoons they waited at the farm for their mother. Joan made herself useful while the boys played amongst the cattle sheds and sheep pens up in the glen or, on wet days, occupied the schoolroom under the eaves, where generations of Beatons had spent their childhood.

With the start of the school holidays, the family had been obliged to spend the entire working day at Tigh na Broch. In the kitchen, Joan learned to prepare and cook vegetables, bake delicacies for the doctor's tea and to make pastry for those delicious pies which were Millicent's speciality. The boys helped McKinnon with the stock. The cattle were kept under cover at this time of the year and there was always feed to prepare, mucking out to be done and any manner of messages to be fetched from the village. For their help in the house and about the farm, Millicent paid the children a few pennies every day. The boys spent theirs at once but Joan had been saving up for the day when her mother would take them on the bus to town to do the Christmas shopping. It was going to be a very special Christmas this year, now that Mairi was regularly employed. There would be money for party food and, with her savings, Joan was determined to buy presents for everybody.

Millicent was surprised at how quickly the children had adapted to the loss of their father. The relationship between McFarlane and his family had, sadly, been pretty tenuous. Of the three children, only Joan remembered him from before the war and even her recollections were hazy. Tam had returned from the Far East a stranger even to his wife, and his behaviour during the twelve months which followed had done nothing to improve matters.

Tam McFarlane's removal to hospital had been a blessed relief for his children. Having insinuated himself into their peaceful young lives, bringing with him suspicion, fear and hatred, how could he have expected them to love him? Why should they have felt any sadness at his passing?

'Would you like to take some messages over to Eisdalsa Island for me this afternoon, Joan?' Millicent asked, as she watched the girl wiping the eggs before replacing them carefully in the basket. 'The boys might like to come too.'

Joan would have preferred to make the trip alone but she could understand how Mrs Beaton might welcome a short release from the children's continuous and usually noisy activity.

'Of course, Mrs Beaton,' she replied happily, before succumbing once again to the irresistible urge to cough.

'Maybe you shouldn't go, with that cold.'

'Oh I'm all right, really I am,' Joan insisted. 'I've had this cough for ages. It's a nuisance, that's all.'

Millicent looked at her doubtfully. A cough like that really shouldn't hang around for so long. Perhaps she ought to mention it to Iain. He would probably give her a linctus to relieve it.

'If your mother agrees, I'd like you to take a few things from the dairy to Mrs Annie Beaton and Dr Stuart. Here's the ferry fare.'

She counted the necessary coppers into Joan's hand and watched her knot them carefully into a corner of her handkerchief.

Excited at the prospect of the expedition, Joan hopped from one foot to the other. 'If it's not too crowded, Donnie might let Tommy and me take an oar.'

'I thought ten years was the age limit for rowing the ferry.' Millicent remembered how her own boys had quarrelled over the privilege.

'Tommy's done it before. He's very big and strong for his age,' Joan explained. 'I don't suppose Donnie realises he's only eight.'

Millicent laughed. How she enjoyed having children in the house again. It made her feel years younger. She yearned for grandchildren of her own but it seemed there would never be any. It really was most unfair. Her daughter Morag was the only one of her children who was married and she had deliberately avoided pregnancy, satisfied with her role of surrogate grandmother to her stepdaughter's children. Despite Millicent's ultimatum, Iain had made no progress at all in the matrimonial stakes and David had made it quite clear that matrimony held no part in his plans for the immediate future. The chances of her ever enjoying the companionship of her own grandchildren were so slim it seemed as though she would just have to make the most of Mairi's bairns while she had the chance.

As soon as Joan had gone off to seek her mother's permission to go to the island, Millicent fetched an old leatherette shopping bag from the cupboard, wiped it clean inside with a damp cloth and began packing it with a hard round cheese, a one pound pat of butter and half a dozen of the brown eggs Joan had collected. As an afterthought she added a pot of bramble jelly which she had preserved the previous September.

'There,' she said, as Joan came back into the kitchen. 'Do you think you can manage all that without dropping it and smashing the eggs?'

Food was still rationed and although regulations regarding farm produce had been relaxed, they could ill afford to lose those eggs, more than a month's ration for one person.

All the way into the village, Joan kept a firm eye on the boys, lashing them with her tongue whenever they threatened to endanger themselves by climbing the boulders that skirted the foot of the cliff. Soon the old manse and the village school came into view. Struggling with the tickle in her throat, Joan covered her mouth with her hand as she felt another bout of coughing coming on. She paused for a moment to recover her breath and called her brothers to her before approaching the two gloomy buildings.

Neither showed any sign of life other than a single light glowing in the parlour of the schoolmaster's house. The children crept by in silence, afraid they might alert 'Baldie' Alexander to their presence. The schoolroom was dark and silent this afternoon, its windows still dotted with cotton wool snow from the end-of-term party.

Outside the village hall, the children paused to study the notice board which was covered with posters about the various events scheduled for the Christmas holidays; a fair and jumble sale for the coming Saturday; a ceilidh on New Year's Eve and, on Ne'er Day, a pantomime! There was an air of suppressed excitement abroad. Tinsel decorations hung in the windows of the little whitewashed cottages. The frosty air was permeated with delicious smells of baking and from open doorways, the sound of carols from the radio added to the festive atmosphere.

The boys skipped along Back Street, shouting and waving to those of their friends who had ventured out on this chill afternoon. They would have stopped to exchange their boyish jokes and to discuss the treats and the presents that Christmas might bring, but Joan hustled them along, anxious to catch the ferry.

'I'm to get a bike, a new one!' Billy McKenzie declared as he stretched his arms out to make a Spitfire and rattled along the street, all eight machine guns firing.

'So'm I, so'm I!' shouted wee Malcolm, following suit.

'You are not so!' declared Thomas. 'Mum canna afford it.'

'What's Mum got to do wi it?' demanded Thomas, coming to a sudden halt and making Joan step out of his path. 'It's Santa brings the presents.'

Joan glanced warningly at Tommy. There was no reason to spoil the illusion for the wee one too soon. She herself had gone on believing in Santa Claus until the second winter of the war, when her mother had taken her into her confidence, explaining that with Daddy away in the Army, there was no money for new toys any more.

'Santa only brings presents to good wee boys,' she told Malcolm firmly. The chances of that epithet being attached to her little brother were so slim that she could consider the matter closed.

'But I want a bike!' he wailed, his eyes filling with tears.

'Och, you'll get something. Dinna fash,' Thomas insisted more kindly. 'Only, I don't suppose it'll be a bike.'

They ran along the rim of the old slate quarry. Long ago it had been engulfed by the sea and now offered a safe haven for the sailing boats belonging to those rich summer visitors whose holiday homes lay empty all through the winter. A rough path led the children past the noisome public lavvies to the old steamer pier, where once, so their mother had told them, you could get a boat to take you all the way to Inverness, or down the coast to Crinan. The children had never seen one of these famous paddle steamers, but there was a photograph of one in Mrs Beaton's kitchen. The caption read, *The Chevalier at Eisdalsa Pier.* Mrs Beaton had once told Joan how she had first travelled to Eisdalsa by steamer, all the way from Glasgow.

The tide was out and the children were obliged to descend the wooden stairs to the lower landing stage where, as luck would have it, Donnie's heavy clinker-built ferry boat lay tied up and unattended.

For a while the boys played around on the pier, clambering on the wooden struts, which were slippery from the still wet seaweed clinging to the timber. Joan, anxious for the safety of her bag of groceries, guarded it carefully from the boy's restless feet. She wished Donnie would hurry. It would be dark by half past four. They would have little more than an hour to get across to the island, deliver the messages and return in daylight.

At long last they heard unsteady footsteps approaching. There was a scrape of heavily studded boots on the path above. The footsteps were accompanied by tuneless whistling and an occasional burst of song. Donnie McDonald, having spent an extended dinner hour at the inn, was full of festive cheer. He swayed as he climbed down the steps and had Thomas not grabbed the ferryman's arm as he took the final flight to the lower landing, he would surely have stumbled straight into the sea.

'Haud this,' cried the ferryman, hauling in the rope and tossing it to Tommy as he stepped clumsily across the gunwale. 'An where's Mairi McFarlane's bairns goin' to on Eisdalsa Island the day?'

'I have messages for Mrs Annie Beaton,' Joan told him, 'and we'll be needing to get back across before dark,' she added. After he returned from the war, Joan's father had taken to disappearing to the village inn most evenings after supper. Her brothers were usually fast asleep before he came back, but Joan had often waited up with her mother for Tam's return. She recognised a drunken man when she saw one.

'Perhaps we had better do the rowing, Donnie,' she suggested pointedly, and Donnie, responding automatically to the commanding tone of a disapproving female, slumped submissively into the stern of the boat, leaving the children to their own devices.

Joan took command. Ordering Malcolm to the bows, she told him to sit still and hold the bag of groceries tight. Then, clambering into position athwart, she took up one of the two heavy oars. Thomas cast off the line and seating himself beside her, took hold of the other.

Working together, they hauled the heavy rowing boat out into the choppy waters of the Eisdalsa Channel. Even at low tide it was deep enough here for those great passenger steamers which had once tied up alongside the pier. The current was strong and the waves slapped menacingly against the planking of the sturdy little craft.

'Speed bonnie boat,' roared Donnie from his perch in the stern, galvanised into full-throated song by the motion of the craft.

'Hauld yer wheest,' gasped Joan. She felt the full force of the tide now. Fearing that they might be carried down the channel and out into the bay she applied herself to her oar using every ounce of strength. The prow of the vessel moved around a couple of points so that it was headed towards the northern end of the channel, directly into the path of the oncoming waves.

Thomas was a strong lad. Keen to show off his male superiority to his sister, he bent his back to the task of propelling the boat through the choppy sea. He was, however, only eight years old and his fledgling muscles soon tired.

'Pull Thomas, pull,' Joan gasped as she felt the bows being forced away from the safety of the harbour entrance for which they were headed.

Donnie, slumped in the stern, was silent now. If he sensed anything of the danger, he was too inebriated to do anything about it. The moment his eyes closed he began to snore loudly.

Terrified and angry at the same time, Joan screamed at him,

'Donnie McDonald, will y'wake up the now! Wee Thomas here canna haud the boat. We are all goin' ti droon!'

Whether it was the tone of her voice or the seaman's instinct for self-preservation, Donnie, abruptly aroused from his slumbers, was suddenly stone-cold sober. He opened his eyes in time to see the harbour mouth slip from view and be replaced by Sgeir Mor-thir, the rocky islet which marked the southern exit from the channel.

'Pull on your oar Joan,' he yelled. 'Thomas, hold yours till I get ti ye.'

He struggled to rise, stumbled to his feet and almost measured his length in the boat in his effort to reach the middle thwart. Changing places with the boy was not easy. The vessel rocked alarmingly and Malcolm, clinging to the prow with both hands and with the shopping bag clenched between his knees, began to cry.

Donnie grabbed the oar. Thomas edged cautiously towards the stern. At first Donnie's added power seemed to make very little difference. The boat gathered speed as she drew closer to the rocks and Joan, casting a glance over her shoulder, saw for the first time the danger they were in. In her panic, she thrust the blade of her oar deep in the water. As it emerged, the sudden loss of resistance caused her to lose her balance and fall backwards. With Donnie's additional pull from his side, the boat slewed around, caught on the rocks and tipped sideways, casting both Joan and her rowing partner into the sea. Thomas, unbalanced while resettling himself in the stern, was also tipped overboard. Dislodged from their rowlocks by the force of the impact, both oars drifted away. At a leisurely pace, the boat turned in its own length, scraped harmlessly against the rock once again and drifted on into the bay, carrying with it a white-faced, petrified Malcolm, still clasping Joan's precious shopping bag between his knees as though his safety depended upon its presence there.

The last vestige of Donnie's alcoholic euphoria was dispelled by the intense cold. He came to the surface gasping and struck out for the shore. Joan, unable at first to get her bearings, paddled to keep afloat and looked around her in hopes of finding her brothers. Thomas bobbed to the surface some yards away and, unable to swim, began to thrash the water in desperation. Joan swam towards him, ignoring the danger that she might be knocked unconscious by his flaying arms.

'Be still,' she yelled at him, 'Just let yourself float. I'll tow you.' Unusually for him, Thomas obeyed his sister's command without question, his wild cries reduced to a pathetic whimper.

Joan struck out for the nearest shore, kicking fiercely with her legs while she grasped her brother by his shoulders. All too soon the cold began to get to her and she felt her strength ebbing away. With one last superhuman effort, she thrust herself backwards and was immediately rewarded with the feel of rocks, slippery beneath her feet. Although she was unable to stand upright on the weed-slimed stones, she managed to pull her brother clear of the water, falling flat on her back as she did so. Sobbing with the pain in her chest and throat, she lay still, only an occasional dry, choking cough indicating that she was alive.

32

Cape Town, November 23rd 1947.

Dear Mum and Dad,

The voyage so far has been uneventful for the most part. We have encountered very little heavy weather, which proved fortunate since we had been at sea no more than a few days when Ellen announced that she was pregnant. I must admit that at first I was more than a little cross with her. She thought I might have delayed our sailing had I known and she was right! Fortunately, apart from a little morning sickness she has been fine so far and there is small prospect of bad weather on the next stage of our voyage. The baby is not due until late in February so we should be home in good time for the happy event.

Meanwhile, we are absorbing the sun and the sea air and getting plenty of rest. There's a mixed crowd on board, mainly Australians who were caught in the UK when war broke out or who volunteered for service in the British Forces. There's plenty of activity if one wants to become involved but for the most part we eat, sleep and read. The food improved after we called in to the Canaries for supplies and here in Cape Town we appear to be taking on quantities of fresh fruit and vegetables, so all augers well for the remainder of the trip.

We have just returned from a brief tour of the town. It's strange to see a place so completely unaffected by the war. Ellen was able to buy cotton dresses to accommodate her growing waistline and quantities of wool for baby clothes. I never even knew she could knit. Mind you, we have yet to see some results! It was so marvellous to be able to shop without clothing coupons! The post is to be collected at noon and we sail on the evening tide. I will write again when we dock at Freemantle.

Ellen sends her love with mine, Stephen.

Stuart Beaton finished reading his son's letter for the third time and took up his own pen to complete his reply.

I ran into Prof Dowson at last week's meeting. He tells me that the Hospital Appointments Board is unlikely to sit again before late February but he promised to telephone if anything should come up before then. It seems that they are definitely going to make a bid for a new School of Anaplastics, so keep your fingers crossed.

Your mother and I are delighted to hear your news about the baby. No doubt she will have plenty to say to you in her own note. You will have to watch that Ellen does not get over tired in all that heat. You've hardly chosen the best time to be there. I understand temperatures can soar to over a hundred degrees in summer. Take good care of Ellen and our grandchild!

My love to you both, Dad.

'Doctor Beaton! Doctor Beaton!'

He heard the shouts even before the hammering on the outer door had begun. Annie arrived before him and pulled it open.

Breathless and perspiring heavily despite the chilly afternoon, Cameron Finlay paused to catch his breath.

'What is it, man?' Stuart demanded.

'An accident, down by the shore, oh the poor wee mites!'

'A drowning?'

'As good as.'

'Who?'

'Its was the ferry boat overturned.'

'Donnie?'

'Och, he's no sae bad. It's Mairi McFarlane's wains is lying there drooned.'

Annie had disappeared and returned with Stuart's medical bag before her husband had time to put on his coat. She insisted he wait while she buttoned him up tight. There was no sense in getting chilled. He'd be no use to anyone if he got sick himself.

'You go on,' she said, thrusting him out the door. 'I'll gather up some blankets and follow you.'

After a while they removed Thomas's weight from Joan's body and she was aware of firm hands dragging her gently above the tide line. Before she could find words to thank her rescuers, she fainted away.

She came to, to find that someone was lifting her arms above her head and pumping air into her lungs. After two or three painful intakes, she felt an overwhelming desire to vomit. They turned her over just in time as she brought up the quantities of the seawater she had swallowed. She fainted again.

When she regained consciousness, Joan found she had been wrapped in a warm blanket and someone was crouching beside her, trying to force hot liquid between her lips. A few yards away the stooped figure of Dr Stuart Beaton stood beside what looked like a heap of rags stretched out on the beach. Her brother! She gave a cry of alarm as Annie bent over her, holding the cup to her lips.

'Its all right dear, Thomas is all right. Dr Beaton is just making sure he is breathing properly before they carry him indoors.'

'Where's wee Malcolm?' The girl struggled into a sitting position, glancing around her in hope of seeing the familiar little figure in his yellow sou'wester and shiny wellington boots. 'He's got your messages.'

Annie, trying hard to show no sign of alarm, thrust the steaming cup into Joan's hands.

'You stay still. I'll be back in a minute,' she said. She got to her feet and hurried away to where a group of islanders were clustered around the sodden figure of the distraught ferryman.

'Its a' my fault,' he moaned, clasping a blanket draped around his shoulders and glancing anxiously every few minutes in the direction of the doctor and the boy. 'I swear to God I'll never touch another dram, no, not ever again.'

His comrades made little attempt to console him. He was indeed to blame.

'D'ye reckon they'll prosecute?' asked someone in the crowd.

Donnie stared at the bystander in dismay. 'What'd I get?' he demanded, his hands trembling so that he lost his grip on the blanket and had to retrieve it from the ground.

'If they'd drowned it would be manslaughter at the very least,' muttered the island's barrack-room lawyer, but no so loudly that Donnie could hear.

'The wee one was with them,' Annie gasped as she joined the group. 'Malcolm McFarlane was in the boat too!'

Those gathered around the ferryman turned on him accusingly.

'You didna say there was anither bairn,' said Wullie Smith. 'How is it you never said?'

Donnie's face dropped. 'I forgot.'

In truth, everything that happened prior to his swapping places with Thomas and taking an oar, was still very hazy.

Immediately the men set off running in either direction along the shore in search of the third child. It was young Douglas Moore who, scrambling out along the skerry of rocks at the southernmost tip of the island, spotted the ferry boat drifting across the bay towards the next group of islands. The bright yellow hat of the little child seated in the bows was clearly visible.

Douglas's feet flew across the uneven ground as he ran back to the main square, shouting for the postmistress as he went. By now all the islanders were gathered at the shore and it took a while to find Christie McWorter and to get her back to her tiny cottage post office. Once in place before the switchboard, it was a matter of moments before she had connected with Mr Dalgliesh at Lunga ferry.

Stuart Beaton had the men carry both Thomas and Joan across the village green to his own house while Donnie, anxious to make what reparation he could, declared he was fit to row his own boat across to Tigh na Broch to fetch the children's mother. On the island, everyone waited anxiously for news of the drifting ferry.

Stuart examined his patient intently. Joan's pulse was racing still. She had swallowed a great deal of seawater and her throat was raw from coughing. Nevertheless, her lungs seemed rather more congested than he might have expected considering how much seawater had already been expelled while they were still down by the shore.

'We'll need to keep her here for a while, Annie,' he told his wife. 'I don't like the sound of her lungs at all. We may be in for trouble.'

Annie, unperturbed at having additional company in the house, simply nodded her head in agreement.

'What about the boy?' she asked.

'He seems to be fine,' Stuart decided, feeling Tommy's brow for any sign of fever. 'Of course, once his sister got him onto his back, he was able to keep his mouth closed. Apart from the shock, he's come out of it pretty well.'

'What a mercy Joan can swim so well,' Annie observed. 'I know she spends a lot of time over here in the summer, swimming in the quarry by the back shore.'

'It's a good thing she does. All of the village children should be able to swim. I think I'll talk to the schoolmaster about giving them lessons.'

'Not you,' she declared. 'I'm not having you diving into that cold water at your time of life.'

'Oh, you stupid woman, of course not,' he replied, but in truth he had meant just that. He sometimes forgot that it was time to hand such responsibilities over to the younger men.

By the time his mother arrived, white-faced and trembling, Thomas was up and about, albeit uncharacteristically quiet. He sat beside a roaring fire in Annie Beaton's kitchen reading some old children's annuals which had once belonged to Stephen. Joan lay on the box bed in the corner of the room, tossing in her sleep and mumbling incoherently.

Sobbing with relief at the sight of her two elder children, Mairi ran to Joan's side, gazed down at her with a perplexed expression and turned to Stuart, anxiously.

'She looks so like Tam lying there,' she said, suspiciously. 'It's just how he was, when he first got sick.'

Stuart pushed her gently aside and felt for himself the now burning brow. Once again he took up his stethoscope to examine Joan's chest. That rattle he had attributed at first to the water she had swallowed, was now more pronounced.

He got Mairi to hold the girl while he applied the stethoscope to her back. Thoroughly concerned now, he tapped at the base of the ribs and was rewarded with the ominously dull sound of lungs clogged with phlegm. It seemed extraordinary that congestion should have set in this rapidly.

'Before the accident, did Joan have a cold?' he asked Mairi.

'A wee cough perhaps, but she's had that for a while now. Drives me mad sometimes, it does. When I canna get to sleep myself.'

Stuart felt he was beginning to understand. When the child coughed up more phlegm he caught a little in a dish and went off into the smaller of the two bedrooms he used as his study.

While he was away, Annie fetched a bowl of lukewarm water and a cloth. She wrung it out and gently wiped Joan's face. It might not contribute much to her recovery but it would give Mairi something to do.

'You bathe her,' Annie suggested. 'It will help to cool her down. I'll make us all a wee cup of tea.'

It was some moments before Mairi, concentrating on the task in hand, paused and looked about her as though she had suddenly missed something.

Annie, placing a steaming cup on the small table at her side, asked Mairi what was the trouble.

'Where's wee Malcolm?' she asked, realising that she had not seen him since she arrived.

Annie gasped. Whoever had gone to fetch Mairi must have neglected to tell her that her youngest child had last been seen alone in the ferryboat, heading for the Sound of Lunga.

'They've gone to fetch him,' she answered lamely, hoping against hope that the child would be returned, unharmed, before Mairi became aware of the danger he was in. Thankfully, she accepted Annie's explanation unquestioningly and returned to bathing her daughter.

When Annie carried Stuart's tea in to him, she found him engrossed in something he was peering at under the microscope.

'I wondered what you were up to,' she said testily, resenting the fact that he had left her to cope alone with a distraught mother who was becoming increasingly alarmed at her daughter's condition. 'Mairi is asking about Malcolm.'

Stuart looked up with a worried frown. Whatever absorbed him was certainly not good news.

'Oh Annie,' he murmured, 'that poor woman. I am at a loss to know what to say to her.'

'Why?' she asked, disturbed by his worried frown.

'Look here. You've seen this before.'

Annie peered at the object under the microscope. Myriad bacteria, multiplying even as she watched, occupied the entire field of vision.

She looked up at her husband, inquiringly. 'Bacilli?'

'I can't be sure mind, not without all the tests, but I think it could be TB.'

There was no need for him to elaborate further. All too often before the war, the two of them had been in close contact with the terrible disease. Tuberculosis had swept through the working-class areas of Glasgow like a tide, following in the wake of long-term unemployment and its accompanying poverty. It was uncommon in Argyll, where the one thing not lacking was fresh air. Recalling the condition of those miserable little hovels beneath the castle walls, however, Annie was not really surprised.

'Tuberculosis is on the increase everywhere,' Stuart reminded her. 'It's no longer associated only with overcrowding and lack of good food. A great many servicemen brought it home with them and such a highly contagious disease was bound to run rife amongst their families. All those aid agencies in Europe whose personnel have been in contact with victims of the war, are reporting increasing numbers of cases in their staff and it's also prevalent amongst returning prisoners of war.'

'But Tam McFarlane didn't have TB, did he?' she wondered.

'Who can say? It doesn't always manifest itself in obvious ways and in any case, McFarlane had enough other problems to mask the symptoms. Iain might well have missed it.'

'So, Tam could have passed it on to Joan?'

'In crowded conditions in damp old buildings with insufficient heating, it's possible.'

'Well, you'd better keep it to yourself for the moment,' she warned. 'That poor woman has enough to contend with for one day. There's still no word of little Malcolm and Mairi doesn't even know he's not on the island.'

'She must be told,' he insisted.

'I realise that,' his wife agreed, 'but another hour or so will make no difference either way.'

'God, what a mess!' Stuart looked so tired all of a sudden, Annie worried about him. Where on earth had Iain got to? Surely someone must have told him about the accident by now? It really was too bad of him to leave Stuart to deal with everything!

When he returned to the kitchen Stuart found his patient awake and coughing. Thomas, crouched over the fire, was absorbed in his book. He hardly looked up as the doctor moved over towards the bed and again began an intensive examination of Joan. Mairi got up and stretched, cramped after her long vigil.

'I'll take a wee breath of air,' she said. 'Maybe I should go along to the post office and make a call. Mrs Beaton will be wondering what is happening. She was so kind, when the men came to fetch me. She'll be anxious.'

Annie reprimanded herself for her thoughtlessness. She should have thought to telephone Millicent herself, but then there had been so much happening. She was so busy with her own recriminations that she hardly registered what Mairi was saying.

'If you'll tell me which house is Malcolm staying at, I'll fetch him. We'll need to get home.'

'I doubt if the ferry is running,' said Annie, reminding Mairi as gently as she could, that the ferry boat had been cast adrift.

'Och, I'll find someone to row us across,' she declared and went to the door.

Standing in the open doorway, she lifted her hand to her eyes and peered across the green towards the harbour. It would soon be dark. The western sky was bathed in a warm red glow which deepened by the minute. Even as Mairi watched, the fiery sun sank below the mountains of Mull leaving behind a dull rusty glow, a fading ghost of the evening's splendour.

'The boat must be back,' Mairi said. 'There's a great crowd of people by the pier and, well I never, is that not the lifeboat from Oban Bay?'

Annie knew now she could keep the truth from Mairi no longer. Apprehensively, she followed the woman to the door and took hold of her arm.

'Mairi, there's something we haven't told you.'

'Ah, there he is at last!' Mairi shook off Annie's comforting hand and pointed.

'Over here you young scamp,' she called. 'Where've you been?'

Across the green, vigorously swinging Millicent's old shopping bag, regardless of its precious contents, skipped Malcolm McFarlane, his yellow oilskin sou'wester pushed back and hanging around his neck on its elastic. His once shiny wellingtons were covered in mud and his face glowed with excitement.

'Hallo, Ma! What you doin' here? Where's Joan and Tommy? They'll be so sick they fell out o'the boat. I had a ride in the lifeboat all the way from Lunga ferry!'

'Lunga ferry? Whatever were you doing there?' demanded Mairi, bewildered, but happy to have all her bairns together once more.

33

IAIN BEATON PUT down the phone and turned to his mother.

'They've confirmed TB,' he told her. 'Joan has been transferred to the Chest Hospital.'

'Oh the poor wee thing,' Millicent lamented. 'I blame myself for not saying anything before. She has had that cough ever since the children have been coming here. I thought it was just a hangover from a cold.'

'It was up to her mother to mention it,' Iain insisted. 'These people are always so reluctant to call in a doctor, just as though I would send a bill to someone in Mairi's circumstances.' He paused, knowing that Mairi was not the only one at fault. 'I should have noticed that cough myself,' he admitted.

'You hardly have time to do more than say *good morning* most days,' Millicent excused him. 'No, it was up to Mairi and myself to spot it.'

'The fact remains that it took a pensioned-off GP to point out the problem. I feel an absolute idiot!'

'The child is in good hands now,' Millicent tried to console him. 'She'll be properly cared for in the Chest Hospital. I suppose it's going to be a long time before she will be well again?'

'Undoubtedly.'

'I thought there was some method of preventing the disease these days.'

'BCG vaccination, you mean?'

'Yes, that's it.'

'It's unlikely that Mairi would have had her children vaccinated –she couldn't afford it. In any case, protection is usually reserved for the immediate contacts of a known carrier, to prevent the disease spreading once it arrives in a household.'

'So the boys and Mairi will get it?'

'Yes, I'll make sure they do.' Unfortunately he had some even more devastating news for Millicent.

'You do understand, don't you, Mairi will have to stay away from the dairy until we can be sure she's clear herself?'

'Oh no, how long will that take?'

'A few weeks at the very least. You'll have to find someone else to help out.'

'Or do the work myself. It would be so much easier if you were to get yourself a receptionist. I simply can't go on doing both jobs.'

Her words brought to mind his earlier encounter with Alison.

'Oh Lord, I forgot,' he said suddenly.

'What? What is it?' Millicent felt she simply could not take any more disasters.

'I have to make a phone call. I'll be back.'

He rushed away to his consulting room and slammed the door. It took some minutes for the switchboard to locate her.

'Alison McKenzie.'

'Alison. It's Iain Beaton. How's things?'

'Iain? What's wrong? You know we're not supposed to take personal calls on the ward.'

'I know. I pulled rank – told them it was a medical matter of some urgency.'

'Oh, I see.'

'Well, you don't really, but you'll understand when I've had a chance to explain.'

'I was expecting you to call sooner than this.' Her tone suggested a reprimand. Well, that's what he deserved.

'It's about New Year. Are you coming or not?'

'I've asked Matron and she says I may take the three days I have coming and add them to the two-day public holiday. That gives me enough time to make the journey worthwhile.'

'Oh good, I'm so glad. What day will you be here?'

'New Year is on the Thursday so let's say Tuesday the twenty-ninth.'

'Great! I'll meet the train at three o'clock.'

'Make sure you do!'

'Trust me.'

If only she could. Catching sight of Sister George in the doorway at the far end of the ward, she slammed down the receiver and went back to her notes.

Putting down the phone Iain started to whistle a little tune as he sauntered back into the kitchen.

'I might possibly have solved your problem,' he told his mother.

'The problem is yours, not mine,' Millicent reminded him. 'What's happened?'

He laid his finger along the side of his nose in that irritating way he had when he had some secret to divulge.

'Wait and see,' was all he would say.

She wondered if the call had been to Alison. She did hope so. She was a nice girl. She felt she could live with such a daughter-in-law.

Alison watched with relief as Sister, having spoken to the patient at the far end, went back into the corridor. She put down her pen and gazed out of the window. Was she about to make a fool of herself again, she wondered? The last time she saw Iain he had been undemonstrative to say the least. He hadn't told her how much he'd missed her nor had he complimented her in any way. In fact, until he picked up the phone a few moments ago, she suspected he had not given her another thought since their meeting in the teashop. She had nothing to lose by returning to Eisdalsa however, and the Beaton's New Year's party promised to be more fun than spending the holiday with her grandmother. What harm could it do to give him this one last chance?

34

MILLICENT WAS BUSY reciting a list of guests as she counted freshly baked mince pies into a tin before storing them in the larder.

'That leaves just the family, the Browns, nineteen, twenty, Morag and Duncan twenty-one, twenty-two, and Annie and Stuart, twenty-three, twenty-four and two or three more in case David manages to get away. There, that should be enough.'

'You'd better put in a couple for Alison,' Iain told her casually. He couldn't keep it from her any longer. His mother needed to know she was coming so she could make the necessary sleeping arrangements.

Millicent stopped what she was doing to stare at him.

'Alison is coming for New Year? You might have told me.'

'I wasn't sure until I called her, sorry if it's short notice.'

Fearing that Alison might change her mind about coming, he had deliberately avoiding telling his mother until the last possible minute.

'No matter, she's most welcome.' She added two more pies before firming down the lid of the tin and sealing it with sticking plaster. 'That leaves just these three for our morning coffee. Is Alma calling in this morning?'

'I expect so,' he answered, frowning as he watched his mother secure the box with a second layer of sticking plaster. 'No wonder I never have any tape when I need it,' he grumbled. 'And by the way, what happened to all the cotton wool? I was sure there was plenty when I dressed old Mrs McColl's ulcer.'

'I used a bit for the Christmas crib,' Millicent confessed.

'We're not in the Health Service yet, Ma. Cotton wool will probably be on prescription then, but at the moment we still have to pay for it ourselves. Oh, by the way I've arranged to pick Alison up at three o'clock on Tuesday.'

'Make sure you're not late this time. You can't use the car as an excuse any more.'

'Yes Mother!' He did wish she would treat him like an adult just once in a while.

'If I was that girl, I'd be wondering what more I had to do, to get you to show you cared.'

'It doesn't do to get too enthusiastic until you're absolutely sure of your ground,' he told her. 'I let that happen once and got my fingers burned.'

'I didn't know you had ever had a girl who was that important to you.'

Millicent was intrigued and rather pleased as well. She had often wondered why he seemed so determined to remain a bachelor, but a blighted love affair would naturally make him more cautious where women were concerned.

'I spent the best part of ten years away from home, Mother. You weren't to know everything that was going on in my life.'

'I know, but you never even mentioned any women friends in your letters.'

'I took this one to dinner in all the best restaurants, lavished good wine and expensive flowers on her and even bought the engagement ring,' he confessed. 'It was my own fault. I ought to have asked her first.'

'Did she have a good reason for turning you down?'

Millicent felt a surge of indignation. How could any woman have refused to marry her son?

'The best. She was already married. Her husband had been taken prisoner at Dunkirk. He was one of the doctors who volunteered to stay behind to tend the wounded.'

Even after all this time Iain found it difficult to reconcile his disappointment at her refusal with his dismay at finding he had allowed himself to be led into deceiving a gallant colleague. 'Which room will Alison have?' he asked, quickly changing the subject.

'I thought the nursery.'

'Right up there on the second floor?'

'Where else?'

'I think you should give Alison my room and I'll go up to the attic. She might prefer to be closer to the bathroom.'

'But what about the phone?'

They had had an extension put in Iain's bedroom to save Millicent being disturbed by night calls.

'Leave it. If everything goes to plan, she'll be having to put up with calls in the middle of the night for years to come.'

'You don't mean you're actually going to marry her?'

'If she'll have me, yes. I haven't asked her yet.'

'Darling, I'm so pleased! Don't make it a long engagement will you. Girls don't take kindly to be kept dangling. She won't hang around forever waiting for just the right moment. The way you have neglected her, one could hardly blame her for thinking you weren't wildly enthusiastic.

'I have to admit she did seem a little cool the last time we met,' he admitted. He hadn't thought much about it at the time but now his mother mentioned it...

'Once we got talking, we got along fine.'

'I didn't even know you'd met her since that time, in the summer. You never said anything.'

Millicent's tone was accusing. Here was she, worrying herself sick about how they were going to manage in the future, and here was he, making his own plans and keeping her in the dark about them.

'I saw her when I went to Edinburgh to visit the war pensions people. I suggested she might come, then. She phoned the other day to say when she'd be arriving.'

'I hope you've written to her since.'

'Well, no. There just hasn't been the time.'

'Oh Iain, you can be so exasperating at times!'

She stumped out into the hall in search of the daily help.

'Mrs Clark! Mrs Clark! Oh there you are. We really must get on with sorting out the bedrooms for our guests. Come with me, please.'

Iain finished reading the paper, folded his napkin and pushed back his chair. He had a few minutes to spare before surgery. Maybe his mother was right. Perhaps he should drop Alison a line to say how he much he was looking forward to seeing her.

35

ALISON MCKENZIE STARED out at the frosty landscape slipping past the carriage window and asked herself once again what she thought she was doing here. Until yesterday when his letter arrived, she had been toying with the idea of making a last minute excuse, extra duties for a sick colleague or some such. She opened her handbag and extracted the single sheet of notepaper with the Eisdalsa Practice letter heading.

My Dear Alison,

I can't tell you how much I'm looking forward to seeing you on Tuesday. The forecast looks like being good for both the 31st and the 1st of January so we are planning a family picnic on one of the nearby, uninhabited islands on ne're day. Uncle Stuart has a spanking new yacht which he is dying to try out. Bring whatever waterproofs you have but don't worry if you have none, Mum can always fix you up with something of hers.

My sister Morag is coming so you won't be the only female of our generation at the party. Since I told them you were joining us, the family have all been dying to meet you.

Please don't feel too intimidated. They're a harmless bunch really.

I'll be there in good time to meet the train. The car is unmistakeable. It's a dark green Daimler – which used to belong to the dowager Marchioness. You'd laugh to see some of the old retainers doffing their caps to me by mistake!

Well I've just heard the surgery bell go so I'd better be on my way.

Longing to see you again very soon,

All my love

Iain

She folded the paper carefully and returned it to its envelope. Such missives were rare. It might be the only letter he ever wrote to her. She tucked it back into her bag and tried to concentrate on the magnificent scenery.

For some time the elderly steam locomotive had been running along the side of a heavily wooded valley between the mountains, pulling behind it three plum-coloured carriages which sported the lavish upholstery, curtained windows and lacy antimacassars of a more affluent period in railway history.

The line had been joined along its route by a fast-flowing river ,which at one moment dashed over sharply dropping rapids while at the next meandered sluggishly beside the track as the valley widened and the hills receded. As Alison stared dreamily out of the window, her reverie was interrupted by a marked change in the sound of the wheels on the track. They were travelling across a causeway built above a stretch of marshland. Ahead lay the wide expanse of Loch Awe and, recognising the place, Alison gave a small sigh of relief.

Another half hour and they would be arriving in Oban.

At the far end of the loch, the railway track followed the river Awe northwest through the Pass of Brander before abandoning the river altogether and cutting a fresh pathway between the surrounding hills. Without the water to distract her, Alison fell to thinking seriously about her future and in particular, Sister Charles' proposition.

It had almost certainly stemmed from something which had occurred a few days after her meeting with Iain Beaton in the tea shop. A colleague, Miriam Jordan, was getting married and the girls had clubbed together to buy her a wedding gift. To make the presentation they had gathered in the lounge bar of a rather dour, tartan-hung hotel, a few blocks from the hospital. The event was tinged with sadness because Miriam had recently been informed that St James' policy on married staff remained what it had always been. As a married woman she would be expected to resign from her post.

'It's so stupid,' complained Alison, 'to think they have spent three years training you to be a Staff Nurse and now, because of some antiquated notion that married women shouldn't work, they're ready to sacrifice all that studying and expense.'

'They were happy enough to employ married women during the war,' a diminutive, golden-haired lass from Peebles complained. 'Even my mum, with four children and her man away at sea, was asked to return to her old job in the Cottage Hospital. Mind you, she got her marching orders as soon as the regular girls were discharged from the services.'

'Why on earth shouldn't a married woman continue working?' Alison wondered. 'Just because she's getting married, it doesn't mean she will immediately have children to worry about. It's not as though it isn't possible to control that side of things.'

'You don't mean by using contraception?' exclaimed the buxom Bridget Malone, horrified. 'Father Doran would never condone that!'

'Why ever not?' Alison exploded. 'What's wrong with planning your family properly? A professional girl ought to be able to earn her keep alongside her husband until such time as she chooses to start her family. She should be able to have her couple of kids or however many she wants, and then go back to work. It makes the best economic sense.'

'It's a sin to prevent procreation by any means,' Bridget insisted, primly. 'Anyway, I can't think of anything nicer than getting married and having babies.'

She placed an affectionate arm around the shoulders of the bride-to-be, who was beginning to look a little uncomfortable at this sudden turn in the conversation.

'I can't tell you how much I envy you, Miriam,' the Irish girl confessed boldly, for all to hear. 'I'd be happy to give up nursing tomorrow, if it meant I was getting married.'

'If you're content to sacrifice all your training to bring up lots of good little Catholics just to please the priest, that's fine by me,' said Alison sharply. 'It still doesn't answer my question. What sense does it make to dismiss a trained nurse the moment she gets married?'

Sister Charles had wondered at the time, if she should accept Miriam's invitation. Now she was sure she had made a mistake. She really ought not to be party to a discussion of this kind.

She put down her glass as though to intervene, thought better of it and allowed the conversation to continue without her.

'Then there's the whole question of living in the Nurses' Home,' Alison took another tack. 'What's so special about living on the job anyway? I can understand that we ought to be within reasonable distance in case of emergencies, and it's obvious that a married women can't live in the Nurses' Home, but why shouldn't she be housed somewhere nearby? There're plenty of suitable tenements surrounding the hospital. Some of them actually belong to the hospital trust. It seems to me, nurses should be able to rent those.'

'But that would mean it was the wife who decided where the couple lived.' exclaimed Kirsty Macmillan who, like Alison herself, had been born and raised in Edinburgh. Such a notion had to be completely alien to any well brought up, Scottish girl.

'What's wrong with that?' Alison laughed. 'I reckon with housing so difficult to come by, there'll be quite a few men looking for a nurse to marry if accommodation is to be provided.'

'Hardly the best reason for marriage, surely?' Sister Charles could not resist the temptation to join in.

'All I'm saying is that there is no reason for sacking a valuable member of staff just because she wants to get married.' Alison stood by her argument. 'What do you suppose the doctors would say if they were required to leave their posts when they took a wife?'

'Oh, but that's different,' protested a red headed girl from Stornoway. 'A man doesn't have the same responsibility in the home, nor is it his job to bring up the children.'

'Why not?' demanded Alison. 'Don't you see that you're all stuck in a rut? You believe that because your mothers and grandmothers were content to be good little housewives, willing to suppress all their personal ambitions in favour of their husband's, that we have to do the same, today! What's wrong with husband and wife sharing the household chores and both going out to work? Why shouldn't a father take a hand in bringing up his own children? He's fifty per cent responsible for them being there in the first place!'

At this outburst Bridget looked shocked; some of the others nodded in agreement.

'Someone's got to look after the kids if a woman goes back to work. Who's going to do it?' demanded another nurse who wanted to support Alison's viewpoint but had experienced rather more of the practical aspects of life within a large family.

'There'll always be someone willing to take care of the children, even when they're of school age,' Alison assured her. 'If a woman has carved out any kind of a career for herself, she ought to be in a position to be able to pay for the day to day care of her children. In that way she will be giving employment to someone else who needs a job.'

Alison was not too sure of the economics of her argument but she was certain that there had to be a less wasteful way of utilising well-trained and dedicated women. Weren't they always complaining that there was a shortage of experienced nursing staff and worrying about the constant drain away from the profession?

'Pay for a Nanny you mean? On our salaries?' scoffed one of the others.

'That's just the point,' declared Alison. 'A nurse's pay should reflect the amount of training and the long and unsocial hours she works. If it did, there would be no problem about a working mother being able to afford child care.'

'Alison, you're beginning to sound like one of those new women Labour politicians. The Betty Braddock of Auld Reekie!' Miriam made an attempt to lighten the discussion. It was her hen-party, after all.

Sister Charles studied the expressions on the faces of the young girls around her. There were several who clearly agreed with what Alison was saying, even though they lacked the courage to stand up and say so in public. There had been a time when Sister Charles herself had been forced to make a choice between taking a husband and pursuing the career she loved. In the event, that decision had been made for her one fine spring day in 1916, by the German shell which had destroyed her fiancé's command post and everyone in it. She glanced across the crowded room to where Alison was engaged in further argument with the reactionary Bridget Malone.

'Then there's the way the medical staff lord it over us.' Alison was getting into her stride now, 'Look how even the youngest doctors treat us; showing off in front of their colleagues, when half the time they rely on the more experienced nurses to keep them from killing the patients.'

'But doctor always knows best!' Bridget protested.

What Alison was saying was contrary to everything their training had taught them. How could she dare to question the superior knowledge of the medical men?

Some of the others laughed, thinking the Irish girl was being deliberately controversial. In fact Bridget sincerely believed what she was saying. A man must be right in all things. Hadn't he the learning and the superior brain-power?

Sister Charles listened to the exchange in silence. Bridget was a conscientious girl and a reliable nurse, but her naïvety, born of an unquestioning loyalty to a stultifying tradition, would prevent her further progress within the profession. She would probably be better off marrying and bringing up a family, for there was going to be little room for the Bridget Malones in the new order of things. Nurses would have to speak up for their rights from now on or they would continue to find themselves treated on a par with cooks and janitors, just as they had been ever since the days of Florence Nightingale. What these girls really needed was a spokesperson of their own. Sister Charles could not suppress a little smile. Maybe she had found them one.

As the end of the year approached, much of the discussion in the Nurses' Home had been about the changes that were to take place when the new National Health Service came into being. There had been plenty of talk both in parliament and in the national press, about how the changes would affect doctors, but little or nothing was being said on behalf of the nurses. Not even at the level of Matron had there been any representation of nurses' views on any of the main bodies formulating plans for the new service.

Only at this late stage had the Royal College of Nursing woken up to the fact that it should be taking part in the discussions and begun to demand representation on committees at regional and district level. They were, however, still content to allow the British Medical Association to do all the talking with the Minister of Health.

The Royal College saw its role as a non-belligerent body, concerned in the main with standards of nursing care and the conduct of examinations. Debate was seldom encouraged and any suggestion of militancy abhorrent. The *Nursing Times*, the accepted organ for disseminating information, carried articles on knitting, birdwatching, fashion notes and the occasional uplifting feature on an example of missionary zeal in some far away land. Nurses' salaries and topics relating to conditions of working were studiously avoided, while the question of representation of nurses on the decision-making bodies was never even contemplated.

On Christmas Eve, Matron approached her senior nursing Sister, Vera Charles, for the name of a suitable representative to attend a national conference. Sister Charles had had no difficulty in making her recommendation. When, three days later, Alison reminded Sister that she was taking leave and would not be returning until the beginning of January, Miss Charles had listened without comment but then, instead of dismissing her, she invited Alison to take a seat.

'There is something I have to discuss with you, Nurse. It might be best to get it over with before you go on leave.'

Expecting a reprimand for some infringement of yet another ridiculous regulation, Alison felt the colour rising to her cheeks. 'Matron has asked me to recommend someone to attend a conference of Scottish nurses to be held in January, here in Edinburgh. I have been asking around, and I find that your name comes most readily to everyone's lips. How would you feel about being asked to represent your colleagues?'

Alison did not know quite how to respond. Naturally, she was surprised and flattered to be asked but it did leave her in something of a quandary. Sister Charles was not to know that ever since her last encounter with Iain Beaton, she had been giving serious thought to the question of marriage and how it would inevitably result in her leaving the profession altogether. In her stand for the right of a married woman to continue in the nursing profession, she had been voicing a plea for herself as much as for anyone.

'You would of course be given time off work to attend,' Sister added hurriedly, misinterpreting Alison's hesitation. 'According to the way matters progress from the first meeting, there may be others. So far as your own advancement is concerned, this could be an important opportunity.'

Alison, although thrilled at the prospect, hardly knew how to respond. It so happened that because of her upbringing, she was remarkably well-versed in workers' negotiations. Her father had been a great spokesman for his workmates in the days before the war, when jobs were scarce and conditions in the factories poor. That was before unemployment and a loss of self-respect had led him to spend endless nights in the pub and long days at the races.

Sister Charles could see that there was something troubling Alison and asked what it was.

'To be truly representative, a delegate should be elected by the whole body of nurses. Otherwise she will have no mandate to speak on their behalf.'

Sister Charles was taken aback by Alison's response. While she applauded the girl's studied approach to the subject of nursing politics, this attitude smacked rather too much of trade unionism. She wasn't sure that it was quite what Matron had in mind!

'I suppose we could arrange a meeting at which your name is put forward,' she conceded. 'I can't imagine that there will be any rival bid for the position, but if it will make you feel more comfortable.'

'I would certainly prefer to see it done that way,' Alison told her.

'Well, you go off and enjoy your leave and I'll see what can be arranged. May I take it you will be willing to stand if such an election does take place?' This time Alison did not hesitate.

'Oh yes, indeed!' She turned to go, paused and turned back. 'I appreciate your asking me,' she said. 'Thank you.'

Was it possible that, just for one fleeting moment, the straight-laced Sister Charles had actually allowed her face to crack into the slightest semblance of a smile?

Alison had left the office feeling extraordinarily elated. Before leaving the Nurses' Home, she had gathered together the latest information on the health reforms from newspapers left lying about in the common room. When she got back, she would make a point of going to the library for a copy of the provisions of the new National Health Act.

This train journey had given her the first real opportunity to consider her options. What if Iain Beaton were to ask her to marry him? Despite his strange way of showing it, she knew that he was attracted to her. At their last meeting, she had had the distinct impression that a proposal had been on the tip of his tongue. With such exciting prospects unfolding for her career however, she was going to find it very difficult to decide. How was she going to respond to his proposal, if and when it came?

36

'WELL, MRS WALLACE, it looks as though Junior will be arriving on time.'
Iain put his stethoscope to one side and completed the patient's notes on
the desk in front of him. His father's records showed that Sally Wallace
had given birth to three babies already and all had gone to full term,
without complications. *Like shelling peas from a pod*, Iain read Hugh's
note with some amusement. There was an illegible squiggle alongside,
pencilled words which he didn't understand. He put a question mark to
remind him to find out what it meant the next time he was in touch with
the maternity unit.

'It might be as well if you were to get yourself into the hospital before
the New Year's holiday, Mrs Wallace. We don't want to go calling the
lifeboat men away from their dinners on New Year's Eve now, do we?'

'I'm not due until the second of January, Doctor,' Sally Wallace
reminded him. 'There's really no need for me to go until the actual day. I
never had a baby in the ambulance yet!'

'That's as may be, but this is your fourth. It's up to you of course,
but I would advise you to get yourself into Oban on the thirtieth of this
month at the very latest.'

'Och well, if you insist, Doctor.'

It was clear that Sally Wallace thought she knew best. She had been
hoping she would see the New Year in with the family. Without her,
poor old Jamie would be left to cook the dinner himself and the children
could be pretty damning when it came to their father's activities in the
kitchen.

'I'll be away then, Doctor,' she said hauling her ungainly figure out of
the chair. 'The bus'll no wait even for the pregnant, and I have to make
the twelve o'clock ferry or I shall miss my lift with Johnny McInnes.'

'Next time I see you, you'll have had the baby.' Iain showed her to the door. 'It should be a particularly happy New Year for you all!' He poked his head around the waiting room door. 'Mr Robertson?'

The waiting room was crowded for a Thursday morning. As always at this time of the year, bronchitis and its associated ills were rife amongst the islanders. Most of them managed to cope using time-honoured remedies. Even so, the pile of files remaining on his desk was daunting. At this rate he would have no time for lunch before he set out to meet Alison at the station. And he had promised to drop in on Alma as usual after surgery. She was bound to have a few problems to be sorted out before the holiday.

Bobby Robertson shuffled in, wheezing and coughing as he stuffed his pipe, still warm, into his trouser pocket. Iain turned to him with an encouraging smile and drew his prescription pad towards him.

37

HE WAS LATE. He knew he would be, despite all his best intentions to be standing there waiting for her on the platform when she arrived.

It was Alma who had held him up. She had received notification only that morning about her own position once the new health service came into operation and she needed to talk. The problem was that all district nurses were going to have to become State Registered. Unqualified but experienced personnel, offered a shorter route to qualification, would still be required to take additional training and examinations.

'I don't know that I'm up to all that study at my time of life,' Alma had complained.

'But you're a relatively young woman,' Iain protested. 'You must be much the same age as David and myself. Forty-one, forty-two?'

'It's not just a matter of age,' she replied. 'I left school at thirteen and went straight into service. It was old Mrs McLean up at Johnstone's encouraged me to take up nursing, just the practical side you understand. The bright girls all went off to the city hospitals to become properly qualified. They were happy enough to have people like me on the wards of the West Highland in those days.'

'I'm sure you could have taken the exams if you'd tried,' Iain insisted. 'I seem to remember you collecting a few prizes at school.'

''I never had the opportunity to stay on after elementary school,' Alma told him. 'My parents needed what little money I could earn by going into service. I was being fed and housed by my employers and that made one less mouth to feed at home. There's no way that I could begin to study anatomy and chemistry and all that stuff with only the three Rs behind me.'

'I don't suppose it would be all that difficult for someone of your practical experience,' he said, trying to cheer her, but he knew from Alison what an SRN course contained and realised it was going to be tough going for someone of Alma's background.

It was a pity, because Alma had qualities often lacking in the more academically able young women who trained as nurses. She was always cheerful and optimistic even with patients who were depressed or in a very weak condition. She was calm with the obstreperous and gentle with the aged. He had come across far less compassionate women on the wards at Edinburgh Infirmary.

'What would you do for a living,' he asked, 'if you have to give up nursing?'

'I don't know. Take a typing course perhaps, work in a shop, who knows.'

'That would be a wicked waste!' he had exclaimed, surprised at the anger her suggestion had provoked. He'd come to rely on her good sense and could not conceive of the practice operating without her. Belatedly, he checked on the time. 'Can we talk about this later on? I promised Mother I'd meet someone off the train. She's going to be furious with me if I'm late.'

Alma was too absorbed with the question of her own future to be wondering who Iain was meeting from the train. It was a pity he had to go all the same, because she had already thought of one solution to her problems, something that directly affected him. It was presumptuous of her, of course, but almost too exciting to contemplate.

38

ALISON WAITED BENEATH the glass canopy of the old Victorian railway station, shivering in the northeasterly breeze which swirled around the stout wrought-iron pillars and whistled through the elaborate filigree of rusted ironwork supporting the roof. She glanced up at the station clock, checked the time once again with her own wrist watch and stamped her feet to keep the blood flowing in them.

It was already a quarter past three and there was still no sign of Iain. Now she was certain her journey had been a mistake. He must have forgotten she was coming, or he'd got the day wrong. His poor timekeeping was irritating but, she supposed, that was what a doctor's wife was for, amongst other things. To make sure he didn't miss his appointments! There I go again, she told herself. He hasn't even asked me yet. Even so, in her heart of hearts she knew he would. What then? What answer was she to give him?

She heard the throaty sound of a car horn and looked up to see him leap from a splendid, if rather elderly, green Daimler. He came striding towards her, obviously concerned and apologetic. Her steely determination began to waver.

'I'm so sorry. Have you been waiting long? Are you absolutely frozen? Would you like to stop off for a cup of tea before we go on home?'

The self-recriminations poured forth at such a rate that Alison had to put up a hand as though to ward them off.

'Tea would be nice. The train was a little early,' she added to ease his conscience. He could not fail to have noticed the platform was deserted and all the other passengers long gone.

He lifted her heavy suitcase as though it was a featherweight and tucking his hand beneath her elbow, led her firmly in the direction of waiting vehicle. In her anxiety to keep pace with him, she stumbled on the cobbled roadway and he strengthened his grip so that she became intensely aware of his closeness.

'We'll put your bag in the car and pop into the Castle for tea.'

After more than three hours on a train without a restaurant car, she was not going to argue. They walked into the carpeted reception area of a rather seedy Victorian hotel and were shown into the lounge, where their order was taken by a gaunt figure in a rusty black morning suit.

'Afternoon tea, please,' Iain ordered.

'Will that be with the bread and butter and pastries?' The waiter looked down his long thin nose in a disparaging manner and sucked air noisily through a hole in his teeth. Iain glancing first at Alison, shook his head.

'Just a pot of tea for two, and perhaps we could have some scones with strawberry jam and cream. If you don't mind,' he added, intimidated by the fellow's obvious disdain.

Clearly, the waiter did mind. The customer was always right, naturally, but the scones were yesterday's leftovers, whereas the bread had come from the baker's that morning. As for the cream, his eyes rolled heavenwards. He heard Iain apologising for bringing her in here.

'It's a bit crumby I know,' Iain said, 'but you looked so cold, I thought we'd best get inside as quickly as possible.'

The waiter stalked off in disgust.

Alison became acutely aware of an increase in tension between them.

'You look absolutely stunning,' he told her. In the warmth of the room, her cheeks had begun to glow. He put out his hand to grab hers. 'I'm so glad you decided to come!'

There was no denying the passion in his tone.

'This may not be the best time or place to say it,' he hesitated.

With a clatter of china and a tiny curse as she caught her heel in a rough piece of carpeting, the waitress stumbled, and the tray she was carrying landed in front of them with a thump. Tea spilt onto the white tray cloth.

Iain was mortified. The waitress made a little noise which sounded very like, 'whoops, sorry!' and Alison tried her hardest not to laugh.

Recovering her poise, the waitress suggested Madam might like to pour. Alison nodded curtly. The waitress departed, fairly sure there would be no complaint from these two. They were too intent on each other, to be worried about a few tea stains.

In silence, Alison poured. Two sugars, she remembered, and just a little milk. As she handed Iain the cup she asked gently, 'you were saying?'

He shuffled uncomfortably, stirring his tea vigorously while plucking up courage to begin again.

'I'm afraid my days for moonlight and roses are long gone. You'd probably prefer a bit more romance, soft lights, sweet music and a bottle of champagne rather than tea in a cracked cup but, well, the fact is, its getting rather crowded at Tigh na Broch.'

Alison's expressive eyebrows shot up. Iain hastened to explain.

'My sister and her husband from Inverlinnie have already arrived and there are others due in tomorrow, so I thought I should tell you, ask you rather, now, while we can have a moment to ourselves.'

'Ask me what?' she asked. She was not going to let him get away with any half measures.

'Oh come on,' he exclaimed, annoyed by her attempt at coquetry. 'You're not going to make me get down on my knees are you? You must know how much I want you to marry me.'

'Then perhaps you should ask me, properly.'

She was unsmiling when she said it. Her mind was in a whirl of indecision. A week ago she would have known exactly what to say. Now she was not so sure. It wasn't just his unconventional manner of proposing, although she might have expected as much from Iain Beaton. No, it was something much more important. At the back of her mind was the prospect of more interesting things to be done than becoming the wife of a general practitioner who had chosen to bury himself in the country. There had been a challenge in Sister Charles' proposal that had excited her and her interest had been aroused as never before.

'Oh, all right then,' Iain was saying, going along with what he understood to be the usual game played by females in these circumstances. Not quite getting to his knees, he grabbed her hand again and whispered, 'Alison, my dear one, will you consent to become my wife?'

Here it was. The moment she had been planning for since that first day they had met on the ward and he had helped her with the laundry. So why hold back? What more could a girl want than this? She recalled her argument with Bridget Malone and she remembered her own words. Why should a woman with a profession she has worked hard to attain, give it all up just because she marries?

Iain couldn't understand why she was hesitating. Surely she must feel as he did? He had neglected her, of course he had. Hadn't he been busy getting settled into the practice? She must appreciate that! After all, it was in her interests as well as his that the practice should flourish. So, what was holding her back?

At last she answered, but the words were not those he wanted to hear.

'I'm not sure,' she said, releasing her hand and playing with the teaspoon while she tried to formulate an appropriate answer. 'I have other things to consider. There's my grandmother, for one. She can't be left entirely alone. Then there's my work. I've studied very hard to get where I am. And there may be greater opportunities in the new Health Service. I'd like to be around when the changeover happens.'

'With regard to your grandmother,' he declared, dismissively, 'I'm sure that a few strings can be pulled to get her into a nursing home here. As for your nursing career, well that experience wouldn't be wasted. A nurse can make an excellent mother. My granny was one before she married Grandpa David. Even Mother did a bit of voluntary hospital work,' he added, not appreciating how condescending he sounded. 'Meanwhile, you can help me in the surgery.'

'As what? Your wife or your employee?'

They both knew that in the new scheme of things, GPs would not be allowed to employ their own wives as secretaries or as nurses. A wife helping in her husband's practice was not going to be paid for what she did.

'I'm very fond of you, Iain,' Alison responded bluntly, 'but since we last met, I've been thinking a great deal about my immediate future and I'm not sure that I'm ready to settle down to married life, not yet awhile, anyway.'

He didn't know what to say. All along he had assumed that she liked him more than a little. He was not a very romantic sort of fellow but he did find her very attractive and even if he had not been too demonstrative, she must have known how he felt. He consoled himself with the thought that maybe this was just a modern woman's way of asserting herself. It was true her reticence made her even more desirable. Perhaps she did need to be courted for a while longer. Well, patients permitting, he had four whole days to devote to her. She would soon see that he was quite sincere.

'I'm not going to give up that easily,' he told her, with a disarming grin. 'I'll ask you again when you've had a chance to think it over.'

Hardly aware of what he was doing, Iain summoned the waitress and paid the bill. He was so distracted, he left an overly handsome tip.

The chill wind caught them with their coats still unbuttoned as they left the hotel. Alison shivered. Enveloping her in his ex-service winter-warm, Iain grasped her around the waist and they hurried towards the car. It's funny, he thought, as he pulled the starter and listened attentively for the almost imperceptible sound of the Daimler's engine, how every significant meeting they had seemed to take place in some really awful café. Maybe things would go better if their meetings were held in more appropriate surroundings.

39

'BEST GET OUT of those wet things as soon as possible, Aunt Annie.'

'We nearly didn't come across,' Annie explained, pulling off her boots. 'Donnie was very reluctant to make a run at all. If it hadn't been for your uncle using all his persuasive charm, we'd be facing a very quiet Hogmanay on the island.'

'So much for the long range weather forecast,' Iain laughed as he squeezed water from his uncle's tweed deerstalker.

'Och, it wasn't all that bad,' laughed Stuart Beaton. 'I've been out in far worse conditions!'

Iain took his aunt's heavy winter coat and hung it close to the hall radiator. It had obviously been an uncomfortably wet passage, if not a dangerous one.

'You must be absolutely frozen. Here, let me take your things.'

Alison held out a hand for the elderly doctor's coat and gloves. Stuart, never slow to appreciate a pretty face, threw a questioning glance in his nephew's direction.

'Uncle Stuart, I don't believe you've met Alison McKenzie. Alison, this is my uncle, Dr Stuart Beaton,' Iain introduced them. 'And my aunt, Annie, Mrs Beaton.'

'Oh, no need to be so formal Iain,' laughed his aunt, and to Alison she said, 'Call me Annie. Everyone does.'

'Pleased to meet you, my dear,' said Stuart and then to his nephew, 'I must say young Iain, you're a dark horse and no mistake. We had you marked down as a regular old bachelor type!'

Iain didn't know whether to be pleased or embarrassed by his uncle's comment.

'Alison is a colleague,' he explained awkwardly. 'We met at the

Infirmary. She's a staff nurse,' he added, in case they mistook her for a doctor.

'Looking forward to the changes in July, no doubt?' Stuart observed casually.

'I'm not sure,' Alison replied. 'No one has as yet considered it necessary to tell us how we are likely to be affected. We've heard a great deal about the doctors, particularly the consultants and how the status of our Voluntary Hospital is to be preserved, but nothing has been said about improving things for us or any of the other people who do the real work!'

Here's a feisty little thing thought Stuart admiringly, regarding Alison with an even keener eye.

'Uncle Stuart is the regional representative for the BMA,' Iain explained, hastily. 'He's supposed to keep us all informed about what is going to happen. Mind you, we see so little of him, I'm no wiser than you.'

'Perhaps you should come to some of the meetings, yourself,' his uncle suggested, teasing, knowing what Iain's response was bound to be.

'What chance have I to go waltzing off to Glasgow every few weeks to listen to a lot of hot air being spouted by a bunch of old men, some of whom saw their last patient ten years ago.'

He knew he was exaggerating, but it was in fact the case that it was largely the senior consultants and retired practitioners who had time to attend meetings.

'At least you have *someone* speaking up for you,' observed Annie. 'I was talking to Alma Livingstone only the other day and she, like Alison here, has very little idea how the new service will affect her and her friends. What she does know however is that she herself will have to retrain if she wants to keep her job.'

'Why, what does she do?' Alison asked.

'Alma is our district nurse,' Iain explained. 'It seems she will have to begin training for full registration within the next six months.'

'I hadn't heard anything about that,' said Alison, feeling unreasonably responsible for the fate of a colleague whose position might be precarious. 'I'd like to talk to her if there's an opportunity.'

'You're sure to meet her tonight. We all end up at the village hall after the Bells. There's a traditional ceilidh,' Annie told her.

'I'm surprised to find you so interested in the future of nursing,' said Iain, provocatively. 'I had the impression that you had no long-term ambitions in that direction.'

He was still smarting a little from her refusal. His first impression had been that Alison regarded her job in nursing only as a means to a suitable marriage. This was the first time he had heard her express any thoughts about the future of the profession within the new scheme of things. She sounded almost militant in her opinions.

'Actually,' Alison spoke with a degree of pride that Iain had not recognised in her before, 'I've been asked to represent my colleagues at a national conference when I get back. It would be useful to have an opinion from someone in a totally different sphere of nursing.'

'Good for you!' exclaimed Annie. 'It's about time the nurses had their say in all this. So far the men have had everything too much their own way.'

'Oh dear,' exclaimed Stuart, 'here we go again.'

Alison looked puzzled.

'Don't take too much notice of him,' Iain excused his uncle. 'Aunt Annie was once a great champion of women's rights, one of the best in fact.

'A suffragette,' Alison recalled what Iain had told her about his aunt. She regarded the older woman with renewed interest. 'My mother used to tell me about the great meetings held at the Glasgow Cross,' she said, 'and about the women going to Parliament to demand the right to vote.'

'Yes, well, it was all a long time ago,' said Annie, catching Stuart's eye and recognising how it pained him to be reminded, even after all these years.

'I sometimes wonder whether it was all worth it,' was all he said however, 'when I hear of the large number of women who don't even bother to cast their vote at elections.' He paused in an attempt to regain control of his emotions, 'when I remember what some people went through, so that they might have that right.'

'But surely that was the whole point,' Alison said. 'The suffragettes went through everything they did in order for women to have the *right* to vote. If they choose not to exercise it, surely that's up to them? What's important is that women may vote if they wish to, just as men may vote or not as they decide.'

'Absolutely,' said Annie decisively, and clapping a hand to Alison's shoulder led her off to the kitchen.

'Let's go and have some serious political talk, Alison, with the people who really matter in this household. Who's here? Have you met my sister-in-law Margaret? She's a writer and another advocate of women's rights. You've met Morag? She's a surgeon, and believe me, that took some courage when she began training, just after the first war.'

40

THE VILLAGE HALL had been built by the slate quarriers at the Marquis's expense in the year he raised his army of Volunteers to protect the coastline of Argyll from a threatened attack by the French. It had begun life as their Drill Hall but for the past forty years it had been the venue for community activities and fundraising of every kind. It served as a theatre for school concerts and the place for dances and ceilidhs; one had been held after midnight on every New Year's Day since the 1860s.

The building was a sturdy structure built in stone, with a solid floor designed to sustain the activities of a company of marching men. There was no give in it for those who danced in light pumps and Alison soon complained of sore feet and begged to be allowed to rest. Iain slipped away to find them a cool drink while she regained her breath and wondered at the resilience of the locals who seemed not to notice the hard floor. To the skirl of pipes they formed their sets and began the intricate movements of an eightsome reel. They laughed and sang, ignoring the rising dust which coated shoes and stockings and soiled the hems of the longer skirts, most of which had been retrieved in triumph from some attic trunk or musty wardrobe, for this special occasion. The men were kilted, the women wore white, each with the colourful plaid of their clan fixed proudly across one shoulder. There were similar events in Edinburgh, of course, but those were not for the likes of Alison McKenzie. Never before had she experienced such a family atmosphere, a closeness in which she should have felt privileged to share. The villagers had made her very welcome. Was she not the guest of the Beatons, a family of long standing in this community and no doubt held in high regard? Nevertheless, she was still an outsider. Watching Iain making his way slowly around the hall, stopping from time to time to exchange words with old and young alike, she felt excluded. She guessed she would always be a stranger here.

'I'm getting far too old for this!' The attractive, dark-haired woman who had taken an empty chair at Alison's side, was perspiring freely and did not hesitate to loosen the lacing of her blouse, easing the neckline to reveal creamy shoulders and a delicate, swan-like neck.

'Ah, that's better!' She fanned herself with her neat little evening bag and as Iain approached, cried, 'Oh, how did you guess. I really needed that.'

She took Alison's lemonade from him and swallowed it without a pause. 'What a mind-reader you are,' she told Iain and stopped abruptly.

'Oh, I'm so sorry,' she said to Alison, 'was that meant for you? How thoughtless of me!'

'Your need seems to have been greater than mine,' Alison smiled. How could she be offended when the woman appeared so genuinely contrite?

'Alison, this is Alma Livingstone, our district nurse. You said you wanted to meet her.'

'How do you do,' said Alison, offering her hand.

Alma took it. So this was the reason for the doctor's abrupt departure on Tuesday. She regarded the younger woman suspiciously. A friend of his mother's, he'd said. His girlfriend, more like.

Alma handed Iain the empty glass. 'Perhaps you should get another drink for Alison,' she suggested rather stiffly, struggling with barely concealed disappointment.

While Iain went for a second glass of lemonade, Alison considered the district nurse with interest. Alma Livingstone appeared somewhat older than herself, nearer Iain's age than her own. She had worn well, nevertheless. Alma's ivory skin was smooth and unblemished. Her blue-black hair, released for the occasion from its usual severe imprisonment, hung in loosely waving tresses almost to her shoulders. With her gypsy style blouse, she wore a skirt of deep red velvet, a perfect foil for those Latin looks. Alison's eyes were drawn immediately to the exquisite cameo nestled on her creamy white throat, an inch above that daringly exposed cleavage.

'What a lovely pendant,' she exclaimed.

'My mother's. It was the only decent piece of jewellery she possessed, poor dear.'

'It's beautiful,' Alison breathed, admiringly. 'Your mother, is she dead?'

'She died last year. A good innings. She was seventy-eight.'

'My mother died when I was twelve. My gran looked after me until I left school.'

Alma's natural instinct was to sympathise with anyone who had been orphaned so young. Despite herself, she found she was warming towards the stranger.

'You've lived here all your life?' Alison asked.

'The last of the litter,' Alma told her. There were eight of us, five brothers, two sisters and me.' Alma said it proudly with only a hint of resentment. One after another, they had grown up and gone away, leaving their little sister to take care of things at home.

'Mrs Beaton tells me you have to retrain if you want to keep your job. That seems a bit hard when you've been doing the work for... how long is it?'

'Fifteen years. Still, it's only right. I should be properly qualified. A district nurse is in the front line when it comes to giving advice and taking care of the bedridden. There are times when I realise just how inadequate I am, believe me.'

'We all have that problem,' said Alison. 'No one can be expected to know everything.'

'This new directive simply helped me make up my mind,' Alma assured her. 'I only took the job in the first place because of mother. It meant that I could live at home you see. Any other form of nursing would have required me to live in the hospital. I did have a chance to go to Glasgow to train properly, but that was a long time ago, soon after father died. Unfortunately my mother couldn't be left on her own.'

Alison thought of her own grandmother and nodded, understanding only too well the obligations that had kept Alma from a proper education.

'What will you do now?' she asked.

'Look for a different job, a nursing home perhaps. I might go back to Johnstone's.' Then, seeing Alison's puzzled frown, she explained, 'a private nursing home at the head of the glen. It's where I started, as a kitchen maid.'

'I don't suppose they pay very well?' Alison did not want this to sound like a formal interview but she was keen to understand the plight of the Alma and others like her. She represented the women who having dedicated their lives to nursing, were to be ousted from their jobs because they didn't have the necessary piece of paper. Surely there must be some way of keeping them in their jobs?

'Have you thought about taking the training course? I understand it's been reduced to six months for people with your experience.'

'I'm too old to go back to the schoolroom now,' Alma protested. I'll find something. Don't worry about me.'

But Alison did worry. She worried about the large numbers of such women whose lives would be shattered by this ill-considered stroke of bureaucracy. Apart from the effect the decision would have on the lives of individuals, it was a serious waste of experienced nurses. Maybe they didn't have all the necessary academic knowledge at their fingertips but they were probably good practical bedside nurses and there would always be a need for them.

'Iain's been a long time,' Alma commented and stood up, waving when she spotted Stuart, who was obviously searching for someone in the crowd. He caught sight of them and made his way over.

'Thank goodness I've found you,' he said to Alison. 'Iain's been called away I afraid. A patient has gone into labour.'

'Not Mrs Wallace,' Alma exclaimed indignantly. 'Iain told her to get into the hospital in good time, but she would hang on for the holiday.'

'He's had to call out the lifeboat. The Lunga ferry has been cancelled because of the weather.'

'How long will that take?' asked Alison, remembering having seen the lifeboat station in Oban, close to the railway station.

'About an hour, I would think. Iain's gone home for his things. He'll go straight on to the ferry landing. He's taken the car so we're going to have to walk back I'm afraid.'

'Will he need a hand?' Alison asked, picturing herself in the role of doctor's helpmate, bedraggled by the storm, standing steadfastly at Iain's side, holding up the oil-lamp for him to see by.

'The midwife is already on the island. They have their own, you know, over there. She would have dealt with matters herself but unfortunately there seems to be some complication.'

There was indeed a complication. Iain could tell at a glance that the baby was not presenting head down and locked into the pelvis as it should be. He applied the foetal stethoscope and hearing nothing glanced up at the midwife, shaking his head. His eyes confirmed her worst suspicions. The infant was already dead.

'Cord?' she asked.

'Probably.'

Sally Wallace, although exhausted by her long travail, was for the moment fully aware of what was happening around her. She sensed the hopelessness in the professional voices.

'He's dead isn't he?' she demanded.

Iain tried to preserve an air of optimism but she could tell from his non-committal response that she was right.

'The baby is not coming out without help, Mrs Wallace. We're going to have to give you a whiff of anaesthetic now and then we'll see what can be done to save him.'

Mrs Wallace did not argue. She was already resigned to the situation.

The midwife placed the gas and air mask over her face as the next contraction began to take hold and as Sally steeled herself against the onset of pain, Iain slipped the hypodermic needle into her vein. In a matter of seconds, the narcotic carried her away into oblivion.

The foetus had not only presented itself feet first in the birth canal but in the process of turning in the womb, it had become entangled with the umbilical cord. As they had suspected, the fleshy rope was wound tightly around the infant's neck choking off all blood supply to the brain. Iain lifted the baby out of the gaping wound in the woman's abdomen, snipped the ligatured cord and handed the perfectly formed, lifeless blue infant to the midwife. Despite all her experience of other equally tragic events, the woman was unable to hold back her tears as she unwound the snake of purple cord from around the infant's head and laid the little body on a snow-white towel. She wiped the tiny body clean and wrapped it tight, as carefully as if it lived, laying it at last in the carrycot prepared with such carefree anticipation a few short hours before.

Iain's attention was concentrated upon the mother. The operation to remove the foetus was in itself a simple one and something he had performed a number of times before. The baby's last urgent struggles had however torn the placenta too early from its attachment to the uterus wall and there had already been considerable haemorrhaging. Now the patient was bleeding so badly that without an immediate transfusion of blood, he feared he could not save her.

He instructed the nurse to set up a saline drip in the hope that the additional fluid would preserve life long enough for him to find a blood donor.

'Who do we have here in the household?' he demanded sharply, packing absorbent cotton into the wound to staunch the flow. 'She needs a transfusion.'

'She has an unusual blood grouping,' the midwife warned, examining the patient's details from her records. 'It's group A and rhesus negative. I remember there was some concern when Sally had her last baby. They were standing by at the hospital in case a blood transfusion was needed.'

The discovery that the rhesus factor could be responsible for infant mortality had been made shortly before the war. It was also well established that a rhesus negative subject could not receive blood from a rhesus positive donor. The chances of such a rare blood grouping occurring in more than one individual within this small island population were negligible.

Iain's contact with his patient had been limited. Not wishing to step on the toes of an experienced midwife, he had chosen to leave the routine examinations to her. Now he cursed himself for not spotting the problem with her blood grouping. He knew, however, that even had he done so, he would have been unable to prevent the baby's death. If only Sally had taken his advice and gone into hospital before she went into labour, the breech birth could have been dealt with in good time and the problem of transfusions for both mother and child would have been solved. Now the infant was dead and the chances were that the mother too would die.

Having checked that the drip was working satisfactorily, Iain left the midwife in charge and went to seek out the anxious father.

41

'I SHOULD HAVE known about that blood grouping. I could have asked the midwife earlier. I saw that hieroglyphic on Dad's notes and never got around to asking about it.'

'And that woman should have got herself into the hospital when you said, instead of messing about at home until the last minute. No one blames you for what happened. You did everything you could.' Alison was becoming impatient with him. The Hogmanay party had been ruined for her. She had arrived back at Tigh na Broch with the others but had seen nothing of Iain until mid-morning the following day. Tomorrow, she must catch the early train back to Edinburgh and here he was, wasting what little time they had left together going over and over what had happened.

They were drinking coffee in the morning room on the sunny side of the house. It had turned out to be a calm day, but with the late start they had missed the tide and Stuart had been obliged to call off their picnic on a nearby island.

With the rest of the family steering clear of the pair, Iain and Alison were attempting, rather self-consciously, to recover the rapport they were creating when interrupted the night before.

As a nurse, Alison understood as well as anyone that a doctor in Iain's position was on duty at all times. She would have been less upset by his abrupt departure had the family not kept on making excuses for him. Stuart had been almost embarrassing in his attempts to act as substitute escort. If Millicent had apologised once, she had done so a dozen times.

From the start it had been obvious that the whole family was conspiring to throw the two of them together. So undisguised was their desire to please, that Alison had begun to suspect their motives. No man's mother could be that keen on his choice of a bride. Had Millicent some other reason for wanting to see him married?

Alison had been disappointed not to find Iain returned by breakfast time but when, at last, she heard his car draw up in front of the house, she determined not to reproach him for his protracted absence. She wanted to make the most of the time that was left. Iain, however, coupled his remorse at the loss of his patient with his apologies for letting her down and as a consequence, an air of deep depression had descended upon them both.

There was every reason to be cheerful on such a lovely day. Alison wanted to suggest that he took her over to Eisdalsa Island. Annie and Stuart had been adamant that she could not leave without visiting their cottage, but Iain insisted on soul-searching, instead of enjoying the break while he had the chance.

'If we had an early lunch we could be over on the two o'clock ferry,' she attempted to persuade him. 'Your uncle said we should not be too long because it gets dark so early and we must cross by six at the very latest.'

'Oh, I suppose we had better go if that's what you want,' he concluded, unwillingly. He hadn't slept for more than twenty-four hours and would gladly have taken himself off to bed. Even he could see that would be no way to treat his guest.

'I'll take a quick bath, just to wake myself up. We'll have a sandwich and then go, okay?'

'That will be fine.' She smiled, trying to show him that she forgave him for neglecting her.

He responded by giving her a quick peck on the cheek but then, just as he left the room, he added, 'I think I'll give them a ring at the hospital. There'll have to be a post mortem and I'd like to be there.'

Alison sighed. Would it always been like this, she wondered? Was she prepared for a lifetime of playing second fiddle to an army of patients? This was nothing like the glamorous lives of those hunky doctors portrayed in the movies.

An insistent ringing broke in upon her thoughts. The telephone was in the consulting room, just down the hall. Was no one going to answer it?

She went out into the hall to look for signs of life. She could hear water running into the bath on the floor above but otherwise there was no sound. Millicent must have gone out to the barn. Alison went into the study and lifted the receiver.

'Doctor's surgery,' she said, mimicking Millicent's mode of answering all calls.

'It's my Robbie,' said an anxious voice. 'He would have waited until the proper time, but he's that bad this morning we'll need to have the doctor, right away.'

'What name?' asked Alison, pencil poised.

'Rab, of course. Didnae I say so?' The woman sounded offended, unable to believe that there might be anyone who didn't know her husband.

'I'm sorry, I'm a visitor here. If you will give me the patient's full name I will get the doctor to call you back.'

'He canna dae that. We're no on the phone,' said the caller, exasperated. The logicality of this conversation just added to Alison's confusion. If they weren't on the phone, how could the silly woman be making the call?

'Then tell me what's wrong and I'll ask the doctor to call round.'

'Just say it's Rab has his trouble. Dr Hugh will understand.'

'Dr Iain Beaton is the doctor now,' Alison said testily. What sort of people were these? They expected everyone to be aware of their own circumstances but were so out of touch, they were not aware of Hugh Beaton's death, nearly a year ago?

'Och aye. The wee laddie. Well, I suppose he'll do all the same. The doctor will know if you say Rab McLeod of Glen Foley.'

'What is the problem?' Alison persisted.

'It's his usual. The doctor will know.' The woman ended this strange conversation before Alison could extract further details. Nothing had been said about its being a public holiday. There had been no apology for calling the doctor out on his day off. Was it a real emergency Alison wondered? As she put down the phone, Millicent came in red-faced and panting.

'I heard the phone ring,' she said. 'I came as fast as I could.' She paused in the doorway. 'Oh dear, did they ring off?'

'I took a message,' said Alison, 'though I can't say it was all that clear.'

She recalled the conversation for Millicent's benefit. Iain's mother laughed.

'That will be old Robbie McLeod in trouble with his piles again. He always manages to want help when it's a holiday and the usual surgery times don't apply.'

'It's hardly a major emergency, then,' Alison said, annoyed that the doctor's attendance should be demanded for something so trivial.

'To Rab it's a major emergency, believe me.'

'Then why leave it until the holiday before he does something about it?'

'Rab has a large farm which he likes to run like clockwork. He'll have calculated that Iain will not be too busy over the holiday so he won't have to waste his time hanging around in the surgery.'

'You mean he deliberately called Iain on his day off?'

Millicent shrugged. 'There's always some who are like that,' she explained, resignedly.

'How thoughtless! Can't they give the doctor a rest for one day in the year?'

'The way Rab looks at it, he's taking a day off from his farming chores so he has the time to spend with the doctor. It's convenient for him you see.'

'But that's outrageous!'

'Not in his mind. To him it's quite logical. Unlike the panel patients, he's the one will be paying the bill, so it's for him to decide when to call out the doctor, even if it does take him until the next quarter-day to get around to settling his account.'

'If I was Iain I'd refuse to go,' Alison declared.

'There are so few paying patients in this practice Iain could not afford to lose one of them. We just have to grin and bear it.'

'That's one thing in favour of hospital life,' Alison decided, 'A day off, is a day off. It would have to be a dire emergency if we were called back to duty.'

Iain appeared, still towelling his hair. In the bright, wintry sunlight, it looked like burnished copper. When he heard about the call, he threw down the towel and began to pack jars and bottles into his medical bag.

'You're not going, without any lunch?' Alison groaned.

'I'm afraid so,' he replied. 'As I remember, old Robbie's always good for a couple of guineas' worth of creams and tablets.' He grinned at his mother. 'Dad always reckoned it was Rab McLeod's piles paid for his best Highland bull!'

Millicent laughed with him at the reminder, but as her son swept out of the house and started up the engine of the Daimler, she was forced to wipe a tear from the corner of her eye.

Alison made no attempt to disguise her annoyance. 'I may as well go and pack my things ready for tomorrow,' she snapped. 'By the time he gets back, it will be too late to go to the island.'

'You could always take a walk up the glen instead,' Millicent attempted to mollify her. 'You can visit the island next time.'

Millicent's words were wasted. By the time she herself reached the hallway, it was already deserted.

42

ALISON'S LETTER ARRIVED by the first post on Tuesday of the following week. Iain, although half anticipating what she would have to say, could not disguise his disappointment. On rereading her letter however, he had to admire her spirit.

Edinburgh, January 6th 1948
Dear Iain,

Please thank your mother for inviting me to spend New Year with your family. They all made me most welcome and I enjoyed my stay in your lovely countryside.

I have thought long and hard about your proposal and am flattered that you should want me to be your wife. I told you before that I did not feel that I could marry you and nothing has occurred since that would make me change my mind.

While I believe that under other circumstances we might have had a successful marriage, I know that I could not endure the life which you want me to lead. I'm a city girl at heart and while I might come to terms with the country way of life, I doubt if I could ever be happy at Eisdalsa. I know I could not endure the inevitable loneliness of a GP's wife, nor could I come to terms with the idea of sharing my husband with a couple of thousand other people, all of whom would take precedence over myself and my children, should there be any.

Since I am able to consider the matter so logically, I can only conclude that I am not in love with you. Were it otherwise, maybe these factors would not even be considered. I have enjoyed our friendship and hope it may continue, but I cannot marry you.

Please tell Alma that I shall be putting her case to the meeting when

I attend the nurses' conference next week. I believe it would be a wicked waste to dismiss people like herself from the service.
My very best wishes to your mother and the rest, Alison.

Iain sat at his desk gazing unseeing at the bleak landscape in his view. She was quite right. Had there been the slightest spark of passion on her part, these reservations would never have been mentioned and if he was absolutely honest with himself, had it not been for Millicent forcing the issue, he would probably never have proposed to her. Now he'd have to confess his failure and his mother would begin hunting for a bride for him all over again.

There was a tap on the door.

It opened a crack to reveal Alma Livingstone in her dark blue uniform coat and small, tight-fitting bonnet. Her face was glowing with the cold.

'Come in Alma,' he said, rising to take her things. 'You look absolutely frozen. Here, come and sit by the fire. I'll get mother to make us some tea.'

'I only popped in to tell you I've been over to Lunga to the Wallace place. John is in a bad state, the older girl, Janet, is coping quite well and the younger ones are simply dazed. His mother's arriving today for the funeral so I expect she'll take a hand, but I think John needs some help to tide him over, something to give him a good night's sleep.'

'I'm going across to Mrs Buchanan later today. I'll make a point of dropping in.' Iain went out into the hallway and called out to his mother. 'Alma's here, any chance of a cup of tea?'

'Won't be a minute,' came his mother's disembodied reply from somewhere at the back of the house.

'I've just had a letter from Alison,' he said, holding up the flimsy sheet. 'She mentions you.' He scanned the notepaper once again. 'Ah, yes, here it is, she says she will be speaking about your case when she addresses the nursing conference that she's attending later in the week. What case is that?'

'It's this question of my having to be State Registered if I want to continue as a district nurse after July. But Alison really shouldn't bother. I've quite made up my mind to quit nursing all together. I'm too old now to go back to school so I'll just have to find a different job.'

'But that's absurd. You're so good at what you do. I shall write to the authorities and make a special case.'

Alma blushed with pleasure. It was the first time he had openly acknowledged her contribution. She wasn't aware he ever noticed what she did.

'No, please don't do that! It's not that I don't appreciate your wanting to help, but I know in my heart of hearts that the ruling is something which has been needed for a long time. Until they are properly qualified, district nurses will never be given the status the job deserves.'

Iain folded the letter and thrust it from him, giving Alma his full attention.

'It's not just a case of visiting the old folks and seeing their beds are clean and they're getting enough to eat,' she explained. 'The district nurse ought to be someone who can offer well-informed advice. She is the first point of contact for the most vulnerable people. They come to rely on a familiar face and they accept what one says even if it's contrary to what the doctor has told them. I'm only too well aware that I don't have the necessary knowledge to be sure that my assessment of a situation is always for the best.'

'Nevertheless,' Iain protested, 'there's a wealth of practical common sense bottled up in that head of yours. I would hate to see it lost to the practice after all this time. You know everyone on the list and I've come to rely on your little hints about who's over-playing their symptoms and who might be hiding something which could help make a diagnosis.' He paused. Despite his protest, he could see she had made up her mind. Nothing he said now was going to shake her resolve.

'What had you thought of doing instead?'

'I wondered about the possibility of going back to Johnstone's. It's still a private nursing home so they may not be quite so particular about the qualifications of their staff.'

During two world wars the neighbouring estate had opened its doors to wounded servicemen but during the last few months, beds had been offered to local people requiring residential care. In July it was to become an old people's home, registered with the local authority.

'I don't know how the new rules will affect private organisations, if at all,' Iain said. 'They'll have to show that some at least of their nursing staff are properly qualified and that rather suggests that unqualified people won't be paid as much.'

He paused, rapidly trying to prepare his own proposition so that she didn't take it the wrong way. The idea had been growing in his mind ever since he had read Alison's letter. His mother would insist he engaged someone to help with the practice, if not a wife, then a secretary, receptionist, whatever you'd call it.

'Look,' he said, 'I have a suggestion to make. You know this practice intimately, far better than I do myself. Your knowledge of what happened during Dad's last years is absolutely invaluable to me. With all the paperwork I shall be handling once the new scheme is under way,

I'm going to need an assistant, someone to keep records and fill in the forms. Government schemes always mean loads of forms. I also need help with day to day jobs like answering the telephone and keeping the appointments book, all those things which help to make a practice run smoothly. Will you come and work for me?'

'I'm no secretary,' she reminded him, not wanting the job just because he felt sorry for her, 'but,' she added, hesitantly, 'I did learn to type some years ago, on an old machine of my auntie's.'

'I'm sure you would do an excellent job,' Iain insisted. 'You're well organised, Alma, and good with people. You have a remarkable ability to calm patients when they are overwrought. I've watched you in action.'

The more Iain thought about it, the more convinced he was that Alma was the ideal person to help him run the practice. 'You don't have to make your mind up immediately, of course. There's no reason why you should leave your present position until you're forced to go, but will you think seriously about it? I can't pay much to begin with but I understand there will be allowances for ancillary staff in the new system.'

He could see that the idea met with her approval. She seemed to glow with an inner excitement and her eyes sparkled as she replied.

'I can't think of anything I'd rather do, Iain, but...' she hesitated to air her greatest concern.

'What?'

'Will the Executive Medical Committee allow it? I don't have secretarial qualifications. Wouldn't it be the same problem as my being a district nurse?'

'If you are already in post and performing satisfactorily, I can't see how they could object. We'll get you a new typewriter and given enough practise, you'll soon become proficient. Come on Alma, what do you say?'

'I'd like the job very much,' was her reply, 'and I don't want to wait to be dismissed. I'll give in my notice just as soon as you like, I have to give them a month.'

'Then do it, right away,' Iain told her, delighted at her acceptance. The practice was hardly in a position to support a paid assistant, but he felt he might persuade Millicent to fork out sufficient cash, just to tide him over until July. A wedding would have cost them a great deal more!

43

CHRISTMAS 1947 HAD promised to mark a turning point in the fortunes of Mairi McFarlane and her children. In the event, it was no improvement upon the year before. Although Iain Beaton had examined Mairi and the boys for signs of TB and found nothing, he was obliged to send samples from the entire family to the Public Health Laboratories in Glasgow. Until she and her boys had been declared free from the disease, Mairi could not return to her work in the dairy, so, instead of splashing out at the festive season, money saved during her brief period of employment had to be put aside to tide her over until she could start earning again. There was no money to spare for Christmas treats. Had it not been for a generous gift of dairy produce sent down from Tigh na Broch and some second-hand toys provided by Alma Livingstone, it would have been a miserable time for the McFarlane household.

For Joan, confined to a hospital bed, the Christmas period was a bleak affair. In the absence of any kind of public transport from Eisdalsa during the public holidays, she had resigned herself to the fact that she would see nothing of Mairi until after the New Year. The nursing staff tried their best to make it a happy time for her but nothing could compensate for the absence of her mother.

Mairi McFarlane had been waiting at the bus stop since ten fifteen, a quarter of an hour before the bus was due. The wait would be worthwhile however, if some passing motorist were to stop and offer her a lift. She turned over the handful of coppers in her pocket, knowing exactly how much was there: ninepence. If she went both ways by bus it would cost her the whole amount, but for a single journey the fare was sixpence and she could spend the threepence saved on a cup of tea and a scone. More importantly, she would have an excuse to sit over it for at least half an hour in the café on the esplanade. Full of hope, she glanced along the road, praying for the appearance of a car or van she recognised.

She looked up at the church clock. Always five minutes slow, it now registered twenty-five past eleven. The bus should be here by this time. Resigned to paying the full fare, and spending two hours wandering in the rain, Mairi stared into the distance expecting to see it rounding the corner.

Standing with her back to the castle gateway, she did not notice the emergence of the estate's ex-Army Jeep until it had ploughed through the puddle at her feet, throwing up a shower of spray and soaking her stockings.

Mairi stared after the vehicle, emitting a flow of invective, which, until her recent experiences with Tam, she would never have been able to voice. Watching the red tail-lights disappearing into the gloom she inspected her soaked shoes and ruined stockings. She would have to spend the rest of the day with wet feet.

She was so engrossed in examining the damage to her footwear and trying to remove the mud from her coat, she didn't notice the Jeep returning until it drew to a halt, its front wheel resting in the offending puddle. She glanced up, prepared for a battle of words.

The driver's expression was one of genuine concern as he leaned out and asked, 'Did I soak you as I passed? I'm awfully sorry. I didn't see that puddle until it was too late.'

His friendly smile faded as he followed her glance and saw that the woman's shoes and stockings were wet through, and the hem of her coat, spattered with mud.

'Oh dear!' he exclaimed, 'I really am most terribly sorry!' Then, remembering where he had seen her before, he added, 'Mrs McFarlane isn't it?'

Mairi had only a hazy recollection of what had occurred on the night when Tam knocked her down and she had cut her head. She remembered Dr Beaton and Constable Christie being there and another man whom Joan had told her was the new factor at the castle.

'Were you waiting for the bus?' he asked. 'Only I just came across it, half a mile outside the village. It's broken down. I was on my way to telephone for a replacement vehicle, that's why I turned back.' He watched her angry expression turn to one of dismay when he added, 'I'm afraid it's going to be a while before they get the bus going, but I was planning to go into town myself this morning so if you don't mind riding in this old jalopy, I'll be happy to give you a lift.'

Her tightlipped expression relaxed suddenly and he saw her smile for the first time.

'Well…' she replied hesitantly. She would not normally accept a ride from a complete stranger, but she was desperate to get to Oban.

'Why don't you hop in, and I'll just run up to the lodge and make the call. I have to pick up a package from the Lunga ferry first, but after that we can go straight into town.'

Not merely a stranger, by his accent, he wasn't even a Scot. Even so, Joan had told her how kind the factor had been on that terrible night and after all, His Lordship had seen fit to engage him, Englishman or not. She supposed he must be all right.

While she stood there silent, rehearsing these unspoken doubts, he introduced himself.

'Peter Parker's my name,' he told her, 'We weren't introduced last time we met.'

He jumped down into the road and took her basket.

'Let me help you up,' he suggested placing his hand beneath her elbow. 'It's a bit higher off the ground than a normal vehicle. I work for the Marquis,' he continued chatting as she settled herself. 'Estate Manager they call me, a rather grand name for what is in reality a general dogsbody. I haven't been at the lodge for very long and I've not had much time to get to know my neighbours.'

'This is very good of you,' Mairi said at last, perching precariously on the rather uncomfortable passenger seat. 'I'm Mairi McFarlane.' She gave an embarrassed giggle. 'But of course, you already know that.'

She paused, wondering whether she should try to make further conversation. 'I never thanked you for helping out that night. Joan, my little girl, told me how kind you were.'

Peter placed her basket at the rear and took his seat behind the wheel.

'How is your head?' he asked. 'All healed up?'

'Long ago.'

The smile she turned upon him was fleeting but he found it electrifying.

'I heard about your husband,' he said soberly as it faded. 'I'm so sorry.'

'It couldn't be helped.' Her voice was flat, betraying no emotion. 'It might have been better had he never come back at all.'

She was silent for a moment, then, with some vehemence she added, 'Those Japs have a lot to answer for!'

He drew up outside the castle gate and jumped down.

As she sat there, perched on the high seat of the vehicle, Mairi noticed net curtains twitch at the windows of more than one of the cottages and felt her neighbours' eyes on her. Well, she didn't care what they thought.

She was getting the lift she needed and her trip promised to be far more interesting than she could possibly have imagined.

Peter Parker re-emerged minutes later, jumped in and started the engine. With a shudder and a deal of rattling, they took off, once again ploughing recklessly through the offending puddle. The canvas top to the vehicle flapped as they gathered speed and the Perspex side screen, which had become warped with use, let in rather more air than Mairi might have wished. However, her feet were drying in the hot air coming up from the engine and she felt herself enveloped in a cocoon of cheerfulness such as she had not experienced in a very long time.

They slowed to pass the broken down bus and Peter Parker called out assurances to the driver that help was on its way. The driver waved in acknowledgement and returned to his newspaper. His passengers sat with their noses pressed to the window, awaiting the arrival of the replacement vehicle, which was unlikely to be there in less than an hour. Mairi was so pleased she would not have to wait with them.

'Have you lived in Castle Row for long?' Peter asked, as they drew away, beginning the steep ascent from the village.

'Since I was married,' she said, making a rapid calculation. 'It must be about thirteen years. My husband was a quarry worker, you see, and the houses are tied to the job. I don't know how long I'll be able to stay there now...'

She bit off her words without completing the sentence. Why on earth should she immediately open her heart to this complete stranger? Even Alma had not been invited to share this, her deepest worry. Ever since Tam's funeral she had been expecting notice to quit.

'The cottages are owned by the Stirling Estates?'

She nodded forlornly.

'Well, I'm not aware of any quarrymen requiring accommodation for the time being, so I see no reason why you should be asked to leave. In any case, if you have to vacate in the future, we'll be obliged to find you alternative accommodation.'

He should know, of course. Wasn't he the factor? It would be up to him to decide if she stayed on in the house.

'I thought the place would be needed by another family,' she said, with relief, then added, 'Mind you, there's no' many would want to live in such an unhealthy cottage!'

She found herself telling him about Joan having contracted TB and how the doctor thought her illness might be due to the house they were living in.

'That's why I'm going into Oban now, to visit Joan. She's in the chest hospital.'

'Oh dear, I'm so sorry. She's such a bright little girl. I did so admire the way she handled things that night; kept her head when others might have panicked. How long will she be in hospital do you think?'

'It could be months.'

'Can't they give her penicillin?' he asked, glancing across at Mairi and noticing how her brow had clouded at the mention of her daughter.

'I don't know *what* they are treating her with,' she replied bleakly. 'They've got her outside on a balcony, supposedly to let the fresh air blow away her infection. Otherwise they don't seem to be doing much for her. Of course, she'll be getting better food than I can afford to give her, plenty of milk and so on, but all that does is make her fat. I have never seen such a collection of sick people looking so rosy-cheeked and bloated as that lot up there on the hill.'

'That used to be the treatment, I know.' Peter had had friends in the forces who contracted tuberculosis, 'But when the Yanks came over in '43, they brought with them this new miracle drug called penicillin, a cure-all for bacterial infections. It's speeded up the recovery time amazingly. You should ask the doctors to give it to your girl.'

'I can see you've not had much experience of hospitals,' she said, observing his robust figure and healthy complexion. 'Doctors don't ask relatives what drugs they should use. They don't even tell you what treatment they're giving and they certainly wouldn't thank me for telling them to use some new-fangled cure-all.'

She'd had a bad time, he could see that. Yet she still had a bit of fight left in her. Peter felt strangely attracted to this woman, despite her mousey hair and shiny country girl's complexion. Her wide-set, brown eyes sparkled now with anger and frustration.

'As for my knowledge of what goes on inside hospitals; I've had my share,' he told her.

The rain was coming down more heavily now and he stared ahead through the streaming windscreen. Against the background of noise from the vehicle, she was obliged to look closely at him watching his lips move, half hearing, half reading what they said.

'My wife was injured in the bombing. Doodle bug it was.'

Mairi had heard about those flying bombs. She could only imagine the terror such weapons must have caused.

'They gave me compassionate leave,' he went on, 'sent me home from the Ardennes. She had been in a coma for more than a week before I got there and she never opened her eyes again. They were feeding her through a tube, simply keeping her alive. I begged them to take away the gadgets and let her die in peace but they kept on hoping she would come out of it. I knew it was no good. In the end they had to do as I said and let her go, but it should never have been such a struggle. Patients and their families ought to have more say in what happens to them and their loved ones. That's why this new Health Service is going to make all the difference. If your little girl is still in hospital when the changeover comes in July, you'll be able to go along there and demand penicillin. That's what I would do!'

Mairi suspected that he was exaggerating the power to be given to the public in the new scheme of things, but she enjoyed listening to him talking. She admired his wide experience and the positive view he took of everything.

They drew up to the curb in front of McCorquadale's Coffee Parlour and she alighted with as much dignity as the utilitarian vehicle would allow.

'I've a number of people to see in town,' he told her. 'It'll probably take me most of the afternoon. What time does visiting end?'

'I always leave dead on four o'clock, so as to catch the bus down here at half past,' she said.

'If you wouldn't mind waiting for a few minutes, I can promise to be at the gates to the hospital by four fifteen.'

'Och, you'll no' be wanting to go so far out of your way,' she protested. 'It's a long way up there by the road. I can take the path straight down, by the steps.'

She pointed out a well-defined route, upwards between the terraces of houses which covered the hillside above the town.

He glanced at the grey, forbidding sky. The rain had stopped but there was no break in the clouds.

'It'll like as not be raining again by then,' he told her. 'Look out for me. I'll be at the gate.'

Without waiting for her further protest, he let in the gear, made a signal to the oncoming vehicles and pulled out into a steady stream of traffic snaking its way sedately along the seafront.

44

DESPITE THE PRESENT setback, Alma was pleased to see that Mairi continued to manage her house, her family and herself in the way she had adopted since she began work at Tigh na Broch. The incentive for retaining her new found self-assurance must belong in part, to the continued attentions of Peter Parker. Following their first chance encounter, scarcely a Wednesday or a Saturday morning went by when he was not there to pick Mairi up as she waited at the bus stop. On these days, it seemed he could always find pressing business to attend to in town, activity which kept him there until soon after four o'clock, when Mairi would find him waiting for her at the hospital gates.

For her part, Mairi began paying greater attention to her appearance. The village hairdresser cut and styled her dark hair regularly in exchange for washing the mountain of towels that that lady managed to get through in the course of a week. At the back of a drawer, Mairi had come across a box of face powder and the remains of an old lipstick. Both were applied to such great effect that when she visited the hospital on the very next occasion, Joan remarked on her improved looks.

'Oh, you do look nice!' she exclaimed when she saw her mother approaching from the far end of the ward. 'What have you done to yourself?'

'Seeing all these other mothers looking so smart, I thought I should make more of an effort,' Mairi exclaimed, blushing a little at the subterfuge. How could she confess to her own daughter that she was enjoying the attentions of a very personable gentleman?

To avoid further questioning, she opened the parcel she had brought with her to display a bed-jacket created out of an outmoded evening gown Millicent had given her for the purpose. The rose-coloured silk had been neatly quilted and made into a short jacket, which tied at the neck with a velvet bow. Although always a good needlewoman, it had been a long time since Mairi had attempted quite such an ambitious project.

Joan, who had never possessed anything so exquisite, squealed with delight and struggled to sit up so that she might try on the delightful garment. The effort made her cough so hard that Mairi feared she would choke.

'Here, drink this,' she begged the child, holding a glass of water to her lips. 'They'll throw me out if you carry on like that!'

Joan held a handkerchief to her lips, trying to stifle the coughs. When she withdrew it, Mairi was alarmed to see flecks of blood in the sputum.

'How long has that been going on?' she demanded. No one had told her that Joan was coughing up blood.

'Oh, that's nothing,' the girl said, casually. 'Lots of people do it. It happens all the time.'

'Oh, does it?'

Agitated by the distressing condition of her daughter and encouraged by the words of her new friend, Mairi felt brave enough to challenge Sister when she came along, smiling and nodding to the visitors as she moved from bed to bed.

'Why did no one tell me Joan was coughing up blood?' she demanded. 'She is getting no better lying here. What are you doing for her other than feeding her up and giving her a bed in the open air?'

'That's the treatment Doctor ordered, dear,' said the woman patronisingly. 'I'm afraid there's nothing more that we can do for her.'

'But there are drugs that can cure her. I know there are. My friends tell me so.'

'And did your friends also tell you how much they cost?' Sister enquired. 'It's not as if your Joan were a paying patient.'

'If there're drugs will cure my little girl, I want you to use them,' cried Mairi, indignantly. 'And if they cost more than the hospital can afford, I'll find the money myself, somehow!'

The nurse, visibly shaken by Mairi's angry outburst, hesitated for a moment before saying stiffly, 'I'll tell Doctor. Maybe something can be arranged!' Then, tossing her head, she stalked away.

While she was unable to work in the dairy until pronounced free of tuberculosis herself, Mairi had hoped to be employed at Tigh na Broch in some alternative capacity. When consulted upon the matter however, the Ministry vet had been quite adamant. With Millicent's herd soon to undergo testing for tuberculosis, even the slightest risk of infecting the cattle must be avoided at all costs.

The time was fast approaching when all dairy cows would have to be guaranteed free of the disease. At present, the rule was that although testing was not yet compulsory, a herd tested and found positive for the tuberculin bacillus was to be slaughtered. For the time being, Mairi must find some alternative means of earning a living. In such a small village and with her young family to be considered, it was not easy for her to obtain suitable employment. The boys were unable to return to school until they had been given the all clear by the Public Health authorities and so, apart from her twice-weekly visits to the hospital, Mairi found herself confined to her home. Having completed all those little jobs around the house which had remained unattended in previous months, she applied herself to making-over some of her husband's clothes in order to provide new school outfits for the boys. Long-neglected skills with the needle now came to the fore and Alma, popping in after one of her visits to the old lady at the end of the row, was astonished to see Malcolm standing impatiently upon a low stool while his mother, her mouth full of pins, hovered around him, making deft alterations to the fall of the half-completed jacket he was wearing.

'I didn't know you were a tailor,' exclaimed the district nurse, admiring the professional manner in which Mairi tackled the job.

'I learnt it from the seamstress in one of the houses where I worked before I was married,' Mairi told her.

'How did you get such a good fit? Did you have a pattern?'

'I drafted my own.' Mairi saw nothing remarkable in this. She had never been able to afford to buy paper patterns.

'I never met anyone who could do that! Have you ever thought of making clothes for other people?' Alma saw the possibilities at once. 'There must be plenty of people around here who would welcome the services of a decent dressmaker.'

'I don't have an up-to-date sewing machine so I never thought about making things for a living,' Mairi confessed. 'I've only got an old treadle machine which was my mother's. Nowadays people use electric ones with all manner of gadgets.'

'I can't see anything wrong with that stitching,' Alma declared, examining the work closely.

'Can I get down now?' demanded Malcolm, fidgeting on the stool and likely to overturn it.

'Oh aye, ye wee monster,' said his mother, releasing him hurriedly from the half completed jacket. Then, tapping him lightly on the buttocks, she cried, 'Away wi' you and play.'

The child scurried off to join his brother in the yard. It was a cold day, but dry. With the threat of disease hanging over them still, Mairi was determined the boys should be out in the fresh air as much as possible.

'I'll tell you what,' Alma said, warming to her idea, 'You could make me a dress and see how it goes. I have a length of material I've been saving for a rainy day. I could do with something new for best. If it goes well, I can put the word about for you.'

'I'll happily make *you* a dress,' said Mairi, grateful for the opportunity to do something in return for all Alma's kindnesses to her. 'But I'll no' charge you a penny for sewing it.'

'Och, we'll see about that when the time comes.' Alma was going to insist on paying for the work once the dress was finished. She took off her coat, determined to get Mairi started at once on this new project.

'I've a few minutes to spare just now. Why don't you take my measurements and you can be drafting the pattern while I go and fetch the material?'

45

'THEY'RE ON THEIR way home! Stephen says they managed to get a berth on a cargo vessel sailing on December 15th.' Annie paused, reading the next few sentences in silence.

Stuart looked up quickly from his copy of yesterday's *Herald*. Until now, he had been listening with only half an ear to his wife's commentary. He much preferred to read Stephen's letters himself but she loved to tell him the best bits as she came to them. Her bleak expression told him that this was bad news.

'What is it?' he demanded.

'Ellen won't be coming with him.'

'What? Why not? What's happened?'

'Her mother is dying of cancer of the liver. Ellen has stayed behind to help her father through the final weeks.'

Annie's eyes filled with tears. She had been so delighted to hear they were on their way. Stephen didn't even mention the baby in his letter. A delay of even a month would mean that Ellen would have to remain in Australia until after the birth. Annie realised she was being selfish, but all she could think of at the moment was her own disappointment at not being present at the birth of her grandchild.

'It seems that it was a last-minute decision on Ellen's part,' said Stuart, taking up the letter and continuing the narrative where his wife had left off. 'They had actually boarded the ship at Freemantle when news came through that Jeanie was dying. Stephen has this interview in Glasgow at the end of February so he couldn't stay behind with her.'

'But she is coming back later?'

'Not until after...' He thought fondly of the tough, wiry little woman from Kent who had met and married Jack McDougal before the Great

War. 'From what Steve says, Jeanie can't have very long to live.'

'But what about the baby?'

'Ellen couldn't sail in her ninth month. The steamer company would never allow it. I'm afraid we'll have to wait a while to see the wee one.'

'Poor Stevie, he must be heartbroken having to come home alone and not to be with Ellen when the baby comes.'

'It happens to lots of people,' Stuart told her gently. There was no need to remind her that it was precisely what had happened to him, when Stephen was born. Then it had been in even worse circumstances. Annie had been told her husband was lost at sea.

'But that was war time,' she insisted. 'Those two children shouldn't have to be separated now. Poor Ellen, to have to go through it all, alone!'

'They're hardly children, dear, and I'm quite sure that Jack will see Ellen has the best care and attention when the time comes.'

He had gone on to Stephen's second page, which he found even more disturbing.

Just before we left Kerrera Station, I had the opportunity to spend a few days down in Adelaide at the invitation of a friend of Archie McIndoe's, Bernard Isleworth, who is the Surgical Director of the South Australia State Hospital. The Adelaide Royal is in the process of extending its facilities and in particular they're setting up a brand new burns unit which is all but completed. It was astonishing to see so many of McIndoe's innovations already installed, not the Heath Robinson devices we put in for ourselves at East Grinstead but purpose-built equipment. It's a Rolls Royce of a set up. I would have given my eye teeth to work in a place like that. I'll just have to hope that Glasgow Infirmary has something similar in mind.

Stuart looked up at Annie. Anxious not to distress her further, he made light of Stephen's comments. 'It seems not everything stopped for the war in Australia. From what Steve says they have gone ahead by leaps and bounds with their hospital building programme.'

He handed the letter back so that she might read the remainder for herself, and hoping she would not read into it what he had. If Stephen failed to get the appointment he wanted at Glasgow University, he might well be tempted to return to Australia.

46

THE WAITING ROOM was full. Iain glanced at his watch. Eleven already and he'd had two urgent requests for home visits even before surgery began that morning. He turned his attention to Mrs Ireton who sat on the edge of her chair, tense, anxious, clearly expecting him to tell her the worst.

She had tried to ignore the dragging pain which had begun to accompany her monthly periods. For a long time she had explained away the extraordinary amount of bleeding to her own satisfaction, concealing from her husband the fact that there had been little respite from her trouble between one period and the next. However, neither he, nor their daughter Isobel, could avoid noticing her extraordinary pallor and increasing lethargy as she dragged herself around the house in an attempt to appear her normal, active self. If they had not immediately been struck by her altered appearance, they could hardly miss the untidy, not to say dirty, condition of a house which had once glowed with unceasing dusting and polishing, nor could they avoid noticing that Helen no longer took any interest in what she wore.

Isobel Ireton occupied the second chair. The look of determination with which she had followed her mother into the surgery, despite that lady's protests that she wanted to see the doctor alone, had now given place to undisguised terror that what she had imagined was wrong with Helen was about to be confirmed.

'Well, Mrs Ireton,' Iain cleared his throat before delivering his diagnosis. The telephone on his desk began to ring.

Annoyed by the interruption, he nevertheless lifted the receiver.

'Surgery.'

'Iain?' It was Alma's voice.

'Who else?' He lifted his eyebrows in a vain attempt to relieve the tension in the room.

'Sorry to disturb you. Are you with a patient?'

'Yes.'

'I'll be as quick as I can. There's a family in Back Street on Eisdalsa Island, the Fergussons, mother, father and two infants of two and three years, all complaining of diarrhoea and sickness. The trouble is severe in the little ones. I think you should see them as soon as possible. They say they rang you earlier on and were wondering if you had been delayed.'

She did not care to relate Mr Fergusson's actual words: 'I don't know what the world's coming to. Dr Hugh would never have kept us waiting this long!' he had declared.

'I'm snowed under at the moment,' Iain said. 'The waiting room's full and I have two other calls awaiting my attention. Do they have any kaolin mixture in the house?'

'No nothing.'

'Damn. I've plenty here, but there's no chance of getting it to them before noon at the earliest.'

'I could come over and pick it up if you can get it ready.'

'Will you? That would be a great help. Meanwhile, get them to drink plenty of boiled water, particularly the babies. They can dehydrate very quickly. I'll prepare a couple of mixtures, one for the adults and one for the children.' He hesitated for a moment. 'You're sure there's no fever?'

'Vomiting and diarrhoea, that's all,' she assured him.

'Sounds like food poisoning. We'll need to look into that later. Try to get them to recall what they've been eating. It shouldn't be too difficult if it's something the babies had too.'

'I'll see you in about twenty minutes,' she replied.

'I'll be ready.' He put down the receiver and turned his attention to his patient.

'There's little doubt in my mind, Mrs Ireton, that this is something quite minor. However, I'd like a second opinion, just to be sure. I'll make an appointment for you to see Mr Kmiecik at the West Highland Hospital. There's every chance that all you'll require is what we call a D&C, a scraping of the womb to remove extraneous tissue. It's a minor procedure; you'll be in and out in a couple of days.'

'And what if it's not as simple as that?' demanded the daughter. 'What if it's something much worse? Will she need a hysterectomy?'

Iain glanced at Helen Ireton, sensing her fear.

'I think we should try to cross one bridge at a time, Miss Ireton, don't you?' he replied, putting the younger woman firmly in her place. Here was one of the new generation of partially-informed laymen, pressing for more information than he was able to give. There was indeed, every possibility Mrs Ireton required a hysterectomy, a procedure which carried with it the certainty of a long and painful period of recovery. 'Mr Kmiecik will decide what is necessary in your mother's case.'

He made a note to call Kmiecik, and ushered the two women to the door.

'If you will call in to the surgery when your appointment comes through, Mrs Ireton,' Iain said, 'I'll give you a letter to take to the specialist.'

When he popped his head around the door of the waiting room, half an hour and several patients later, Iain was surprised to find that the number of people had dropped considerably. Alma Livingstone, who had been chatting animatedly with two of the ladies, looked up expectantly.

'Ah, Nurse, will you come through to the dispensary,' Iain grinned, relieved to have a moment's break from the never-ending stream of stuffy noses, chesty coughs and cold sores which seemed to be the major reason for the extra-large number of patients this morning. He had forgotten how much he loathed February, the wettest, windiest and gloomiest month of the year in Eisdalsa!

'I thought there were more people waiting,' he observed as he opened the dispensary door and selected a number of items from the array of bottles arranged neatly above the marble work bench.

'I had a talk with one or two people and found their problems weren't all that urgent,' she told him. 'I suggested they might come back later in the week when you weren't so busy. I hope you don't mind.'

'That was very good of you, Alma,' he said as she closed the door behind her. 'I'm sorry I haven't had a chance to get this ready for you.'

'Oh, that's all right,' she assured him. 'I'm only too glad of a chance to sit down for a moment.'

She perched on the high laboratory stool beside him and watched as he carefully measured ingredients into a tall glass jar.

'I don't expect to be doing this kind of thing for much longer,' Iain told her. 'Once medicines are on prescription, free of charge, there'll be standard packaging and labelling of most things. The basic dispensing of pills and mixtures by GPs will be a thing of the past.'

'What will Mrs McColl do when she can no longer demand her special pink bottle, I wonder?' laughed Alma.

It had been one of the first services she had performed for him on his arrival, revealing the secret of Mrs McColl's bottle. The woman suffered from chronic dyspepsia brought on, according to Hugh Beaton, by over-indulgence in shellfish. After trying a number of proprietary brands of stomach powders and anti-acid solutions, he had turned to an ancient recipe of his father's, sodium bromide, bismuth and liquid chloroform coloured with a touch of cochineal to make it pink. Mrs McColl swore that the concoction did wonders for her condition and reappeared regularly demanding further supplies. On one occasion, when Hugh had forgotten to add the cochineal, she returned the bottle next day, declaring the *white stuff* was not a patch on what she had had before. Hugh had taken back the bottle, topped it up with water, added a dash of pink and handed it back. She went away quite satisfied, never to complain again!

Iain agitated his mixture of kaolin, to which he had added a little liquid chloroform, then transferred it to the medicine bottle. He looked up to see Alma smiling at him.

'What?' he demanded.

'I just enjoy watching you work,' she answered. 'You always seem so focused on what you're doing. Are you aware that you draw your lips over your teeth and stick out the tip of your tongue when you're concentrating?'

'My mother used to tell me off about it when I was little,' he confessed, watching her instead of looking at what he was doing.

'Oh, damn!' he exclaimed, as a portion of the mixture overflowed onto the worktop.

'Sorry, my fault,' she apologised, reaching across him for a cloth to mop up the mess.

Carefully placing the bottle out of harm's way, Iain removed the rag from her grasp.

'I'm beginning to wonder what I would do without you, Alma Livingstone,' he murmured. 'Promise me you won't go off and leave me here to cope on my own.'

'Why should I do that?' she asked. 'Haven't I given in my notice to the Council just so as I can be here to help you all the time?'

'I just thought, well, you're a smart woman. Anyone would be pleased to give you a job. You might be offered something better paid than a doctor's receptionist.'

'Who says I want to be anything other than a doctor's receptionist,' she argued, 'so long as you're the doctor.'

Was she playing with him? Was this yet another of those feminine games?

'Meaning?' he asked.

'Meaning that I have come to enjoy working alongside you, Dr Beaton, and I would be happy to spend the rest of my life doing just that. I don't care if it's as nurse, receptionist or parlour maid.'

His heart turned a somersault. While he had been wasting his time, dreaming of what might have been had Alison not turned him down, Alma had been shielding him from the demands of the more inconsiderate patients and guiding his hand through the labyrinth of general practice. He studied her face intently, realising for the first time the smouldering depths in her extraordinary, gypsy eyes. He stroked the silky skin of her milk-white throat and brushed those delightfully sculptured cheekbones with his lips, making them glow rather more fiercely than Alma might have wished.

She could hardly believe she'd been so outspoken. 'I'm sorry,' she broke the lengthy silence with a shy apology. 'I shouldn't have said that.'

'Why not, if it's true?'

He kissed her properly then, a warm lingering exploration of her lips and then a deeper, more forceful penetration in which he thrilled to the touch of her tongue on his own. It was Alma who broke away.

'I can't breathe!' she exclaimed. 'And besides, you have patients waiting. Here, let me do that!'

She grabbed the bottle, wiped off the surplus where he had spilled the contents and gave him the label to write out.

'Who's this for, the adults?'

Quickly regaining his composure, Iain nodded, picked up the measuring cylinder and began to prepare a weaker mixture for the children.

'Tell them I'll call in later today to see how they are progressing,' he said. 'If it is a mild food poisoning, they should all be feeling better in a few hours. Did you ask them about the source of the infection?'

'I tried to make sense of what Mrs Fergusson was telling me but she was obviously feeling very unwell. I didn't press it.'

'Never mind, I'll try to track down the offending foodstuff for myself. Let me know if you hear of anyone else complaining of similar symptoms. A lot of people consider sickness and diarrhoea something they can deal with themselves. Not everyone bothers to report it.'

'I'll keep my ears open.' she said, with just the hint of a smile.

She picked up the two bottles, both now neatly labelled, and prepared to leave.

'Alma' he called to her as he busied himself returning bottles and jars to the shelves.

'Yes?'

'I'm so glad you're staying.'

'Yes. Well, I'd best be getting along.'

Wearing an enigmatic smile, which completely transformed his normally serious expression, Iain poked his head around the waiting room door.

'Next patient please!'

47

STEPHEN BEATON WAS early for his appointment, so rather than take a taxi, he had decided to approach the university by way of Kelvin Park. The air was clear and cold but even so there were signs that winter would soon be past. The bare branches of the weeping willows had already changed to that rich brown colour which precedes the catkins. On the riverbank, snowdrops and crocus crowded beneath leafless alders. The volume and variety of the spring chorus startled him. These were the first birds he had come across since disembarking at Southampton, and he was surprised how sweetly their song contrasted with that raucous cacophony produced by a flock of parakeets or a lone kookaburra.

Crossing the stream by a little wooden bridge, he mounted the zig-zag path to the plateau above, entering the university building by way of its nineteenth-century Gothic cloisters.

Struck by the extreme youthfulness of the students gathered beneath those shadowy walls, he wondered how they would regard someone like himself. No doubt they would see him as an old fogey, as he had once labelled *his* professors. As though in answer to his question, despite the fact that he wore no academic gown, one small group stepped respectfully out of his way, making Stephen feel very old indeed.

Well, a gown might be mandatory, but that didn't mean he had to sport the pin-stripe trousers and black jackets worn by those earlier academics. The day of the uniform, military or otherwise was now past.

Here and there, he spotted older men looking strangely out of place in their undergraduate gowns. One or two seemed to be nearer to his own age. Remembering that many of the pilots and air crew he had come across had interrupted their studies to go and fight, he supposed these men to be resuming their education where they had left off in 1939. He could imagine them being the keenest of students, intent on making the most of this second chance.

The committee room to which Stephen had been directed was situated in an unfamiliar part of the building. Feeling like a stranger in his own home, he was obliged to make enquiries as to how to get there.

'Och aye,' said the porter, appreciating Stephen's confusion. 'The Medical Appointments Board, is it? They'll nae doubt be wantin' to avoid a' the dust and noise down at the Infirmary.'

'Building work?' enquired Stephen envisaging some splendid new extension. The new school of anaplastics, perhaps.

'War damage repairs,' explained the fellow, 'though to my mind, it's a new hospital entirely that's needing built.'

'Maybe that will happen soon, with the new Health Service.'

'Och, dinna expect too much frae all that talk, Doctor. There'll never be enough money for all the work this old hospital needs doing.'

Such was the scepticism of the ordinary man in the street, thought Stephen. 'I'll believe it when I see it,' was the general impression he had garnered from every quarter, as he had made his way north from Southampton. In its newspapers, radio and general conversation, the nation appeared to view the National Health Service proposals with a wry humour. It would be a good thing if it ever happened, but wasn't it all pie in the sky?

Even if the general public welcomed the idea, according to the *Lancet* the medical profession was largely opposed. Amongst the politicians, there appeared to be little respect for those responsible for the scheme. He recalled some of the headlines he had seen: CHURCHILL DESCRIBES MR BEVAN AS 'THAT SQUALID NUISANCE'; LORD MORAN HITS OUT AGAINST PROPOSALS FOR VOLUNTARY HOSPITALS and RICHARD LAW WARNS, HEALTH SERVICE PROPOSALS LIKELY TO INCREASE MATERNAL MORTALITY IN CHILDBIRTH.

This last was sheer scaremongering of the worst kind. Any sensible person must realise that the exact opposite had to be the outcome. Extensive improvements to pre- and post-natal care were outlined in the plan, not to mention better maternity units throughout the country.

On a more positive note Stephen had read, 'Junior doctors support the new Health Service.' It seemed that the medical students had formed themselves into a political group, the Association of Medical Students and Junior Doctors and, for the first time, there was a voice speaking on behalf of the rank and file in the profession.

Stephen was inclined to agree with the porter. It could be a while before they saw any tangible differences, like new buildings and better equipment. The money for the health service had to come from somewhere so those whose earnings were great enough would contribute through their taxes. The difference now was that everyone would be entitled to the treatment they needed, whether or not they were able to pay.

'Mr Beaton?'

The receptionist broke into his deliberations, quite startling him.

'Yes?'

'You may go in now.'

The woman returned immediately to her typing and Stephen stood up, straightened his tie for the umpteenth time, and ran a finger around inside his too tight collar.

His holiday in Australia had not only improved his tan and filled his hollow cheeks. He had put on several inches in certain places. Helping out on the farm had thickened his biceps and broadened his shoulders to such a degree that this morning he had struggled to get into the demob suit which had hung on him like a sack a few months earlier.

He entered the heavily panelled Board Room to be confronted by an unexpectedly large number of people arranged along one side of an immense table. The only vacant seat was placed facing them.

With a polite nod and a cheerful, 'Good morning gentlemen,' he took the empty chair.

He was disconcerted to find that the Chairman was an old adversary of his student days, Sir Harold Digby Smythe, now retired but at one time the Medical Superintendent of the Infirmary.

Stephen cast a smile in the direction of the one friendly face, that of Professor Dowson, his old mentor, but he searched in vain for any others that he knew. Six years was a long time to have been absent from the scene. The older men who had taught him, those who had held things together here while the younger doctors went away to war, had now departed and their places had been taken by ex-servicemen.

As he read the name plates displayed in front of each of the Board members, Stephen thought it strange that a well qualified man should choose to cling on to his naval rank. SURGEON COMMANDER MCCLUSKEY appeared somewhat out of place in this setting. It seemed that MAJOR BICKERSTAFF, too, found it impossible to discard his obviously much valued rank. The armed services had provided a man with a certain sense of security; you knew where you stood in the pecking order, as it were. Could it be that these chaps actually felt insecure in Civvy Street?

'Now then, Wing Commander Beaton…' It obviously pained Stephen's old adversary to use such a distinguished title for a former pupil, and a maverick at that!

'Plain Mister will serve just as well,' Stephen assured him politely. 'I was demobilised nearly six months ago.'

He had not intended to imply any criticism of either the Major or the Surgeon Commander, but they both shuffled uncomfortably in their chairs and the Commander turned a rather deeper shade of puce.

'Very well, *Mr* Beaton, if my colleagues will allow me, I shall kick off with a few questions of my own.'

Sir Harold glared at those seated alongside him as though daring any of them to oppose him. Meeting no opposition, he continued. 'We have in front of us a very impressive list of your achievements while serving under Mr Archibald McIndoe at the Queen Victoria Hospital in East Grinstead. A unique and most rewarding experience I am sure, but was it not a trifle limited?'

In writing his application, Stephen had assumed that these gentlemen would be interested in what he knew about plastic surgery. That was, after all, what the job was supposed to be about.

'I'm sorry, Sir. I don't quite understand the question.'

'It's simple enough my dear fellow. At first sight it would seem you have a very narrow field of experience. Was that all you did during your time in the RAF? Tidying up the damage to a few mutilated pilots so that their wives and girlfriends would find them more presentable?'

Sir Harold was well known for his sarcastic wit. Stephen should not therefore have been surprised by this shallow interpretation of what had been achieved at East Grinstead. The insult was, however, directed not merely at himself but at the man whom he venerated above all others. He rose to the bait.

'To describe Mr McIndoe's achievements in terms of simple cosmetic surgery is to misunderstand completely the achievements of the unit at East Grinstead,' Stephen replied coldly. 'These men were not merely disfigured by scorching. Many had lost flesh and even bone, from extensive areas of their bodies. In other times and in the hands of a less skilful surgeon, many would have died. There is a deal of difference between effecting an improvement on otherwise healthy tissue and the work we were carrying out. Where do you obtain grafts and to what do you stitch them, when more than two-thirds of the body's surface has been destroyed? In order to reconstruct these men, McIndoe had to devise unique methods of treatment, inventing special instruments, even having to redesign the beds and the plumbing, in order to enable us to work while giving the least pain and discomfort to our patients. The surgery was painstaking, laborious and often deeply distressing. We could not heal the bodies if the minds were not wholly in accord with our objectives, but by working together with the full cooperation of our patients, we were able to reconstruct lives which would have been written off ten years earlier. We returned many of those highly trained and very valuable young men to the battle.'

Here Stephen broke off his tirade, overcome by the memory of those brave, often foolhardy, young men who, after agonising months of repeated surgery, could not wait to climb back into the cockpit of an aeroplane.

In an attempt to allow Stephen time to compose himself Professor Dowson entered the discussion. 'I would point out to the Board,' he said quietly, 'that Mr Beaton joined the RAF at the outbreak of war, having already completed the first year of his residency at this hospital. He was primarily assigned to general medical duties and no doubt attained, at that time, a far wider experience than his application suggests. If there is some concern that his later experience was within a limited field, perhaps we should ask him to describe the work he did prior to his attachment to the Queen Victoria Burns Unit.'

Grateful to his mentor for this intervention, Stephen now launched into an account of the surgical work accomplished on the air base at Manston and at the Margate Cottage Hospital, which the RAF had shared with the civilian population of the town. He described the emergency work he had carried out during countless air raids on the base and the work done with the WAAF personnel employed there. It was a formidable list of operations, one which left Sir Harold Digby Smythe looking rather small. Stephen's victory was a hollow one, however, for it was made at the expense of any last shred of goodwill that might have existed between himself and the Chairman.

A wizened old gentleman seated to Stephen's right chose this moment to lean forward and demand in a wavering voice, 'Beaton? There was a young RAF surgeon of that name who organised our students to go out and deal with casualties during the bombing of the Clydeside in '43. Was that you, young man?'

Dowson, grinning, nodded his head vigorously while Digby Smythe glowered thunderously beneath lowered brows. Stephen knew how Digby Smythe must hate to be reminded of the incident. The nice old gentleman had done him no favours in mentioning it.

On the night of February 15th 1943, Glasgow experienced a devastating aerial bombardment which destroyed much of the Clydeside's residential area. Stephen, enjoying a rare spell of leave from his RAF duties, had taken a team of medical students out to the first-aid stations, thereby saving a great many lives. Unfortunately his intervention had been in direct contravention of Digby Smythe's orders.

The newspapers had made a story of epic proportions out of the incident and although Digby Smythe, as Medical Superintendent, had been credited with the decision to send the students to the rescue, he had never forgiven Stephen his insubordination.

At the far left-hand end of the table, sat a figure Stephen found vaguely familiar. While remaining quiet throughout the discussion so far, he had nevertheless listened intently to Stephen's answers, taking careful note of all he said. To cut short the unwanted discussion of Stephen's exploits in the Glasgow blitz, Digby Smythe decided to introduce the stranger to the regular Board members.

'Gentlemen, I have the great honour to introduce to the Board Mr Malcolm Fraser of the Medical Faculty of the Midwest. Although a Scot by birth, Mr Fraser is a figure of international reputation in the field of plastic surgery. For a number of years he has carried the banner of Scottish medical science across the sea to our brothers in arms in America. It is a great privilege to welcome him here today and to have the benefit of his immense experience in selecting the right man to head our new School of Anaplastics.'

Malcolm Fraser was the archetypal successful medical man. His carefully contrived casual hair style was undoubtedly the work of one of Glasgow's more exclusive barbers. The jet black, waving tresses, with their distinguished streaks of silver-grey at the temples, contrasted sharply with the short-back-and-sides style of the others around the table and appeared to have been designed to inspire confidence in the most distressed and bemused of patients. His impeccable, hand-sewn three piece suit, in fashionable charcoal grey, disguised an abdomen which gave more than a hint of transatlantic overindulgence and was undoubtedly the work of some expensive cutting room in Savile Row. An Italian silk tie and matching kerchief, drooping with studied nonchalance from his breast pocket, provided an exotic splash of colour in the otherwise plain ensemble.

From the moment he had set eyes on him, Stephen had the impression that he and Malcolm Fraser had met before, but it was not until the man began to speak that he remembered the occasion. The recollection so startled him that he scarcely heard the first question.

Leaning far back in his chair in lordly fashion, Malcolm Fraser addressed the candidate in an educated Scottish accent which, without doubt, owed its smooth and rounded tones to an expensive English public school. He had however assumed, more recently, just sufficient of a transatlantic twang as to be acceptable on both sides of the ocean.

'Tell me Beaton, do you see any future for anaplastics within the compass of a National Health Service which is free at the point of treatment?'

'Of course.'

'How would you answer those who, like the Chairman, suggest that plastic surgery is generally not life-saving and therefore should be paid for by the patient?'

'Who is to say that plastic surgery is not life-saving? It depends whether you consider that *quality* of life has any importance in the scheme of things.' Stephen was warming to his argument and Fraser, trying to lead him into an explanation which would enlighten the more sceptical of his audience, encouraged him to elaborate.

'How do you mean, *quality* of life?'

Stephen responded at once.

'We can heal a burn leaving unsightly tissue, puckering of skin and ghastly twisted features, and declare the patient fit to return to his place in society. This was often the case in the days when the only treatment available was to cover the wounds with Acriflavin and hope for the best.'

Only Stephen and perhaps Professor Dowson observed the change of colour in the Chairman's countenance. It was an old battle which he had fought with the reactionary consultant.

Ignoring Digby Smythe's discomfort, Stephen continued, 'McIndoe's method is to avoid the shortening of tendons and puckering of skin by keeping the burned areas hydrated and sterile using salt baths and by applying grafts as soon as possible, not waiting until the shortening has already taken place. If the first graft sloughs off we apply another and another, until the wound heals sufficiently to attach a permanent skin covering. It is a long-winded approach and inevitably costly, but the results are very much more satisfactory for the patient. To go through life permanently disfigured is a trial which all too often results in the victim giving up entirely, either becoming a permanent cost to the State by hiding away in some institution, or by ending it all in suicide.'

There was a painful silence following this blunt exposition. The hiatus was suddenly filled by a cough, emitted from the gentleman on Digby Smythe's right hand. His name plate suggested a lay member of the panel. He was in fact The Honourable Cyril Meecham MP, representing the Ministry of Health.

'You should understand, Dr Beaton,' Meecham explained, 'that the Ministry has yet to be convinced of the necessity for establishing a School of Anaplastics within the structure of this particular teaching hospital. The enormous cost of installing equipment and trained staff, in addition to the extensive bed occupancy required, would seem likely to demand an excessive proportion of the limited budget which is available for a Government-funded scheme. It is felt that patients requiring cosmetic surgery should bear the cost of treatment themselves or where appropriate, it should be paid for by their employer's insurers. Because of this, we consider that the work should be restricted to those Voluntary Hospitals which continue to opt out of the scheme. The Western Infirmary expects to be included within the National Health Service.'

Stephen's immediate reaction was one of anger. Had he been persuaded to return here, leaving his pregnant wife and her dying mother behind in Australia, in order to be interviewed for a post which might never exist?

He caught the warning signals in Professor Dowson's expression and, trying to control his very understandable annoyance, took a deep breath and returned to the debate.

'My interest, sir, is not in correcting those inconsistencies of Nature which some find disagreeable. I have no time for those who demand surgery for reasons of vanity. If there are plastic surgeons prepared to spend their time on such operations, good luck to them, and as you say, let the patient pay the bill. One cannot, however, place such people within the same category as the pilot whose hands have been destroyed while he continued to control his burning aircraft to avoid crashing onto a built-up area, the tank commander whose face has been scorched beyond recognition, or the infantryman unfortunate enough to find himself too close to a flamethrower. In peacetime there will still be casualties of this kind: the fireman who rescues a colleague from a burning building; furnace workers injured in the course of their dangerous duties; the unsuspecting housewife caught unawares when her gas cooker explodes. Are these casualties to be left to their own devices once the initial healing has taken place? Do they not deserve as many of the State's resources as the Saturday-night drunk who falls down in the street and breaks his leg?'

Malcolm Fraser, unconsciously tapping his gold Parker pen on his blotter, appeared to applaud this outburst. It was exactly what he had anticipated when he had persuaded Digby Smythe to invite a representative from the Ministry to be present at Stephen's interview. If there was one person in the country who could persuade the Minister that anaplastics was a worthy discipline for investment, that man had to be Stephen Beaton.

Meecham made no further comment. He nodded sagely, wrote at length on the pad before him and as the Chairman took up the debate he deliberately removed the top sheet containing his notes, folded it and committed it to his inside pocket. Whatever his reaction to Stephen's outburst, the man from the Ministry was clearly determined to record every word.

With a light knock on the door, the receptionist entered, whispered a few words to the Chairman who nodded and replied *sotto voce*, 'We shall be just a few moments now, I think.' The woman left the room and

Digby Smythe invited any further questions from the Board.

Professor Dowson leaned forward to address his own questions.

'I believe it would be right to say that amongst your other duties, whilst working with Mr McIndoe you instructed RAF personnel who later carried out your procedures in other military hospitals?'

'Yes, from 1943 onwards we had a continuous training programme in operation for both surgical and nursing staff.'

'And you had every faith in the ability of these trainees to carry out your procedures unsupervised?' the Chairman interposed eagerly.

'Oh yes, Mr McIndoe would not agree to the certification of any candidate who did not meet his own high standards. You have to understand that the philosophy behind the treatment was of equal importance to the surgery itself.'

While Dowson indicated his understanding of Stephen's explanation with a nod and an encouraging smile, Digby Smythe scowled and others, including the man from the Ministry, seemed somewhat bemused.

An older gentleman whom Stephen associated with his earliest days as a student now questioned his teaching experience.

'At East Grinstead you appear to have moved very quickly from the status of pupil of Mr McIndoe, to instructor in his methods,' he observed.

'I did,' Stephen replied, 'and I am quite sure that in normal circumstances both he and I myself, would have opted for a longer period of training, but at the time it was a question of sheer necessity. It was impossible for just the two of us to deal with the influx of casualties being sent to us by medical units up and down the country. It was also necessary to train specialist nurses. This was accomplished by Mr McIndoe's own team, who were largely RAF medical orderlies and Princess Alice's nurses who had qualified within the service. We all worked for months without leave, until there were sufficient numbers of staff trained in his procedures.'

'You will be aware of the ongoing discussion regarding the training of doctors, Mr Beaton,' the old gentleman pursued his point. 'As a result of your teaching experience, do you have any observations to make about the curriculum currently employed in general medical training?'

Stephen's answer was one he had rehearsed frequently in the staff common room at East Grinstead. 'Too many teaching hospitals rely on a traditional curriculum to the exclusion of more recent advances in medicine. This is because doctors generally take up teaching when nearing the end of their careers. Their knowledge and experience are of course valuable, but these older men have a tendency to stick with what they were taught themselves, rather than introduce any new ideas. As a consequence, new graduates are forced to reject a large body of obsolete information the moment they set foot in the wards.'

Stephen paused, expecting some kind of protest, but no one interrupted.

'Perhaps we should be examining what we already teach in order to prune out those areas which are no longer relevant. There have been a great many changes as a result of our wartime experiences and no doubt under peacetime conditions, developments will continue apace. It is becoming increasingly difficult for an undergraduate to absorb everything he is asked to remember. Soon the task will be quite impossible.'

The Chairman was becoming restive. Stephen's remarks would certainly been taken personally by Digby Smythe who had never been recognised within hospital circles as any kind of an innovator.

He moved on hurriedly.

'Maybe the time has come for us to concentrate more on understanding basic anatomy and physiology in the first place, teaching our new doctors how to observe their patients fully and diagnose their problems from a study of the whole person. There has been far too much emphasis placed on specialisation, so much so that quite obvious symptoms are overlooked because the consultant is concentrating on the one area of the body he knows well! Instead of demanding that our students learn their text books by heart, we should encourage them to look up the most suitable methods of treatment and the most appropriate drugs for the purpose when they are presented with a particular case, rather than expecting them to commit whole sections of the *Materia Medica* to memory!'

A few heads were nodding in agreement, although it was clear to Stephen that there were many greybeards around the table who were unconvinced.

'I am sure that my colleagues have found your observations interesting, not to say unusual.' The Chairman, with customary sarcasm summarised their collective response. 'You will receive details of the post offered and of the contract which you will be expected to sign, should you be appointed. Do you have any further questions concerning the appointment?'

'From what this gentleman said,' Stephen indicated the Ministry representative, 'am I to infer that there has been no definite decision to build this new anaplastics unit?'

'We have every confidence that Mr Meecham will be reporting favourably to his Minister, Mr Beaton. The plans should be going ahead without delay.'

'But no decision has been made?'

'Not as yet, no.'

'Then may I ask *when* your appointee might be expected to take up the post?'

'Almost immediately; we thought that for the time being, the incumbent would contribute to the General Surgery programme as well as carrying out what anaplastics work comes to hand using the present facilities. There would of course be an opportunity to teach the theory behind McIndoe's method.'

Stephen was flabbergasted. It could be years before they got around to equipping a specialist burns unit. How dare they expect him to waste his time waiting around in hopes that one day he would get the facilities he wanted?

'Are there any further questions?' asked Digby Smythe, taking Stephen's silence as acquiescence.

'No, thank you.'

There was no point in making any further statement. He looked across at Dowson, wondering how his old friend could have suggested he make this fruitless journey.

'Good. Now, if there are no further questions for Mr Beaton?' Digby Smythe looked to either side and seeing no reaction from his colleagues, concluded, 'we will ask you to leave us to our deliberations. My secretary has your address in the city?'

'I am staying at the Grosvenor Hotel.'

'Very well, we will contact you there within the next day or so.'

Digby Smythe wound up the interview with a few frosty words of thanks to the candidate for his attendance and as he left the room, Stephen overheard him address the meeting.

'We shall be interviewing a number of candidates for the post of orthopaedic registrar later this afternoon gentlemen, but before we take our lunch break, I wonder if you will indulge me. I have had a second, last minute application for the anaplastics post.'

48

'MUM? WELL, IT'S over!'

'How did it go?'

'It's a bit of a mess. I'll explain when I see you. Nothing from Ellen in the mail?'

'Not since you left, dear.'

Communications ship to shore had been impossible. Only in the gravest of emergencies could passengers use what limited facilities there were, but he had written to her from both Colombo and Cape Town. She must surely have received at least one of his letters by now. Why hadn't she written in reply?

The baby was due towards the end of February, not much more than a week away. He had hoped to find a letter from Ellen waiting for him when he reached home, but there had been nothing. True, he had been upset by her last-minute decision to remain behind, but he had understood her need to stay with her mother until the end. In the heat of the moment he may have said things he later regretted, but he could think of nothing which would have prevented her from writing to him.

On his return to Eisdalsa the previously week, his mother had shown him a letter she had received from Jeanie McDougal, written in a faint, rather spidery hand. It must have been posted not long after Stephen's departure. Jeanie spoke of how pleased she and Jack were about becoming grandparents and reported that Ellen was well, although finding the heat rather tiring. It appeared that Jeanie's condition had reached some kind of a plateau, for she spoke of herself as feeling a lot better. Stephen couldn't help resenting this period of remission, which had simply delayed the inevitable and served to keep him apart from Ellen.

'I shall be staying on here for a few days,' he told his mother over the phone. 'They'll be letting me know the result of the interview quite soon, and I'd like to look up a few old friends. Also, there are some arrangements I need to make.' He paused, trying to make his voice sound as casual as possible. 'You will ring me, here at the hotel, if anything comes from Ellen?'

'Of course.' Annie wrote down the number he gave her and hung up. The poor boy was obviously worried at not hearing from Ellen. Should she send a cable to Jack, she wondered? Just to let them know how anxious Stephen was. She picked up the phone once more and called the exchange.

The instant Stephen replaced the receiver the telephone rang again. It was a public phone, the call might be for anyone. He looked up and down the hallway, wondering if someone might be expecting a call. There was no one. He lifted the handset. To his surprise, the call was for him.

'May I speak to Dr Stephen Beaton, room 305?' The voice was vaguely familiar.

'Speaking.'

'Ah, I'm glad I caught you, Beaton old chap. Malcolm Fraser. We met a few years ago and at this morning's interview, of course.'

How could Stephen forget!

'What can I do for you?' he asked, sharply.

They had first met, when was it, 1942 or 1943? It was Hogmanay, he remembered. Ellen was with him and Squeaky Piper and the rest of the crew. They had gatecrashed a party at the invitation of one of the WAAFs on the station, and she had turned out to be the sister of this chap Fraser, plastic surgeon to the rich and famous, with the most cynical view of medicine that he had ever come across.

'Can you spare me a half hour of your time? I think we should meet.'

Stephen's reply was unenthusiastic. 'I suppose so. Where do you suggest?'

'The bar of the Grosvenor is as good a place as any. Shall we say six o'clock?'

'I told Digby Smythe we should have let you in on it right from the start, but he seemed to think you would be opposed to any hint of collusion so we agreed to trust you to speak your piece, which you did, admirably, I'm pleased to say!'

Fraser knocked back his double whisky and demanded another. 'On the rocks this time, barman,' he called, with that transatlantic bray Stephen found so irritating. He turned to Stephen, apologetically, 'I know it's a bad habit. Picked it up in the States, y'know – taking ice in the whisky I mean!'

Stephen sipped at his drink and refused a second. There was something in this over-hearty approach that he did not trust. For all his bombast, the fellow was nervous. Of what? Of Stephen's response to whatever Digby Smythe and Fraser had cooked up between them, presumably.

'Wouldn't it be a good idea if you were to get to the point?' he asked abruptly.

'Okay, here's the way it is.' Fraser settled back in his chair, swilling what was left of his second dram around the glass so that the ice made an chinking sound.

'You saw the attitude displayed by that fellow Meecham this morning. The boys at the Ministry are becoming highly suspicious of any moves which might suggest we were carving out chunks of the Health Service provision for ourselves.'

'I don't understand. I was under the impression that there would be no private practice within the Health Service.'

Stephen wondered what this man, who had already made it clear that his allegiances lay on the other side of the ocean, was doing interfering with the British Government's plans for its own people.

'Ah, you've been out of contact for a while. Things have changed a bit. The consultants have gained a few concessions, d'you see? It's now accepted consultants will keep a few private beds in State Hospitals, for their own fee-paying patients. It's a good arrangement all round. The consultant gets his extra fee, and the hospital charges the patient the earth for the privilege of staying in a private room. The cost to the hospital is minimal, just a few extra cleaners and a nurse or two, young, pretty, special uniform – you know the kind of thing; while the consultant has access to any paramedical facilities the hospital can provide.'

Stephen understood well enough. In order to win over the major consultants, Bevan had had to give them the right to continue to demand heavy fees from those patients willing to pay and gullible enough to think that they were gaining an advantage by so doing.

'What do these *private* patients expect for their money?' he asked.

'As I said, a room to themselves and extra-special cosseting...'

Stephen finished the sentence for him '...and a place at the front of the queue for treatment.'

'Well, yes. Only to be expected, old boy.'

'And where does the new School of Anaplastics fit into this happy arrangement?'

If Fraser recognised the ice in Stephen's tone he chose not to show it.

'Digby Smythe hopes to persuade the Government to fund the

construction of an anaplastics unit and you know yourself how much that's likely to cost. It'll be for accident and emergency work of course,' he treated Stephen to a conspiratorial wink, 'but once the unit is completed, he aims to offer cosmetic surgery on a private basis. It will be a lucrative spin off for the hospital. The money can be used for further research into the discipline.'

Stephen was not so naïve as to be persuaded by that kind of temptation. He had already experienced sufficient of hospital politics to know that there is never any guarantee of funding for research purposes.

Fraser, misinterpreting his doubtful expression, continued, 'A decent plastic surgeon with the right backing might expect to make a substantial addition to his ordinary income from the State.'

'There's just one thing puzzles me, Fraser.' Stephen had dropped any pretence of friendliness towards his visitor. The change did not go unnoticed now. 'What's your interest in all this? Forgive me, but I thought that you had already joined forces with the Yanks.'

'Ostensibly, yes. The fact is, your man McIndoe has caused quite a stir over in the States. He's been lecturing and demonstrating, strictly to the profession of course, but word has got out in the popular press. People are clamouring at the doors of all the major hospitals for his kind of surgery and the fact is, old boy, we don't yet know enough about it to carry out the procedures satisfactorily ourselves. There's a demand for British-trained plastic surgeons and since chaps like you seem unwilling to come out to the States to do your stuff, people over there are queuing up to come here!'

'Ah, now I see.' Stephen finished his drink and stood up. 'You drum up the trade over there, no doubt taking a handsome commission for yourself, while we perform the business over here, using facilities provided by the taxpayer. But since these patients of yours will have money and influence, they can expect immediate treatment, no matter how trivial, while real emergency cases wait in line for a bed. Well, let me tell you Mr Malcolm Fraser, I didn't like your attitude when we first met during the war, and time has not changed my impression of you one iota. While you and your kind were making yourselves a nice comfortable dugout over there in the States, the rest of us were trying to keep things together here. The minute the chaps who saved your bacon begin to look as though they might possibly benefit from the sacrifices they've made, you and all the rest of the evil, small-minded characters like you start looking for a piece of the action. What's your main objective? Are you determined to destroy the National Health Service or does it come down to sheer old-fashioned greed? Knowing what little I do of you, Fraser, I would plump for the latter.' Stephen paused for a moment, in order to swallow the remainder of his whisky. 'Well, let me tell you this, my friend,' he leaned across the low coffee table between them so that he was looking the other straight in the eye, 'neither Archie McIndoe nor I myself would want to work under the conditions you've just outlined. I can't believe any member of the East Grinstead team would give your rotten plan a second thought.'

He got up to leave.

'You're not going so soon, old man?'

'I don't believe we have anything more to say to one another,' Stephen replied, coldly.

'Oh but we have. I thought you wanted this Chair of Anaplastics.'

Stephen hesitated, wondering what was coming next.

'What has that to do with it?'

'What we've been talking about, it goes with the job, d'you see?'

'So you're some kind of envoy from Digby Smythe, is that it?'

'That's about the size of it,' Fraser agreed.

'And if I refuse to become involved with your little scam?'

'We appoint the other chappie.'

'The fellow who came in at the last minute, you mean? I caught sight of him as I left. I can't say I remember him being part of our team. Did we train him?'

'No. Seemingly he didn't meet McIndoe's requirements. I must say, he was very honest about it. Nice young fellow. Good looking too. Should appeal to the old dears.'

'What experience has he had in plastic surgery?'

'Towards the end of the war some of the RAF hospitals set up their own burns units, as you know. Our chappie spent a few months helping out. I expect he learned enough about the general principles to get by. He has a good reputation as a general surgeon and he does have one other tiny advantage.'

Stephen would have bitten off his tongue rather than ask. Fraser did not wait for him to do so.

'He's Digby Smythe's nephew.'

He might have known it. Apart from a couple of moments when habit got the better of him, Digby Smythe had appeared uncharacteristically impartial throughout the interview. Not so surprising, Stephen realised now, when a decision concerning the appointment had already been made!

'So, you intend to advertise the hospital to your rich American friends as a centre of excellence in plastic surgery, based upon a surgeon who knows little or nothing about it?' Stephen was even more scathing in his condemnation of Fraser's plan.

'Only if you force us into it.'

'Oh, I see. It'll be my fault if your little scheme backfires.'

Fraser made no reply but called for another drink.

'Why don't you sit down again, old boy, and we'll talk about it some more. I'm sure we can come to some amicable arrangement.'

Stephen was not to be mollified. 'I see it all now,' he said explosively. 'You need my name on the paperwork in order to persuade the Minister. I did wonder why Digby Smythe should have contemplated having me on the staff. We go back a long way, he and I, and we have never seen eye to eye about anything.'

'As a matter of fact, it was Dowson who proposed you, but I have to say, Digby Smythe jumped at the idea.'

Stephen couldn't believe his father's friend had had any part in this conspiracy.

'Let me just say this,' Stephen went on. 'I may not be the most fervent patriot on this earth, but I do believe in a social order which includes fair treatment for all, no matter what their circumstances. I believe in this Health Service, and I believe that the men who fought the war in order that you and those like you might save their skins, have more right to claim treatment for their ills than our rich cousins from across the water. If the Yanks want medical services which we can provide, by all means let them have them, but at the full cost, not by taking priority over facilities fought and paid for by the ordinary men and women of this country. Do we understand one another?'

He found he had raised his voice to such a level that others in the quiet bar could not help but overhear. When he had finished he thought he heard a murmur of approval from some of those around him. Looking neither to right nor left he made for the exit, allowing the doors to swing to behind him. By the time he reached the reception counter he had made up his mind.

'Can you give me the address of the nearest travel agent?' he enquired.

'You'll find a Thomas Cook's in Argyle Street.' The girl in the crisp white shirt with a tartan tie looked at him curiously. He had only recently returned from Australia, she remembered him telling her so when he booked in two days before. What kind of a man came home from so far away and made arrangements immediately to go abroad again? She watched him as he made for the lifts. That was the sort of man she could go for, a mature, well-travelled professional, a businessman perhaps? She studied the room chart, *Stephen Beaton FRCS*. She dreamed.

Stephen was fuming, accusing himself of gross stupidity. Why had he not immediately taken up the offer from that chap in Adelaide? While the Australians might not be planning a National Health Service on the British pattern, they were years ahead in terms of hospital building. From what he himself had observed, no matter what scheme the Government introduced to pay for it, they were clearly determined to provide a service to cover all aspects of health care and there was no doubt in Stephen's mind that Australia was going to be a great place for anyone engaged in research at the frontiers of medical science. The very least he could say for the Australians was that they valued the good health of *all* of the people and not just the favoured few.

Fearing to raise her hopes unnecessarily, he had said nothing to Ellen about the possibility of his working at the Adelaide Royal. When Bernard Isleworth had offered him the Chair of Anaplastics in their new School of Surgery there, Stephen, although sorely tempted, had refused on the grounds that there was perhaps a post awaiting him in Glasgow. Isleworth had nevertheless agreed to hold over his offer of an appointment until the outcome of the interview in Glasgow was known. Stephen recalled his parting words: 'We've done our best to provide the right environment for this work, Beaton, but we need a team leader of your stature and experience in the field. Mind you, Steve, I can't keep the offer open indefinitely. I'll need to know by the beginning of March whether or not you're coming back.'

Stephen stepped out of the lift and fumbled for his key. He had so much to do. He must send messages to Ellen, and to Isleworth in Australia, and he must let his folks know when he planned to return to Eisdalsa. Then there was the call he would have to make to Professor Dowson. He had to satisfy himself that his friend knew nothing of Fraser's scheme.

That evening, having composed a cablegram accepting the Adelaide post, he wrote a brief note to Digby Smythe explaining that, after consideration of all aspects of the post offered, he was withdrawing his application. His other letter was to Arthur Meecham, outlining Fraser's plan to exploit the Health Service and embellishing it with his own caustic comments. This last, he tore immediately into tiny pieces, substituting a copy of his letter to Digby Smythe and enclosing with it a covering letter to Meecham. If the Junior Health Minister had any sense at all, he would read into it exactly what Stephen hoped, that there was a flaw in the Infirmary's proposal for a new anaplastics unit.

He checked out of the hotel the following morning and as he handed in his key, he asked for the duty manager. 'I'm expecting a letter by special delivery, some time today or tomorrow. It will be from Glasgow University. There's no need to redirect it to me. Perhaps you would be kind enough to return it to the sender?'

49

'AUNT MILLICENT IS quite determined then?'

'Absolutely, the farmhouse has been made˙ fit for her to move in whenever she wants. The new beasts she has bought are doing exceptionally well, despite that nasty scare earlier on about TB.'

Stephen was trying to show an interest in the family gossip which, together with village news, seemed to be the only topics in his mother's conversation these days.

'Iain is trying to set the practice to rights before the Ministry inspection and it looks as though he will soon have someone to help out with the practice.'

'Getting married at last, is he? Well, it's about time he took the plunge.'

'No, nothing like that.' When she first heard of the arrangement, Annie thought there might be a chance of a wedding but nothing had been said. 'Alma Livingstone has to give up her job as district nurse, so she's going to work for Iain in the surgery.'

'Things must be looking up if he can afford to pay staff.'

'It seems he can claim an allowance for a secretary when the NHS kicks in.'

'You seem very certain it will.'

'Your father is quite sure the majority of ordinary doctors will sign up in the end.'

'Only half the membership bothered to reply to the last referendum,' Stephen reminded her.

Eaten up with frustration now that he had decided to return to Australia, he found it difficult to show any interest in the machinations of his colleagues in the BMA. Following the withdrawal of his application for the post at the Western Infirmary, he had begun the tedious process of formally applying to emigrate and now awaited clearance from Australia House in London. Having been told he might have to wait a full month for the next available berth aboard a ship sailing for Freemantle, he had even made enquiries about flying, but was disappointed to find there was still no regular passenger service.

Stephen turned the pages of the newspaper in a desultory fashion, not really interested either in its contents or in the subject of the conversation.

'There's to be another referendum in May,' Annie went on. 'Stuart says that will be the crucial test. Of course, they won't be absolutely sure until the moment comes for the mass of doctors to sign on.'

Stephen glanced through the window of the cottage and saw Christie McWorter turn into the square, escorted by a motley collection of dogs belonging to various households on the island. He concentrated hard, willing the Postie to walk across in their direction.

In response to Annie's request for news, a cablegram from Jack McDougal had told them that Ellen was well and that arrangements had been made for her to go into the new hospital in Kerrera to have her baby. There had been little change in Jeanie's condition however, and Ellen was kept busy organising the household. There was still no word from Ellen herself. Maybe today a letter would come.

Christie McWorter was taking her time, moving from door to door with her postbag which seemed unusually full for this time of the year. Her canine escort crowded around the open doorway, their tails wagging furiously as each received a titbit set aside by old Mrs MacDiarmid at No. 53. At last the entourage resumed its leisurely tour of the houses and Christie, passing by two cottages which she knew to be deserted for the winter months, made directly for Annie's door. Stephen was there before she could lift the knocker.

'Good morning, Stephen,' she said, smiling. 'There's something for you today.'

Stephen waited eagerly while she fished around in the depths of her sack, the inquisitive noses of the two largest dogs getting in her way.

'Och, wull you twa beasties get oot o' the way, just,' she muttered, thrusting them aside.

Stephen could not hide his disappointment when she withdrew a number of what were clearly business letters, posted in Britain. Finally she handed over a large white envelope crossed in thick blue pencil and accompanied by a post office form for him to sign.

'Registered post,' she said importantly, 'sign here.'

He did so, his heart sinking. Nothing from Ellen yet again.

'Ah good,' said Christie, inspecting his signature. 'I always like to get those out of the way. It's such a responsibility you understand.'

Carefully she folded away her precious form and then rummaged again in the sack.

'There's a catalogue for Mrs Beaton and a couple of letters for the doctor. Dr Stuart that is. It's funny there being two doctors here now,' she giggled.

With a strained 'thank you', Stephen accepted the little bundle and was about to shut the door when Christie suddenly let out a cry of triumph.

'Michtie me! I nearly forgot. These things are so flimsy they get stuck between the other letters.'

It was a thin blue envelope with printed form for the address and an airmail stamp across the top.

Stephen snatched it from her with as little grace as a starving man offered a bread roll. Annie, who had followed him to the door, saved the situation by her cheerful intervention.

'He's been waiting for word from Australia, Christie. Now we can all have a bit of peace,' she laughed. 'Won't you come in for a cup of tea?'

If Christie McWorter had felt the least bit affronted, Annie's explanation and pleasant invitation were enough to appease her.

'Thank you Annie,' she said, 'another time perhaps. I've that many packets to deliver today. Best be getting along.' She turned away, the dogs jostling for position as they accompanied her to the end cottage where bacon rinds and even the occasional meaty bone might possibly be on the menu.

Stephen cut open the special envelope as instructed, careful not to tear into any of the writing inside. He hated these things. The aerogram was a recent invention. If you wanted a letter sent by airmail anywhere in the world, it was this way or not at all. He scanned the tiny writing, screwing up his eyes to see what she had managed to cram onto it. Clearly there was much to say and not much room to get it all in.

I'd written several letters, surface mail, before I could manage a trip into town to get some of these special airmail forms. I hope you've received the others okay. They told me at the post office that surface mail can take anything up to two months if you happen to miss the mail ship. At best it still takes six weeks! I've had one letter from you, posted in Cape Town. Nothing since. I expect you've been pretty tied up since you got back to Scotland so I'll forgive you.

He'd written twice since he docked in Southampton. She must be right about the time letters took. He hadn't imagined it to be quite so long.

Mother has been a lot better since Christmas, when she had a nasty turn and we had to send for the doctor. He gave her some tablets to take when the pain got bad and they seem to have done the trick. Junior has been behaving pretty well. He's very active as soon as I lie down at night but I don't mind. It's no worse than having you beside me, kicking out in your sleep! I hope you get this before the interview because I want to wish you luck. I trust the job will turn out to be all you hoped. I wish you could have been here for the last week or two before baby is born but what will be, will be, as they say! Dad has been great. He has taken his promise to look after me so much to heart he never stops fussing. We have arranged for me to go into the maternity ward the week before baby is due so that there won't be any last minute dash. I want everything to go smoothly so I can get back here to the farm as soon as possible. Ma really needs me. The girls are very good but she is now heavily dependent on Dad and myself. Everyone sends New Year greetings to the Eisdalsa folks.

The signature, '*Your loving Ellen*', was crammed into the margin, there being no more space available. He experienced a pang of remorse at that last bit. Jeanie would be relying on her daughter just now. The Aboriginal servants were able to perform the necessary household chores but it was family love and support that was needed in these final weeks. How selfish he had been, thinking only of his own loneliness and disappointment. It was comforting to know that both Jeanie's and Ellen's treatments were in good hands.

Once Ellen had been made fully aware of her mother's condition she would not rest until Stephen had visited the local hospital in Kerrera to discuss Jeanie's case with her doctor. Stephen had been impressed by the young man he met there, a general practitioner with the wide range of skills needed by someone working alone in the outback, where travelling time was a crucial factor in every emergency. Together, they had gone over Jeanie's treatment in minute detail but apart from suggesting a couple of additions to the list of painkilling drugs, Stephen had been able to contribute very little. Reassured by the fact that the Flying Doctor Service would soon be fully operational, Stephen had been able to convince Ellen that there was nothing further that could be done for her mother.

Despite the bitter words they had exchanged in those few moments before the ship sailed, her letter carried no hint of reproof for his sailing without her. She had even wished him well for his interview. Having read the short letter for a second time and assured himself that he had not missed even the slightest nuance, he folded it carefully and tucked it into his pocket.

Annie watched him covertly as he read, and was relieved to see him smiling at last. Stephen had said very little about Ellen's decision to remain behind to look after Jeanie, but Annie suspected his tension was caused by something more than a few weeks separation. Had there been a quarrel, she wondered? Anyway, he seemed happy enough now.

'Ellen says she's sent several letters by surface mail,' he told his mother. 'They must still be on their way. You'd think things would have been speeded up a bit by this time.'

If it had taken so long for his own letter to reach her from Cape Town, perhaps it would be best to send a cablegram right away to let her know he was coming back as soon as possible. He had already posted one long letter, describing what had happened at the interview and his narrative had sounded like the script for a Whitehall farce. He'd omitted the rather less pleasant aspects of his encounter with Malcolm Fraser, however. Recalling that particular conversation, he shuddered involuntarily and Annie looked up again, demanding sharply, 'What is it?'

'Don't you feel it a bit chilly in here,' he asked, covering up. He stooped to put a few more lumps of coal into the stove.

'How is Ellen?' Annie ventured.

'Fine. She says the baby is pretty active now. Jack has made arrangements with the hospital and everything seems to be under control.'

'Oh good,' Annie smiled across at him. 'I'm so glad.'

Only then did Stephen turn to his other correspondence. He began with the envelope he had been asked to sign for.

'That looks a bit official,' his mother remarked, wondering if perhaps it was another job he had been applying for.

'It's from Australia House, my application for immigration.'

Annie's heart missed a beat and she found herself struggling for breath. Fighting down an overwhelming feeling of nausea, she managed at last to speak, her voice even and under control.

'You've definitely decided, then?'

'I'm afraid so, Mum. That business at the Infirmary simply made up my mind for me. If guys like Digby Smythe are so determined to put their spanner in the works, I can't see any way the National Health Service can succeed.'

'But his interest is only in this one very narrow field isn't it? There can't be many other forms of surgery which would attract such large sums of money from private practice.'

'Who knows? Anyway, plastic surgery is what I do, only I want to combine it with genuine medical practice and research. I don't intend to get mixed up with a bunch of people who are determined to milk rich widows of their fortunes by pandering to their egoistical fancies!'

'You make it all sound so petty. Some people require your kind of expertise because they genuinely feel that something about their appearance is seriously affecting their lives.'

'In that case, what they need is a psychiatrist not a plastic surgeon,' Stephen replied caustically. 'I could never be reconciled to a system which put some wealthy woman's long ear-lobes before a child disfigured in a motor accident.'

'But why can't the two go hand in hand?' Annie really did not understand why both her men were so adamantly opposed to a combination of private and State provision.

'There's nothing wrong with a private health scheme if those operating it are prepared to pay for it, but that's not the case here,' Stephen told her. 'What Digby Smythe and his ilk are after is for the Government to build and equip the new hospitals using public money. They then expect to access the facilities for their private patients.'

'I still don't see why that should affect the public health provision in any way,' Annie protested.

Stephen had to take a deep breath.

'What they don't bother to mention is that they will be giving their private patients priority over NHS patients. Why else would these people be willing to pay more money than they need? Neither Beveridge, nor Aneurin Bevan, nor even Tories like Willink for that matter, intended that there should be a private sector within the system. These pirates expect to accommodate their special patients in the best facilities the State hospitals can provide, employing highly qualified staff, trained at the tax payer's expense. Experienced nurses and doctors are already in short supply. If their services are to be prioritised, the ordinary man in the street will find himself pushed way back in the queue while the consultants line their pockets with private consultation fees in addition to a generous income paid by the State. The hospital committees will of course claim that the additional charges for accommodation will benefit the hospital as a whole, but the element of privilege will remain. That's what neither Dad nor I can stomach. You above all people should be able to understand that!'

Annie nodded thoughtfully, allowing him to continue without interruption.

'It's not the system our Servicemen were promised while they were still fighting on the battlefront. Bevan has been manipulated by the BMA until almost every facet of the scheme has been altered in favour of the consultants. Well, I'm sorry, but I for one am not prepared to sign up to such hypocrisy.'

A slow handclap from the open doorway alerted them both to Stuart

Beaton's unannounced appearance.

'Fine words, son. It's a pity you weren't at the meeting I've just attended. The press were there in force.'

'What was the outcome?'

'Oh, the usual. The big boys were shouting the odds about the sanctity of the consultant's position, claiming the Government aims to steal the Voluntary Hospitals' nice little nest eggs of trust monies, that kind of thing. Patient's rights didn't figure in the discussion and there was no mention of the GPs and how they're going to fare in the big shake-up. The chaps with large practices in the big cities will be supported in their efforts to form Group Practices, but no one has any bright ideas how to lessen the burden on the one-man country practice. If Iain even gets his subsidised receptionist, it'll be a miracle.'

'What will happen to the scheme if the doctors vote against?' Annie asked.

'Back to the drawing board, I suppose,' suggested Stephen.

'Well, in that case, surely it will be up to men like yourselves to see that this time the plan is properly devised,' Annie suggested, hoping to shame Stephen into remaining. She didn't know how she was going bear it if he went all that way away, for good.

'Maybe,' said Stephen, 'but it's a battle for the younger men to fight now. Don't misunderstand me, Mum. I want the scheme to succeed. No one could be more in favour of it than I am. If I thought I could make one iota of difference by staying here, I would do so. It may be selfish of me to choose this way out but I know that in Australia I can do the work I have prepared myself for these past few years. I will be teaching the next generation of Australian surgeons, so let's hope some of them will come here and work, once this lot have sorted themselves out. I'm past forty, with a great deal of skill and experience at my fingertips which I need to use *now*, not in ten or fifteen years time when the hospital committee and the Government have made up their minds where to invest whatever money they've been allocated. The appointments board was more interested in what I could contribute by way of general surgery than in anaplastics. In Adelaide I can move straight in and get on with the job I'm equipped for. The anaplastics suite there is already in place. It's just waiting for the right man to lead it and I happen to believe that man is me.'

There was a pause in which Annie and Stuart exchanged glances, not quite knowing whether to be disappointed in, or proud of, this son of theirs. He noted the unspoken exchange and added, less stridently, 'So, incidentally, does the chief of surgery there.'

He handed his father the official looking letter from the Australian

Department of Immigration which stated that since his appointment as Head of the School of Plastic Surgery at the Adelaide State Hospital of South Australia was confirmed, other immigration formalities were waived. He was free to enter Australia at any time, for the period of his employment in this capacity.

'I thought it took weeks to get a letter from Australia,' said Annie. 'You only cabled them last week.'

'This was posted in London,' Stephen said, 'it's from the High Commissioner's Office.'

He passed the top letter to his father and continued reading, this time a note from Bernard Isleworth himself.

February 28th 1948
Dear Beaton,

I can't tell you how delighted we all are that you have decided to join us! In view of the urgency of the situation, this letter will be reaching you via the diplomatic bag, hopefully in just a few days from now.

The Australian Government has arranged for your flight to Adelaide by RAAF transport, so that you may arrive here in time to accompany an Australian delegation to Japan in April. We have been asked to participate in an international commission to review the condition of people affected by the atomic bombs on Hiroshima and Nagasaki. It seems likely that the hospital will be offering remedial treatment to survivors of the initial effects of radiation. You will appreciate that this is new territory for all of us and offers unlimited opportunities for research. I cannot over-stress the urgency of the situation and trust you will make haste to join us at your earliest convenience. Details of your travel arrangements will be forwarded from London.

Annie was torn between dismay at Stephen's imminent departure and pride in this acknowledgement of his achievements. Stuart was filled with admiration for his son.

'Congratulations, Steve!'

He clasped Stephen firmly by the hand as he thumped him hard on the back. Annie still held back, tears welling in her eyes. The battle for her boy was already lost.

'Australian war veterans and Japanese citizens need my skills as much as any one else, you know, Mum.' Stephen coaxed gently, hoping she would understand. 'The Hippocratic Oath doesn't say anything about caring only for the British people who are sick.'

Stuart had been examining the travel instructions which accompanied the communication from the Australian High Commission.

'They say you should telephone Northolt as soon as possible to check on flight arrangements. How long do you think it's going to take you to get away?'

'First off, I'll need to get word to Ellen. If I've to report directly to Adelaide, there'll be arrangements to be made there before she can join me. I'll need to find somewhere for us to live, and I'll have to have what little we've collected by way of household furniture and our personal effects packed up for shipment. Fortunately most of our stuff is in storage down in Surrey and it will only take a word to Pickfords to have it shipped directly to Adelaide.'

'Ellen does know that this move to Adelaide is on the cards?' Characteristically, Annie, having recovered from the immediate shock of hearing Stephen's decision, now set herself to addressing the practicalities of his departure.

'Oh Lord!' Stephen exclaimed. 'The fact is I never even told her about the offer from Bernard Isleworth. At the time, I was so certain of the job here in Glasgow, I didn't want to raise any false hopes we might stay in Australia. I think she'll be delighted to stay on, but as you say, Mum, I should ask her.' He paused, wondering what would be the quickest method of contacting her.

'Don't they have a telephone?' Annie asked.

'No, the distances are too great and the population too isolated to lay cables to every homestead. They rely on radio. Now, that *is* a possibility. If I can get a telephone message to Southern Cross, they may be able to contact Jack McDougal by radio.'

The tiny front room of Christie McWorter's cottage, where the switch board for the island exchange was housed, was barely large enough to hold Christie and her equipment. Stephen waited impatiently in the minute hallway. Christie had made contact with the Glasgow main exchange and for some minutes the two operators had been conversing in short sentences, between interruptions from other callers.

'Hallo, Glasgow?' Christie, suddenly fully alert, listened intently to what she was told and then pulled out the plug connecting her to the exchange and removed her headphones.

'They've established a link through Perth with the radio station at Southern Cross,' she told him importantly. 'Glasgow will ring back when the radio link with Kerrera Station is ready.'

'Did you ask how much all this is going to cost?' Stephen was getting concerned. He had heard horrific tales of the cost of trans-oceanic telephone calls and was beginning to wonder if he had enough cash with him to cover it.

'They will let us know soon enough,' said Christie. Then, understanding his concern, 'I can always take a cheque.'

At the thought of writing a cheque to pay for a telephone call, Stephen blanched, but he knew he would have to face up to the bill like a man.

'There's maybe time for a wee cup o' tea.' Christie got up from her seat and edged past him, making for the equally tiny kitchen at the back.

'You can stay here, just in case they ring back while I'm gone. You saw where to push in the plug?'

Stephen nodded but prayed she would be back in place before the call came. He could not bear to think that some error on his part might interfere with things after all this trouble.

He need not have feared. Christie was back with steaming cups of tea and a plate of fresh-baked scones minutes before the exchange rang back and it was Christie herself who was the first to hear Australia calling.

She spoke into her microphone, indicating to Stephen that he should pick up the handset on the wall.

'Australia? Hello Australia? This is Eisdalsa Island in Argyllshire, Scotland, with a call for Mrs Ellen Beaton.'

She paused, listening for the reply, then nodded to Stephen.

'Ellen?'

'Stephen?'

Her voice was faint and the sound distorted by atmospherics but he would have recognised it under any circumstances.

'Marty Fields said he was relaying a long distance call. Where are you?'

'Would you believe, Eisdalsa!'

'But I don't understand. How did you get my message so quickly?'

'Message? What message? I've just had your airmail letter.'

'Jack sent a cable as soon as the baby was born.'

'You mean? Are you okay?'

'Fine, and little Hugh is fine as well!'

'Oh darling, you're wonderful! He's got everything he needs? Ten toes, enough fingers?'

'He's perfect, even down to the red hair.'

'And Jeanie?'

Ellen hesitated, the sparkle going out of her voice in an instant.

'Not so well. The doctor says it can't be long.'

'Poor darling, having to cope with this all alone. I wish I was with you.'

'Dad's been wonderful, taking charge of everything and bossing everyone around. You wouldn't recognise him!' She paused before asking, 'If you hadn't heard about the baby already, why were you calling? This must be costing the earth.'

'It is, so I must be quick. I've been offered a job at the South Australia State Hospital in Adelaide. Shall I take it?'

There was a moment of complete silence broken only by the wheezes and squeaks of static.

'You mean, you're coming back here?'

'If you would like me to.'

'Of course I want you to only...'

'What?'

'There's still mother, and now the baby.'

'Of course. I don't expect you to come to Adelaide right away. Not until everything's sorted. There'll be lots of preparations for me to make. I'll need to find a house for us and it'll take time settling into the new job but at least I'll be able to get up to Kerrera, once in a while.'

'Stevie.'

'What?'

'I love you!'

'I love you too.'

'Hurry back.'

'Yes, faster than you can imagine. They are arranging for me to fly!'

'When?'

'A matter of days, just as soon as I can get away. I'll have to go straight to Adelaide and contact you from there. Sorry, time's up. I love you. Give the baby a big hug for me. Goodbye for now.'

There was a click and the line cut.

50

'THERE'LL BE THE usual family gathering at luncheon on Sunday, I suppose?'

Iain's question was asked casually, as he and his mother lingered over breakfast with minutes to go before the first patients arrived. 'It's just that I thought it would be nice to invite Alma to have a meal with us to seal our agreement as it were, a little celebration of her coming to work here. Sunday seems to be the only day when we can be reasonably certain of not being interrupted.'

'Well, Annie and Stuart will be expecting to come,' Millicent hesitated. She too would like to invite Alma as he suggested; she was just a bit surprised that it was he who had been the first to think of it.

'The trouble is,' she went on, 'with Stephen likely to leave any day now, I was rather expecting it to be a larger family gathering than usual this Sunday. Annie was hinting that perhaps Morag might like to come down to say goodbye.'

'It's not as if Alma doesn't know everybody,' Iain insisted. 'I don't see why we can't celebrate her joining us with all the family here. After all, she's going to be a part of the practice.'

'Well, if you don't think she'll feel out of place.' Millicent could see that Iain's had not just been a casual suggestion, and she didn't want to disappoint him.

'That's all right then?' He wasn't going to give his mother a chance to change her mind. 'I'll tell her twelve thirty, shall I?'

Wisely, Millicent refrained from further questioning. Perhaps there was more significance to this invitation than he was letting on, but she had learnt her lesson over the Alison affair. She had wondered if, in attempting to throw them together, she had put Alison off the idea of becoming Iain's wife. She was determined not make the same mistake again.

Despite her resolve to make no comment, however, as she went about her various duties that Thursday morning, Millicent could not help musing on the possibility of Alma as a daughter-in-law. It would be rather strange were Iain to marry a girl from the village, whose father had been the ticket clerk on the steamer pier. Richie Livingstone had been a leading member of the Free Church, of course, and as an elder, he had been much respected in the district. Maybe it wasn't such a bad idea.

When, at eleven o'clock, with the waiting room empty and only a couple of routine house calls to be made, Iain welcomed Alma to their weekly meeting, Millicent made sure she was on hand to provide coffee and shortbread. If she hoped to intercept some signal of a new, more intimate, understanding between the couple, she was to be disappointed.

Seeing the shortbread biscuits, Alma's first words were about the unfortunate illness that had laid low all four members of the Fergusson family.

'Did you have any results from the tests?' she asked.

They had eventually managed to extract from Mrs Fergusson a list of foods that might have been the cause of the food poisoning. Choosing only those items which all four members of the family had consumed, they had been able to whittle down the list to four items: milk, a meat pie which Mrs Fergusson herself had made from meat freshly purchased from the travelling butcher, boiled fish and shortbread biscuits from Jessie Moran's bakery on Eisdalsa Island.

Iain had sent samples of all four items to the laboratories in Glasgow for analysis.

'No, they found nothing to suggest that any of the samples was responsible. We may never know what caused the outbreak. Without refrigeration the chances are that any protein food left at room temperature for a few hours, or not properly cooked, could have been the source. Mrs Fergusson was pretty hazy about what everyone had eaten. Thank goodness no other families had the same problem. That would have suggested the source was the suppliers and not the individual household.'

'Anyway, the Fergussons got over it quickly enough,' Alma said. 'Mrs Fergusson is determined to keep a bottle of the kaolin mixture in her medicine cabinet from now on. She said it was like a miracle how quickly the trouble dried up.'

'Better for her to take more care how she stores her food,' Iain remarked. 'The ideal, of course, would be a refrigerator in every household but without electricity, that's just a pipe dream.'

'There's talk of the supply being brought down from Oban within the next few years,' said Alma.

'I won't hold my breath.'

Iain was more concerned with the immediate future.

'This episode reminded me of something we discussed when I first took over; Mrs Moran's shortbread.'

'I thought you said the laboratory had cleared all four samples.'

'They did, but that doesn't necessarily mean that Jessie Moran is absolved from all suspicion. There is no running water to any of the cottages on the island other than Stuart and Annie's, and even they have a chemical toilet. Jessie Moran is contravening the regulations by selling food cooked on premises that don't conform. She should have water piped to the house, separate basins for preparing food and for washing her hands and most important of all, a proper drainage system.'

'But there's no possibility of a mains sewage system ever coming here,' Alma protested.

'Septic tanks are the answer, or even a properly controlled cesspit would be acceptable, but earth closets are not. I'm going to have to make a report to the Sanitation Department.'

'You'll cause a great deal of ill feeling on the island.'

'Can't be helped I'm afraid.'

'What will happen when the Sanitary Inspector finds out?'

'He'll probably make her stop selling the shortbread until she has made the necessary improvements.'

'I believe she depends upon her sales, to supplement her pension. She's been a widow for some years.'

Iain shrugged. 'I've been very remiss, doing nothing about it so far. This recent scare has just highlighted how important it is for people to obey the rules.'

Alma could see he was right. Nevertheless, she would hate to see him ostracised by the villagers, for treating one of their number in a high-handed manner.

'Jessie is a reasonable enough woman,' she observed, 'maybe, if you were to go and have a talk to her about it before you put in your report, she wouldn't take it so badly.'

Sinking his teeth into one of his mother's own home-baked shortbreads, Iain smiled at her earnest expression.

'You're absolutely right, as usual,' he said, picking up the plate and offering it to her. 'I don't know what I'd do without you to keep me on the straight and narrow.'

She beamed at him and selected a piece of shortbread.

'Another cup of coffee, anyone?' Millicent asked, coming upon them unannounced. 'Has Iain asked you about Sunday yet?' she demanded.

Alma looked mystified.

'Oh yes, I almost forgot.' He said it casually enough, even though he had been working up to the moment when he would ask her.

'Mother wondered if you would like to come to lunch on Sunday, a little celebration of your joining the practice.'

'That would be nice; thank you Mrs Beaton.'

'We usually have a few of the family here on a Sunday,' Millicent hastened to warn her. 'Iain's cousin, Stephen, is staying on Eisdalsa Island at the moment, and Dr and Mrs Stuart usually come along.'

'I won't be intruding?' Alma looked a little alarmed at the prospect of confronting so many of the family.

'Not at all, they'll be delighted to see you,' Iain exclaimed. Under his breath, so that only Alma heard, he added 'and so will I.'

Sunday luncheon at Tigh na Broch had turned into something of a celebration. News of the birth of a son to Ellen and Stephen had put everyone in party mood. At the end of a particularly splendid meal, Stuart raised his glass to toast the baby.

'To little Hugh, the first of the next generation of Beatons, destined to carry on the family tradition, poor little bugger!'

'He might be a horse-doctor,' Stephen warned. 'His mother would prefer it.'

'Or a poet, or a bank clerk?' suggested Alma who, after a glass or two of wine, felt much more relaxed in company with this close-knit family.

Her presence had surprised some members of the family. Annie in particular was quick to notice a change in her nephew's attitude towards Alma. He was never far from her side and when the conversation centred upon family matters, it was he who offered the necessary explanation which would include Alma in their reminiscences and conjecturing.

'Quite right, Alma,' said Annie, taking up the point. 'These Beatons are too ready to assume that everyone is going to be a doctor. It would be nice if someone did something different for a change.'

Alma blushed. 'Oh, I didn't mean to imply any criticism. I just think that children should be allowed to make their own decisions about what they do in life.'

Stuart looked up sharply. He remembered Alma's father being something of a bigot, with strongly held views about women's place in the order of things. His attitude had obviously affected his daughter's outlook on life.

'Would you have taken up something other than nursing, had you been able to choose,' he asked.

'No, but I would have gone to Glasgow and trained properly,' she replied. 'I had every opportunity to do so, but my father refused his permission for me to go.'

'If you'd taken your SRN you wouldn't be coming to work for me,' said Iain. The satisfied grin he bestowed upon his new receptionist did not go unobserved by any of the female members of the company.

Alma returned his smile and Millicent expertly turned the conversation in another direction.

'How are the negotiations going, Stuart,' she asked. 'We haven't seen you since your last trip to London.'

'Well, the service will definitely get off the ground in July,' Stuart replied. 'The Executive Committee of the BMA is going to find there are more of its members than they expected in support of the scheme, even as it stands. We haven't heard from the ex-service voters yet and if we can only get all the ordinary GPs to cast their votes, the referendum in May will be the turning point!'

'That might be easier said than done,' suggested Iain. He had come across an extraordinary apathy amongst the few colleagues he met in the course of his daily round.

'Some of us are working on it,' Stuart assured him. 'You may be pleasantly surprised at the outcome. The changes are going to come about, first of all, in the administration arrangements. General Practitioners will be immediately affected, but new hospital building and the setting up of facilities such as the burns unit at the Western Infirmary will have to come later.'

Stuart turned to his wife with a sympathetic shrug. 'I'm sorry to have to say this Annie, but Stephen was absolutely right in making his decision. The chances are that, had he accepted the appointment at the Western, by the time he took over his new premises he would be due for retirement.'

'So, when are you leaving?' Morag enquired of her cousin. 'Mother said something about your having to fly.'

'I have to be at Northolt on Friday,' he told her.

'The RAAF is looking after him,' Annie explained with a touch of pride. Even her unhappiness at the imminent departure of her son for Australia could not deflect her satisfaction that Stephen's work should be so highly valued by his adopted country.

'How long does it take, Duncan?'

Millicent's son-in-law had travelled extensively before and during the war, he ought to know. 'Will he be flying non-stop?'

'No. They have to stop once or twice to refuel and change crews. There'll probably be a couple of nights in a hotel.'

'I don't have the details, but the flight is scheduled to touch down in Canberra on Monday,' Stephen told them. 'After that, it's a fairly short hop to Adelaide by the internal air-passenger service. They already have a pretty comprehensive system of routes across the continent and apart from the scheduled airlines, no end of the larger spreads have their own airstrips. Some farmers own their own light aircraft. They're decades ahead as far as travel is concerned. Down there you'd hardly know there had ever been a war.'

'Apart from the cemeteries and the veterans' hospitals,' Stuart observed dryly.

Despite his concern for his mother's feelings, there was no disguising Stephen's excitement at the prospect of his new life.

'I might take up flying again myself, once I get settled,' he added. 'What's the point of having a licence if you don't use it?'

The thought of Stephen flying alone, in a small aircraft, across the vast Australian desert wastes, made Annie blanch and Stuart, placing a comforting arm about her shoulders, was quick to give his assurances. 'There'll be regular flights to Australia in no time at all Annie. We'll get out there to see them, never fear.'

'Stephen, you'd better make sure you get a house with plenty of spare room,' said Morag. 'It looks as though you could be inundated with visitors.'

'We'll be amongst the first,' Duncan added.

ALISON MCKENZIE SAT forward in her seat, the better to hear what was being said. The hall was crowded. Naturally enough, women were in the majority but there was a fair sprinkling of men. Some of those would be psychiatric nurses, she realised, but many were ex-servicemen, experienced sick-berth attendants and medical orderlies who had decided to remain in the nursing profession at the end of the war. Many of them had taken the opportunity, while in the Armed Services, to sit the examinations for state registration and amongst their number, the first male nursing sister to be appointed to a large general hospital in the south of England. It was he who stood at the lectern now.

A spare, agile figure of a man, no more than five foot two or three at most, he wore an immaculate white shirt; its short sleeves set off sun-browned, muscular arms, giving a hint of exceptional strength. He spoke in a northern accent, which was difficult to identify accurately because it had been honed by the years and mingled with a dozen different dialects. His voice rang out above the squeaks and whistles of an inefficient public address system.

'I represent the recently formed Association of Male Nurses, Madam Chairman. At this first joint meeting of associations of workers in the nursing profession I would like to take the opportunity to declare our solidarity with our female colleagues and to appraise them of certain matters which affect my members in particular.'

There was some shuffling and muttering in the body of the hall. This terminology was not what the women were used to.

'Like many other male nurses, it was quite by chance that I became a member of this profession. A spell as a patient in a TB hospital opened my eyes to the importance of nursing and when I had recovered, I volunteered for service as a medical orderly in the RAF.

'I came to love my work, Madam Chairman, and knew early on that I had found my vocation. While serving as a medical orderly, I handled every form of disability from dysentery and prickly heat to frostbite and gunshot wounds and towards the end of the war I worked in a severe burns unit in Sussex. Imagine my disappointment therefore when, on returning to civilian life, I found my options, as a male, were limited to nursing in psychiatric hospitals or in long-stay institutions for the chronically disabled, where my muscle power was the capability most regularly called upon.'

Here there was general laughter. The women were only too happy to acknowledge their inferiority where strength was called for.

'The excuse given for excluding most of the men from general nursing was that they were not registered. It has taken my male colleagues four years, continually challenging the system, before being granted permission to be examined for state registration, even though the Board of Trade certificates issued to service personnel covered most of the curriculum of the General Nursing Council, with the exception of Midwifery and Gynaecology. When the men applied for additional training to bring them up to SRN standard, this was refused on the grounds that men could not nurse women in labour. How can it be that a male obstetrician is acceptable in the labour ward, but a male nurse cannot be a midwife? In an emergency, policemen and ambulance drivers have delivered babies, even fathers have been known to do it.'

There were murmurings around the hall. It would have been difficult to say if these were of agreement or disapproval.

'I've listened to this morning's discussion on low salaries and the antiquated rules which say that nurses must resign when they marry. My members agree with you. Nurses should be allowed to continue working after marriage. Having graduated, they should be free to live outside the hospital if they wish.'

He paused for a flurry of applause.

'As for salaries, I will ask you now to consider the position of the male nurse. If it is difficult for a single woman to manage on the miserable money offered, even to the most senior grades, imagine how much more difficult is it for a man with a wife and family to support. We men have no option but to find somewhere to live outside the hospital. There is no subsidised accommodation in the Nurses' Home for us, nor are we compensated for the additional expense of living out.

'Since men are regarded as suitable only for nursing psychiatric or permanently disabled patients, we are excluded from the major training establishments, employing fully qualified nurse tutors. There are only a very few male nurse tutors who, like myself, received training while still in the Services. Women may be struggling to reach the top in other professions, Madam Chairman, but in nursing it is the men who are the second-class citizens.'

The murmuring had turned into audible protest. Many women viewed the prospect of men in senior nursing posts with alarm. This was the only profession where women could hope to rise to the very top. Once they got a firm foot on the ladder, the men would undoubtedly be going for the top jobs. At present, equal pay for male and female nurses was the norm, but in other professions, equal pay was just a pipe dream. How long would it be before differentiation was introduced, once the men had access to every branch? Despite Government claims of equal opportunity for the sexes, there were still very few women barristers or surgeons and there were no women company directors, university professors or judges. While some nurses believed it was imperative that men must be admitted to the profession if nurses were ever to receive appropriate salaries and working conditions, there were others who feared the introduction of men to SRN status would be the thin end of the wedge.

The red light began flashing on the lectern. It was time for the speaker to bring his address to a close.

'The problems we have been discussing this morning, Madam Chairman, result from blatant exploitation of our talents, by both the voluntary hospitals and the municipal authorities. This is largely due to the fact that, in the past, nurses have had no one to represent their interests. Our employers rely on our loyalty and dedication. They take advantage of our weakness as negotiators, and assume that our principles will prevent us from withdrawing our labour. But, ladies and gentlemen, withdrawal of labour is the main weapon in the arsenal of other workers, why not in that of the nurses?'

The unrest was now palpable. These militant words seemed more appropriate to a shipyard than a hospital. The fellow was in danger of being booed off the stage.

'The first aim of my members, Madam Chairman, is to improve the status of every nurse, of either sex, and in every sector of the profession, by demanding representation on committees at all levels of the negotiations. Why should we be expected to wait patiently with our begging bowls, while the BMA negotiates the best terms for its own members, with no thought for those of us who work alongside them? Let's face it, they can't manage without us and they know it!'

Despite the uneasy feeling that his earlier words had evoked, and the suspicion that they were harbouring a belligerent trade unionist in their midst, these final sentences had alerted the audience to the real purpose of their meeting. They seemed to have warmed to the wiry little man whose sincerity was unquestionable.

Bartholomew Alloysius George Gage, Baggy to his friends, sat down to applause which grew in volume as the full import of what he had said filtered through, even to minds which had been trained by a century of tradition to unquestioning acceptance of the status quo.

'Our last speaker referred to every nurse, in every sector of the profession,' the Chairman consulted her order papers. 'Our next speaker is Miss Alison McKenzie, who wishes to make a statement on behalf of the district nurses. Miss McKenzie.'

Alison walked briskly to the podium, her pulse racing. She had dreamed of this moment all week and had many times practised her speech in front of the mirror, but as she looked up and saw five hundred faces turned expectantly towards her, her throat closed and her mind went blank.

She remembered her father's words when she told him she was going to address this conference: 'Head up, deep breath, find a spot on the wall above their heads and talk to it. On no account allow yourself to look directly at anyone, or you'll find yourself being distracted by their expression.'

It was the first time he had taken the slightest interest in what she was doing. When he learned that she was representing her colleagues at a nurse's convention, her father had suddenly become quite animated, wanting to know what she intended saying and giving her valuable advice about her delivery.

'Madam Chairman,' she began, her voice lost in the vastness of the hall and strangled by her nervousness.

There was unrest in the audience as they strained to hear her. She began again, leaning a little closer to the microphone.

'I'd like to tell you a story about a woman, we'll call her Mary. Mary grew up in the 1920s, leaving school at the age of thirteen. She was clever enough to go on to secondary school, but her dad considered education would be wasted on a girl.'

There was a general murmur of disapproval.

'Mary was put into service in a private nursing home where, as luck would have it, she encountered a housekeeper who saw in her potential for something better than domestic service. She suggested a career in nursing and introduced Mary to the matron of the local hospital. As a nursing apprentice she learned to make beds and empty bedpans. She also exercised her previously acquired skills of scrubbing floors and dusting and polishing and became expert at counting laundry.'

There was a titter from the hall, but Alison's now clear, ringing tones had arrested their attention and the noise quickly died.

'She was soon learning to take blood pressure and fill in a temperature chart and was even allowed to hand out the medicines prescribed by the doctor and dispensed by the staff nurse. Most important of all, she discovered that she had a certain way with her patients. She could coax them to make those painful efforts which led eventually to their recovery. She managed to give them the will to overcome the inevitable. She encouraged despondent relatives when there seemed to be no hope of recovery. She was in fact exactly what is required of a good, practical, bedside nurse. The ward sister valued her services and even the houseman occasionally recognised her existence.'

There was a sympathetic laugh from somewhere. They were listening, she could feel it, but she must get on before she lost their attention.

'In order to be able to live with her elderly, widowed mother, at the age of thirty Mary transferred to the District Nursing Service and took a six weeks' training course, at her own expense, in order to satisfy the requirements of the Queen's Institute. For ten years she has worked in the district for a pittance, making more bearable the lives of her patients, most of whom are elderly, lonely and bedridden. She has become loved and respected by the community she serves.'

She paused to give emphasis to her next words. The assembly was silent.

'On July 5th 1948, Mary will receive an ultimatum. Take unpaid leave and get your SRN, or quit!'

So great was the tension she had developed that one could hear the rustle of paper as someone moved.

'All those years of dedication and attention to her work are now as nothing. Unless Mary can pass these wretched examinations, she must go.'

Alison drew a long breath and looked directly at her audience.

'Colleagues, we can't afford to lose the skills, the experience, and the expertise of those of our sisters who learnt their nursing at Nellie's elbow and never had the opportunity to take written examinations. I ask you to consider the plight of those nurses without formal qualification. If we are to believe our politicians, the next generation of school leavers will all be equipped to take on the levels of training that those of us who are privileged to be SRN have received. Meanwhile we *must* retain those nurses who have been long in the profession but who may not have the necessary academic background to absorb the new technologies. They are still needed to exercise the basic, but equally important, skills of the bedside nurse. I propose, Madam Chairman, that this meeting approach the Minister, demanding implementation of that section of the Horder Report of 1942 which recommended a recognised category of Assistant

Nurse, with a progressive salary scale and transferable pension benefits similar to those accorded to SRNs. Experience should be taken into account as well as paper qualifications.'

She sat down to tumultuous applause.

Alison was still trembling in the aftermath of her performance when a small white card was passed along the row and thrust into her hand. On one side was printed *The Association of Male Nurses*, an address and telephone number and at the bottom *BAG Gage, Hon. Sec.* She turned the card over to find written in a neat hand.

Congratulations! We must meet. I'll be beside the Nurses Benevolent Society stall after this session. It was signed, *BAG Gage.*

'I thought perhaps a coffee between sessions?' Baggy suggested. 'I have to leave after the afternoon discussion groups, so this is the only opportunity we have to get things fixed up.'

Alison had responded to his request out of interest. Now she regarded the man with more than a little apprehension.

'Here, let me take that,' he said, grabbing her smart little brief case.

Now she had to follow him, whether she wanted to or not.

He wove his way through the throng of delegates all seeking their morning coffee, guided her to a seat and summoned the waiter.

'Coffee or tea?' he asked.

'Tea, please,' she said weakly, still trying to regain her composure.

'And something to eat? Toast perhaps?'

She nodded.

'Two rounds of buttered toast, thank you.' The waiter departed and Baggy leaned forward.

'You spoke well,' he said. 'Done much of this sort of thing, have you?'

'My first time,' she confessed.

'Well, no one would ever have believed it.'

'Thank you.'

'Don't thank me. Could be, you'll come to regret ever having stood up in public at all.'

'I don't understand,' Alison said.

'Of course you don't. Why should you? The fact is some of us, from different branches of the profession, have formed an action group in order to try to implement some of these ideas we have been discussing this morning. It's no use our sitting here telling each other our woes. We have to get the message over to the public and if we are to get things straight before July, we have to work fast. How many members of the Press did you spot in the hall?'

Alison shook her head.

'It wasn't many, take my word for it. The only reporter taking notes was from the *Nursing Times* and you can imagine how that transcript will be manicured and sweetened before it gets into print.'

'What's this got to do with me?' Alison wanted to know.

'You've got what it takes, girl. The minute you got going, you had them spellbound. Talk like that to the General Nursing Council or more particularly, the Parliamentary Committee deciding the details of the health service, and we might get some of our points over.'

'I never anticipated that my little contribution this morning could lead to anything more,' she told him, unable to suppress her excitement.

'Well, I want you to think about it. We are drawing up a list of members who would be willing to stand for office, representing the interests of the nurses on the various bodies involved in the planning. May I add your name?'

It took very little deliberation for her to decide. She had been excited by the power she felt as she addressed that audience. She felt sure she understood sufficient of the nurses' concerns to represent them. Why shouldn't she follow in her father's footsteps? He, of course, had eventually lost his job in the 1930s because of his union activities, but she put that firmly out of mind when she replied.

'If you think I can contribute anything...'

'So your answer's yes?' he asked.

'Yes.'

'Good girl. We'll make a Member of Parliament out of you yet.'

'Oh, I don't think so,' she laughed, but she couldn't help feeling flattered, all the same.

52

THE RINGING OF the telephone brought Iain suddenly awake. He reached out in the half light and fumbled for the receiver.

'Dr Beaton?'

'Yes.'

'It's Charlie Stevenson.' The man sounded breathless as though he had been running.

'Yes?'

'Nurse says it's time.'

'Oh okay, I'll be there as soon as I can.'

'Thank you, Doctor.'

'That's all right Mr Stevenson and, Mr Stevenson.'

'Yes?'

'Don't worry, the midwife knows what she's doing. There'll be plenty of time for me to get there and even if there's not, she can manage very well without me.'

There was a moment's silence in which Iain could hear the man's continued heavy breathing, then he managed to blurt out, 'Okay, Doctor.'

'So don't go having an accident on the way back, you understand? Babies in the middle of the night are one thing, broken necks are something else!'

'I understand Doctor.'

'I'll see you in about half an hour.'

'Thank you.'

The receiver was slammed down at the other end of the line. Iain replaced his more carefully, and dragged on his trousers over his pyjamas. It might be the beginning of June, but the wind had been howling since early last evening and it had been raining heavily for hours. It was going to be cold and miserable out there.

Millicent was waiting for him in the kitchen when he got downstairs.

'I heard the telephone,' she explained. 'I've made some tea.'

'I really ought to be going,' he hesitated, sorely tempted by the welcoming brew.

'Oh, come on, another five minutes won't do any harm.'

Iain grinned at her over the steaming cup.

'This is really too bad of you Mother,' he told her. 'The idea of putting the telephone in my room was that you wouldn't have to be disturbed.'

'I know, but I woke at the first ring. Force of habit I suppose.'

'Thanks, anyway. I feel much better for that.'

He put down his cup and pulled on his heavy-duty waterproofs. Millicent handed him his medical bag and he strode out to the car, confident that it would start on the first pull.

What a blessing he had accepted Cyril Lord's offer of a better car. He couldn't see the old Armstrong Siddeley starting after a night like the last. With headlights on full power, he set off down the drive and swung into the main road. The surf was pounding the shore, the tide higher than he had ever seen it. In one spot, sea water swept right across the road beneath his wheels and Iain wondered whether the road might be undermined. The Council had been promising to reinforce the beach at this point for years and never got around to it.

At the bottom of the hill he put the car into low gear and crept upwards, knowing from experience how many small rivulets would have developed in the night, bringing down mud and other debris to make the surface treacherous. At the summit of the brae he encountered yet another small landslide and felt the rear wheels sliding on a patch of mud. For one sickening moment he found himself peering down the steep slope to the valley floor.

For years before the war, there had been promises of road widening at this danger spot, but the job would necessitate the removal of a quantity of the bank above and the estimated cost had been prohibitive. The outbreak of war had put paid to all such projects, and even now it was going take a major disaster before anything was done to make the corner safe.

With a sigh of relief, Iain turned away from the sea and headed across the brae on the road to Lunga ferry. Once he had topped the brow of the hill, he could put on a little more speed and took a series of sharp bends at a little under forty, something he would never have done in daylight. As it was an hour or so before dawn, he didn't think he'd encounter any other vehicle on the road. He was soon to be proved wrong however, for as he approached the flat plain which surrounded Seileachan Bay, he saw headlights approaching and was forced to pull in to a lay-by to allow a nippy little sports car to tear past him. The driver gave him only a cursory acknowledgement before gunning his vehicle to even greater speed. By the time Iain had pulled out again, the other car had already disappeared over the crest of the lowest slope.

At the approach to the church, Iain turned onto a narrow unmade track and soon found himself in the yard of Stevenson's farm. He switched off the engine and waited for a moment, hoping for a slackening of the wind which had been gusting forcefully ever since he left home and was now accompanied by a heavy shower of rain. There was nothing for it but to make a dash for the house. He opened the car door and sank to his ankles in farmyard manure.

'It's at times like this,' he muttered, pushing past Charlie Stevenson, who waited anxiously in the dimly lit porch, 'that I remember with some regret the comfortable little hospital job I had in Edinburgh!'

Despite himself, Charlie was forced to smile. Then, having helped to remove the doctor's outer garments, he offered him a dram before he got started.

'After the job is done, Mr Stevenson,' Iain replied, 'I'll be glad to wet the baby's head with you. Just now, I think I'd best keep my wits about me.'

He took the stairs two at a time and found the familiar figure of the midwife awaiting him on the narrow landing.

'You timed that just right, Doctor,' she assured him, pointing him to a nightstand with a jug of hot water and a basin.

'Baby is presenting very nicely,' she whispered, 'although I think you may have to make a snip or two. She's overly distended already.'

'We'll see.' Iain followed her to the bedside.

Iain disliked cutting the mother if it could be avoided, but in this case it did appear necessary. A few clean cuts would heal faster than a jagged tear. No need for additional anaesthetic. With what Molly had already endured, a couple of quick nips with the scalpel wouldn't hurt that much. Telling Mrs Stevenson to draw deeply on the gas and air, he made three small incisions in the skin restricting the infant's head. His action was immediately rewarded when, at the next contraction the baby's head came clear and the infant actually began to cry.

'Everything's fine, Molly,' the midwife reassured Mrs Stevenson, wiping perspiration from the young woman's beaded brow. 'Try not to push too hard next time, it's just the shoulders to come out now.'

With a sudden flurry of activity, the baby tumbled into the waiting hands of the midwife in a gush of blood and water.

'Oh, it's a lovely wee boy, Molly. Just wait a minute and you shall see for yourself.'

Iain busied himself with ligatures to the cord, ceremonially offering it to the midwife to cut. While he waited for the afterbirth, the nurse carried the infant away to wipe him clean and wrap him up tight before placing him in his mother's arms.

Meanwhile Iain attended to Molly, finally making three neat sutures where he had been obliged to cut her.

Molly Stevenson, her long travail over at last, was all smiles as she held her baby.

'Thank you, Nurse,' she said weary but content, then beaming up at Iain, 'Thank you too, Doctor.'

'Always happy to oblige.' He smiled at her, as he checked her pulse one last time.

When a birth went as well as this, it compensated a little for those other times where things proved to be more complicated or, as in the case of the Wallace's baby, they had a tragic outcome. Through no fault of his own, Iain's first birth in private practice had been a disaster which he was unlikely to forget.

Until now, Iain, completely absorbed in what he was doing, had been quite unaware of the passage of time. He glanced at his watch and was startled to find that it was already nearly eight o'clock. He would need to hurry if he was to be in time for morning surgery.

Charlie, who at the first word from the nurse had flown up the stairs to see his wife and baby son, now turned away from the bed.

'You'll not be going before you've had the dram I promised you, Doctor,' he insisted.

Iain was weary and ready for his breakfast. The last thing he wanted just now was whisky. Nevertheless, he allowed his host to precede him down the stairs to the kitchen where they toasted the baby in the finest Bruichladdich.

'Do you have a name for the boy?' Iain asked.

'Oh, he'll need to be Charlie, like his dad,' replied the farmer proudly, 'but Molly has a mind to call him after you too, Doctor, so with your consent, he'll be Charlie Iain Stevenson.' He savoured the names as they rolled off his tongue.

Although he had to confess that Molly herself had done all the work, most ably assisted by the midwife, Iain took the compliment in the spirit in which it was offered and felt immensely proud. With the post-war baby boom currently in full swing, he thought he could look forward to there being a spate of little Iains born in the neighbourhood.

He pulled on his shoes, grateful that despite his intense anxiety, the farmer had found time to clean off the muck for him and give the doctor's heavy brogues a decent shine.

'I'll need to pick my way carefully this time,' Iain grinned, thanking Charlie for taking so much trouble. 'It would never do to get them all muddied again.'

'The rain's been off for an hour or more,' Charlie told him, 'so it shouldn't be too bad outside, but you'll need to watch your driving. My cowman tells me there are a number of landslips along the road.'

'I'll take care,' Iain assured him. 'Tell Molly I'll call in again tomorrow sometime, but if you're worried about anything get someone to ring me.'

Carefully avoiding the quagmire which last night had caught him unawares, Iain climbed into his car. In moments, he was pulling out onto the main road, headed over the brae towards home.

53

AFTER YEARS OF covering considerable distances each day on her bicycle, Alma regarded the three-mile pedal to the surgery as modest exercise to set her up for the day.

Leaving home just after half past seven, she aimed to be at Tigh na Broch by eight, usually finding the road pleasantly devoid of traffic at that hour. As she pedalled along the quiet lanes this bright summer morning, she found herself in close communion with Nature, sharing with the gamekeepers and ferrymen sightings of wildlife generally denied to later risers.

After last night's storm, the clouds had cleared and the wind had dropped to a gentle breeze from the southwest. In the full flush of summer, still wet leaves hung heavily from the overhanging branches, sparkling in the sunlight. From the hedgerows the heavy scent of hawthorn blossom mingled with that of new-mown hay.

She topped the rise and came in sight of Tigh na Broch, its dark, slated roof glistening in the morning sunshine. A weasel ran out from the hedge, narrowly missing her front wheel. She braked sharply, encountering a muddy patch on the bend, and slithered to a standstill. Dismounting hurriedly to avoid toppling over, she looked down at the muddied surface and up at the scar left behind by the shifting topsoil. It was then that she noticed the heavy imprint of motor tyres, not parallel with the grass verge as one would expect, but straight across the road towards the cliff edge where quite suddenly they disappeared.

Standing on the very edge of the tarmac, she peered over and found she could see right to the foot of the steep incline.

A bright red sports car lay on its side, almost buried in a clump of brambles. How long had it been there, she wondered? It certainly hadn't been there when she left for home the previous evening. There was no one about, so the accident must have already been dealt with. The car had probably been left there until someone could send out a towing vehicle from one of the garages. She was about to turn away and remount her cycle, when she saw a slight movement. She craned right over to get the best possible view. Yes, there it was again. Something white fluttering in the breeze. She concentrated hard on the driver's side of the vehicle hoping to see some other sign of life and was rewarded by an arm, raised above the shattered windscreen and waving feebly. The driver was still there! Maybe she was the first on the scene, after all.

If she climbed down the slope, she could reach the car in a few minutes and perhaps help the driver if he was injured. She glanced across the low lying meadows towards Tigh na Broch. What if she found she could do nothing alone and needed to summon help? She would have to waste precious minutes running to the house for assistance.

Deciding that the better course would be to make straight for the house, alert Iain and then return to the scene of the accident, she jumped on her bike and coasted downhill, picking up speed as she swept along the shore road and up the drive towards the house. Flinging down her cycle she hammered on the front door. When there was no immediate answer she shouted out.

'Iain! Mrs Beaton!' Receiving no answer she hurried around to the rear and entered the kitchen. It was deserted. Millicent must be out in the barn.

She went into the hall and lifted the telephone receiver.

'Operator, this is an emergency.'

'Who's calling?' drawled the familiar voice of Mrs McWorter.

'This is Alma Livingstone. I'm speaking from Tigh na Broch. There's been an accident on the brae. A car has gone over the cliff and is lying on Mrs Beaton's ground. Call the police and I believe an ambulance will be needed. The driver seemed to be alive when I first spotted the car from the hill.'

'Just leave everything to me, Nurse. Where shall I say to find you?'

'I'm going across the fields to see if there is anything I can do. Dr Beaton seems to be out on a call. Maybe when you've summoned the police, you'll try to contact him?'

'I'll do what I can.'

She rang off and Alma ran into the surgery to gather up a few things she thought she might need. She wrote a very hurried note for Millicent which she left prominently displayed on the kitchen table and set out across the meadow at a run.

The car's fall had been broken by a thicket of willow saplings and brambles which was probably the reason why it had not broken up on impact. It lay on its side with two wheels pointing skywards. Alma reached out tentatively towards the bonnet, the only part of the vehicle she could touch without tearing herself to pieces on the bushes. The metal was stone cold. The car must have been here for some time. Regardless of the thorns and prickles, she parted the thicket and approached nearer to where the driver ought to be. A low groaning sound seemed to come from somewhere beneath her feet.

She discovered the driver, hanging upside down and wedged in his seat, his legs trapped underneath the dashboard. One arm hung limply over the side of the car, while the other hand gripped the edge of the windscreen for support. The canvas top had been ripped open revealing the rest of the driver's body. A formidable lump had been raised on his brow and the side of his face showed extensive bruising. What caused Alma the greatest alarm however, was the quantity of blood which had soaked through the torn sleeve of his thick tweed jacket and collected in a pool on the leaf-strewn ground. He must have been bleeding freely for a long time.

She crept in closer so that she could address him directly.

'Hallo there. I've sent for help. Someone should be here quite soon.' When there was no response, Alma tried again. 'Can you tell me your name?'

The driver groaned.

Alma knew it was important to keep him awake, so continued to talk to him. 'I'm Alma Livingstone. I work for the doctor. His house is just over there. You'll be fine just as soon as he gets here.'

The man groaned again and looked as though he might be losing consciousness.

Alma, realising too much time had been lost already, set to work on the bleeding arm. She took out the scissors she had brought and cut away the sleeve of the jacket, a very expensive garment which went with the high-powered sports car. With both jacket and shirt sleeves removed, a gaping wound was exposed in his forearm. In addition, the limb was fractured just below the elbow. With a strip of bandage, she created a tourniquet, checking her watch to ensure that she did not restrict the blood flow for too long. Having satisfactorily restricted further blood loss, she bandaged over the wound and prepared a makeshift sling to support the dangling arm. Then, with superhuman effort, she managed to ease the driver into a slightly more comfortable position. Although still tilted almost upside-down, she had managed to slide him sideways sufficiently so that his good shoulder was now supported by the door. Next she attempted to free his legs but soon realised that they were firmly trapped beneath the dashboard. He would have to be cut free. She cursed herself for neglecting to tell Mrs McWorter to call out the fire brigade as well. Sometimes the police carried bolt cutters, or there might be something suitable at the farm. As soon as Iain arrived she would go and see what she could find.

Having done all she could to make him comfortable, she covered the man with the travelling rug she had brought with her, tucking it securely around him. She had also brought a small flask of brandy but feared to give him any. Perhaps it would be best to leave that to Iain.

All the time she worked, she kept up a very one-sided conversation, believing the man to be only semi-conscious, but hoping her voice would reassure him.

'That was a terrible storm last night,' she observed. 'That corner's an absolute nightmare at the best of times. I bet you took it a bit too fast. It's easily done if you're not familiar with the road.'

He groaned again and his free hand came up to touch his battered brow.

'Here, let me see if I can ease that a bit,' she said, drawing a bottle of witch hazel from her bag. She dabbed at the place for a few moments and the tension clearly eased, because the creases on his brow almost disappeared and she realised that he was a great deal younger than she had at first imagined. Why, he was little more than a boy.

Her patient now seemed to be so relaxed that she feared he would go off to sleep. That would never do. She continued talking, louder and more rapidly.

'Wherever were you going, along this road in the early hours? It's not as though it goes anywhere, beyond the village.' She glanced at her watch. It was time to release the tourniquet.

At least the moaning had stopped, for which she was thankful. She looked up from what she was doing, to find that the poor fellow was actually smiling at her, although the smile changed quickly to a wince of pain as he attempted to shift his body into a more upright position.

'Stay still, now,' she urged. 'We don't want to disturb that poor arm any more than necessary, do we?'

There was nothing more she could do for him. She crouched beside him, holding his good hand and talking.

'How well do you know the islands? Did you know that once there was a great industry here, manufacturing roofing slates that were sent all around the world?' She continued telling him about her ancestors who had worked the slate and those of her family who had emigrated to New Zealand in the last century. 'One of my cousins came back to fight in the war,' she told him proudly. 'Fancy that, all the way from New Zealand.'

Running out of conversation for the moment, she checked her watch.

It was time to loosen the tourniquet yet again.

She untied the knot in the bandage and waited until the blanched skin below the elbow began to turn a more healthy pink. As fresh blood flowed again from the wound, she retied the tourniquet, tightening it using a scalpel for a tommy-bar.

Where was Iain? He must have got her message by now. All she could do was to sit and wait.

She continued to talk to the motorist from time to time, trying to establish some kind of rapport with him, but although he kept his eyes constantly upon hers, he never actually spoke. She began to wonder if the knock on his head had affected his speech.

Well, she'd managed to keep him awake so far.

She pulled out her watch again and saw that nearly half an hour had passed since she got here. With the rescue vehicles having to come out from Oban, there could be no relief for the best part of an hour. Iain, however, might appear at any moment. Releasing her hold on the victim, she stood up and stretched her cramped limbs then peered across the thicket seeking some sign of life from the house. After a moment, she began waving, excitedly.

Millicent came in from the cowsheds just as Iain's car crunched to a standstill on the gravel forecourt. She went to the front door to let him in. He looked exhausted, poor dear, and with surgery in half an hour, he would hardly have time for a shower before breakfast.

She herself had gone back to bed after he left and had slept only fitfully for a further couple of hours. At last she had given up trying and decided to get up and get on with the day's chores in order to give McKinnon a pleasant surprise. She too was ready for her breakfast.

'You go and freshen yourself up,' she suggested. 'What would you like for breakfast? Bacon and eggs?'

Gratefully, Iain stripped off his coat and stumbled up the stairs. Millicent went into the kitchen to prepare the meal.

In a few seconds she was back, shouting to him from the foot of the stairs.

'Iain! Iain! Come down at once! There's an emergency.'

Iain was to remember little of his wild dash across the fields. Except for one incident. At the gate between one field and the next, the ground sloped upwards rather sharply and after so much rain, the entrance had become a quagmire. His legs gave way under him and he landed face down in the mud. Struggling to his feet, the thought crossed his mind that Charlie might not have bothered with his shoes after all, for they were plastered again for the second time in one day! The next minute he was bounding across the second meadow. He could see Alma now, waving to guide him to the spot while, on the road above, a police car had pulled up and two uniformed figures were scrambling down the cliff.

Alma had left nothing for him to do except administer an injection of morphine to relieve the pain. What was really needed was a transfusion to restore the patient's blood volume but that must wait until they got him to hospital. Despite Alma's administrations, the chances of the man surviving seemed very small.

'One good thing in his favour,' Iain told her later, 'is that because he was head down, what blood remained was concentrated in the vital organs. That may have saved him.'

The police had already alerted Cyril Lord, who was able to drive his recovery vehicle across the meadows to the site. He had the tools to tackle the job of cutting the victim out, but even so it was a long time before the driver's legs were freed and he was lifted clear. While the men wrestled with the mangled wreckage, Alma remained at the motorist's side, talking to him and reassuring him. Even when, at long last, they strapped him to the stretcher, she insisted on climbing alongside him up the steep slope to the road. As Iain and Alma stood side by side watching the ambulance men settle their patient, she began to tremble. A policeman handed Iain a blanket and he wrapped her warmly before leading her away to sit in the back of the police car.

'Perhaps you would be kind enough to drive us back to the house, Constable?' he requested. 'Miss Livingstone needs to rest.'

'Of course, Doctor,' he replied, 'if you don't mind waiting while we take a few measurements. We must do it before these tyre marks are obliterated by other vehicles. After that, we'll be glad to run you back.'

He paused, wondering whether he should question Alma just at this moment. She was clearly suffering from shock.

'I don't suppose the lady managed to find out when the accident took place?' He addressed his question to the doctor. 'It's clear the vehicle has been down there for some time.'

'I think I can tell you that,' Iain told him. 'The car passed me on the road as I was attending an emergency call, it would have been about five o'clock. Mr Stevenson, my patient's husband, will no doubt give you a more accurate time for my arrival at his house.'

'That's very helpful, sir. Thank you.' The constable made a note in his book and went off to join his colleague.

'I left your spare bag and all your stuff down by the wreck,' Alma worried.

'I'll fetch it later, if necessary,' Iain assured her. 'With a bit of luck

Cyril will have collected everything up. More importantly we have to get you back to the house and into bed. You've had quite a time!'

'Oh, I'm all right, just a bit shaky, that's all. What about morning surgery?' she demanded, wearily.

'I expect Mother will have sent everyone away by this time. Do you realise it's nearly eleven o'clock!'

By the time the policemen were ready to leave, Alma had dropped off to sleep with Iain's arm around her. He looked down at her white face, the deep shadows beneath her lids telling their own story of the morning's ordeal. She had done well. What a nerve the authorities had to suggest she wasn't competent to be a nurse.

He tapped his fingers impatiently on the back of the driver's seat, willing the policemen to be done with their task. After a few more minutes he studied Alma's face again. In sleep, the anxious frown had disappeared. She was wearing very well for forty, he thought, a lot better than he was himself. In fact, she was a very attractive woman, and smart, too. She'd done everything possible for that motorist under the circumstances.

'Silly bugger didn't deserve such good fortune as to have Alma save his life!' he said to himself, remembering the reckless way in which the young man had taken the road over the braes.

'What was that, sir?' enquired the policeman as he and his companion climbed into the car and slammed the doors.

'Oh nothing,' Iain replied. 'That chap was going at quite a rate when he passed me,' he observed. 'Probably took the bend too fast.'

'Yes, that's what we think. Mind you, the surface must have been treacherous after the rain. The real truth is, the road needs widening so the curve can be reduced. I'll put it in my report.'

Iain wondered what difference that was going to make, unless of course the driver should be dead on arrival at the hospital.

'Did you discover who he is by any chance? He's not a familiar figure in these parts.'

'Bill here recognised him,' the driver indicated his companion. 'His name is Montieth, a nephew of the Marquis, I believe.'

'That would account for the expensive sports car, certainly,' Iain observed, dryly. His next thought he kept to himself. If it *was* a nephew of His Lordship's who had nearly killed himself, maybe the road would be put right, after all.

54

'I DON'T KNOW how we managed without you all those weeks,' said Millicent as she watched Mairi pour the last batch of milk through the cooler.

Mairi put down her bucket and tucked a stray hair under her neat white cap.

'I really enjoy this, Mrs Beaton,' she responded happily. 'I can't say the same for my other job though. Once I've finished wee Molly Stevenson's wedding dress, that'll be it. I'll no care if I never thread another needle in ma entire life.'

'Alma tells me that there is a queue of women waiting for your services,' Millicent said. 'Are you sure that you're doing the right thing by turning them down?'

'Dressmaking is fine when you're doing it for yersel,' Mairi told her. 'When it's for someone else and you have to get it done on time, and all the worry of will it fit and will it suit, no, I canna say I enjoy it.'

'At least young Joan will soon be well again as a result.'

Millicent had so admired Mairi's tenacity in demanding the penicillin treatment which had undoubtedly brought about her daughter's rapid recovery. Her earnings from dressmaking had paid for the drug.

On her return to work in the dairy, Mairi had managed for some weeks to continue with her sewing, so that by the time Joan was due for discharge from the hospital the family's finances could run to a new coat for Joan and shoes for everyone.

The continued attentions of Peter Parker had contributed greatly to Mairi's revival. Amongst the islanders, Peter was now accepted as her regular escort and when they were together, Mairi positively blossomed with self-confidence.

'My brother-in-law was asking me the other day if you had heard anything more from the pensions people?' Millicent remarked.

'Och, I should have let you know, the doctor having been so good, writing a' those letters.' Mairi looked genuinely contrite.

'No need to apologise,' said Millicent immediately. 'He was just curious, that's all.'

'I mentioned to Alma a letter Tam had got from an old comrade,' said Mairi, 'and she suggested we should write to him to see if he could remember the incident when Tam was hit over the head. The man wrote back with a description of what had happened in the prison camp and even got his version confirmed by a couple of others who were there. And now Tam's case has been put to the Pensions Board again with the new evidence, by a lawyer friend of Mr Parker's.' Mairi blushed when using the name.

'Let's hope there'll soon be some good news,' said Millicent.

Mairi could not suppress a grin, 'It's not that important now I'm working again and...' should she tell Mrs Beaton now? She would have to know soon enough, 'well, you see, Peter Parker and me, we're going to be married.'

'Oh Mairi, I'm so pleased for you,' cried Millicent, giving her a generous hug. It was the best news she had heard for a long time. 'You deserve a little happiness, my dear. Congratulations!'

'Of course,' said Mairi earnestly, 'I can't expect Peter to support the children, especially as they get older. If we get something from the pensions people it will come in handy for their education. I'll put it by for them.'

'Have you made your plans for the wedding?'

'It'll no be a grand affair. Just a quick trip to the Registry Office, both having been married before. Peter is keen to have his family up from England, though where they're all going to stay, I can't imagine.'

'There's plenty of folk on the islands do bed and breakfast at this time of the year,' Millicent said. 'I'm sure you'll manage. If there's anything I can do to help, you must let me know.'

'We need two witnesses,' Mairi told her. 'Obviously Alma Livingstone must be one, but Peter being new here and no' knowing a lot of people, we were wondering if the doctor would stand up for him. Do you think he might?'

'I think you'll find Peter has only to ask,' Millicent assured her. 'Had you not considered being married at St Brandon's? You're both widowed so there's no reason why you shouldn't be married in church.' Millicent loved to attend weddings in the little church over the hill.

'We're neither of us keen on the kirk,' Mairi replied with unusual vehemence. Her first wedding had been in the church and look where that had got her. A simple exchange of vows was all either of them wanted.

'Well I shall expect an invitation, wherever it's held,' Millicent told her firmly.

All this talk about weddings only served to remind her of what might have been. She could not avoid the familiar pang of regret that Iain's relationship with Alison had come to nothing.

55

IAIN PARKED THE Daimler on the pier, apologising to his lady companions for the distance they must walk to the Council Offices. 'I daren't risk leaving the car outside in the road. They're getting pretty hot on parking these days.'

'It hasn't taken long for people to get back to using their cars, has it?' observed Alma, teetering on high-heeled shoes on the rough cobbles and using this as an excuse to cling to Iain's arm. 'One wonders where they get the juice.'

'There's always a way,' said Iain, 'especially in places like this where distances are so great and bus services so poor. Most people can find a reason for demanding extra petrol coupons.'

'It makes you wonder what parking is going to be like when they lift the restrictions,' Millicent remarked, grasping hold of Iain's other arm as the road became steeper.

'What's the time?' Alma asked, craning to see the face of the station clock between the rooftops. 'I promised Mairi I'd be there in time to see her dress was okay.'

'I don't know what all the fuss is about,' said Iain. 'You woman can make such a meal of an affair like this. They're only going to stand up and affirm their marriage vows in the front of a few friends. What does it matter what Mairi's dress looks like?'

'You only get married once,' protested Alma and then, seeing him grinning, she gave him a slap on the backside.

'You're wrong anyway,' he laughed. 'They've both been married before!'

'Oh, you know what I mean!'

They struggled on up the hill, turning into the side street just as Peter Parker's car pulled up before the offices of the Argyll County Council.

'Well that's a cut above the old Jeep,' observed Iain watching Peter hand Mairi out of the front passenger seat of a sparkling grey Silver Ghost.

'The Marquis suggested Peter take the Rolls out of mothballs for the occasion,' Alma told them. 'He's even sent along his chauffeur to drive it.'

'I suppose it's just a coincidence that Lord and Lady Montieth are coming to the castle in August,' Iain observed dryly.

'You old cynic you,' said Alma. 'Why can't you give the Marquis credit for a generous gesture?'

'Because I've never known him to do anyone a good turn without having a damned good reason,' Iain replied harshly, sounding just like his father. 'You don't think His Lordship might have thought it convenient to have the Rolls in good working order in time for his holiday in the summer?'

Alma, however, would have nothing ill said of the Marquis. 'It was kind of him to think of the Rolls,' she insisted. 'Mairi deserves a decent car to take her to her wedding.'

Since his nephew's accident, His Lordship had been in close touch with Dr Beaton, ignoring Kmeikic and the staff at the hospital and depending on Iain's reports of the young man's progress. His Lordship's thanks for the service rendered to the young man had been profuse and when Iain had pointed out that it was Alma who had been first on the scene and rendered the vital first aid, he insisted on giving her a suitable reward. On hearing from his factor how Alma was obliged to travel around the district by bicycle, His Lordship had decided to buy her a car. Despite the shortages, he seemed to have access to anything he wanted so Alma was taking driving lessons from Peter Parker.

'Oh, doesn't wee Joanie look a treat in that dress!' Millicent exclaimed as Mairi's daughter alighted from the Rolls and turned to wait for her brothers. 'Mairi said she'd been staying up until the early hours to get it finished.'

While the two women enthused about the outfits which Mairi had created for herself and her daughter, and marvelled at the unusually well-polished appearance of the two little boys, Iain appraised the groom with a critical eye. Since the evening Peter Parker had called to ask if he would act as his witness to the marriage, the two men had become the best of friends. With Peter Parker, Iain had spent many an evening mulling over the pros and cons of marriage, Peter unsure if it was a good idea to take a second wife whilst the first was still fresh in his memory, and Iain wondering if, after half a lifetime of bachelorhood, he was ready to forego his freedom.

For Peter the decision had not been a difficult one. Having been married once to a woman whom he had loved dearly, it astonished him to find that he had been blessed with this second chance of happiness.

'What about the children?' Iain had asked him one evening when, after a chance meeting in the local inn, they had strolled together to the end of the pier to watch the sunset. 'It's one thing to take on someone else's woman, but his kids as well...'

'Mairi has done a fine job bringing them up,' Peter told him, and there was no denying the pride in his voice as he said it. 'Despite their previous experience of having a man about the house being so terrible, they've shown no sign of resentment at my presence. I reckon I can make a reasonable stab at being a father, given the chance.'

'Three's quite a handful though,' said Iain. 'Do you expect to have any more, of your own?'

'We'll see.'

Peter had not managed to father a child in six years of marriage to his former wife, although whether the fault was with her or with himself, they had never discovered. With Mairi, he believed he would be happy whatever happened. Should they have a child of their own it would be a bonus, but he wasn't going to lose any sleep over it.

For his wedding, Peter Parker had exchanged the comfortable leather-patched tweeds which he always wore for a smartly cut, navy-blue pin stripe. His silver tie and the pink carnation in his button hole were all that distinguished him from the trickle of clerks, councillors and officials passing up and down the stone steps and in and out through the heavy oak doors to the dilapidated old building which was the county seat of Argyll.

The decade prior to the outbreak of hostilities had been lean years for the farming and fishing community of Oban and the regular influx of tourists, the mainstay of the town's economy, had dried up as a world-wide recession hit hard in the 1930s. Although the war had brought a form of prosperity to this Argyllshire town, when both the Royal Navy and the Coastal Command of the RAF had found a use for the sheltered harbours of Oban and Tobermory, none had settled upon the local infrastructure. Additional accommodation had been provided at the hospital for service casualties and some church and other buildings had been refurbished to provide recreation centres for the troops, but none of the public buildings had received any attention.

Within the Council Offices, the room set aside for marriages was larger and somewhat more elaborately furnished than others in the building but one could not avoid noticing the damp patches on the ceiling or overlook the elaborate nineteenth-century cornices, which were crumbling from lack of maintenance. The sole attempt to create any air of festivity was an expertly arranged floral display positioned beside the highly polished, elaborately carved old desk.

As the guests began to gather, however, the colourful dresses and flowery hats of the ladies lent colour to the scene and by the time the Registrar entered ahead of the bridal party, the room had acquired a surprising air of excitement and a real feeling of occasion.

Mairi looked radiant. She had studied the latest fashions for the design of her deceptively simple blue dress. It was A-line, calf length with a full skirt falling from a pinched in waist. The bodice, with its scooped neckline and short sleeves, displayed her neck and shoulders to perfection. Alma was struck by the change in her friend's hair, once so mousey and drab. After long months of careful cutting and regular washing, it shone in the sunlight seeping in through the high Victorian windows, and was magically transformed by the multitude of colours in the stained glass. The bride turned to her daughter and handed her a neat little posy of yellow roses. She glanced across at Alma and smiled and as her head moved, the concoction of yellow and white flowers and feathers which adorned her neat cloche hat danced.

'By the authority vested in me, I now declare you husband and wife. You may kiss the bride.'

Peter Parker turned to his new wife and carefully lifting the wisp of veiling covering the upper part of her face, kissed her. There was a general flurry of congratulations from the guests and a few muted cheers before the signing of the register could begin.

Alma and Iain, who had stood one on either side of the bridal pair throughout the short ceremony, now moved together, patiently awaiting their turn to witness the signatures.

Millicent, admiring the tall figure of her son, resplendent in Highland dress, and the slim figure of the smartly dressed woman at his side, imagined for a moment that it might be they who had just been married.

Hastily, she dismissed the notion. Nothing short of a church wedding would do for a member of the Beaton family, although she had to admit, this had been a surprisingly moving occasion. Bereft of the frills and fussiness of a full blown church wedding, there had been a solemn dignity to the ceremony.

The formalities over, many in the company were moved to tears by the sight of Joan, taller and altogether more mature after her long illness, throwing her arms about her new step-father and kissing him as though formally accepting him as her father. While she turned to give her mother a hug, the boys stepped forward and solemnly shook Peter by the hand. Millicent's eyes met Alma's. They exchanged satisfied smiles acknowledging their mutual conviction that Mairi had made the right decision.

The wedding party that night was held in the village hall. All the islanders were invited; His Lordship's tenants, neighbours and friends of many years, even Tam's workmates from the slate quarries had come to wish the couple well. Peter's English guests, having been accommodated in various households across the island, were clearly enjoying the Scottish hospitality and revelling in the unusual experience of a true Highland wedding.

Following a long-held tradition, His Lordship had provided a haunch of venison to add to the wedding feast. A table, heaving with good things which had been conjured up out of the meagre rations allowed for such functions, stood at the back of the hall and beside it the landlord of the village inn dispensed liberal measures of whisky and his own, locally brewed, heather ale.

Mairi had become isolated after Tam's return from the Far East and there were many of those present tonight to whom she had not spoken in more than a year. For her, it was a time for healing old wounds and renewing past relationships. Tam's behaviour on his return from the war had soured his memory in the minds of certain islanders but that had nothing to do with Mairi herself. There was not a soul present would deny her this second chance of happiness.

'I shall never forget how much of this I owe to you,' she told Alma, as they repaired their make-up in the Ladies, towards the end of the evening.

'Nonsense, I had nothing to do with it,' Alma replied, colouring with embarrassment.

'Oh but you did. Without you, I would still be sitting in my own squalor, wallowing in self-pity. Do you think Peter would have thought anything of the scarecrow you saw that time, when Tam had malaria?'

'I'm sure you and Peter would have come together, no matter what,' Alma insisted. 'You were made for each other.'

'When we go to live in the flat at the castle, you'll not be a stranger?'

Mairi's plea was from the heart. When Peter had told her that, at His Lordship's insistence, he and his new family were to occupy the suite of rooms traditionally assigned to the estate manager, Mairi had been terrified.

Peter had dismissed her fears at once.

'It's not very grand, you know. The rooms are big and difficult to heat and the furnishings are pretty old. The best thing you can say for the place is that there's plenty of room and the children will have space of their own. The views are good though. I'm sure you'll soon have it looking like home.'

'I'll come and see you as often as time will allow,' Alma promised. 'Of course, I shall be pretty busy at the surgery.'

'Are you looking forward to starting your new job?'

'Yes, really excited! Iain has had some alterations made to the layout of the ground floor. There's now a proper reception desk. It all looks very efficient.'

'I'm going to miss Tigh na Broch,' said Mairi a trifle wistfully. 'I really liked working for Mrs Beaton. After all she has done for us since Joanie's illness I feel I'm letting her down.'

'I'm sure she doesn't believe that at all,' Alma reassured her. 'At least you've had time to train Peggy McClaren to take your place. Mrs Beaton won't be entirely without help.'

'And I've promised to lend a hand whenever there is a rush on,' Mairi added eagerly. 'We've produced a really fine new cheese you know. I'd like to be there to see it launched.'

'I'm certain that Mrs Beaton will be glad of any help you can give her,' Alma reiterated, 'but what's most important, you'll have time to concentrate on your family. You have a fine man in Peter Parker so don't you go neglecting him for the sake of some old cheese.'

They left the cloakroom arm in arm, laughing.

The last waltz was announced. Soon the party would be breaking up. As the music of the 'Gay Gordons' gave place to the first bars of 'Who's Taking You Home Tonight', bride and groom took to the floor. Right on cue, Iain swept Alma into his arms and he too steered his partner expertly around the room. Soon they were joined by the entire company, a kaleidoscope of colour constantly moving in the soft light of a dozen oil lamps swinging high above their heads from the rafters of the old drill hall. With the floor so crowded, it was becoming unbearably hot. Iain looked down at his partner, her dark head resting against his shoulder, and experienced a depth of feeling which was quite new to him. Holding her more tightly, he steered her towards the rear door to the hall and whispered in her ear. Leaving the dance by mutual consent, they wandered outside.

On this, the shortest night of the year, even at midnight it was still light enough for them to see where they were going. As they strolled across the grass towards the beach, music from the hall mingled with the crashing of surf along the shore.

Alma's light summer dress was no match for the evening breeze and she was unable to suppress a shiver as they topped the mound of waste slate thrown up by winter storms and began their descent towards the water's edge. Iain removed his jacket and placed it around her shoulders but it was the warmth of his body through the thin stuff of his shirt that gave her the best protection from the night wind.

'Tired?' he asked.

She nodded. 'It's been a lovely day.'

'You must be quite exhausted.'

Alma had been up since dawn helping Mairi to prepare for the wedding. Until this moment, the excitement had kept her going but now she began to feel the effects of the long day.

'I do hope Mairi's troubles are all in the past,' she said, gazing out at the waves breaking restlessly around the southern tip of Eisdalsa Island.

'I'm sure they're both going to be very happy,' Iain said. He continued to gaze out to sea as he went on. 'Do you know what I was thinking today during the ceremony?'

'No?'

'I was wishing it was us, standing there, exchanging our vows.' As he turned her in his arms, the wind caught her hair, blowing it across her face. He lifted the wanton locks out of her eyes and brushed her cheek with soft surgeon's fingers. 'I'm going to have to ask you to come and live with me, Alma Livingstone, for sure as God, I can't live without you.'

'I didn't realise it was to be a residential appointment,' she said quietly, teasing.

'If you marry me, I'll not be able to offer you a salary, but I can guarantee it will be a job for life.'

For an agonising moment she pretended to consider his offer. At last she asked, 'When do I start?'

'You mean, you will? You'll really marry me?'

'Of course, I gather you need someone to answer the phone when you're not there. I presume it sometimes rings before eight thirty in the morning and after five at night?'

'You've been talking to my mother.'

They were both laughing now.

'And you don't mind being a doctor's wife?'

'I can't think of anything I'd like better.'

'Oh Alma, I do love you. How about you? Could you ever bring yourself to love me too?'

'With a little practise I think I might.' Then, recognising the anxiety her bantering had provoked she admitted, 'I think I have loved you ever since you sat next to me in class and pulled my plaits!'

'I never did. Did I?'

Her answer was smothered by his kisses. Tender at first, becoming fiercer as their passion mounted. Alma felt her knees buckle until he was supporting her entirely. It was as though her whole body was melding with his.

Their kissing was interrupted by an increase in the volume of sound as all three doors to the hall were flung wide, illuminating the surrounding tarmac.

Party-goers poured out from every door. Those who had come from a distance made for their vehicles with a deal of door slamming and a few raucous toots on their horns. Those who had arrived on foot formed up into companionable groups and made off down the road singing and laughing as they disappeared into the night.

'Come on, I'd best get you home. If we stay here any longer people will start talking.'

Iain straightened his kilt and ran his fingers through his unruly locks. Alma returned his jacket and ran back towards the hall. 'I'll just get my coat,' she called back over her shoulder. She emerged a few moments later and hurried towards him where he waited beside the Daimler.

'What about your mother? Won't she need a lift home?'

'Uncle Stuart will look after her,' he replied. 'He and Annie are staying the night at Tigh na Broch.'

He helped Alma into the passenger seat and went around to his own door. Climbing in beside her, he paused for a moment, devouring her with his eyes.

'What's the matter?' she asked.

'Nothing, I was just wondering.'

'What?'

'How you could possibly put up with an idiot like me, for the rest of your life.'

'Why an idiot?'

'To have been working with you for all these months, without realising.'

'Realising what?'

'How much I love you.'

He took her in his arms once again and this time their kiss lasted a lot longer.

56

THE WOMAN WAS in her early sixties. Iain thought he ought to recall her from his childhood but he couldn't quite place her. According to his father's records, she had lived in the village all her life apart from a spell in service up at the castle before she married.

He had led her to the couch and discreetly pulled the curtain around her while she removed her garments. She had been embarrassed to have to strip down to her skirt and sat forward now, in a vain attempt to hide her flabby bosoms.

He asked her to sit up straight which she did, finally abandoning all modesty and looking him straight in the eyes as he felt first one breast and then the other, gently squeezing and pulling until he came at last to the place she had first indicated. She gasped and he handled her even more gently. Yes, it was quite unmistakable.

'Of course, it might only be gristle,' he suggested, giving some cause for hope. The lump was the size of a walnut, situated in the left breast. 'There's certainly something there,' he said, feeling again to confirm his approximate assessment of the size. The tumour was already well developed in which case there would almost certainly be secondaries. Any hope of recovery depended on immediate action.

'I think we shall have to get a specialist to have a look at this, Mrs Muir. I'll make arrangements right away.'

'Is it bad, Doctor?' she asked, anxiously. All modesty forgotten she looked down at the affected breast and her hand came up automatically, to the exact spot.

'Not if we've caught it in time,' he said. 'Do you think your husband can get you to Glasgow, probably before the end of the week?'

'Oh dear, so soon? Is that really necessary, Doctor?' she pleaded. 'Murdo's that busy, what with the harvest festival and a'. Can it wait till the end of the month?'

Of course! That was how he knew of her. Murdo Muir was an elder of the kirk. He remembered now. He'd been master of one of the coastal steamers when they were still running, just before the war.

'Mrs Muir, if this is what I think it is, it won't wait, harvest festival or no. I would like to make an appointment for you to go down to the Western Infirmary, this week if possible. Now, are you able to get there under your own steam or would you like me to arrange transport?'

'Och, that'll no' be necessary,' she protested. The thought of having to accept the doctor's charity was too much for her to swallow. 'We'll manage on the train.' She reached for her bra, anxious to cover up the source of her embarrassment. Iain pulled the curtain across and turned away to write the letter she would require to take with her.

'I'll make the call now,' he said when she was once again fully clothed and in command of herself. 'If you'll just go back to the waiting room for a few moments, I can give you a date right away.'

She pulled on her outdoor coat and stood up, holding her capacious handbag by handles which were badly worn. 'Thank you Doctor,' she said and then added anxiously, 'Now, how much will that be?'

The immediate problem was to pay the doctor. How they were going to afford the expense of the train fare to Glasgow and seeing a specialist, she did not know.

'Mrs Muir, you must know all about the new Health Service?' Iain turned round to face her, incredulous. 'I thought everyone had heard about it. Have you not filled in one of these new registration cards? You should have had one each, delivered by the postie.'

He held out a sample of the card and she glanced at it casually.

'Oh that, yes I do remember seeing something like that. Lord alone knows where I put them. Is it important?'

'Well yes, it is,' Iain told her. 'If you think you've lost yours, Miss Livingstone at the reception counter will give you some more. You must fill one in for every member of the household and send them off at once, particularly as you're going to be receiving a lot of attention in the next few weeks.'

'And your bill?' she asked again.

'There's nothing to pay, Mrs Muir. That's the whole point of the new service.'

'Oh, but I thought that just applied to the destitute, like the old Poor Law.'

'No, this is for everyone, from the poorest to the richest in the land, free health care for all. You'll have to pay for it through your taxes of course, but at the time when you need help the most, everything will be provided free of charge.'

Her relief was obvious.

'Oh, I see. Does that mean the hospital and all?'

'Everything, medicine, operation, nursing care, even travel, if necessary.' He allowed these last words to hang in the air. There were pamphlets in the waiting room explaining how one could claim travelling expenses. He felt sure she would see them while she waited. No need to embarrass her further with explanations. He watched Mrs Muir leave the room, pulling the door to behind her. His father had always said it was the genteel poor who were most tricky to handle.

A few moments later, he took Mrs Muir's letter out to the reception desk. His mother's morning room had been made into a pleasant well-lit waiting room with a good view across the garden towards the sea. The old waiting room was now the reception area and dispensary with a hole cut into the wall and covered by a sliding glass panel. Behind this Alma sat to greet patients and take telephone calls. She was attending evening classes twice a week at the High School in order to master the new typewriter they had bought her.

'Mrs Muir has an appointment at the Glasgow Infirmary for Friday afternoon, Miss Livingstone. Will you make her out an appointment card and see she has one of those travel pamphlets. Oh, and give her as many registration cards as she needs. They seem to have mislaid the lot at home.'

'Not another one. That's the third family this week hasn't registered yet!'

Alma would have liked him to call her by her Christian name but she understood his concern to have a proper, business-like approach during surgery hours.

He had been granted a secretarial allowance because of his bachelor status and the fact that he now occupied the house by himself. Until they were actually married, there was no reason why Alma should not be paid for her work. It seemed sensible, for the time being, to keep their impending marriage to themselves.

'They'll sign up the minute they need a doctor,' Iain laughed. 'Who's next?'

'Kirsty McBain. She's not the first on the list, but Mrs McBain is in the waiting room with the two kiddies. I'm sure the other patients will be glad to have them go first.'

The McBain children were not Alma's favourites. Wild was a mild description for their antics.

Iain poked his head around the waiting room door.

'Kirsty McBain?'

Seven-year-old Kirsty let go the mutilated teddy bear which she had been wresting from her five-year-old brother and trotted across to him confidently. Mrs McBain took longer, hurriedly gathering up the toys the children had strewn all around the floor.

The basket of toys had been Alma's idea, to keep the children happy while waiting. Sometimes, as on this occasion, it caused more problems than it was worth. When his sister went out with the doctor, the prospect of having the toy box to himself was too great a temptation for Donald. As his mother grasped him firmly by the arm, he screamed with rage.

'Come along now,' cried Mrs McBain, 'or Doctor'll carry you off in his black bag!'

This threat was sufficient to quell the noise. She tucked the child under her arm and carried him, hiccoughing and weeping, out into the corridor where she set him down and wiped his face with a nearly clean handkerchief and a lot of spit.

'Now then,' said Iain when he had them all settled. 'What can we do for Kirsty today?'

'It's just the medicine you gave her last week, Doctor. It's all used up and you said to go on taking it for two weeks.'

Iain withdrew the child's treatment record from the manila envelope which carried all her details; name, date of birth and National Health Number.

'I prescribed penicillin for two weeks, taking one spoonful three times a day. You should have had sufficient in the one bottle.'

'Oh well, it was wee Donnie y'see.' The woman had the grace to look a trifle uncomfortable. 'He would have a taste of his sister's pink medicine,' she explained, 'an' he liked it so much that whenever she got hers, I had to give him a drop on the spoon too.'

'The penicillin was to kill the bacteria in Kirsty's throat, Mrs McBain. Giving it to Donnie is not a good idea at all.'

'Och, it'll do him no harm,' she shrugged her shoulders dismissing the doctor's warning. 'It might even do him a bit o' good if there are bugs about.'

Silently Iain cursed the wiseacre who had thought of making up the penicillin dosage for children into an attractive pink syrupy liquid. He could see this becoming a regular problem. How was he going to explain bacterial resistivity to this silly woman?

'We don't yet know what the long term effects of taking antibiotics like penicillin will be, Mrs McBain,' he said, doing his best to keep his explanation simple. 'It is possible that certain bacteria will become accustomed to the drug and it will lose its effectiveness. It would be much better to keep Donnie away from it until he really has a problem.'

The woman sniffed, unimpressed by the doctor's explanation.

'I'm prescribing a further dose for Kirsty which will last just this week, but it's only for Kirsty, mind.'

He turned to Donnie.

'As for you young man, if I hear that you've been taking your sister's medicine again, I'll get your faither to give you a good skelping. You understand?'

The infant glanced suspiciously at the black medical case which Iain kept ready to hand for emergencies. Wide-eyed, he nodded solemnly.

Mrs McBain, with her children in tow, swept out into the hall, triumphant.

Iain sighed. A few months ago the woman would have been content with a bottle of Gee's Linctus from the pharmacy for her daughter's sore tonsils and he would never have set eyes on either child. Balancing the past against the present however, he knew that catching Kirsty's tonsillitis in good time had avoided an unpleasant tonsillectomy. He just hoped that the boy would never need a life-saving course of penicillin himself.

The stream of patients into his surgery that morning seemed endless. Most were genuine cases. A few had come along, curious about the new system and anxious not to miss out on any benefits owing to them. When, later in the day, he voiced his concerns to Stuart Beaton, the old man simply laughed.

'It's a nine-day wonder,' he prophesied. They'll soon tire of hanging about in the waiting room.'

'I had old Walter Fairlie in yesterday. He's eighty-five years old and has been bald as a coot ever since I can remember. He only wanted me to give him a chitty to go and get fitted for a wig.'

'What ever did you say?' demanded Annie, trying hard not to laugh.

'I told him wigs were intended only for those who had had surgery or some disease which had caused their hair to fall out suddenly. I didn't like to say that free wigs were reserved for women and adolescents, because I'm not sure what the position is on premature male baldness. I can't imagine that the resources committee had it in mind to place hair on every bald male head in the country.'

'There are lot of minor details that particular committee failed to address,' Stuart agreed. 'No doubt it will all be straightened out in due course.'

'The best thing that has resulted from this is our direct access to the hospitals.' Iain related his experience with Mrs Muir. 'In the past I'd have been lucky even to get someone to speak to me about her over the phone. I rang this morning and they agreed to see her right away. She's going down to Glasgow on Friday.'

'Poor woman,' said Stuart, who knew the family well. 'I hope it's not too late.'

'Well, at least she'll have the best possible chance down there. Kmiecik could have done little for her at the Cottage Hospital.'

'It was lovely to see young Joan McFarlane looking so fit and well at the wedding last month,' observed Annie.

'I must say, I was surprised she was able to be there,' observed Stuart remembering the day, months before, when he had correctly diagnosed TB in the child. 'I would have expected her to be in the chest hospital for eighteen months at the very least.'

'The miracle of penicillin,' Iain reminded him, but Stuart still seemed sceptical.

'I just hope the cure is a lasting one,' he observed, remembering the cycles of acute illness followed by a period of recession which had been the pattern of the disease in the old days.

'The pity of it is,' added Millicent, 'poor Mairi was obliged to make clothes for half the parish, as well as working part time in the dairy, just to get together enough money to pay the medical bills. If she'd waited a month or two longer, she'd have had the treatment for free.'

'I'm sure Mairi feels that every penny was well spent,' said Annie. 'But I'm mighty glad that people in her position will not have to worry about paying for such treatment in the future.'

'Amen to that,' Stuart agreed.

'How's Alma getting on in her new job?' Annie asked.

'Splendidly,' Millicent told her. 'We couldn't have made a better choice, could we Iain?'

'What?' At the mention of Alma's name, Iain had become lost in his own private thoughts. 'Oh no, she's doing an absolutely marvellous job.'

'For a start,' Millicent told them, 'she already knows many of the patients and has a fair idea what is likely to be an emergency and she's able to recognise both maternal panic and hypochondria. She's really a tremendous help. It's relieved me of an enormous burden as you know. Now Mairi is married, she has very little time to help out in the dairy and I'm kept busy most of the time.'

'So, everything in the practice is now under control, is it?' Stuart's question was directed at Iain. He might not be as observant as Annie in some respects, but even he could see that his nephew's mind was elsewhere.

'Eh? Oh yes. I've been showing Alma a few simple procedures in the dispensary,' Iain responded. 'I can't envisage us ever having a pharmacist of our own in the practice so I'll need to go on dispensing the more common drugs myself. If I don't, some patients will never get around to collecting their prescriptions. Many of the older ones hardly ever get into town.'

'You should see the boot of his car,' Millicent chimed in. 'It's just like a chemist's shop.'

'Heard anything from the folk up at the castle yet?' Iain's uncle enquired with a wicked grin at his wife. 'The last time I spoke to His Lordship, he was up in arms about the whole scheme. *"You'll not get me queuing up for me med'cine with the bloody hoy polloy,'* was what he actually said. *'Bloody quack can come here as he's always done, when I want 'im. We pay 'im enough for it!"'*

'I must check to see if he's registered here or in Taymouth,' said Iain.

'Unlikely to find he's registered anywhere at all,' said Stuart.

'Well in that case he can go hang,' said Iain. 'He still owes the practice five guineas for Dad's last visit to the castle, nearly two years ago.' He paused to scribble on the cuff of his white shirt.

'Oh Iain,' said his mother, 'I wish you wouldn't do that. It makes laundering so difficult.'

'So you haven't entirely forsworn your housewifely duties, Millicent?' Annie observed.

'We can hardly expect our receptionist to do his dirty washing now, can we?' Millicent grinned. 'As soon as the electricity comes in, he can buy a washing machine and do his own. Then we'll see if he goes on using his cuffs for a notepad.'

'I was only reminding myself to get Alma to send another bill to His Lordship,' Iain excused himself, truculently. 'She can include a couple of registration forms at the same time, just to stir the old boy into action.'

'You could lose a valuable private patient,' Stuart warned.

'I don't intend to have any private patients,' Iain told him. 'That's one thing in which I am totally in agreement with old Steve, as well as being free for all, the service must provide equal access to treatment. There oughtn't to be special privileges for those who can afford to pay to jump the queue. If people want private medical care, they can look for it outside the NHS.'

'There speaks my brave socialist,' said Annie.

She might have been joking but in truth, she was mighty proud of both the boys. She hated the thought of Stephen having to go half a world away in order to do his work in the way he wanted, but she supported entirely his reasons for going. Iain too was sticking up for his principles. That was good. Nothing much could go wrong with the system while people like Iain and David were working it.

'Did you ever get the final result of the doctors' referendum, Stuart?' Millicent asked suddenly. In all the flurry of activity in handing over the practice and expanding her work in the dairy, she had lost track of what had been happening in the medical world.

'All I can tell you is that ninety-five per cent of doctors, including both GPs and hospital doctors, have signed up to the scheme. Those who have failed to do so are mainly the senior consultants in those Voluntary Hospitals which are opting out, and men with lucrative practices in Harley Street.'

'That's amazing,' said Iain, 'when one remembers that only a few months ago the BMA was claiming figures of less than fifty per cent in agreement. It just shows how out of touch the guys at the top really are.'

'Not all of them,' Annie objected, glancing across at Stuart. 'Your uncle had a few words to say you know, all along the line.'

'It's a good job we had a few real doctors on our side,' Iain agreed.

'What news of Stephen and Ellen?' asked Millicent, busily pouring second cups all round.

'They have a house with a view over the ocean,' Annie told her. 'The baby is thriving and Stephen seems to have landed a plum job. He doesn't say a lot about what he's doing, but it seems he will be going to Japan again, very soon, to give some lectures on burns treatment to the doctors there.'

'And Jack McDougal, how is he managing without Jeanie?'

'Ellen says he's getting on well on his own. He has a friend with a private plane who gives him a lift down to Adelaide every once in a while.' She spoke enviously. 'I wish we could just jump on an aeroplane ourselves, and be in Australia in a few hours.'

'One day soon they will be starting a proper passenger service,' Stuart assured her. 'You'll be one of the first to use it, I promise you.'

If only she shared his confidence. Hopes and dreams were all that was left to them now, thought Annie, as she studied her husband in the fading light. She had noticed lately how frail he looked in late afternoon, when the shadows began to fall. In the past it had been she who was the weaker of the two. She had been the one to be fussed over and cosseted, but now it was Stuart who showed the wear and tear of half a century of hard work and bloody conflict. Recently he had come to rely more and more on her strength and determination. Annie prayed he would live long enough to see his son again, and little Hugh.

Millicent had worn the best. Bronzed by her days in the open air, she looked good for another twenty years, better than any of them in fact. She was lucky to have one of her children still at home and Morag was only a couple of hours' drive away. If Iain would only surprise her and take a wife, she still had time for a grandchild or two!

As though reading her thoughts, Stuart asked suddenly, 'Whatever happened to that pretty girl you brought home last New Year's, Iain?'

'Alison McKenzie? Oh, she's making a name for herself in nursing politics, I believe. She was recently appointed as the Royal College of Nursing's representative on the General Nursing Council.'

'Good for her!' said Annie.

'Funny thing, I had the distinct impression that you and she were planning to get together.' Ignoring the kick Annie aimed at his shin, Stuart continued, 'she was a nice lass, I thought she'd have made an ideal doctor's wife.'

'I think she's too dedicated to her work to consider anything as mundane as being a wife and mother.' Iain tried to sound casual, but he still smarted from Alison's rejection.

Millicent had long since ceased to worry about Alison. Anyone could see Alma Livingstone was ready to accept Iain like a shot. It would be an ideal match. They worked so well together. Alma had been quick and eager to learn what was required of her in the practice and she was so obviously fond of him. How could Iain be so blind? If he didn't act soon, Alma was likely to give up waiting and marry someone else.

'What news of David?' Stuart asked, aware, somewhat belatedly, that his previous choice of subject had created a certain tension in the room. 'How has the changeover affected him?'

'I was talking to him over the phone only the other night,' said Iain. 'He's full of plans for running a sheltered workshop within the hospital grounds. Actually, he's advocated the useful occupation of psychiatric patients as a means of rehabilitating them, for a long time. He's convinced it will work.'

'Good luck to him,' said Stuart. 'One has to admire someone who devotes his life to the mentally disabled.'

'You've left out David's other news,' said Millicent, happily. 'Go on Iain, tell them.'

'Oh yes,' as though the matter was of secondary importance, 'he's getting married.'

'She's what they call a psychiatric social worker,' Millicent chipped in eagerly. 'It's going to be her job to find employment places and somewhere to live for patients released into the community. She'll keep an eye on them, see they take their medicine and report in regularly for check-up.'

'A posting which, so far as David is concerned at any rate, appears to have been an unqualified success,' laughed Stuart.

Annie did not see this as a subject for levity.

'Society is going to have to learn to accept responsibility for the less able and the inadequates of this world,' she insisted, 'especially when it's often society which has made them what they are. There should be a place for everyone on this planet, but so far it's only the smartest and the richest have managed to find it. Now, maybe, it will be the turn of the rest.'

'When is the wedding to be?' Stuart asked, hoping to divert his wife from one of her favourite topics.

'Oh not for some time yet,' said Iain. 'In the New Year, perhaps.'

It seemed to Iain that this was as good a time as any to drop his own bombshell. 'Which means Alma and I will be able to get in first with the wedding presents.'

Millicent's mouth fell open. 'Do you mean what I think you mean?'

'Yes, Mother! We are going to be married just as soon as it can be arranged. I intended to wait for Alma before saying anything, but on second thoughts, perhaps it's best for you to be prepared before she gets here. I don't want Uncle Stuart introducing the subject of Alison in front of my fiancée!'

'You'll have to tell her, surely,' said Millicent rather primly.

'Tell her what? That her best beloved was turned down in favour of a seat on the General Nursing Council? I don't think so!'

Even Annie looked a trifle shocked.

'It's always better not to have secrets, dear,' she suggested.

'Oh come on, Aunt Annie, I'm just kidding. The girls met at the Hogmanay do, don't you remember? Alma knows all about Alison.'

'Oh, you were only teasing,' said Annie, relieved.

'Anyway, dearest, I couldn't be more pleased,' Millicent threw her arms about him and gave him a kiss. 'I know you and Alma are going to be very happy.'

All four fell silent for a while as they watched the setting sun transform the western sky into an artist's pallette of colour. Suspended above the darkening hills of Mull, the great orange orb splashed the gathering clouds with reds and yellows, pink and purple. To the south and west, the islands in the Sound were suddenly cast into sharp silhouette while the drawing room at Tigh na Broch was suffused with a warm orange glow.

Common hopes and expectations, fond memories and sad ones, hung together in the air, clothing them all in that blanket of belonging which families accept without question and the rootless and lonely can only envy. While Annie and Millicent yearned for those who were absent, the men wondered about the future and hoped there was yet time to change things for the better.

Stuart's remaining days would be occupied mainly with the past, a few regrets perhaps but, for the most part, happy memories.

For Iain there was a bright road to follow, marriage to the woman he loved and a challenging future. He looked forward eagerly to both.

Down by the wall which separated the garden from the meadow beyond, Millicent's prize herd was gathering, ready for the evening milking. They could hear Sorlie McKinnon already out there, calling the beasts home. Soon, Millicent would go to help him.

With a frisson of excitement, Iain watched a new black Ford Prefect saloon slow down as it reached the road works at the top of the hill where, thanks to the insistence of the Marquis, they were already making improvements to that dangerous corner.

The little car took the downward slope with care, gathering speed only when it had reached the comparative safety of the shore road. As Alma turned into the drive, the first of the evening's patients stepped aside to let her pass.

This was Iain's signal to go back to work. He stood up. 'Duty calls.' At the door he paused to address his aunt and uncle. 'How about you two waiting until after surgery is finished and catching the late ferry for a change? We could all have a drink to celebrate my engagement.'

Without waiting for their reply he strode out into the hallway. As he did so, he studied for the hundredth time the contents of the little square box he had collected that morning from the jeweller's in Oban.

When he heard the Ford pull up on the gravel forecourt he snapped the box shut, returned it hastily to his pocket and opened the door. 'Good, I'm glad you're early,' he greeted her with a kiss.

She looked at him in surprise. There were people coming up the drive, supposing they saw…

Taking Alma by the hand, he led her into his consulting room and closed the door firmly behind them. 'Our secret's out,' he confessed. 'Mother knows. So do Stuart and Annie. I'm sorry. It just seemed the right moment to tell them.'

'Oh Iain, I'm so glad.' Alma flung her arms around his neck. 'I know we agreed to wait, but it's been awful these past weeks having to stop myself saying anything to your mother that would give any hint.'

'I know. Anyway, it's all over now. I'll write to the Executive Committee tomorrow to let them know. It was nice having a paid helper for a while.'

'Oh, I see. Perhaps you'd rather I stayed single. We could always live in sin.'

Iain had caught sight of the first of the evening's patients arriving at the surgery door. 'I don't think Mrs Gillespie would approve,' he laughed. He pushed her from him and fished in his pocket for the little box.

'We're having a wee celebration after surgery,' he told her. 'Annie and Stuart are staying on especially. I thought you might like to wear this.'

He watched her closely as she opened the box and took out the ring.

'It's beautiful,' she breathed.

'Here, let me put it on for you.' He slid the handsome solitaire diamond on to the third finger of her left hand, closed her fingers over and kissed them. 'I can't wait for it to be a solid gold one,' he said, smiling down at her.

An impatient hand struck the bell on the reception counter.

'The sooner we get to it, the sooner they'll all be gone,' Alma said, kissing him lightly on the cheek. 'Thank you for the ring.'

'I love you, Alma.'

'Yes, I believe you do,' she answered, still wondering what she had done to deserve such happiness.

They kissed again, ignoring the bell as it rang a second and a third time. On the fourth ring they parted. Iain took his place behind the desk, where he made much of straightening his tie and fixing his stethoscope around his neck. Alma, her colour charmingly heightened, went out to the reception counter.

'Good evening, Mrs Gillespie. I'm so sorry to keep you. There was a little emergency.'

Self-consciously she swept a stray lock of hair out of her eyes. The diamond flashed in the last rays of the sun.

Mrs Gillespie could not have failed to notice it. By morning, news of the doctor's engagement to his receptionist was certain to be all over the islands!

The Islands that Roofed the World

Mary Withall

ISBN 0 946487 76 6 PBK £4.99

Easdale, Belnahua, Luing & Seil: The Islands that Roofed the World

Come over the 200-year-old bridge which crosses the Atlantic to the charming, yet scarred, Inner Hebridean Slate Islands.

The Slate Islands lie off the west coast of Argyll. Slate has been taken from their shores from earliest recorded history and the richness and quality of the deposits meant that in the 18th and 19th centuries slate quarrying was one of the most important industries in Scotland. The Breadalbane family owned the land of Easdale and its surrounds for over 400 years and of course roofed their own buildings in slate as well as many important buildings, including Cawdor Castle in Inverness-shire and Glasgow Cathedral. Their 18th century ownership of Nova Scotia ensured international trade, and it is therefore unsurprising to find public buildings in eastern Canada roofed in Easdale slate.

The geology, the industry, the people and their way of life: this is the story of the Slate Islands past, present and future, told by the Easdale Folk Museum archivist, with affection and admiration. Easdale remains unique, an island that has no roads and cannot support heavy vehicular traffic. The islanders today are working to retain its delicate environmental and economic balance in a way that is feasible in the modern world.

Luath Press Limited
committed to publishing well written books worth reading

LUATH PRESS takes its name from Robert Burns, whose little collie Luath (*Gael.*, swift or nimble) tripped up Jean Armour at a wedding and gave him the chance to speak to the woman who was to be his wife and the abiding love of his life. Burns called one of 'The Twa Dogs' Luath after Cuchullin's hunting dog in *Ossian's Fingal*. Luath Press was established in 1981 in the heart of Burns country, and is now based a few steps up the road from Burns' first lodgings on Edinburgh's Royal Mile. Luath offers you distinctive writing with a hint of unexpected pleasures.

Most bookshops in the UK, the US, Canada, Australia, New Zealand and parts of Europe either carry our books in stock or can order them for you. To order direct from us, please send a £sterling cheque, postal order, international money order or your credit card details (number, address of cardholder and expiry date) to us at the address below. Please add post and packing as follows: UK – £1.00 per delivery address; overseas surface mail – £2.50 per delivery address; overseas airmail – £3.50 for the first book to each delivery address, plus £1.00 for each additional book by airmail to the same address. If your order is a gift, we will happily enclose your card or message at no extra charge.

Luath Press Limited
543/2 Castlehill
The Royal Mile
Edinburgh EH1 2ND
Scotland
Telephone: 0131 225 4326 (24 hours)
Fax: 0131 225 4324
email: sales@luath.co.uk
Website: www.luath.co.uk